LUCIFER AND THE CHILD

Lucifer and the Child

by

Ethel Mannin

Swan River Press
Dublin, Ireland
MMXXIII

Lucifer and the Child
by Ethel Mannin

Published by
Swan River Press
at Æon House
Dublin, Ireland
in May MMXXIII

www.swanriverpress.ie
brian@swanriverpress.ie

Cover design by Meggan Kehrli
from artwork © Lorena Carrington

Set in Garamond by Ken Mackenzie

Published with assistance from Dublin UNESCO
City of Literature and Dublin City Libraries

Paperback Edition
ISBN 978-1-78380-770-3

Swan River Press published
a limited edition hardback of
Lucifer and the Child on 30 April 2020

Contents

Merely the Natural Plus

Rosanne Rabinowitz

Ethel Mannin (1900-1984) was a best-selling author who had written more than one hundred books but is virtually unknown today. Her output included fiction, journalism, short stories, travelogues, autobiography, and political analysis. All of her books have been out of print for decades—until now.

Born into a working-class family in South London, Mannin was a lifelong socialist, feminist, and anti-fascist. In the 1930s she organised alongside the Russian-born American anarchist Emma Goldman in support of the Spanish anarchosyndicalist forces and their struggle against Franco. Later, she agitated for the Indian independence movement along with her husband Reg Reginald. She was an advocate for African liberation movements and one of the few, even on the post-war left, who stood up for the rights of Palestinians. Iraqi critic and educator Ahmed Al-Rawi has described her as a post-colonial writer, which was unusual among British authors of the time.

In her lifetime Mannin was also known for her famous lovers, including Bertrand Russell and W. B. Yeats. In fact, it was the Yeats connection that had me trawling internet archives and second-hand bookshops while researching my tale "The Shiftings"—a ghost story exploring her relationship with the poet—for Swan River Press's anthology *The Far Tower: Stories for W. B. Yeats* (2019). But I first discovered Ethel Mannin years ago, when I was a teenaged history obsessive with a special interest in labour and radical history. The figure of Mannin's comrade "Red" Emma Goldman, described by FBI director J. Edgar Hoover as the "most dangerous woman in America", held a powerful fascination for me. In the course of my reading I came across a vivid description of Goldman giving a speech, which was an extract from Mannin's historical novel *Red Rose* (1941). This brought me to my local library looking for Mannin's work.

While I couldn't find *Red Rose* or anything about Mannin's political activities, I did discover old editions of *Venetian Blinds* (1933) and *Lucifer and the Child*, which was first published in 1945. *Venetian Blinds* is a realist novel about the price paid for upward mobility, starting with the excitement of market day on Battersea's Lavender Hill and ending with loneliness in the suburbs. It reminded me of early George Orwell novels such as *A Clergyman's Daughter* (1935) and *Keep the Aspidistra Flying* (1936), which were also about crossing class lines—albeit in the opposite direction.

After the relatively straightforward social narrative of *Venetian Blinds*, the ambiguous supernaturalism of *Lucifer and the Child* was a surprise. It is a story of witchcraft—or is it? I already had an interest in supernatural fiction but did not expect to find it in this context. Set mainly in the crowded streets of 1930s East London, the story begins when young Jenny Flower strays from a school outing in the countryside where she encounters a Dark Stranger. He could be Lucifer, or he could simply be a very imaginative and charismatic sailor.

In a passage reminiscent of Arthur Machen's "The Great God Pan" (1894) Mannin portrays the wonder and absolute awe of a city child encountering the forest for the first time: "Sometimes there were breaks in the bird-song and then everything was very still, as though every leaf of all the millions was holding its breath and waiting, and you also waited and listened and heard your own heart beating."

While observing a dragon-fly Jenny discovers that she is not alone. A Dark Stranger has also been watching; he steadies her as she reels in surprise at its take-off. All adults had been the enemy to her but this one is "the bringer of new things". For the first time, she sees a life beyond her council estate, her school, and a family that does not know what to make of her. A new world opens up, one where she potentially wields power. Jenny is ushered into the "Goetic life", a process that evokes another noted work by Machen: "The White People" (1904) in which a curious girl is initiated by her nurse into dark ceremonies and the "most secret secrets" of the countryside.

Similarly, the Dark Stranger introduces Jenny to fairy rings in the grass and tells her how the Little People made them by dancing in the moonlight. He shows her a big yellow toad under a boulder. He reveals deadly nightshade, witches' bane, hemlock, poisonous mushrooms. He spins her tales of tree-witches and wood-spirits, nymphs and dryads, fauns and satyrs. She also comes to learn that she might be descended from two sisters burned at the stake many centuries ago.

Jenny is a solitary child who joins in the noisy games of the other children but does not have any true friends among them. She would rather spend time with Old Mother Beadle in Ropewalk Alley. Regarded as a witch by the local children, Mrs. Beadle supplements her pension by telling fortunes and selling concoctions of herbs to induce abortions. And in this capacity, she also guides Jenny into a world of magic.

Meanwhile, Jenny's family views Mrs. Beadle as a bad influence. So too does Marian Drew, a teacher who takes an interest in her pupil and aims to "save" her from a descent into the irrational and ultimately evil "Goetic life". Though Marian is a vicar's daughter she's not entirely straitlaced. She holds progressive notions of educational freedom and creativity, perhaps reflective of Mannin's interest in the Summerhill school of A. S. Neil, who advocated a libertarian education system in contrast to the more rigid teaching of the time.

Marian and the Dark Stranger form a relationship characterised by sharp physical attraction and equally intense debate. He asks Marian: "Do you really know where reality ends and fantasy begins? Are you quite sure that the images of your mind have no reality?" Indeed, themes regarding the transcendent and the commonplace run throughout the novel, and at one point he says to Marian: "Another drink and you may begin to understand that the supernatural is merely the natural plus."

Lucifer and the Child is the only full-length work of speculative fiction from Mannin, who usually described herself as an atheist and rationalist. However, she was also a journalist, a seeker of curiosities and always keen to investigate. In one of her many volumes of autobiography, *Privileged Spectator* (1939), Mannin recollects a visit to a swami that Yeats admired. "For my part I was willing to try at least once my vibrations on a higher plane." She gives a scathing account of her meeting with a well-fed, well-dressed individual expounding on the virtues of poverty. She had little time for mysticism or the pomp that often surrounded it.

Yet a powerful charge of the numinous and strange runs through *Lucifer and the Child*, despite its realism—or possibly because of it. Like Machen, Mannin also takes inspiration from London itself as well as the natural world. "Its interminable greyness and its high dockyard walls can make it as oppressive as a prison, but it has its moments—the occasional crumbling grace of a Georgian doorway, the sudden impression of a ship crossing the road as it moves into a basin, the unexpectedness of a lamp bracket jutting from a wall, of a capstan marooned in an alleyway, of funnels thrusting up at the ends of streets, and always the smell of the river with its faint, fugitive hint of the sea."

Within this evocative cityscape we find a toad that is "strange and unknowable, like the moon" and step into Mrs. Beadle's house: "Ordinariness stopped outside. The dilapidated door opened on to a new world. The world to which she belonged." And in one of his arguments with Marian, the Dark Stranger suggests how the "spirit of the past" haunts people and places; a kind of spiritualism without the supernatural that would now strike a chord with modern psychogeographers.

The novel even touches on cosmic horror: "Enchantment was for her the deep forest through which she moved with deadly nightshade in her hand and an adder at her foot; it was her head upon the shoulder of the Dark Stranger, and starless night and the hunting cry of the owl; it was earth-light on the moon and no shade from the sun, and no living thing in the desolate volcanic wastes, and loneliness unutterable, the loneliness of space and dead worlds and infinity."

Meanwhile, a dry humour underlies much of the narrative. For example, Marian's thoughts about two do-gooding colleagues: "She reached the point at which she felt that if either of them referred once more to 'the paw', when speaking of the working classes, she would scream . . . " I also chuckled when reading about the pious antics of local "cadets" joined by Jenny's brother Les, who dedicates himself to marching and playing trumpet with them. "At the hall the cadets learned 'First Aid' and 'Signalling'; they also did 'physical jerks', and took turns on the parallel bars and the ropes. Before they left, Mr. Wilson, their group-captain, a pale young man who was the Sunday-school superintendent, gave them a little talk on manliness and uprightness, clean thoughts and tongues, and the avoidance of something vaguely referred to as 'bad habits', and then they marched home again." Such light-hearted observations grow darker as in the story's background fascism continues to rise and conflict engulfs the world in the "sinister year 1936, with the dress-rehearsal for the coming world-war taking place in Spain".

Mannin had been active in groups such as Workers Relief for the Victims of German Fascism and the Spanish Medical

Aid Society. Looking back from the mid-1940s—she finished writing *Lucifer and the Child* in 1944—no doubt 1936 must have seemed an ominous turning point. And though the novel is rooted in the everyday lives of its characters, Mannin shows us that world events are never far away. She makes this connection explicit when Marian tells the cadet captain that she disapproves of "encouraging militarism" and boys "playing at soldiers" instead of creatively expressing themselves as individuals. Marian warns: "It's only a few steps further on in this direction before they're wearing jackboots—actually and spiritually!"

Mannin was a contradictory woman shaped by contradictory times, a prolific writer who produced an odd and imaginative book so unlike her others. *Lucifer and the Child* remains a rich portrayal of inter-war London and an engaging story of a girl who sought to escape it through myth and magic. And at the end of the book, the reader is left with another question: is the Dark Stranger really so "dark" after all? Or is he instead the "bringer of light", a source of new things and knowledge in a world beset by evil far greater than any mischief wrought by a mythological fellow with horns? In effect, *Lucifer and the Child* is a story about the desire for a different life than the one we're allotted and the extraordinary measures some may take to move beyond it.

"There is never any name for the impact of strangeness on the commonplace, that *je ne sais quoi* that ripples the surface of everydayness and sets up unaccountable disturbances in the imagination and the blood," Mannin writes. With this sensibility *Lucifer and the Child* will at last be recognised as a classic of strange fiction and a work to be enjoyed by contemporary lovers of the genre.

Lambeth,
South London,
3 March 2020

Lucifer and the Child

Author's Note

"*Here was the strangest pair
In the world anywhere . . .*"

– Ralph Hodgson

The reader, having read this tale, may ask, "But was the stranger really Lucifer, and was the child really a witch?" I can only answer—for those who are apt for the "willing suspension of disbelief", the stranger could have been Lucifer, the child could have been a witch. On the other hand, for those not so apt, everything recounted of this strange pair is open to natural, materialist explanation.

For proof corrections and patient assistance with various queries which arose in the writing of the book I am indebted to Mr. G. Turner, and for permission to quote the lines from his poem to Mr. Walter de la Mare.

E. M.

Part I

The Dark Stranger

"What can a tired heart say,
Which the wise of the world have made dumb?
Save to the lonely dreams of a child,
'Return again, come!' "

– Walter de la Mare

Chapter I

The Horned One

On the 18th March, 1618, Margaret and Philippa Flower were burnt at the stake at Lincoln, England, for witchcraft. They were sentenced by the Chief Justice of the Common Pleas, Sir Henry Hobbert, after examination by distinguished magistrates and trial by appointed judges. They confessed to entering into communion with familiar spirits for the accomplishment of evil practices, and to periodic visions of devils. Their mother, who was arrested with them, protested her innocence; she called for bread, crying, might it choke her if she were guilty of the charges made against her. It is recorded that she took the bread into her mouth and instantly fell down dead. Whatever the possible explanation this is historic fact.

Whether Jenny Flower, born Hallowe'en, 1924, was a descendant of this Lincoln family, is open to conjecture. She knew nothing of the possible significance of her name until she was thirteen—though she became acquainted with the facts of the Goetic life long before then—and she never wept again after that, for by that time she had completed her noviciate and was fully possessed, and it is said a witch has no tears.

The exact nature of her possession is open to analysis; nowadays people do not reckon to be possessed of devils, though various people who watched Jenny Flower grow up prophesied that she would end up by "going to the devil"—which for them was another way of saying going to the bad, for of Lucifer as "Light Bringer", "Day Star", and "Son of the Morning", they knew nothing.

But the story properly begins on a summer day in a forest in 1931, when, before she was seven years old, she met the Dark Stranger for the first time. It was the first day of August, which happens to be Lammas—but how should the godly know that they held a Sunday School treat on a witches' sabbath?

Jenny, in spite of all the injunctions from the woman she knew as mother to "keep with the others", and to hold the hand of one of "the big girls" all the time, in spite of all the shepherding and nagging of anxious teachers and helpers, had contrived to get lost. She was not in the least alarmed. She had made the excuse that she "wanted to go somewhere" and had skipped away down a grassy glade and plunged in amongst the tall trees. She was tired of holding Gladys Thompkins's hot and sticky hand; tired of the shouting and yelling of the other children, and of the fussy clucking of the grown-ups. She did not want to run in the egg-and-spoon race with the under-sevens, under the direction of Mr. Deakin, the curate, who had thick glasses and a loud, booming voice and called the children "kiddies", nor did she want to play rounders, or enter competitions, or collect wild flowers under the guidance of kind, religious Miss Mattingley. She did not want to be organised at all. She wanted to be solitary and free.

She plunged on through the trees until she could no longer hear the cries of the children, the commands of the adults, and there were no sounds but the tweets and chirrupings and trills and whistlings of birds. Sometimes there were breaks in the bird-song and then everything was very still, as though every leaf of all the millions was holding its breath and waiting, and you also waited and listened and heard your own heart beating. It was her first forest, her first school treat, and therefore her first visit to the country. There was a little recreation ground beside the river in that part of London's dockland where she had been born and bred, and a few sooty trees; and there was a row of trees, acacia and almond and ash, edging the concrete of the courtyard of the housing estate on which she lived, planted there by a thoughtful borough council which believed that a few trees on a working-class housing estate made "all the difference", like access balconies. So they did; people exclaimed, "What nice flats!" instead of "What horrid tenements!" The trees and balconies showed; the bath crowded into the scullery didn't. But the trees didn't do very well, because immediately opposite them, tall warehouses rose up and shut out the sunlight; between the blocks of flats and the warehouses the trees were at the bottom of a dark ravine, and they were thin and sickly with struggling up to the light. There were trees, too, round the church, with its pale, ornate tower like something off a wedding cake; these trees did a little better; they were less hemmed in, had more room to breathe, but by high summer they were dark and sooty, and they drooped over tombstones and neglected grass graves. Trees that formed great arches of green and gold light Jenny Flower had never known till that day in the forest. Nor any pool except the Pool of London. Now she found herself beside a little pool half covered with small white water-lilies and speared by rushes and bannered with wild yellow iris, and it was pure enchantment. She stood like a small wild animal at the edge of the pool, very still, rapt, and the tall dark figure in the shadow of the trees at the other side of the pool stood as motionless watching her.

In that long moment there was drawn the magic circle, round the pool, round the forest, round the brief candle flame that was the life of Jenny Flower.

She looked up, compelled by the dark gaze fastened on her. Perhaps it was the heritage of darkness in her own blood, but what she saw did not frighten her.

The tall figure emerged from the shadow of the trees, and she stared at him through the straight, lank, black hair which partly covered her face, and curiosity and interest warred in her with a defiant hostility. All adults were her natural enemies, and horns and cloven hoof could make no more difference than wings and halo. Apart from the horns he might have been a seaman, with his shabby dark clothes, the silk "choker" round his neck, the heavily studded belt round his middle. He looked a little foreign with his bright dark eyes and sallow skin, and a certain strangeness in the long, thin cast of his face, but Jenny was used to Malays, Lascars, Kanakas, Chinese, and one man was not more strange than another. It was a lean, hungry, slightly wolfish face, with lines bitten deep into it, the mouth a little crooked and bitter, but when he smiled the expression was gentle, a curious tenderness invading the lips and eyes.

He smiled now. "Hullo, witch!" he said.

"Witch yourself!" she answered him, truculently.

"You're wrong there, little one," he told her. "A witch is always female. I could be a sorcerer, a wizard, a demon, a warlock, or the devil himself, but not a witch."

He removed the antlers, and sighed. "I quite understand why kings don't go about wearing their crowns," he observed. He hung the antlers on a branch of a tree, and regarded them a little ruefully, and the child demanded, "Where did you get those things?"

He turned his bright dark gaze upon her again. "Perhaps I was born with them. Perhaps I found them in the forest." He came round the pool's edge and stood beside her. "Look—there's a dragon-fly—there on that leaf. He's just hatched out. See his wings quivering? He's drying them in the sun."

He knelt down beside her, put an arm round her, and together they watched the opalescent shimmer of the drag-on-fly's wings vibrating in a tremendous urgency of new life.

10

Suddenly the brilliant shining thing rose into the air, transparent wings outspread, electric blue body flashing in the sunlight. The child shrank back a moment, startled, as it darted forward. She gave a little gasp, then laughed, excitedly, turning in the arm that encircled her, looking direct into the dark face, all hostility melted, trust flowing in her. This stranger was not the enemy; he was the bringer of new things.

"What else?" she demanded, eagerly.

He laughed and rose and took her hand and commanded that she followed him.

He showed her and told her various strange things, and they were not the sort of things that Mr. Deakin or Miss Mattingley would have showed her and told her. He showed her the fairy-rings in the grass and told her how the Little People made them dancing there by moonlight. He lifted a boulder and showed her a large yellow toad—"And if you stare at it long enough it will die, but you must look it full in the eyes, and with hate." He showed her deadly nightshade, witches' bane, dragon-wort, hemlock with its smell of mice, and brilliant poisonous fungi like crimson and orange lanterns under the trees. They found a lizard sunning itself on a boulder, and an adder slithering in a ditch. He told her how to distinguish between the stinging nettle and the dead nettle; between an adder and an ordinary grass-snake. He showed her how to cure a sting from a nettle with the juice of a dock-leaf, and all that was poisonous and reptilian she saw through the eyes of enchantment.

When they were tired with wandering under the great arches of the trees, and in the hot sunny clearings where the tall, dry grasses hummed with insects, they sat in a cool brackeny hollow and he told her of tree-witches and wood-spirits, of nymphs and dryads, fauns and satyrs, and she listened with wonder and delight. In turn she told him about the Sunday School treat and how she had run away from the others. She confided to him that her eldest brother, Les, didn't believe in God, or

Heaven or Hell, or any of the things they learned at Sunday School, and she had told Les she didn't believe either; but this was only what they whispered together secretly—they would never dare say it to anyone. It was like bad words. She spoke breathlessly. Sometimes, she said, her brother twisted her wrist to make her say bad words. Once their mother caught him at it and said she would tell their father, and when he came in from work she told him and he took off his belt to them both. Their mother said they would go to Hell when they died and burn in everlasting fire. She gave a little shiver, remembering.

"But I don't care," she concluded, and the eyes that looked out through the tangle of hair were bright with defiance.

The stranger smiled. "Then you will go to the devil."

She repeated, "I don't care!"

He gave her a long searching look, then said, softly, "No, you won't care."

He picked up a snail and put it on the back of his hand and they sat watching it for a little, then suddenly he flung it away and said abruptly, "It's getting late. I must take you back." He fingered the label with her name and address pinned to her grubby cotton dress.

She protested, "I don't want to go home!"

"One day you won't. But that day is not yet. Come."

He pulled her to her feet and she fetched up against him, the top of her head against his belt. She was a thin, under-sized little thing. She smiled up at him with a child's coquetry.

"Carry me!" she commanded.

"All right—witch!" He swept her up into his arms.

"Witch!" she mocked him, but her thin arms were tight round his neck.

He carried her through the forest, from which the green and gold light was withdrawn. Now the undergrowth was invaded with shadows, and owls called in the tree-tops. There was an owl that seemed to be following them. Jenny shivered and buried her face in his shoulder, but the shiver was excitement rather than fear. The stranger looked down at her and smiled, but he said nothing.

In the train, dragging up through the straggling grey outskirts of the city, she slept in the hollow of his arm. The green countryside fell away behind them, a receding tide, and they faced into a grey increeping tide of mean streets. The sad hunting cry of the owl was replaced by the mournful hoot of ships on the darkening river.

It was still not quite dark when they left the tram. In one hand she clutched a wilting bunch of wild flowers, and with the other she clung forlornly to her companion. The dirty pavements gave back the heat of the day, a stale, used heat, airless. There was a smell of fried fish; the din of an automatic piano and drunken voices as they passed a pub on a corner. People lounged at open doors, and a sweaty smell of bedding and unaired rooms seeped out of the houses. Children played hop-scotch on the pavement with shrill cries, and shrieked in pursuit of one another.

Jenny said, as they approached the housing-estate, "I'll get a hiding for not coming home with the others."

He told her, "If you do, there'll be the devil to pay!"

"Where do *you* live?" she asked him.

"In Hell."

"That's only a place in the Bible. It's not real."

"It's real enough."

She persisted. "It's where people are s'posed to go when they're dead. Like Heaven."

"The living go there, too, to both places. But I was thrown out of Heaven young and pitched into Hell. I get on very well there, all things considered."

"Where do you really live?"

"They call it Paradise Court, but Hell's Backyard would have been a better name."

"Is it near here?"

"Near and far. It's across the river."

"Take me there!" She lifted her face to him, beseeching.

"One day, but not now. You're not old enough yet—to cross that particular river. But I'll be about when you want me."

She demanded, with a child's directness, "Where will you be?"

He answered her, carelessly, "Somewhere—you'll see."

They had stopped beside the low wall that ran along under the scrawny trees.

He bent, suddenly, and she felt his lips cold on her forehead, then he strode away into the dusk, and Jenny, with lagging steps, crossed the courtyard to the barracks in which she lived. She would get a hiding, for sure. But she didn't care. What the hell! It was an expression Les was always using. She repeated it now, under her breath, and it gave her a curious courage.

She did not get the hiding, as it happened; Mrs. Flower was gossiping in a neighbour's flat; her husband was at the pub, and when she returned Jenny was in bed and asleep, and Mrs. Flower believed in letting sleeping children lie. In the morning she listened impatiently to a confused story of the return journey, having already made up her mind that "the devil alone knows how the child got back". . .

Chapter II

Nell Flower

The couple whom Jenny knew as Mum and Dad were not in fact her parents, but this, also, she did not know until she was thirteen. Her mother was the young woman she knew as Auntie Nell—pretty Nell Flower, barmaid of the Six Bells, Limehouse. As to Jenny's father, as Nell herself explained to the lady almoner at the hospital at which Jenny was born, "It whittles down to one of three." But which of the three must forever remain one of Nature's secrets. They were all merchant seamen, and, as the lady almoner acidly observed, if you did not know the father of your child it was something to know his calling, and no doubt in years to come the child would be interested to know at least that much about her father. Nellie tossed her pretty head. She was eighteen, and she knew more about life than the lady almoner would ever know. Or so she believed. When Nellie Flower said life she meant men. She would like to have been certain, all the same, and she was always searching the child's face for the revelation of the secret—without finding even the faintest clue. Jenny was not like anyone except herself. She might have been a changeling.

Having failed to abort the child, Nellie was determined to get her adopted as soon as possible. Everyone at the hospital, the matron, the ward sister, the nurses, the lady almoner, tried to dissuade her, but Nellie was as indifferent to their poor-little-mite pleas as to their you-ought-to-be-ashamed-of-yourself censure. She had never wanted a child, and she did not want the one which, as she put it, had been "wished" on her. It seemed almost too good to be true when her brother Joe and his wife offered to relieve her of it. They had two boys, and Joe's wife, Ivy, dearly wanted a little girl, but she had had an operation after the birth of her second boy and she would not be able to conceive again. In Joe's view that was "fine", but Ivy had cried. She was, in her own words, "passionately fond" of children, and had been prepared to bear half a dozen boys in the hope of a girl ultimately. Little girls were so sweet; you could dress them so pretty. When Joe's young sister, Nell, "got into trouble", and having been unable to get rid of it, had brazenly declared that if she had to have it nothing should make her keep it, Ivy had secretly resolved that if the child turned out to be a girl she would persuade Joe to let her adopt it—always provided, of course, it wasn't a black baby, or anything like that. With a fast little cat like young Nellie there was no knowing . . .

She said nothing to the girl of this idea, but when the child was born she went with Joe to the hospital, and to her delight Nellie's baby was a girl, and not black—or brown, or yellow, or deformed—but just like any other new-born baby. It was even, she thought, a little like Joe. You would, after all, expect a family likeness. Joe was quite agreeable to the adoption of the child. It would be helping young Nellie out, and since Ivy's heart was set on it and she couldn't have any more of her own . . .

"No one shall know she's not our own!" Ivy declared, a proposition to which the child's mother was only too glad to agree. Ivy's eldest boy was six, the younger child three, and it was easy to introduce the new baby as their little sister—which the doctor had brought in his black bag as he had brought them. Shortly after the adoption of the child the Flowers moved across the river to the new working-class flats, where, with an entirely new set of neighbours, it was easy for Ivy to pretend the new baby was her own. As everyone in the family, both her own and Joe's, knew about her operation it was impossible to pass the baby off to them as her own, but she seldom saw any of them, and there was no reason why Jenny, as she grew up, should ever know that her Aunt Nellie was, in fact, her mother.

It was much better the child shouldn't know, Ivy argued. It was "not very nice" to be illegitimate, and in the circumstances relating to Nellie it was particularly shameful.

So Jenny, whose name was Flower anyhow, was brought up as one of the Flower family and accepted by Les and Stan as their sister, and Ivy prided herself on showing no favouritism. All went very well until Jenny was about five years old, and then it began to be evident that she had "bad blood" in her. She became one of those children who will kick and scream and throw themselves to the ground rather than do anything they do not want to do, and upon whom force has no effect except to heighten stubbornness and hysteria. Ivy knew only one way to handle such situations and that was by force, so that from time to time the most violent battles raged between herself and the child, and in these battles she was always defeated. Jenny could be thrashed within an inch of her life but she could not be made to do what she had made up her mind not to do. There was nothing for it but for the exhausted Ivy to refer the matter to her husband. Joe would take off his belt to the child and threaten to dam' near kill her, and very nearly did; but his only victory would be the child's physical collapse. He never succeeded in putting "the fear of God" into this adopted child as he did into his own children who would resort to any lies, subterfuge, compromise, or downright capitulation, to escape a "belting".

"She'll be better when she goes to school," Ivy said, and looked forward to that day.

But she wasn't. She shamed Ivy by playing truant, so that the school-board man came round. She strayed away and got lost and had to be brought back by a policeman, as though she were a lost dog, and it was a nice thing, said Ivy, having a copper marching up to your front door, and all the neighbours talking. She shamed Ivy, too, by playing with all the roughest children in the neighbourhood, and by getting herself as dirty as they were. Ivy prided herself on keeping the children "nice". It was a basic principle of her life that though you were poor there was no excuse not to be clean. And being clean meant keeping your place nice, keeping the children nice, looking "decent" when you went out. It meant you didn't run down to the shops in your overall, or go about all day with your hair in curlers; it meant seeing to it that your husband had always a clean shirt, ironed and aired and mended, ready to put on on Sundays; it meant that your children didn't have "things" in their hair—there were a lot of children with "dirty heads" at the school Les and Stan and Jenny attended; they were always known as "the dirty children", and sat apart from the others until they were clean—it meant a hot bath for the whole lot of you every Saturday night (the same hot of water did for all three children, of course) and in the hot weather washing your feet during the week as well. To be herself "clean and decent", and to achieve this for her family, was Ivy's objective in life. Decent meant not getting into debt, not going into a pub except with your husband, never taking a drop too much—not being foul-mouthed, like so many of the women; it meant keeping yourself to yourself, not letting the children run the streets, getting on with your neighbours and the tradespeople, not making eyes at other men. It meant being everything that Mrs. Oliver in the flat below was not. Mrs. Oliver was everlastingly in the family way; as soon as ever she was about again after a confinement she'd "fall" again; the neighbours waited and watched for it. And Mrs. Oliver didn't care. She slopped about best part of the morning in a dirty old dressing-gown—"asking for trouble", Ivy called it, and told Mrs. Oliver so, "to her face", but, "I don't have to ask", is all Mrs. Oliver said, brazenly. Mrs.

Oliver neglected her "place", her children, her own person. She and her husband stayed till closing time at the pub on Saturday nights and came home "tiddley", That and the dressing-gown were the reason for her large family. Ivy was convinced. It was disgusting. Ivy really worried about Mrs. Oliver and her large family and her goings-on.

But her biggest worry was Jenny. She did not like to admit that the child was unmanageable, but the fact remained that she was. It was enough to turn you against the child. She would not acknowledge the fact, but she did turn against her. That she herself was at fault, that her whole tactics in relation to the child were completely wrong, could not possibly have occurred to her. She was convinced that she loved children. According to her lights she did love them. But they were not lights that could ever light anything in a child. She "loved" children, like so many others, so long as they were good—that is to say, obedient, respectful, docile. And in Nell Flower's daughter there were none of those qualities.

Soon after the Sunday School treat she tried discussing the matter with Nell herself. After all, she was the child's mother . . . as though the biological fact had anything to do with understanding the child.

"She's a little devil and no getting away from it," Ivy complained. "Goodness knows what bad blood she's inherited through her father!"

Nell demanded, not unreasonably, "What's it to do with me? You've had the upbringing of her. You took her on knowing the circumstances. If you can't manage the kid you'd better go to the police about her and have her brought up before a Children's Court, and then they'll shove her in a reformatory out of your way."

Ivy was highly indignant. "You ought to be ashamed of yourself, talking so unnatural. Anyone would think you hadn't any natural feelings!"

"If I hadn't the kid wouldn't be here!" Nell pointed out.

"That's about the only thing you *have* got any feeling for!" Ivy retorted, and, as she said afterwards to Joe, could have bitten out her tongue the moment she'd said it, but really she was goaded into it . . .

Nell regarded her insolently, her fine dark eyes scornful under the curling fringe of pink ostrich feather of her hat. It was hard to realise, Ivy thought, that she was only twenty-five, but she was so hard! She seemed to Ivy, who was thirty-five, years older than herself.

"What else is there?" the girl demanded.

Ivy was, as she described it to Joe, completely taken aback. "Well, reely," she stammered, "what a thing to say!"

The girl smiled, derisively, "Well, go—I'm all ears!"

Ivy reddened. "There's—love, isn't there?" she forced herself lo say. It was almost as though she had been forced to say something indecent.

"Love! You bin going to the pictures too often! Call it what you like, it all comes to the same thing in the end. Calling it fancy names don't make it different. Here, I've had enough of this. I'm going!"

She got up and slung a fox fur round her shoulders. She was smart. Ivy thought, no getting away from it. She wouldn't mind having that suit—except, of course, that she could never wear it; she hadn't got Nell's figure—so beautifully slim.

"If you go by Wharf Street you'll meet Jenny coming from school," Ivy said, helplessly. "She'd be sorry to miss seeing you. She thinks the world of her Auntie Nellie. It's why I thought you might be able to do something with her."

"The kid would probably be all right if you didn't go on at her so."

"I like that!"

The girl smiled. "When I do hand out a bit of motherly advice you don't take it! So long. Give my love to Joe."

She was gone, leaving behind her a cloud of cheap, sweet scent. Ivy flung open the window on to the balcony and flapped about with a duster.

Then suddenly she sat down and began to cry. "Reely, to talk to me like that—a married woman of my age! The little slut! The dirty little slut! I won't have her coming here. They ought to be locked up, girls like her! She's nothing but a tart. Why does she come here? She's not reely interested in the kid, for all she brings her clothes and sweets. She's got no feelings for anyone except herself. Men, that's all she's interested in. Men and dressing herself up to fetch them. But if she thinks I'm going to let young Jenny go to the devil in the same way she's mistaken. I'll make her mind if I have to break every bone in her body . . . "

(2)

Nell, walking away down the narrow lane between the blocks of flats and the tall warehouses was asking herself the same question that Ivy had asked—why did she go there?

It wasn't to see her brother: she could see him any day of the week in the Six Bells, or find him at the warehouse where was a hand. It certainly wasn't to see her fool of a sister-in-law. Or because, on her half-day, she had nowhere else to go. She had plenty of places to go, and all of them a dam' sight more amusing than visiting at Ivy's. It wasn't for love of the kid, neither. Well, then, what was it?

Some men loading flour from a warehouse into a lorry "cheeked" her as she tippeted past on her four-inch heels. One of them sang a catch from a popular song, "Ain't—she—sweet?" She smiled faintly and tossed her head. Cheeky things. It gave you a warm feeling, all the same. Men. Well, what else was there? Clothes. But that was all part of it. Having a good time, enjoying life—it all came back to men. It you didn't enjoy life you might as well be dead. People like Ivy—what did they

21

get out of life? Slaving their guts out at housework; nagging at the kids; always frightened the old man was going to drink the pay-packet before he got home on a Friday night, or go off with some other woman; going to the pictures once a week, scraping and saving to get something new to wear, wearing yourself out trying to bring up the kids to be respectable—to lead the same sort of life. She wouldn't succeed in that with young Jenny. The kid had the devil in her. She was her mother's daughter; and her father's.

At that point she always had the sensation of having run up against a blank wall. The child's father. The one that had made her pregnant. Who had done *that* to her—slipped one over on her. Who? Who? What did it matter? What difference did it make? The kid wasn't like anyone except herself. But it must come out in her eventually. It must come out in her face. It couldn't be hidden for ever.

At the back of her mind she knew that the unanswered question was the sole reason for keeping in touch with the child; the sole reason she went to Ivy's. There was this secret hidden in the child. One day she must strike a clue. Once she had found it, once she knew, the child could go to the devil for all she cared. But she had to know. She had to know.

She turned out of the lane flanked by the warehouses, with the wharves and river on their other side, and into a side road of old grey houses whose squalor was relieved by an occasional acacia tree. She had told herself, on leaving Ivy's, that she had no intention of meeting Jenny coming from school; nevertheless she turned into Wharf Street, that led down to the main road and the school.

A straggle of children were already at the bottom of the road, skipping from kerb to gutter, gutter to kerb, taking flying leaps at the lamp-posts, chasing one another across the pavement, darting out into the road. Their shrill cries and shrieks came to her a long way off. Little hooligans, her mind said, but she smiled, faintly, and it was not the derisive smile she had turned on her sister-in-law. Kids. You had to laugh sometimes. They didn't give a dam', kids didn't . . . There was that unacknowledged alliance between herself and them.

Jenny recognised her almost as soon as she turned into the street. "That's my Auntie Nell!" With a loud whoop she broke away from her gang and came tearing along the pavement.

As she came up with Nell she gave a flying leap at her that nearly knocked her over.

Nell caught at her and steadied herself, laughing.

"Steady on!"

Jenny's hair was in her eyes; her face, hands, arms, legs, were dirty. Her cotton dress was dirty—though it had been clean on that morning.

"Where you going?" she demanded, refusing to be shaken off, her arms tight round Nell's waist, her face upturned, alight with eagerness.

"To the West End. And keep your grimy paws off my clean blouse, or I won't be fit to be seen. Let go, there's a good girl."

Jenny let go instantly.

"What you goin' up West for?"

What d'you think? To have a good time, of course."

"Take me with you!"

"You're not old enough."

They began to walk back in the direction of the river.

"Hurry," Nell urged, "we don't want all your gang tagging on." She inquired, as they quickened their step, "How are you getting on at school?"

"I've gone up," Jenny announced, triumphantly.

"Good Lord, you don't say! I bet that was a shock for everyone!"

"I wanted to be in Miss Drew's class. She's nice. She doesn't smack anyone, and she reads us stories during sewing. And she lets us leave the room when we like. If I'm good she's going to take me to the Zoo one Sat'd'y."

"Mind they don't keep you there—in the monkey house!"

Jenny gave her a small punch. Nell laughed. "What else you bin up to?"

"I went to our Sunday School treat last week. I got lost in the forest and a man brought me home."

"The devil he did! You're starting young!"

"He was nice. He had horns on his head at first. But he took them off."

"What on earth are you talking about?"

"Well, he did!" Jenny answered, with a child's conclusiveness.

Nell laughed. "Sounds like the devil himself!"

They had come out under the high grey walls of the warehouses. A flight of steps led up to a narrow alleyway, at the end of which another flight dropped down to the muddy foreshore of the river.

"Come here," Nell commanded. Jenny came to her, and Nell lifted her up and planted her half-way up the steps. "Let me have a look at you!"

She brushed the hair back from the child's forehead and gazed at her searchingly, holding the small dirty face between her hands with their long pointed nails and flashy rings. The secret of the child's blood—it must be written there. It must be! It was—if only she could read . . .

Jenny stood quite still, looking into the dark searching eyes. Auntie Neill often took her face between her hands and stared at her like this. She didn't mind; she never wanted to kick and scream and stamp with Auntie Nell. There was nothing she wouldn't do for her, and do instantly. She loved her.

After that long searching moment Nell took her hands from the child's face and lifted her down. It was no good. The kid wasn't old enough yet. Nothing showed in her face. She could be anybody's kid.

"I must go," she said. Then remembered. "You must be good," she added, severely. "Why are you so naughty at home?"

"I can't help it. I've got bad blood."

"What nonsense! Who says so?"

"Mummy."

"Her!" Again that tacit alliance. She made another effort. "You must try."

She looked at the child, uncertainly. It was difficult to know what to say. Jenny waited, expectantly, looking up at her, like a puppy waiting for another stick to be flung for it to gambol after. But Nell merely said, briskly, "Well—run along now. And don't forget what I said—be a good girl."

"Come again soon," Jenny urged, walking away backwards.

"Look where you're going," was all Nell said.

But it didn't matter what she said. She was on the child's side, and the child knew it, and it was all she needed to know.

She skipped along, a thin, dirty, under-sized wisp of a gutter-kid, chanting a little foolish song they sang at school when Miss Drew took them for games:

As I was going up Silver Hill
I met a piece of paper;
And what do you think
Was written upon it.
Merrily danced the Quaker.

But as she approached the blocks of flats she ceased to skip and sing and her bright face clouded over and became sly and furtive again as her spirit darkened. She would probably get a hiding for making her dress dirty; she would certainly get a scolding for being in late; she would have to wash up the tea-things, and she would be given other odd jobs to keep her out of mischief. Les and Stan would be allowed to go out to play in the courtyard (but they would sneak away down to the river and paddle under the old barges at the foot of the steps). She would not be allowed out, because she was "not to be trusted" . . .

But one day the man with the horns would come for her; he would come out from behind a wall, he would come round a corner, she would look over the balcony and he would be waiting in the yard below, and he would say, "Hullo, witch!" and she would run to him and no one would be able to stop her, and he would gather her up in his arms again, and take her back to the forest, the deep forest that was full of green and gold light, that was full of shadows and the cry of owls. If ever they came back it would not be to this place; they would cross the river into Paradise Court . . . which the man said was Hell, but everyone knew that Paradise was another name for Heaven. Though whichever it was it wouldn't matter, since he would be there, to watch over her and protect her, for ever.

Chapter III

Witch's Kitchen

From the oasis formed by the new blocks of council flats the grey wilderness of dockland slum flows for miles, out beyond the Isle of Dogs and Limehouse to Deptford and Greenwich, and almost, it seems, pouring out with the river into the sea. Its interminable greyness and its high dockyard walls can make it as oppressive as a prison, but it has its moments—the occasional crumbling grace of a Georgian doorway, the sudden impression of a ship crossing the road as it moves into a basin, the unexpectedness of a lamp bracket jutting from a wall, of a capstan marooned in an alleyway, of funnels thrusting up at the ends of streets, and always the smell of the river with its faint, fugitive hint of the sea. To Jenny, born and bred there, it was an endlessly adventurous and exciting world. There were steps down to muddy beaches where you could paddle; there was the swirl of water under the moored barges, the inrush of the wake of a tug, the perpetual movement of the river's traffic, the tall forests of cranes along the wharves, the loading and unloading of ships, the swoop of gulls—always something to see, something to watch, always something happening. She was one of London's noisy, grubby, lively dockland kids, shrieking and yelling with them, sharing their life of the mean streets and the river, yet not of them. She shared their activities, played and quarrelled and fought with them, but formed no friendships amongst them. She had only one friend, and that was not another child but an old woman—a repulsive old hag known locally as "Old Mother Beadle",

Mrs. Beadle lived in Ropewalk Alley, which was reached by a crumbling flight of steps down from the street above; at the other end it ran out to a wharf and a small wooden pier used by the river-police. Mrs. Beadle's house was one of a shabby row; at the front of each house, facing into the alleyway, there was one window upstairs and one down, and a front door opening immediately on to the pavement. On hot evenings people sat on their doorsteps or brought chairs out on to the pavement, to get the air, and to gossip. The inhabitants of Ropewalk Alley were considered "a rough lot" by the people who occupied the neat council flats; they declared that only people with no self-respect would live in such a place. In due course it would be swept away and its inhabitants forcibly moved up in the social scale; in the meantime they lived cheerfully enough, with the bugs in their layers of dirty wallpapers, and rats under their rotten floor-boards, and considered themselves, a little aggressively, as good as anyone else.

It was impossible to visualise old Mrs. Beadle in one of the clean and tidy new flats; she was essentially of Ropewalk Alley. Her clothing appeared to consist mainly of rags and bits of sacking, and her house swarmed with cats. She was hideous and extremely dirty and regarded by her neighbours as "queer", though not to the point of being "not all there", for there was plenty of evidence, one way and another, that she "had her head screwed on all right". She augmented her Old Age Pension by telling fortunes—palmistry and crystal-gazing—and selling concoctions of herbs for the inducing of abortions. There were plenty who swore by her; and she had a quite considerable clientèle for both departments of her activities. It was her boast that the police could never "pin anything on" her, and she was right, for they never did, though she caused them some uneasiness.

The children of the neighbourhood called her a witch, and "dared" each other to knock on her door and run away. They were afraid of her, and excited by their fear. If they saw her moving behind the dirty windows with their bedraggled curtains, they sang out to her "Old Mother Beadle! Can't thread a needle!" dancing about on the pavement in front of the house, but at the slightest sign of her approaching the window they darted wildly away. From a safe distance they called after her in the street, as she strode along like an old scarecrow with a man's battered felt hat pulled down over her face. She always ignored them, but they never wearied of the sport. The adults of the neighbourhood had a curious respect for her and continually rebuked their children—completely without effect—for tormenting her. She was supposed to be a person of some education. According to one story she was the widow of a ship's doctor—hence her knowledge of medical matters. Another story was that she had been a stewardess in a ship; another that she was really a "certificated" midwife, and thus "knew a thing or two". But no one ever dared to ask her anything about herself, and she never volunteered any information. She was a mystery to those who thought about it, but few of them ever did; they were used to her and accepted her. She was useful to them, too. She would always come in when anyone was in labour, till the midwife came . . . though the midwife was always furious when she found her there and always turned her out, opening windows after her and flapping about with a towel dipped in disinfectant. But the women of Ropewalk Alley were on her side against the midwife with her mania for fresh air and Lysol and everything just so. They didn't believe the midwife when she told them, curtly, that it was all nonsense that a lot of heartburn before the child was born meant it would be born with a good head of hair, and that it was mere superstition that if a woman was frightened by a mouse when she was "carrying" and put her hand to her face the child would be born with a birthmark like a mouse on its face. The evidence was all on the side of the midwife, but still they didn't believe her; just as they went on believing in "Old Mother Beadle" even when her prophecies failed to come true. She was supposed to have second sight, and the reputation for being a "wise woman" persisted whatever the evidence against it. She was useful to them in other ways, too; she could always be relied on for a pinch of tea or sugar if ever you were short—though if you didn't repay it you never got another. You could borrow a shilling off her any time you were short of the rent—and you paid it back promptly at the end of the week because you were not quite sure what she would do if you didn't. It was not that she would come round and give you a black-eye—the usual Ropewalk Alley method of settling an argument—but that you had the feeling she could do things other people couldn't. Perhaps you didn't exactly believe in spells and all that sort of thing, for all some people said Old Mother Beadle was a witch, but all the same she was queer. No getting away from it. There was a woman once who paid her back a shilling she'd borrowed with a bad coin. Mrs. Beadle took it back to her when she had had it refused at the stores in the High Street, and the woman denied that it came from her. Mrs. Beadle didn't say anything; she merely pressed it hard into the woman's hand and went away, and that same evening the woman upset a kettle of boiling water over that hand . . . There were several stories like that, so you didn't take chances with Old Mother Beadle. There might be nothing in all the stories, but all the same you never knew.

Ivy knew all about Mrs. Beadle from Nell. Nell had been taken to her by a friend when she was "in trouble", and despite the fact that Mrs. Beadle's herbal brew, absolutely guaranteed to do the trick, had done nothing more than give her diarrhoea, she in turn had taken people there, on the principle that what doesn't work in one case might in another—the old Ropewalk

Alley principle that you never knew. She took her sister-in-law there once to have her fortune told, because she was always trying to read the future in tea leaves at the bottom of her cup, and Nell said that wasn't the way to do it, and why didn't she have her fortune told properly, read in her hand, or in the crystal. Ivy was finally persuaded to go with her to Mrs. Beadle's, but the moment she got inside the house she "came over faint" and ran out. She said she had never known anything like the smell. You could cut the air with a knife, she declared.

Jenny made Mrs. Beadle's acquaintance by running an errand for her. She was playing truant from school, and swinging, bored, round the iron posts at the street end of the alley, when the old woman came to her door and called to her. Jenny did not share the other children's fear of her; but then she was altogether without fear. She ran the errand, was duly rewarded with a penny, and invited into the house. She was aware neither of dirt nor evil smell. She was entering the witch's house, and it was high adventure. The dark back room into which she was taken swarmed with cats of every kind, and the old woman addressed them affectionately, calling them her darlings. There were cats on the mantelpiece, on the dresser, on the table, in the hearth. They writhed round the old woman's and Jenny's legs and rubbed their heads against their knees; the place was moving with them.

Jenny picked one up and fondled it, rubbing her face against its head.

"Fond of cats?" the old woman demanded.

Jenny nodded.

"Have one," said the old woman. "Help yourself."

"My Ma wouldn't let me keep it," Jenny said, ruefully. "She doesn't like cats. She says they give her the creeps."

Mrs. Beadle grunted. "It's human beings that give me the creeps," she observed. "Like a piece of cake?"

Jenny nodded again and Mrs. Beadle lifted a tin from the dresser and took out half a seed cake. She cut off a hunk and handed it to the child, who accepted it silently. It was one of the first things she liked about Old Mother Beadle—that she didn't expect you to say Please and Thank You.

"You're Jenny Flower, aren't you?" The old woman stood by the dresser, a cat on her shoulders, looking hard at the child.

One more nod from Jenny; her mouth was too full for any other answer.

"I thought so. I thought I couldn't be wrong."

It did not occur to Jenny to ask her how she knew.

"You don't like school, do you?"

"Hate it!" Jenny managed to answer, between mouthfuls. It was before she had moved up into Miss Drew's class.

The old woman cackled. "That's right. Lot of dam' nonsense, school. Nobody ever learned anything worth knowing at school. You can always come here. Plenty to learn here. Look at that. Know what that is?"

"That" was a fly-blown reproduction of a photograph of the moon.

"It's the world," Jenny hazarded.

"It's a world, all right, but not this one. It's the moon. You can see the mountains. Great ranges of 'em. Volcanic, too. If you were up there you'd see the stars when the sun was shining. You'd get earth-light instead of moon-light. You'd see full earth and new earth instead of full moon and new moon."

Jenny looked from the picture of the moon to Mrs. Beadle's face, wonderingly.

There was a curious glitter in the old woman's eyes, and a suggestion of suppressed excitement in her voice, as she added, "That's more interesting than the geography they teach you at school, isn't it? Now come and meet Horace."

She led the way out of the kitchen and through a small scullery with a rough stone floor into a yard. She poked about, moving an overloaded garbage bin, a zinc bath, and an unemptied cat box, and then pointed:

"There he is, the precious!"

A very large toad squatted by the drain. Jenny stared, fascinated. She could not have said what fascinated her about the creature. It was just that it was strange and unknowable, like the moon.

She sank down on her haunches beside the creature, and it rolled its eyes and blinked and inhabited its own secret world. You could not fathom what went on behind its amber eyes, what stirred in its cold amphibian blood; it was the colour of earth, and cold as a stone. It had no part in the surrounding world. It was indifferent and apart. It had no grace of beauty, only the agelessness and coldness of a stone. But you could see a pulse throbbing under the warty skin—the pulse of life. It was like something from the mountains of the moon. In Jenny's mind it was linked with the strange things the old woman had been telling her about the moon. It was a part of all that other-world strangeness that for her had a more vivid reality than the commonplace.

She remembered the toad the stranger had shown her under a stone in the forest, and how he had said that if you stared it directly in the eyes, with hate, it would die. But she had felt no hate, no repulsion, and she felt none now; only a kind of awe, the sense of being in the presence of a mystery.

"There's great virtue in a toad," said the old woman. "It only has the evil eye for them that hate it. In the old days the poison of a toad was used to cure the plague and other sicknesses. Nowadays they fling stones at him—to teach him to be a toad! And d'you know why they do that?" The old woman's voice rose and her pale eyes became steely with anger. "They do it because they're afraid of something they don't understand. People always fear what they don't understand. It brings out the venom in them. The seed of the serpent!"

The old woman's words flowed over Jenny like waves on a seashore. There amongst the shingle at the bottom of her mind, some small imperceptible rearrangement was left by the inrush, something was deposited with the ebb. She did not need to understand. There was this natural affinity with the strange, with the things that other people found evil, poisonous, repellent, this as yet submerged knowledge of something outside of the daily commonplaces of living.

Enchantment was for her the deep forest through which she moved with deadly nightshade in her hand and an adder at her foot; it was her head upon the shoulder of the Dark Stranger, and starless night and the hunting cry of the owl; it was earth-light on the moon and no shade from the sun, and no living thing in the desolate volcanic wastes, and loneliness unutterable, the loneliness of space and dead worlds and infinity. It was the mystery of the toad living out his secret life beneath a stone, between the garbage bin and the drain. It was this dark "witch's kitchen" moving with cats.

After that first encounter she was always in and out of the grimy evil-smelling house, and Ivy came to hear of it and said that it had got to stop.

"That horrible old woman! Dirty old troll! She ought to be locked up! I won't have it! D'you hear me? And I mean what I say! So mind."

Jenny heard all right; she could hardly do otherwise, as Ivy's voice, shrill at the best of times, became a screech that could be heard in the surrounding flats when she was angry. She heard and she fully understood, but she had no intention of "minding".

When she was sent out to play in the yard, with instructions to "go out and stop out", but not to stir beyond the yard or she would get a "hiding", instead of slipping away to the "rec."—as the riverside gardens were invariably called—she would speed like a hare down the long grey street that led to Ropewalk Alley. She looked in nearly every day on her way from school, and when Ivy complained of her being late home, would say that she had been "kept in"; being sent on errands afforded her other opportunities, for who was to know how long she had been kept waiting in the shops?

These visits to Mrs. Beadle were pure enchantment. Once across the threshold of that unsavoury house and she was filled with the wonder and excitement of strangeness. Ordinariness stopped outside. The dilapidated door opened on to a new world. The world to which she belonged.

On the hottest day the kitchen range was always going, and the old woman was always brewing strange concoctions in a big black cauldron. She would wander miles to gather weeds from a bit of waste ground for her brews. Some were supposed to be good for rheumatics, some were to be used for liniments, some were merely supposed to be healthful infusions; others had more sinister uses—though Jenny knew nothing of that till later. In the room above the kitchen there were bunches of every kind of herb, dried and hanging on the walls, or sealed in jars whose outsides were thick with dust and cobwebs. There were ancient books of simple and herbal remedies, and even stranger books dealing with "magical confections", "unctions", "potions", "philtres". And one book older and bigger than the rest which was *The Book of Magick*, in which there were pictures of Demons, Vessels of Wrath, or Iniquity, inventors of evil things and wicked arts. Fallen Angels, and a strange thing called an Incubus. There were in the book detailed instructions for the raising of these evil spirits, nocturnal, diurnal, and meridional. Jenny could not read the text, but she was never tired of looking at the pictures; she gazed long and fearlessly at their fearsome faces, and she learned their names, becoming as familiar with Apollyon, Belial, Asmodeus, Mammon, Theutius, Ophis, Astaroth, Abaddon, and the Spirit of Anti-Christ, as other children are with Cinderella, Red Riding Hood, Aladdin, Sinbad, and the Good Shepherd, and as fascinated by their stories. She could gabble the Abracadabra with much greater ease than she could repeat the Athanasian Creed. She never mastered the Catechism—and thus never came to Confirmation—but in a catechism of sorceries and secret things she would have passed with honour long before Confirmation age. And she did, ultimately, come to Confirmation, though not of Holy Church.

In this upper room where the herbs and old books were kept there were also, on the walls, yellow and crumbling Magick Tables of the Planets, their Intelligences and Spirits, with representations of their Seals and Characters. The old woman explained that before a Familiar Spirit could be raised it was necessary to find out to which planet his nature agreed, but all this belonged to the mysteries of Ceremonial Magic and was best not tampered with, for raising a devil was one thing, but getting rid of him again not so simple . . . It was better to keep to the wisdom and sorceries of Natural Magic, and if there were questions to be asked of the future there was always the crystal. Only it was better not to ask.

Witchcraft, said the old woman, was as simple or as complicated as you chose to make it.

She said a number of things like that which meant nothing to Jenny. She was always mumbling and muttering, and addressed the cats as often as the child, but, though she did not understand, nothing left Jenny quite untouched; the waves went over her and ebbed, leaving no outward impression, but there was that imperceptible disturbance of the shingle of ideas at the bottom of her young mind.

The Chart of the Characters of Evil Spirits fascinated her particularly and she was always returning to it. These Characters included certain simple things simply depicted. There was Water—which recalled for her the pool in the forest; there was A Creeping Thing, which looked to her like the lizard the Stranger had shown her; there was a Serpent, which reminded her of the adder; there was a Flying Thing, which made her think of the owl which had followed them with its sad lost cry when they were leaving the forest, and, finally, of the things she recognised and understood, there were Horns such as the Stranger had worn.

In addition there was Flame, a Sword, a Scourge, and a Crown, but these did not interest her, offering no association of ideas.

When she told Mrs. Beadle about the Stranger and the forest, and pointed out to her on the chart the things she had seen there, the old woman gave her a long strange look. "We shall have you saying your prayers backwards yet!"

At that Jenny laughed. "Oh, but I can do that now! Listen—I'll show you—"Jesus gentle, mild and meek—"

But the old woman seized her and clapped a hand over her mouth. "No," she said, sharply, "No—not yet—"

Chapter IV

Marian Drew

To say, simply, that Marian Drew was the daughter of a country vicar is to state a truth which nevertheless suggests something untrue—the picture of a dull, pious home life, narrow, conventional, smothering. Whereas, in fact, life in the Reverend Charles Drew's vicarage, set

down amid the cherry orchards of the Welsh border country, more nearly resembled that of a circus than of a normal country parsonage. To the stranger within those shabby gates there was a sense of trampling and bellowing and perpetual uproar; of numerous noisy activities all going on at the same time—a child howling, someone banging away at the piano, someone hammering, someone yelling to someone else, and someone shouting to the yelling one to "Shut up!" The Drew family was large and energetic; Mrs. Drew decided early on that it was quite unmanageable and that it was best to let it go its own way, and that the most unmanageable person of the whole family was the vicar himself.

He was a fierce, angry little man who could never get over the fact that the Western world which claimed to be civilised and Christian was, in fact, nothing of the kind, but eaten out and in with the lust for Money and Power, and hurtling in a Gadarene headlong descent to its own destruction—and in moments of bitterness he had no wish to save it, no wish to be a voice crying in the wilderness. "And I am one," he would complain, in a great roar of anger, "I am one! And it makes me sick. Because it's no use! No use! No use! Humanity is beyond saving. It's rotten through and through!"

His family were used to these outbursts and paid little attention to them. That is to say the children paid no attention. But Mrs. Drew never got used to them; they always made her sigh. She felt very deeply for Charles and his disappointment in the human race. She suspected that he was really a saint—an angry and rather difficult saint, but a saint all the same. But in these moods of righteous anger and despair Charles would have none of her either. He would roar at her, too. "It's no use you sighing and nodding your head, Katie. You're a miserable sinner, too. We're all miserable sinners! All worms! I don't know why the Almighty doesn't send another flood and wash humanity clean out of existence and give the earth another chance—a chance to breed something different! Something wholesome—something guaranteed not to defile the face of the earth!"

In other moods he would insist that one must believe that humanity was capable of salvation, that one must go on struggling to let in a little light for the sake of the few who were not worms, the few who had what he called "spiritual vertebrae", the few who would survive the Gadarene descent, the few who were not involved in it. At these times he would insist upon the value of the voice crying in the wilderness—insist upon it angrily, as though someone had denied it such value, glaring at his family, who would have been the last to deny it. Despairing or armoured with faith he was always fierce. It was a private joke amongst his children, as they grew older, that he was the fiercest Christian who ever preached the gospel of love and meant it.

During the first years of her married life Mrs, Drew would allow herself to be drawn into arguments with her husband, pointing out his inconsistencies, attempting to answer his enormous, unanswerable questions—"What does it all mean?

What are we going to do about it?"—but she gave it up in time. With her large family. she had, increasingly, too many other things to think about. In any case it was no use attempting to argue with Charles. He had a way of steam-rollering everything you said. Or of just not listening, but of plunging after his own ideas down the labyrinthine ways of endless intellectual perspective. She came to realise, too, that he didn't really want an argument, or even a discussion, but only to relieve his feelings. To a certain extent he did it from the pulpit—which was why his congregation dwindled away. But what did he care whether he was liked in the parish or not? He had a contempt for popular parsons as for popular politicians. He had a contempt for all yes-men. Any charlatan or mountebank could win an easy popularity by always saying the right thing on the right occasion, by kow-towing and avoiding the unpleasant and the controversial, by evading, and being tactful and charming. But Jesus Himself was reviled and persecuted, so why should Charlie Drew, a mere country parson, struggling ineffectually to let in a little light, care what people said about *him*?

"If only Daddy wouldn't go *on* so!" his children said of him, amongst themselves, as they grew older.

But they loved him and respected him, the fierce, angry, roaring little man who loved them so much that it made him angry to think of it. He accused them of not having a brain between them, and when they passed exams, and acquired degrees, and, generally, creditably acquitted themselves in their chosen spheres, he would bellow at them that any fool could get a degree by swotting enough, that it didn't prove anything, that the biggest fools he knew were all M.A.'s . . . but he was proud of them, and they knew it.

Johnny, the eldest, took a medical degree and went off to India—"of all places!" snorted the vicar—to set up a dispensary in the jungle; David lived up to his name, studied Welsh—"*Welsh!*" said the vicar, scornfully, though it was an old love of his—and disappeared into a Welsh university; Richard wanted to paint, and did—"the young fool!" said the vicar, but he had one of his paintings framed in his study and every visitor to the house was commanded to admire it, "Because," he would declare, aggressively, "whether you realise it or not, that boy can paint!" And the visitor, with the vicar's blue eyes blazing at him would not think of disagreeing. But it was true; Richard Drew could paint. He went to Paris and contrived to live there, and sent occasional post-cards home, and his father kept them tied in a bundle in his desk amongst his old sermons. Joan also studied Welsh, and followed her twin, David, over the border, to work in a public library. In due course she took her exam, and passed it with distinction and became a fully fledged librarian. Her father called her a "blue-stocking" and accused her of having all the knowledge and knowing nothing. "Books!" he roared, "Better if they were all burnt, every one! Encouraging people to get their ideas at second-hand instead of thinking for themselves! Reading when they ought to be creating! If we all lived properly we'd have no time for books!" But every room in the vicarage was full of books, and the walls of the vicar's study were covered with them from floor to ceiling. What is more he was frequently seen reading a book . . . and he kept Joan's photograph on top of his desk and dusted it every day with the sleeve of his coat, no one being allowed to do any dusting in the study, though sometimes when he was out Katie would slip in and what she called "run a duster round", meticulously careful not to move anything, so that he wouldn't know.

Gwen, the youngest, who was beautiful—"and brainless," said her father, who felt himself forced to libel her to offset the fact that he adored her—married a local farmer's son at eighteen, settled down happily as a farmer's wife in the district, and produced a child at the end of the first nine months almost to the day. Charles christened the child himself in his own church, which had the wilderness of the vicarage garden on one side of it and a cherry orchard on the other. He did it with a lump in his throat and tears in his eyes and despised himself as "a sentimental old fool". He confessed it freely that he always cried at weddings and christenings, but funerals, he would declare, were often funny. The names given the child in his baptism were Charles Edward Morgan, but to the Drew family he was never anything but Charlie Two.

Whenever he looked at his grandson Charlie One found it very difficult to go on being fierce and angry and disappointed in the human race. Through a new-born child, untouched by the world, you could reaffirm your faith, rediscover the vital belief that man was born good but corrupted by civilisation; you could believe again that in the beginning God made Man in His Own Image. Man fell from grace, it is true, but inspired prophecy had promised that "a little child shall lead them . . . "

Gwen came to stay at the vicarage for a few weeks every summer—she liked to come for the cherry picking—and at these times the old house which seemed to Charles and Katie more of a great empty barn every year as the young people went from it, took on new life again. Joan always contrived to take her holidays to coincide with Gwen's visit, and Richard—even Richard—would come from Paris for a week. Marian and David couldn't get away at that time, and Johnny, of course, was in India, but there were always other young people to fill up the spare rooms and bring the house "to itself", as they called it, again. Katie got a little confused sometimes; she was never quite sure exactly who was staying in the house, or how many would be in for any given meal, whether it was fourteen or fifteen, but Charles would roar at her, what did it matter? She fussed too much; she was too much of a Martha; couldn't they all go out into the orchard and eat themselves silly with cherries? Weren't there gallons of last year's perry still in the casks? And if Katie protested that young people couldn't live on cherries and perry he would roar back that it was time they learned . . . Katie would sigh; Charles could be very trying at times with his impatience of practicalities.

It was worrying and it was difficult, but all the same it was the happiest time of the year, the cherry picking, with "golden Gwen"—Dick's name for her—about the place again, and her lovely baby, and all the other young people with their bright clothes and their eager voices and their laughter, and the evenings, the lovely long, light, June evenings, with everyone a little gay on perry, and Joan looking quite unlike a young lady librarian—Joan with her hair falling over her face and a red handkerchief round her neck, standing on a table in the middle of the drawing-room and playing an accordion as movingly as she played the organ in church on Sundays, whilst the others sat about singing "The Queen was in the Counting-House" to the tune of "Come all ye Faithful"—no one singing more lustily than the vicar himself—singing German drinking songs picked up on holidays abroad, singing the choruses of French music-hall songs, introduced by Dick, and such English classics as "Pollywollydoodle" and "Frankie and Alfie" . . .

Those were the carefree days of the nineteen-twenties. In the big cities there were tea dances and dinner dances and "wild parties" and Bright Young Things; but the Drews amongst their cherry trees knew as little of all that as though they were set down on an island of the Outer Hebrides. The First World War had not touched them; Johnny had been a medical student of eighteen when it had ended, Richard an art student of sixteen, Marian a school-girl of fourteen, Gwen a child of eight, the twins only two years older. Charlie Two made his appearance in 1929, by which time the outer world had sobered up before the threat of financial collapse, but when life at the vicarage was still in riotous full swing, Gwen's visits with her son adding considerably to the riotousness.

One feature of those visits was that on Sunday mornings Charlie Two would be wheeled into church in his pram, which was parked at the top of the aisle, beside the Drew family pew. People were a little startled at first, even scandalised, but anyone who didn't like it, said the vicar, could stay away, for what was the church for if it was not to be a family place? So Charlie Two lay on his back in the pram almost under the lectern, and waved his arms and kicked his feet in the air and made glugging noises, whilst Charlie One read the lessons and delivered his angry sermons, glaring round the church whilst he enunciated the gospel of love for all men, and Gwen rocked the pram with one hand and turned the pages of her prayer book and her hymn book with the other, and the people who were outraged stayed away, but the people who had stood by the Reverend Drew all along accepted the pram and the baby along with everything else that was unusual about their vicar.

All this, then, lay behind the simple statement that Marian Drew, London council school-teacher, was the daughter of a country parson. She had decided quite early on that teaching was her vocation—"As if one blue-stocking in the family weren't enough!" groaned the vicar—and that it must be in some way related to social work, and she had gone to the jungle of London's dockland in the same spirit as Johnny had gone to the Indian jungle. Richard called it, mockingly, "the family missionising spirit"; he respected them both, but he had to mock for the same reason that his father had to roar; he sat about at cafés in Montparnasse and the Quarter and talked mockingly of the country parsonage from which he'd "escaped", and of his doctor brother in India, and his school-teacher sister in London, "up to their necks in good works"... and in spring, when the chestnuts of the Luxembourg gardens wore a country freshness of young green, he would steel his heart against the insidious memory of the cherry trees in a white foam of blossom round the great barn of a vicarage and the little church, telling himself, resolutely, that there was nowhere to touch Paris in the spring.

All the Drew exiles, Johnny in India, the twins in Wales, Richard in Paris, Marian in London, were homesick in the spring, but Marian more than any of them; then more than at any other time she would have the sense of being enclosed in a wilderness of bricks and mortar, beyond the reach of the spring's green tide. But her vocation lay in that wilderness—though why it had to be London instead of a Welsh mining district, or Tyneside, or Clydeside, she did not know, any more than Johnny could have said why it had to be India for him, and not Arabia or the Mexican interior or the Malay Peninsula, or any other place in which he could have served as usefully. She and her eldest brother and her father had one great objective in common—what the Reverend Drew called "letting in a little light", which was another way of saying fighting ignorance and superstition and stupidity, the vicar for the sake of spiritual values essential to human happiness and "the Good Life", Johnny for the sake of physical health, his preoccupation being the human body, Marian for the sake of the children whom she saw as the chief victims—physically and spiritually—of adult ignorance, superstition, and stupidity. She wanted that all children should have as happy and natural a childhood as she and her brothers and sisters had had. When she was fourteen she mothered the twins, aged ten, and Gwen, aged eight; when she was sixteen she declared her intention of marrying young and having a large family—six at least, like her mother, three boys and three girls, one son as brilliant as Johnny, one as gay and good-looking as Dick, one as scholarly as David, and one daughter as clever as Joan, and one as lovely as Gwen, and one who would be all the things she was not but would like to be . . . But it didn't work out like that; it was the little sister who made the early marriage and started a family. The young men who came to the vicarage liked Marian well enough; in fact they liked her very much, and some even thought her attractive, with her pale oval face, dark hair and soft, gentle, dark, eyes, but they did not fall in love with her; they fell in love with Joan, who was quite the least good-looking of the three sisters, and who was not interested in marrying and having children, but belonged with her twin brother in a world of books, and Welsh poetry and Welsh music and Welsh legend. By 1930, when she was twenty-six, and living and working in London, Marian began to be resigned, telling herself that perhaps it was better this way—to devote herself to a number of children instead of merely to some half-dozen of her own. It could still happen, of course, the lovely miracle of falling in love, of having someone in love with oneself, and of bearing children as the outward and visible sign of that love; but she attached importance to having children young enough to be young with them; if love and marriage and children happened now, in her late twenties, it would not be the dream as she had dreamed it.

It had never been her intention to go to London's dockland merely to teach routine subjects—in whose value she had no belief—in a council school. The school teaching was merely a means to an end, the end being contact with children outside of the school, and, through that, approach to their homes and parents. It was, as she saw it, the parents who needed education, not the children. Contact with social workers and probation officers confirmed her belief that it was the parents who were responsible for anti-social conduct in children, not any natural badness in the child itself. The natural creative tendencies of the child were thwarted and twisted into destructiveness; love was corrupted into hate, a child's natural courageousness and honesty into fear and insincerity. You could only redirect the "badness" and destructiveness in a child back into goodness and creativeness through love—the only kind of love a child understood, by being on the side of the child; by eliminating punishment, moral or physical, you eliminated fear, and by casting out fear you cast out hate, and made room for a free, natural, spontaneous love to flow in the child again. When children ceased to be unhappy and afraid—and a child with hate and fear in it was innately unhappy—they would cease to be what was commonly called "bad". This was as much an article of faith with her as that human beings were capable of salvation was for her father . . . despite the black, angry moods in which they were all worms, all doomed and damned in a Gadarene self-destruction.

Early in 1931 she achieved an ambition by organising, with two other women, a Children's Club, the object of which was to take young adolescents off the streets and provide them with interests other than Hollywood films and ogling each other at street corners. For six months she lived with her colleagues. Miss Hawkins and Miss Pritchett, in the rooms above the Club, which was a converted shop. At the end of that time she reached the point at which she felt that if either of them referred once more to "the paw", when speaking of the working classes, she would scream. They were in their middle-thirties, spinsters and—so they frequently declared—proud of it, impatient of women who believed that love, marriage, children, were the deepest fulfilment for Woman; they were ardent feminists, acutely conscious of the sex inequalities operating against women, and never doubted, since they read *Time and Tide* and the *New Statesman* and voted "Labour", that they were "progressive". They had boundless energy and unswerving devotion to their various causes. One of their avowed causes was "the emancipation of the working-class woman". It appeared that what she had to be emancipated from was her "sex inferiority" and her meek "subjection" to the male in rôle of husband. They had to be made politically conscious. It was appalling, declared Miss Hawkins and Miss Pritchett, how they never bothered to use their vote and echoed their husbands on all political matters. "My hubby says—" Shocking! They had, too, to be freed from the idea that there were certain things that were specially women's jobs and certain things that were essentially men's jobs. It was true, they said, that some women would be incapable of driving a railway engine if they tried all their lives, but this was also true of some men . . .

Marian found all this feminist generalisation and assertion both tedious and exhausting. They "went on" about things so. But they had money and organising ability and fell in with her scheme for a children's club. She relied on the fact that they had so many other "causes" that after the first novelty of running the club had worn off they would be only too glad to leave it mainly to her, which proved to be the case. They held Committees—which was so much less tiring than "coping" with all those romping, roaring children. Children in social and psychological theory were one thing, but children in the flesh, particularly East End gutter kids, merely gave one a headache. It was different for Drew, of course—they always used surnames—she was, after all, a school-teacher.

Marian parted from them, except for purposes of Committee, at the end of six months. She needed, she said, to live nearer the school, and she had found a room overlooking the Pool which would save her a tram journey. They "perfectly understood". She had the feeling that they really did understand and were relieved. Their relief was a fact. They conceded that she was "good" with children, and "really quite wonderful" with the mothers, that she was a great asset to the club, with her school-teacher's "knack" in the handling of children—they were frankly terrified of some of the older ones who came to the club, the big boys who seemed to them such hooligans. positively young gangsters, and the sophisticated young girls of fourteen and fifteen, lipsticked and worldly and earning their own livings at an age when the previous generation had still worn gym slips and blue serge bloomers bagging down to black cashmere stockings—but her lack of enthusiasm for feminist causes they found at times very trying, certainly to live with. She needed almost as much "education" as the mothers themselves.

They also considered that she had no sense of humour because she never thought stories of the droll sayings and mis-pronunciations of charwomen, "and people like that", funny. To Miss Hawkings and Miss Pritchett "the paw" were in many respects "perfect screams". They discussed them with affectionate amusement, imitating their accents—convinced that they were all completely without aspirates and all talked with a Cockney accent. "The paw" were comical; lovable—they wouldn't hear a word against them, they declared—but comical. Like some peculiar species in a zoo, Marian would think, angrily. It never for a moment occurred to these lady social workers that they condescended to these people they professed to love and admire, that their very jocularity with them was condescension, since they would not have dreamed of behaving in similar fashion with people of their own class. They called it being free and easy, "getting on with" the working class, making them feel at ease, and that the people they thus condescended to might laugh at them behind their backs—"them and their la-di-da voices"—was unthinkable, still less that they should resent them, "poking their noses in where they're not wanted!" With their class obvious, in their voices, their manner, their clothes, even in the set of their hair, they honestly believed that working-class people accepted them as one of themselves, unaware of any class differences, that they did not think of them as "ladies".

Marian had no such illusions. She was well aware that as a school-teacher—with all that that suggested of superior education—and "one of the ladies that ran the club", and as a spinster, the children's mothers regarded her as completely remote from themselves. And she was remote from them, she would tell herself, both as to social background, education, and experience. The most she could hope for was that they should like her, trust her, regard her as a friend. She organised evenings for the mothers; she got up discussions, and when the discussions lagged she sat down at the piano and coaxed them out of their shyness into community singing. She started a small lending library, which in addition to romantic fiction rather better than their usual tuppenny paper run of reading included simply written books on birth-control and marriage, and the sex education of children. In time the mothers began to come to her for advice—what to do about Teddy and his fits of temper, since tanning the hide off him didn't seem to have any effect, and there might be something in what she had said in there always being a reason for badness in children; what to do about young Elsie aged fourteen who was boy-mad, and, gradually, in time, for the address of that birth-control clinic she had mentioned. At first they hesitated to discuss such personal matters with her, because she was a spinster, and it "didn't seem right"; but she overcame that diffidence by making it clear that knowledge of "the facts of life" was not confined exclusively to the married, and that no modern intelligent person expected them to be. It took time and patience to break down their prejudices and get them to discuss their problems simply and frankly, in discussion groups, and in their private conversations with her, but she had endless patience because she had endless sympathy. They had to be helped because of the children. If their sex lives were wrong their nerves were frayed and they were irritable with the children, nagging at them and punishing them; if they had unwanted children it was unfair to the children themselves. And in addition to all this they had to be helped to understand children, shown that loving a child was not rubbing its chest when it had a cold and boxing its ears for its own good when it didn't "mind," but allying themselves with the child, and this was the most difficult light of all to let in, because of the heavy, close-drawn curtains of fixed ideas encountered at all points.

It was slow, uphill work, and it would have been easy to have become disheartened at times, but she persisted, as her father did in his parish, believing in the value of the single brand snatched from the burning.

But the one mother she most wanted to meet, whom it seemed, increasingly, it was most important to meet, steadily refused to come to the club socials and discussions, and that was Mrs. Flower.

Chapter V

"Meet We No Angels?"

Marian's interest in Jenny Flower was excited by her colleagues' warnings against the child. They were all extremely glad when she passed out of their hands, and all expressed their sympathy for "poor Miss Drew" when she moved up into her class. She was quite unteachable, they declared, and no amount of punishment made the slightest difference, either to her conduct, which was abominable, or to her inattention to lessons. And she could learn, they all insisted, if she made up her mind to it, because she was by no means a dull or stupid child; she was, quite simply, a little devil, and if Marian Drew imagined that her psychological theories of love-and-kindness were going to work in this case she was in for a very big disillusion. The child ought to be in an industrial school, some of them went so far as to assert, adding that she would probably end up as a graduate of Borstal . . .

To all of which Marian merely observed, with a smile, that "she sounds interesting!"

Jenny moved up into Miss Drew's class with every intention of "playing her up". What else were teachers for? It ought to be easy with Miss Drew; she wasn't "strict." There were several teachers like that; they never smacked you, or kept you in, or gave you lines to write—"I must pay attention" one hundred times—or sent you out to "governess" for "the stick"; instead they took you aside after class and "jawed" you; if you were "soppy" you broke down and cried and promised to be good in future, but if you were like Jenny you merely tossed your head and laughed and were cheeky. All such teachers were "softies" and you played them up all you knew; you thought them "soppy" . . .

Where Jenny made the mistake was in assuming that Miss Drew substituted moral persuasion for punishment. It did not take her very long to realise that it was impossible to play Miss Drew up; "playing-up" a teacher meant annoying, harassing, embarrassing, and generally tormenting her; but Miss Drew seemed not to mind what anyone did; she made no attempt to keep order, and for a week the class was in an uproar; after that it became a bore; as Miss Drew didn't mind, and as there was no excitement of evading punishment, or seeing other people overtaken by it, there ceased to be any point in creating a disturbance; as there was no discipline to defy there was nothing to be defiant about. Other teachers, unable to keep order, got red-faced and flustered; they raised their voices, they banged on the desk—it was fine and exciting. Miss Drew merely went on marking exercise books and waited for the din to subside.

The first day in Miss Drew's class Jenny slipped a snail inside the teacher's desk at the first opportunity. Several of the children knew that Jenny had done this and waited expectantly, with excited whispers and giggles, for the teacher to lift the lid of her desk . . . Marian knew from the whispers and giggles that something, some "surprise", was in store for her. When she opened the desk and discovered the snail making a slimy trail across the cover of an exercise book, she took it out and put it on the top of her desk, then unfolded a pocket magnifying glass and proceeded with great intentness to examine the creature through it, watched with no less intentness by the children. They had expected her to be startled, horrified, indignant, to demand of the class as to who had done this thing—then they would have had the fun of playing her up by not telling, or by declaring that one of "the good girls" had done it. After a few minutes Marian looked up, smiling. "Anyone like to come and look through the magnifying glass?" she inquired. The children were still further abashed; no one moved. Marian looked at Jenny, and Jenny, fascinated as always by something she did not understand, got up and came forward. The snail through the magnifying glass was as fascinating as the dragon-fly on the forest pool, as the mountains of the moon, as the toad in his secret world. The snail was also a strange secret thing inhabiting a private world. She peered through the glass, and Marian looked over her shoulder, one arm round her, drawing her close, not merely the small child's body of Jenny Flower, but something in the child herself. Jenny suddenly turned in the circle of the teacher's arm and smiled, as she had turned in the circle of the stranger's arm after their examination of the dragon-fly. . . .

Later in the day, when a sympathetic colleague inquired of Miss Drew as to how she had got on with "that dreadful little Jenny Flower", she was astonished to receive the reply, "Oh, we're great friends. I'm taking her to the zoo on Saturday. She's interested in Gastropoda . . . "

On that Saturday at the Zoo Marian learned a great deal about Jenny's background; she learned about "Mum" and "Dad" and "Stan" and "Les", and "Auntie Nell" and "Old Mother Beadle"—and someone in a forest who had worn horns on his head. One of the reasons why she wanted to meet Mrs. Flower was to fathom the mystery of this horned one. Not that she believed he had horns, but to find out if possible in what this curious fixation in the child's mind was rooted. She was convinced that Jenny was not "making it up", that she had seen something which had made a vivid impression on her mind.

For her part Jenny didn't understand why Miss Drew should be so puzzled. Mrs. Beadle wasn't. She began to talk to Miss Drew about Mrs. Beadle. At first she had told her only that she lived in a house full of cats, that she had a pet toad, and that everyone called her a witch. But gradually she began to tell the teacher some of the things Mrs. Beadle had taught her—about Belial and Apollyon, and Demons and Furies, and the Magick Tables, and the Chart of the Characters of Evil Spirits, upon which was all the things the Stranger had shown her in the forest, the Flying Thing, the Creeping Thing, the Serpent—and the Horns.

"And Mrs. Beadle can call up evil spirits," Jenny continued, triumphantly.

"No," Marian said, sharply. "That's all nonsense. There are no such things as evil spirits!"

Jenny made no answer. She knew that Miss Drew believed in God, in Heaven, surrounded by Angels, and that Mrs. Beadle believed in the Devil, in Hell, surrounded by Evil Spirits. And she herself believed in Mrs, Beadle. Mrs. Beadle had all the evidence. Miss Drew couldn't "prove it" about God and his angels, but Mrs. Beadle could prove it about the Devil and his Evil Spirits. You could raise the Devil himself if you knew how, and Mrs. Beadle did know how. It was all there in the old books, in the tables and charts, and in the stars. It was all a great mystery, but it was real—as the stars were real, and the fat yellow toad with the pulse beating in his throat, and the shadowless mountains of the moon.

Jenny, not yet seven, could not reason about it; she could not urge, as an adult might have done, "You believe in God, therefore you must logically believe in the Devil. You can believe in neither God nor the Devil, in neither Heaven nor Hell, but you cannot logically believe in one and not the other. That people do not believe in the Devil and Evil Spirits nowadays is because—leaving lip-service to the Church out of it—they don't fundamentally believe in God. They neither love Good nor hate Evil. They are full of confusion and cannot distinguish one from the other. When it comes to the point they don't know God from the Devil. They don't know that what they have made of religion is the very Devil. When they worship what they call God they worship everything that is anti-life; when they go to what they call the Devil they embrace life. They have turned God into the Devil, and the Devil in turn becomes that Supreme Good—happiness, beauty, love, zest for living—which is God."

Jenny's belief in Evil Spirits was bound up with her fearful belief in God; her excited, defiant denials of God in the secret sessions with "Les" were part of that fearful belief; you knocked on God's door and ran away and cocked a snook at Him from a safe distance—that was not so very safe, because God, terrifyingly, was everywhere. But in Mrs. Beadle's kitchen you were safe from the wrath of God, because Mrs. Beadle was in league with all those Evil Spirits and Fallen Angels who were against God but had a similar strange and terrible power. And greatest of all the fallen angels was Lucifer, the Devil himself, who had been thrown out of Heaven for his pride and arrogance, which offended God—who was a jealous God. When Mrs. Beadle told her about Lucifer Jenny could hear the Stranger saying, "I was thrown out of Heaven young," so that when she thought of Lucifer she had a vision of the stranger—the stranger with horns on his head. When Mrs. Beadle referred to him as "The Prince of Darkness" she thought of evening closing in on the forest and the stranger lifting her up in his arms, lifting her up, as it seemed to her, into the deep darkness of the trees, and the owl following them with a wild cry, like something lost and afraid. When the old woman referred to Lucifer as "Son of the Morning" Jenny saw the stranger beside the sunlit pool, and the dragon-fly with his quivering, shining wings. Lucifer as the "Day-Star" was most natural; Lucifer belonged to the stars. What more natural, since he had fallen from Heaven? What more natural than that his should be the morning-star, that shone on when all the other stars had faded, since he was of all the fallen angels the greatest, Lucifer the Light-Bringer, and Son of the Morning?

Miss Drew would say, "You mustn't believe these things," and Jenny didn't understand. It was all in the Bible, about Lucifer, Son of the Morning, fallen from Heaven, and Miss Drew believed in the Bible. Jenny was bewildered by the teacher's unbelief, but she accepted it as part of the general strangeness of grown-ups.

But Marian was worried. It was not right that a child should have all this strange, dark knowledge—which even if dismissed as superstition could not be as lightly dismissed in its influence on the child's mind. It was morbid, unhealthy. She decided that if she could not meet the child's mother—and it seemed that without forcing herself upon her she couldn't, and she was not prepared to intrude in that way, like any "lady social worker"—she would meet this Mrs. Beadle. She asked Jenny to take her to her.

Jenny looked doubtful.

"I'll have to ask her first. She doesn't like visitors."

To the old woman she said, "My teacher, Miss Drew, that I told you about, says she would like to come and see you."

"Why?" the old woman demanded.

Jenny shrugged. "I dunno."

"We don't want any school-ma'ams here," Mrs. Beadle declared.

"She's nice," Jenny offered, feeling, vaguely, that Mrs. Beadle was not being just to Miss Drew.

"Nice!" The old woman jabbed angrily at a mess of stinging-nettles and dock-leaves simmering in the big cauldron on the kitchen range. "They're all 'nice', all the Sunday-school teachers and church workers and social workers and probation officers and lady almoners and the rest of them that come poking their noses into the poor people's houses! Let them keep their children's clubs and their clinics and their welfare centres, and leave the poor to live their own lives in their own way!"

She went on stirring the brew, and muttering, "Interfering! Poking in their noses! Patronising . . . "

Jenny said no more about it. It was clear that Miss Drew was not wanted. Nor did she really want her to come there. She could not imagine her in that kitchen amongst the cats; she felt that she would shudder away from the toad; and that she would not approve of all that was magic and exciting in the upper room. She would not fit in. She belonged in a quite different world. The world that held God and the school and the policeman; and everything orderly and clean and neat. Without thinking of it in those terms she knew that Miss Drew was on the side of the angels; and she herself belonged with Mrs. Beadle on the other side, with the fallen angels.

She told Miss Drew, "Mrs. Beadle doesn't like school-teachers, she says."

Marian laughed. "I'm sorry. But didn't you explain that I was rather special in that line?"

"I said you were nice."

"But it made no difference?"

Jenny shook her head. "You wouldn't like it there," she said. "My Mum went there once, and it made her sick. She says I'm not to go there. She says Mrs. Beadle ought to be locked up."

Well, anyhow, Marian thought, she had Mrs. Flower on her side in this matter. Between them they ought to be able to do something to save Jenny from the powers of evil. The moment that thought came to her she was startled at catching herself out thinking of it in those terms. Wasn't that attaching rather too much importance to what was, after all, no more important in the long run than the traditional fairy-tales in which most children were interested for a time? In the child's fantasy-world what did it matter whether Lucifer or Aladdin rubbed the magic lamp and summoned up the genie who made all things possible?

But behind the intellectual argument there was an instinctive uneasiness. Something beyond reasoning insisted that it was not just a case of an ignorant and probably slightly mad old woman filling a child up with a lot of superstitious nonsense about witchcraft. The child had met the "horned" stranger before she had met the old woman. She had "recognised" various occult symbols on the magic charts. There was something in all this occultism which spoke to something in the child's psyche. She was a wild and strange and difficult child. In the Middle Ages such children had been burnt as witches . . . and that that thought should come to her also startled Marian Drew. The practice of witchcraft might be no more than an expression of diabolical illusion, or of primitive pagan superstition, but that it could be as much a force in human life as Christianity itself was not to be denied. "Hell may give one what one wants as easily as Heaven"—and one may go to the stake as easily for a heresy as for the true faith. Nowadays no one forfeited their lives for either, but they still had souls capable of being damned—if not in hell-fire in a hell-upon-earth of black and twisted and tormented living.

She began to study witchcraft—in the scientific writings of Sir James Frazer, Charles Williams, M. Summers—and knew a curious sense of confirmation in the discovery that three women of the name of Flower had been charged with witchcraft in the seventeenth century. She became more intent than ever on meeting Mrs. Flower or old Mrs. Beadle, but though she failed in this, on Hallowe'en she met someone much more important to her investigations.

Chapter VI

Hallowe'en

The fair came once a year, at the end of October, and encamped on a piece of waste ground. Ivy always took the children. It was the final excitement before Christmas. And it made, said Ivy, "a little treat" for Jenny's birthday. She enjoyed it herself, too. It was a bit of excitement and made a change from the pictures. It was best to go in the evening, when everything was lit up with fairy-lights strung across the fair ground, and the torches were blazing on the stalls. Also, if she could get Joe to go along, it was nice to leave the children to themselves for a while and slip away to the pub. Altogether it made quite a pleasant little outing.

Joe took a lot of coaxing before he would go anywhere with his family. He was a dark, morose man, with very little to say even in his comparatively lighter moods. Ivy had met him at an ex-servicemen's dance—a local affair—in 1919; not that Joe Flower danced; but he was a member of the club that organised the dance, and he went along to all its functions for the sake of what he called "a few pints with the boys". Ivy was introduced to him and was fascinated by him; she thought him quite extraordinarily good-looking with his thick black hair and his long, rather sagging face, and that he was "different", because he did not flirt or crack jokes, and she wondered what went on behind his sombre eyes. As a matter of fact, nothing of any interest went on, but Ivy was convinced that "still waters run deep", and all her life she continued to believe that there was more in Joe Flower than there was, and all her life he continued to fascinate her by his dark, empty strangeness. Joe, who had never had any success with women till then, was fascinated by the fascination he clearly had for this young woman who so brazenly flirted with him. She roused his sensuality, and she gave herself to him with a readiness which astonished him, and she went on doing so until one day it occurred to her that not once had he said he loved her or called her by any soft, tender name. It came to her that he was merely "taking advantage" of her, and resentment flared up in her. He took her for granted, that's what. She'd been a fool, an infatuated fool. Well, next time he wouldn't have it all his own way. Next time, to his astonishment. Ivy refused. "All this time you've never said a word of love to me," she accused him, "nor nothing about being engaged or anything. And it's not good enough, see?"

Joe didn't see what Ivy was suddenly making a fuss about. Anyone would think he'd seduced her, the way she was going on, and if anything it had been the other way round; besides, on her own admission he wasn't the first. But what he did see, quite clearly, was that she meant what she said, and that from then on it was marriage or nothing.

"We can get married, if you like," he said, in his slow, heavy way. "I didn't know that was what you wanted. You shoulda mentioned it before."

"Mentioned it!" Ivy said, bitterly. "I s'pose it's not the man's place to mention a thing like that to a woman, is it? Oh, no! But you wasn't backward in mentioning something else, was you? You didn't forget to mention that! Oh, no!"

"I've said I'll marry you, haven't I?" Joe protested.

In this spirit they got married. Marriage did not cure her passion for him, nor did it turn him into a romantic lover or a loving husband. She never got used to his undemonstrativeness, and she never forgave him. She alternately nagged him and cajoled him.

"You do love us, reely, Joe, don'tcher ?" she would plead.

"Wotcher leadin' orf about *now*?" he would demand. "I married yer, didn't I?"

Then she would what he called "create". It was always on the same theme—that he had only married her when he found he couldn't get what he wanted without it.

It always had the same effect on him. "If that's how you feel about it," he would say, "we'll pack up on all that."

Then he would come and go silently, not speaking at all beyond the barest necessity. He would send messages by the children—"Ask yer mother where my clean shirt is—" "Tell yer mother I won't be in for tea—I'm going along to the club." The children were not deceived; they knew Mum and Dad weren't "speaking", and they counted the days, and made guesses as to who would "give in" first, and Ivy would feel humiliated and ashamed before the children, and finally before Joe himself, because it was always she who gave in, unable to bear it any longer. She would have the feeling that he could go on like that indefinitely. She would lie awake in the double bed at nights listening to his heavy sleeping breathing; she knew he wasn't pretending; he could and did sleep; he went right away from her and lived his own life enclosed within himself, silently, secretly. She couldn't do that. She was all on the surface; she had to give out all the time; she couldn't turn back into herself as he could. She got "upset". She couldn't eat or sleep during those times when he was withdrawn from her, and it angered her that it all made no difference to him; he had done without women before she came along, and he could, it seemed, do without them again. But she wasn't like that, and it humiliated her.

There was never any passionate reconciliation between them. He waited for her to give in, and eventually she gave in and spoke to him, and he answered her as though nothing had happened, and everything went on again as though there had never been that black interim of silence and withdrawal. She would try to "have it out" with him, but it was no good; it took two to make a scene, and Joe wasn't having any. She could "create" as much as she liked; he merely turned his back to her and went to sleep, or, if it was daytime, relapsed into silence, went away from her in himself.

She complained that he was "no company" to her; in the evenings he would sit reading his paper till bedtime, or he would go down to the club. When he stayed in she would sit mending—there was never any end to the mending—and she would tell him bits of gossip about the neighbours, and family gossip, and he would grunt, or say "Oh?" but she never felt he was really interested. Unless it was something about the children, and then he would make a comment or ask a question. Anything about his sister interested him. He would never hear a word of criticism of her, and it infuriated Ivy; he was so strait-laced where everyone else was concerned. If she remarked what a "one for the boys" young Doris Oliver—aged fifteen—was and that she would be getting into trouble one of these days, he would mutter that if she was his daughter he would put her across his knee. And he would add that if young Jenny went that way he would hold her, Ivy, responsible.

She would flash at him, "If Jenny goes that road it'll be her mother coming out in her!"

"You've had the upbringing of her!"

"You're a nice one to talk—" She could never resist it. "What about you and me before we was married?"

"I wasn't the first. The slice off the cut cake's never missed."

He could be beastly, could Joe, when he liked. He said a number of things like that. Ivy called it throwing her past up at her, and she never forgave him. What about his sister's past?

"That's none o' your business!" he would assert.

Ivy would seethe with resentment. It was all so unjust! But there was nothing she could do about it. He made her miserable more often than not. Sometimes she would revolt and ask

63

herself what she got out of being married to him. But deep in herself she knew it was no good asking herself that; she had to have him; he hurt her and disappointed her, endlessly, but she never hated him. He had a kind of dark power over her. As though he had put a spell on her . . .

Every year when the fair came the old romantic longings would be revived in her. She persisted in the illusion that given the right romantic setting Joe would respond romantically to her. She should have known by experience that he was incapable of such response, but every year the distant music of the fair roundabouts stirred her, made her feel sentimental and romantic and full of the old soft foolish longing that just once he should "say something nice" to her—tell her she wasn't a bad-looking woman, that her hair looked nice, admire her new jumper, tell her he loved her—even if he only said, "You know I do," to her question. And they would go to the fair, and go on the roundabouts and the swings, with the children, and try to knock down coconuts and lose money trying to win rubbishy dolls in games of chance, and Joe would pot at clay pigeons with an air-gun, and before closing time they would slip away and have a drink at the pub on the corner, though he didn't really approve of women going into pubs—and she would have a gin-and-lime, and feel softened towards him, a yearning softness, and she would believe that just this once, just this one evening, he would respond to her in the way she wanted . . . but he never did. He remained stolidly himself. And he always wanted to leave before the fireworks, because he didn't like the children being out late, and it was a shame because the fireworks were the thing the children liked best.

On Jenny's seventh birthday the boys said, discussing the visit to the fair, "Let's go without Dad—it's more fun!"

That year, for the first time. Ivy made no effort to get her husband to go with her to the fair. It always upset her to disappoint the children about the fireworks, and now that

Jenny was seven she was quite old enough to be allowed out late just once in a while. Besides, it was on a Saturday this year; they could all have a "lay-in" the next day, with no school to get up for. Joe was so strict with the children. They would enjoy themselves better without him; and it wasn't as though he really enjoyed the fair. Come to that, you would be hard put to it to say what he did enjoy . . .

That year, therefore, instead of Joe, Ivy invited little Mrs. Grigg from the next-door flat to go along with her. Mrs. Grigg was intending to take her little girl, so they might as well go along together—Mrs. Grigg's little Nora, the same age as Jenny, was everything that Jenny was not—a nice, well-behaved, obedient child, like a little doll, Ivy always said, so pretty with her fair hair, and such a sweet child, always so clean and tidy; she would have loved just such a pretty sweet good little girl. But what could you do with a child like Jenny? She was such a wild-looking little thing, like a little gipsy. It was a physical impossibility to keep her clean and tidy for five minutes, and as for obedience she simply didn't know the meaning of the word. Mrs. Grigg was always saying how Jenny was "the spitting image" of her father—meaning Joe, and to console Ivy she would suggest that the child had Joe's "awkward" temperament, just as she had his darkness and thinness. There was something in it. Ivy would think; after all, Jenny was a Flower. Joe and Nell were different in their natures, it was true; there was nothing wild about Joe, but Nell was awkward in her own way, as stubborn as they made them, and nothing you could say to her made any difference; she just looked at you with her dark eyes and retired into herself—and Jenny did that all the time. The Flowers were like that; it was as though they went inside themselves and slammed a door in your face. The younger boy, Stan, took after Joe, too; he was a thin, silent child, and given to sulking. Les was more like Nell—there was something wild in him. Either way, wild or morose, it was bad blood, the Flower blood . . .

Ivy sighed as she dressed herself for the fair. If only Joe were different; if only he were like little Mrs. Grigg's hubby, who spoke so nice to her you'd think they were a courting couple still. If only Les was a nice quiet serious boy like Mrs. Bruce's Alfie, who had won a scholarship and was now at a secondary school, and a credit to everyone. If only Stan was a nice little mother's boy who would make up for the wildness of Les and Jenny. Above all, if only Jenny were the dear little girl she had so hoped she would turn out to be.

It was all so disappointing when you'd done your best to be a good wife and mother. Oh well! She dabbed a bit of rouge above each cheek-bone. You couldn't have it all ways. Joe after all was the best-looking man on the whole estate; all the other hubbies looked so ordinary beside Joe. And Les and Jenny were bright children—no denying it; and Stan was a nice little chap, even if he was a bit awkward at times. To-night whilst the children were watching the fireworks she and Mrs. Grigg would slip away together and have a couple of drinks and a good old jaw . . . The distant music of the fair seemed to come closer; she felt excited and gay—and at the back of it all she was ready to cry her heart out, for no reason. No reason at all. Since she knew—who better?—that you couldn't have it all ways . . .

(2)

The repetitive rise and fall of the music ground out by the roundabouts worked no less insidiously in Jenny's blood, exciting her, drawing her like a magnet. It had been throbbing in her all day, like a beat of tom-toms, coming near and then receding, beating up the excitement to an almost intolerable pitch. For the last two years she had been made restless by the Fair music on Hallowe'en, but this year it stirred her as never before.

She did not want to "walk nicely" in front of the two mothers, with Mrs. Grigg's Nora, whom she regarded as "a soppy kid"; she wanted to run on ahead with Stan and Les, and ahead of them, too, for they stopped to swing round lamp-posts, to dart about in the road playing "He", and to hop along the hop-scotch squares chalked on the pavements. She would have liked wings, so that she could have flown straight to the very heart of the Fair, the great pulsing, pounding swings-and-roundabouts heart of it. Her mother and Mrs. Grigg walked so slowly, talking all the time. It always astonished Jenny how much grown-ups found to talk about. You would think they would come to the end of all they had to say. She kept tugging at her mother's skirt and urging her to "Come on!" and whenever she did it her mother pulled her skirt away from her and gave her a slap, warning her that if she had any more of it she would take her straight back home, "So mind!" Jenny didn't "mind". She knew quite well that there was no question of turning back now that they had set out, and if her mother tried to send her nothing would induce her to go. If anyone had been able to convince her that she would burn in hell-fire the following morning if she went to the Fair that night she would still have gone.

They got there at last, pushing their way through the crowds, the roar and clatter breaking over them like a great rough sea. The giant racer roared and plunged with its screaming cargoes; the swings swung up into the air, always on the point of turning right over, and always falling back in time; miniature motor-cars crashed into each other on a crazy moving track; terrifying screams came from the haunted castle; men and women, boys and girls, slid on mats down the spiral run from the top of a high tower; men and boys shot with air-guns at clay-pigeons and celluloid balls bouncing on jets of water, watched by admiring women-folk standing behind them; people lost their pennies at games of chance and failed to knock down coconuts or win the gaudy dolls displayed on the stands, and the painted horses with their grinning scarlet mouths, the ostriches, the swans, the

67

little velvet chariots of the roundabouts whirled and plunged on a torrent of music poured out from the glittering column at the heart of it all.

Jenny forced her way through the crowds to the roundabouts, clutching the pennies her mother had given her, gazing, rapt. Oh, but the roundabouts was a Spanish dancing lady tossing gold and crimson skirts. It was a fountain pouring out music from a basin of gilt and mirrors. There was nothing in the world but that tumult of music and movement that flowed over you in a golden sea, that beat in your body, that made you blind and deaf to everything else. Something in you shouted; something in you sang; a great shout of song, tossed in amongst the paint and plush, the gilt and mirrors, and you climbed up on to the back of a swan and clung to its neck and rode right in under the rushing golden fountain. You had wings at last, and you flew above the surging torrents of music, you whirled on and on for ever . . .

And then somehow you were moving, shakily, down wooden steps that still slowly revolved; you set foot on earth again; you felt a little sick, and very dizzy, and it was difficult to walk. Les and Stan clamoured for another "go", but their mother said, "No, they would be sick, and look at young Jenny as white as a sheet."

"Feel all right, ducks ?" Mrs. Grigg bent down to her, peered into her face, took her hand.

She tore herself away from Mrs. Grigg's hand. Oh, but of course she was all right, if only they would leave her alone! Les and Stan were bowling pennies across a board marked with numbers, and the man in the middle of the stall kept scooping in the pennies, but still the boys remained. Mrs. Grigg was trying to throw rings over a doll at which Nora gazed wistfully, and when she had used all her rings Mrs. Flower had a go, but it was no use. The women laughed ruefully. "They always see to it it's arranged so's you can't get a ring on the good things," Ivy said, and Mrs. Grigg smiled at Jenny and Nora, and said,

"Never mind—we'll go and try for a coconut." The boys joined them, and Les knocked down a coconut, and then they all went off to the haunted castle.

But none of all that meant anything to Jenny. She wanted the swings, the roundabouts, the flying boats that swung out into the air till they were almost flat, the grand racer that hurled you up steep wooden hills and flung you down as though it meant to kill you—she wanted everything that lifted you from the earth, gave you wings, however briefly.

As it was her birthday Ivy allowed her to go on everything once, always prophesying that she would be sick, always wishing that she would be content to go on the children's things, like little Nora.

By the time they had "done" almost everything it was beginning to get dusk and the crowd was beginning to move towards the enclosure at the edge of the fair-ground where the set-pieces for the fireworks display were erected. There was the great favourite, "The Fire of London", waiting to be kindled into flaming action. Rows of eager children were already seated on the ground in front of the press of adults. The Flower children squeezed in and trampled their way to the front, disregarding various angry demands as to what they thought they were doing. Nora hung back, being a well-conducted child, but Ivy was impatient to get the children settled so that she and Mrs. Grigg could slip off to the pub and have a nice talk. The roar and rocket was beginning to make her head ache. She pushed Nora through to the front, told a woman who protested to mind her own business, rescued Mrs. Grigg from an argument with two more women, and dragged her out of the crowd, urging her to "take no notice".

When they got clear of the enclosure she slipped an arm through Mrs. Grigg's.

"Now we can have a bit of peace and quiet," she said. "The kids won't budge for a good half-hour."

They elbowed their way through the crowd and came out to the road which they crossed into the "peace and quiet" of a crowded saloon-bar.

There was a minor fireworks' display before the big piece was set off. That was the grand finale. Rockets shot up into the air to dissolve into showers of red, green and blue stars, or showers of "golden rain". Fountains of golden fire sprayed up from the earth; Catherine wheels spun round; Roman candles blazed, spluttered and faded, and all the time the crowd exclaimed with loud "Oh's!" of wonder and long-sighing "Ah's" of pure bliss. But it was all nothing to what was to come, nothing but a prelude. The moment of ecstasy was when the flames limned the Elizabethan houses and the Old London Bridge into outline, and then crept up round them to destroy them. It was so realistic, some said, that you could almost feel the heat from the blazing buildings, and instinctively you drew back. But Jenny craned forward as though she would plunge into the flames, and there was a terrible intensity of desire in her that the flames should burn and blaze with increasing fury. Something in her shouted in a frenzy of exultation. It was as though she had been born only for this—to witness this conflagration, to will it on—on . . .

And then, straining forward, ecstatic, at the edge of the flames she saw the Stranger, his face lit by the glow, and as she looked he turned his head and looked full at her and smiled, then the illumination where he stood flicked and faded and there was only blackness where he had been. Instantly Jenny was on her feet, forcing her way through the crowd, pushing, trampling, ducking, ignoring the angry shoves from the people with whom she collided. That when she got clear of the enclosure and came out into the fair-ground again he should be at the exit, as though waiting, seemed to her completely natural.

She flung her arms round his waist and felt the heavy studs of his belt cold against her face.

He lifted her up and she felt his kiss cold on her forehead.

"You didn't come—all this time!" she cried, clinging to him still when he set her down.

"You didn't need me," he stated. "I said I'd come if you needed me."

"You came to-night!" There was wonder in her voice and in her face, lifted to his.

"Naturally. It's Hallowe'en."

"It's my birthday!"

"I have a present for you."

From an inner pocket he took out a small coral necklace. He held it up a moment for her inspection against the light of a naphtha flare. She gave a little exclamation of delight and he asked, "You know what it is?"

"It's coral. We learned about it at school."

"It's coral, and coral is a very ancient charm. The Romans hung it round the necks of the children to protect them from evil. To this day Italians still wear it to protect them from the evil eye. Do they teach you all that at school?"

She shook her head. "Mrs. Beadle tells me things like that, though. They say Mrs. Beadle's a witch. She knows about magic."

He bent down and fastened the coral round her neck.

"So long as you wear it you will never be ill and no one will be able to put a spell upon you."

He took her hand. The crowd was beginning to stream out from the fireworks enclosure, pouring out like a black tide.

"I must find my brothers," she said. "I was with them in there. Ma said not to leave them."

"They must come out this way. Keep a look out."

She kept a look out, and suddenly she saw Miss Drew, and at the same moment the teacher saw her and broke out of the crowd.

"I wondered if I'd see you here, Jenny."

Jenny cried, excitedly, to the stranger, "This is my teacher that told me about the coral," and then to Miss Drew, "He's given

71

me some—look! Because it's my birthday. It's a charm—you didn't tell me that! It's magic!"

Marian turned from the child to the tall dark figure, and he gave her a long strange look from which she seemed unable to break away.

Jenny stared from one to the other, wonderingly.

"You two will know each other next time," she said, a little impatiently.

The stranger said, slowly, "Yes—we shall know each other next time."

Marian laughed, nervously. "I'm afraid Jenny didn't introduce us properly. She omitted to tell me who you are."

"She doesn't know."

"I'm not sure that I should approve of her speaking to strangers—"

"We're not strangers. We met in a forest on Lammas Eve."

She was startled. "Then it's you she talks about. She said you had horns—"

"I had horns."

Jenny suddenly darted forward, tugging at Les's arm as he pressed forward with Stan behind him.

"Where you bin?" the boy demanded.

She said quickly, "I wanted to go somewhere. Then I met my teacher. Wait for me."

She turned back to the other two. "I'll have to go." She looked from one to the other, helplessly. "I'd sooner stay with you," she added, forlornly. It was at the stranger she looked as she said this, and she fingered the studs on his belt.

He touched the coral at her neck.

"I'll be about," he said. "You know what it says in the Bible—'Seek and ye shall find.' "

Marian said sharply, "You could leave the Bible out of it!"

He smiled. "Surely the devil may quote scripture?"

Les tugged at Jenny. "Come on," he said.

"I must go," Jenny repeated, and allowed herself to be pulled back into the dark stream of the crowd, but over her shoulder she saw Miss Drew and the stranger no longer looking after her but walking away together. He had a hand at her elbow, steering her through the throng, and suddenly something blazed up in Jenny, so that she cried out loud, "Why did she have to come along?"

But in the crush no one heard her, and she had a sense of being engulfed in black waves. On the fair-ground the lights were going out, one by one.

Chapter VII

Magic Casements

Marian said, as they turned away, "I'd like to talk to you. I've been wanting to meet you for a long time—though I never hoped to." She was frowning.

He murmured, taking her elbow, guiding her, "I can only hope the cloven hoof doesn't embarrass you!"

She said sharply, "You can drop out that stuff! It's about all that I want to talk to you. You are doing the child a lot of harm, filling her up with all that nonsense."

He smiled. "If you will forgive my saying so, school-teachers also fill children up with a lot of nonsense."

"You can call it that if you like—I wouldn't altogether disagree. But at least it's the sort of nonsense that does no harm—"

"Not even all the perverted history?"

She looked up at him. "Look here—who are you? What are you? You look like a common seaman."

"Common or uncommon, I am sailing in the morning."

"Where?"

"The seven seas."

She cried, thoroughly exasperated, "I wish you'd stop talking in riddles!"

"Lest hearing with your ears ye understand not?"

"You can leave the scriptures out of it!"

"The devil is entitled—"

She made an angry exclamation, but it was lost in the crowd that jostled them apart. They came together on the road and again he took her elbow.

"Have you any objection to the Seven Bells?"

"I know nothing about pubs."

She was making no attempt to conceal her hostility, but he continued to smile faintly, the crooked smile that made his lean face a little wolfish.

She let him conduct her down unfamiliar narrow side-streets and they came to the river, a grey glimmer between a dockyard wall on the left and a flight of steps on the right.

The Seven Bells was at the top of the steps. It was shabby and ramshackle; it looked as though it might at any moment collapse into the river, a pile of rotting timber and loose tiles. There poured out from it a babble of rough voices and the hollow music of an automatic piano.

Marian's companion pushed open the swing-door, stood aside for her to enter. The hot yellow light of the interior was blinding after the misty greyness outside; there seemed no air. People stood pressed close, like trees in a dark forest. The people who sat at the tables ranged along the walls were like so much undergrowth, half-submerged by the trees.

She murmured, confused, "It seems very full!"

"It's Saturday night. What will you drink?"

But she had no idea. She said, vaguely, "They wouldn't have cider, I suppose?"

"Lady, this is a sailor's tavern, not the village inn! You'd better join me in the sailor's drink—rum."

He shouldered his way through the crowd, towards the bar. She looked after him and was aware of a certain grace in the tall lean figure. Who was he? What was he? Well, but she knew who he was; he was a merchant seaman. Just a little better spoken than most, perhaps, a smattering of education; or perhaps of a different class from most . . . Well, whoever he was she was

75

resolved to make him talk sense, to drop this mystery nonsense of horns and cloven hoof.

With that resolve she felt more confident in her strange surroundings and began to look about her, interested.

Near her, a shabby man with a peaked cap, an angry red face, and a greasy white silk scarf knotted round his neck, leaned menacingly over a woman who sat at a table, a glass of stout before her, gazing fearfully up at him.

"I truss you w'en I went away, di'n' I?" he demanded, violently, "I truss you, see!"

The woman moved her hand nervously up and down the glass without lifting it from the table. Even her shabby frivolous hat, with its bedraggled wisps of veil and crumpled faded flowers, had a guilty look. Guilty and afraid. Her manner suggested that once she left that place and went outside there was no knowing what her companion might do to her. A black-eye might be the least part of it. Meanwhile she could only gaze at him, sheepishly, speechless, defenceless, hypnotised by his anger.

Something of the woman's fear communicated itself to Marian. She had the feeling of being in a jungle—there was the steamy heat, the sense of hidden lurking danger. People thick as trees in a dark forest. Thicker, and much less comely.

Trees where you sit
Shall crowd into a shade.

But not people. They merely crowded into a sweating density of moist red faces and foetid armpits. The density of a wood was all peace and coolness and green shade. The density of the human jungle was all restlessness and heat and yellow glare. Its smell was animal. The smell of the menagerie. The animal robbed of the natural animal dignity and decency.

The woman at the table said, hopelessly, "I could explain—if you give me the chanst!"

But he wouldn't give her the chance, Marian thought; he wasn't the sort of man who would give anyone a chance. The woman was safe until closing-time, but only till then, and she knew it. Her knowledge of it was in her fixed hypnotised stare and the movement of her hand up and down the glass of stout.

Marian looked away from them to the bar, where her companion was talking to a dark-haired barmaid with a scarlet mouth and a pink satin blouse, the low V of which was fastened by a Woolworth "diamond" brooch. She had fine dark eyes, the lids smeared with blue grease, and her eyebrows were like antennae. She and the man talked and laughed together with the easy familiarity of people who know each other well, Marian thought, and then as she watched the girl turned aside to serve another customer, and the man picked up his drinks and moved away, working his way back between the people, a glass in each hand.

Marian relieved him of a glass and he said, "That barmaid I was talking to is Nell Flower."

"Flower?"

"Yes. 'Auntie Nell' to your Jenny. She's pretty, isn't she?"

"In a hard sort of way—"

"She's had a hard sort of life. If you wouldn't find it too cold we might go outside."

"I'd prefer it."

They went out through a frosted glass door on to a deserted wooden verandah that ran the length of the house, above the river. There were a few iron tables and chairs piled upon each other against the wall. It was not cold, but the wind whipped freshly along the river.

He said, "If we go to the far end we'll be out of the wind."

They went to the end of the balcony and round the corner of the house, and leaned there on the wooden balustrade.

"It's like leaning on the rail of a ship," Marian said, then lifted her glass, a little nervously. "Well—*bon voyage!*"

"Thank you, Lady." His voice was ironic. He drained his glass and placed it on a window-sill behind him.

Marian sipped her drink and he watched her, amused. "You don't like it?"

"It's very strong."

"Not stronger than the damson wine you drink at the vicarage."

She started. "Who told you I was a vicar's daughter?"

"You've just told me yourself!"

"I didn't tell you about the wine—"

"Don't they always drink home-made wines in English country vicarages?"

"But who told you about the vicarage?"

He shrugged. "It's not interesting, Lady."

"Why do you like to make such a mystery of everything?"

Her tone was impatient. He smiled.

"What is the mystery, Lady?"

"Well—to begin with, who are you?"

"As from to-morrow—fireman in the *S.S. Seven Seas Spray*. Or are you going to tell me there's no such ship?"

"I know there's such a ship, and I know she's sailing in the morning—the father of one of the children in my class has signed on in her."

"Very well, then. What else?"

"Presumably you have a name, even if Jenny doesn't know it."

"I have several names."

"One would do. What name did you sign on in?"

He laughed. "John Smith!"

She stared at him. "A false name?"

"What do you think?"

"I think," she cried, thoroughly exasperated, "that you are an impossible person!"

She was so angry that she drained her glass, though until that moment she had no intention of finishing the fiery little drink. Its fieriness seemed to mount to her brain, and she said, violently, "I don't care who you are or what your real name is—you've no right to fill a child up with a lot of superstitious nonsense. She really believes she saw you in the forest with horns on your head."

He sighed. "Must I tell you again that she really did?"

"If it's true—why had you?"

"It happened to be Lammas—which is a witches' sabbath. There are four in the year, and to-night also happens to be one."

"But as I don't happen to be a child you can't persuade me that you are horned?"

"A child needs no persuasion to believe in magic. It believes in it naturally. Adults, in whom magic is dead, do their best to persuade it not to believe. Sometimes, with the aid of school-teachers—" he smiled, "they succeed. Then the child is what they call educated. In other words it is turned into a little humbug and hypocrite, full of falsity and fear—an adult in miniature. But no one will ever succeed in educating Jenny Flower. She was born on a witches' sabbath, and no one knows who her father is—"

"You mean she has what is commonly called bad blood in her?" Her tone was contemptuous.

"Bad and good are matters of definition, Lady, like right and wrong."

He took her empty glass from her.

"Another drink and you may begin to understand that the supernatural is merely the natural plus." He held up her glass. "You'd like the same again, I take it?"

She said, still scornful, "Couldn't you produce it out of a handkerchief or down your sleeve?"

"Conjuring tricks. Lady, are not magic. Your conjuror is an excellent person, but he is interested in sleight of hand, not the supernatural."

He began to move away. She said, quickly, "Not another drink for me, thanks. I must be going."

He turned and looked at her. He stood in shadow and she could not see his face. He seemed so tall that he filled the world. She caught herself out in the sudden fantastic thought and amended it. He was a tall, dark barrier between herself and that safe-lighted world of pub chatter and familiar streets and everydayness. He did not so much stand there as confront her.

"We must both be going," he said, "but not yet. I'll take you when it's time."

She laughed, nervously, clutching at that matter-of-factness blotted out by the tall, dark shadow.

"Don't be silly—I can't stay here till closing-time."

He said, simply, "You'll stay with me till the end of the night. Wait here."

Her heart quickened with anger. "Is this supposed to be hypnotism—or what?"

"You have the conventional mania for labels. Call it what you like—you'll wait."

He picked up his own glass from the window-sill and moved off down the verandah. A fan of yellow light spread out over the wooden floor of the verandah for a moment as he pushed open the door of the bar, and there was the momentary thump of the automatic music and the thick blur of voices.

Marian turned back to the river. She picked up her handbag and gloves from the wooden ledge of the balcony. To go one had merely to walk down the verandah and pass in through the door into the hot crowded saloon bar, to slip through the crowd and out into the street. Getting drinks at the bar he would never notice her go. But she must go at once. She must go now, or it would be too late. He must be shown that whereas it was easy to auto-suggest a child of seven, it did not work on an adult person of nearly twenty-seven. It was such impertinence to talk to her like that—as though she were a child. "You'll wait." It was so impudent—and conceited! You'll wait, indeed! But go now, now. Don't stand staring at the river. Staring at the wake of a police-boat scurrying through the darkness; staring at the lights, red and green; staring at the pale arc of light above some scaffolding on the opposite bank; staring at the shadowy hulks of warehouses, feeling drowsy with the soft lip-lip of the water, with the night wind that had the smell of the sea on it, feeling as though you could stand there . . . till the end of the night.

He put the glass into her hand and kept an arm round her shoulder.

She said, a little faintly, "I was just going—"

"We are both just going." His free hand closed over hers that held the glass and lifted it to her mouth.

She said, with the glass near her lips, "You could get drunk on the fumes alone!" It came to her that it was like the last moment before going under an anaesthetic—the final clutch at consciousness . . .

"Not, mind you," as she said to him later, though when she said it and where she had no idea, "that one passes out on two drinks—not even sailors' drinks, but just—just—that you feel so drowsy and it's easier to slip away . . . slipping down the river on the evening tide, and everything becomes an effort. Why make an effort? Not, mind you, that one is not perfectly aware of what one is doing. One has one's handbag and gloves. Remembers one's address. One is not familiar with the streets, but one can always ask the way . . . to the end of the night. Supposing one asked a policeman that? "Yes, Miss, first right, second left, then keep right on . . . right on . . . "

He took the latch-key from her. "Let me."

It was he who found the switch at the top of the stairs, opened the door, found another switch, flooding the room with a soft warm light diffused through the parchment shade of a table lamp. There were shelves of books, autumn leaves, a slender branch of crimson berries sprayed out across a bare pale wall, curtains blowing out from an open window above the river, a low divan with a row of brightly coloured cushions ranged along the wall. He smiled, and now it was the gentle smile that Jenny knew.

"Come." He led her over to the divan and she sank down; he arranged cushions under her head, lifted her feet. She sighed.

"You see, I brought you here safely," she said, drowsily, then her body relaxed and she slept.

He sat in an armchair beside the table lamp, a little distance from the divan; he sat quite still and did not take his eyes from her.

When sleep ebbed from her, like grey mist rolling back along a river, she lay for a little looking at him, and she saw him as Jenny had seen him the first time, with horns on his head. She saw the branching shadow of them on the ceiling. She gave a little scream and rolled over, burying her face in the pillows.

He went over to her and she felt his hands on her shoulders and heard his voice, saying quietly, "It's all right. There's nothing to be frightened of. Look at me!"

His voice compelled her and she twisted her head and looked at him, fearfully, then, as she stared, relief came into her eyes.

"I must have been dreaming—I thought—you had horns!"

Then, as realisation began to assert itself more vividly, "What are you doing here?"

"You brought me." He smiled.

"I brought you? I don't even know you! I know what happened—the drinks went to my head. I'm not used to spirits. You brought me home. You took advantage of my condition—"

He laughed outright at that.

"Lady, that I never did!" He caught her hands, gripping them tightly. "Marian, Maria, stop playing the outraged vicar's daughter—your father isn't that kind of a vicar anyhow!"

She stared at him. "How did you know that?"

"You told me so yourself—at great length. You sang me 'Adeste Fideles'—but with different words—"

She gave a cry of dismay, but he laughed again and pulled her close to him, then released her hands and enclosed her in his arms.

"You told me also that your name was Marian—which is a corruption of a holy name—"

Suddenly she laughed herself. "And that appealed to your sense of blasphemy, I suppose?"

He gazed at her, wonderingly. "Have you really stopped being angry, Marian, Maria? Are you really laughing?"

She leaned her head against his shoulder.

She gave a little sigh and said, irrelevantly, "Why did I have to wait for you so long?"

He put a hand under her chin and tilted up her face. "Perhaps," he said, before he kissed her. "Perhaps because you didn't believe in magic—"

Not until morning and the room was full of a grey cold light and she was alone did she remember that she still did not know his name.

Chapter VIII

Perilous Seas

At home Jenny accounted for the coral necklace by saying, simply, that after she had left her brothers, towards the end of the fireworks, "to go somewhere", a gipsy had given it to her. Ivy merely observed that she had told her before she mustn't speak to strangers, let alone take things from them, and let the matter go; the rebuke was purely mechanical. Her general management of the children was to find out what they were doing and tell them they mustn't and as often as not she told them they mustn't without troubling to find out; they in turn accepted the rebukes as a matter of routine. Jenny lied about the necklace instinctively.

But to Mrs. Beadle she showed it with pride, and told the truth triumphantly.

"It was him I met at the Sunday-school treat. But he didn't have horns this time!"

"Your old flame, eh?"

The expression meant nothing to Jenny, but the word "flame" brought back the whole scene.

"It was when the fireworks were on, and London was burning. The flames went right up to the sky! It was lovely. And he was standing right in the flames."

The old woman smiled. "You're quite sure he didn't have horns that time?"

"Oh, no," Jenny said. "I'd have noticed. But afterwards, when Stan and Les came up, he went away with Miss Drew." The eager light went out of her face as she said this.

"What are you pulling a long face for? He gave you the necklace, didn't he, not her!"

Jenny turned a couple of "Catherine wheels" across the kitchen, and then came and stood by the old woman stirring her everlasting brew in the big black pot.

"At school to-day she asked me what his name was. I didn't let on I didn't know."

"What did you say?"

"I told her it was Lucifer."

The old woman looked up. "What made you say that?" Her tone was sharp.

Jenny stood first on one foot and then on the other.

"It's what I call him in my mind."

"Why?"

"Because Lucifer was the Prince of them all, wasn't he? More important than any one—'cept God."

"What did she say to that?"

"She didn't say anything. She smiled. I thought she'd say I mustn't say things like that. She always used to when I told her magic things."

Mrs. Beadle went on stirring her brew, and Jenny hopped across the kitchen, first on one foot and then on the other, dodging the cats. She was never still for long. "Always on the go", was how Ivy described it and was always telling her to stop jigging about, for goodness sake, anyone would think she had St. Vitus's dance . . . For Jenny one of the joys of being at Mrs. Beadle's was that there were no mustn'ts and stop-its.

Suddenly the old woman looked up from her stirring. "Have you seen your Auntie Nell lately?"

"She came to tea Sunday. She brought me a new dress and a box of chocolates for my birthday! She had a new hat with a lot of blue veil behind, like a mist. She looked lovely. She had stockings so thin you could see the little hairs on her legs, and ever such high heels."

"Does she know you come here?"

Jenny shook her head. "She wouldn't like me to. She always says I must be good and do as Ma says, and Ma says I'm not to speak to you. I'd get a hiding if she knew I came here. Miss Drew says I mustn't either, but I don't care what *she* says!"

"I thought you liked her."

"I don't any more."

She came close to the old woman, catching at her black ragged skirt.

"I want to ask you something."

"Well, go on—out with it!"

"In those books upstairs it tells you how to make spells, doesn't it?"

"What about it?"

"If you put a bad enough spell on a person they'd die, wouldn't they?"

"People have been known to."

"But no one could ever put a spell on me whilst I'm wearing the coral!"

"There was a spell put on you when you were born, Jenny Flower!"

"Nobody put a spell on me!" There was both defiance and pleading in her voice.

"Oh, yes, they did! Lucifer himself! You ask him next time you see him. He'll tell you."

"Will he tell me?" She was suddenly excited. "When will I see him? When will he come?"

"The next witches' sabbath."

"When will that be?"

"Not for a long time yet."

"This year?"

"No. Early next. Christmas comes first."

"I don't care about Christmas!" That was true; Christmas meant relations—"visitors"—aunts and uncles and cousins, and Postman's Knock and other silly boring games; Christmas was not just one day; if it had been just the one day in which you hung up your stocking and got an orange in the toe and something sticking out at the top, and the excitement of waking up in the early morning before it was light and squeezing the stocking and trying to make out what was in it and going to sleep again—if it had been just that it would have been something to look forward to; but it was not just that one day, it was several days, and all of them Sundays, with best clothes and not being allowed to run in the streets, and visitors, and good behaviour, and silly games. "What comes after Christmas?" she demanded.

"Candlemas."

"Candlemas." She repeated the name with satisfaction, savouring it. She had a vision of lighted candles in a row, wavering against a darkness in which stood someone tall and strange, smiling down at her. You half-closed your eyes and the pointed yellow flame of the candles became stars. Somewhere in the visionary dark an owl called . . . Like a ship's siren in the night. Like the hoot of the roundabouts in their wild dance.

"Last time it was Hallowe'en, wasn't it?"

"You should know, Jenny Flower! Did you stay awake till after midnight, as I told you, to keep your soul at home?"

"I couldn't. I did try, but I was so sleepy when we got in from the Fair."

The old woman looked at her. "What did you dream?"

"I dreamt I was grown up and London was on fire, like in the fireworks piece!"

"How old do you reckon you were?"

"I was sixteen. I had lipstick and high heels, like Auntie Nell. It was exciting! The flames reached up to the sky . . . "

87

She skipped round the room again. Hallowe'en and souls and their final resting-place had no significance for her.

Mrs. Beadle went on stirring.

(2)

Marian wanted to take Jenny home with her for Christmas; she promised a Christmas tree that reached to the ceiling and holly growing wild in the woods, but Jenny didn't want to go. She had "turned against" Miss Drew since the night of the Fair. She didn't want to "play her up" in class because of this change of feeling, but she no longer wanted to have anything to do with her out of class. She no longer trusted her, though she could not have said why. From time to time she dreamed that Miss Drew was dead. Waking she did not wish Miss Drew was dead, but only that she would go away. There was no need for her. It was better without her.

Marian was aware of this change of attitude and knew that the cause was jealousy and was determined to overcome it. If they could all three be friends then he would cease to be a bad influence on Jenny, and the child would cease to be jealous. "He!" If she didn't discover his name soon she would have to follow Jenny's example and take to calling him "Lucifer"—it was too ridiculous! As always when she thought of him her blood stirred and she drifted into a reverie. She had let him make love to her, a man of whom she knew nothing but that he had signed on as fireman in a cargo boat and was sailing in the morning; a man whose name she hadn't even known, and didn't know now . . . and yet that, somehow, seemed the least important thing of all. What did it matter what people were called? Or how old—or young—they were? It was not what people were called, or how many years they had lived, that mattered, but what they were as people. But that, also, she didn't know. He was merely a dark presence, a strange smile.

Ah, but be honest, Marian, Maria; he was more than that; he was a man who had taken you unresisting into his arms—as though you had been that girl behind the bar—you, whom no man had kissed till then.

The colour always rushed up into her face, hotly, with the memory. It was possible to blame the "sailors' drinks" for that episode, but what excuse could be made for the fact that she had never ceased to think about it, not with shame and dismay, but with a longing that became an obsession . . . as though in kissing her he had put a spell upon her . . . so that his strange thin face looked up at her from the pages of the exercise books she sat correcting, and smiled at her across the heads of the children in class. So that in long sleepless nights in her room above the river she gave herself up to endless fantasies of his step upon the stair and of herself running to let him in—

"I run, I run, I am gathered to thy heart."

Though she did not know his name, nor anything about him; though no word of love had passed between them, and she had no name for what she felt for him. Was it love? Could you love someone of whom you knew nothing? Your mind asked the question, and your blood answered that you knew nothing except that you wanted him back . . . to feel his lips cold on yours again.

Cold as the kiss of Lucifer. Oh, but that was ridiculous! The scientific study of witchcraft, an inquiry into occult philosophy, was one thing, superstitious acceptance of that philosophy quite another. Perhaps a man's lips are always cold. Perhaps it was only imagination. How is virgin inexperience to know? One could not know; but one could keep clear of superstitious fancies. One was nothing if not rational.

That she had no sense of guilt about this strange episode was part of her rationality. She would lie staring at the insomniac darkness, listening to the ships' sirens, infinitely sad out there in the black night, listening to the swish of the river as a police-boat sped past, or a string of barges cleaved the water; listening to the sounds from the street—the singing of drunks going home, the maundering voices of the men, the shrill voices of the women, all tremuloso and sudden bursts of high hysterical laughter—and long for him, achingly, intolerably, without shame, this stranger of whom she had cried, "Why did I have to wait for you so long?"

But this freely acknowledged longing, this rational lack of shame, deserted her, curiously, in her parents' home. There, in the narrow bed of her childhood, of her innocence, the memory of Hallowe'en troubled her like an unconfessed sin. But to whom could she confess? Certainly not to that fierce saint, her father, nor that gentle saint, her mother. Certainly not to her brothers and sisters. They were all so wrapped in innocence. All, that is, except Richard, but instead of coming home for Christmas he had gone South in search of the sun. Richard was not innocent, but she could not tell him either. He would merely be amused. He would make a droll remark; perhaps even a cynical, rather brutal remark. Even in Montparnasse, he might say, it was usual to know one's partner's name, even if it was only an assumed one. "Really, my dear," she could hear him protest, "don't you think you were rather overdoing the unconventional? Just a shade too informal?" John would say that, too, in all probability. And it was all remote from the Celtic twilight which enveloped Joan and David, and from the warm, safe, happy domestic world in which Gwen lived with her young husband, with Charlie Two, and the baby sister born in 1930, and with a third child already on the way—golden Gwen who grew lovelier every year, as though her beauty throve on happiness. Gwen who had achieved what had been Marian's own dream—romantic love, happy marriage, lovely children. Marian envied her passionately, but without jealousy. It was right that Gwen should have such rich happiness; but it increased her own sense of loneliness in what had happened to her. Hers was no warm, safe, happy love, but only wildness and strangeness, and no home in it.

When they sang "Adeste Fideles" in church on Christmas morning she was quite sure that neither of the twins, nor Gwen, thought of the other words they sung in their riotous moments to that lovely tune; they were wrapped in innocence and pure in heart and free to worship; they were the faithful of whom they sang, come to adore; they were on the side of the angels. But she could only think of the Stranger, reminding her, smiling, that she had sung those other words to him on that dark walk home of which she remembered nothing—and she filled with shame, and a sense of blasphemy. Her mother whispered to her at one point that she couldn't remember whether she had put the potatoes in beside the turkey in the oven before they had left the vicarage, and did Marian remember? Because if she hadn't there would be no time to bake them now, when they got back, they would have to have them plain boiled . . . Domesticities intruded upon her mother's Christmas worship; she was Martha, and careful, and troubled by many things. It didn't matter; you could bring your worries into the church, just as you could bring in the babies and the pram; the church was a home; the first church had been a stables, with a baby, and shepherds—rough peasants in from the fields. But that dark Hallowe'en interlude, that could not be brought into the church—the church that was a home.

Marian knelt in prayer, her face buried in her hands, but she could not pray. She had a desolating sense of homelessness; of drifting upon a wild dark sea, and her desolation was intensified by the realisation that if anyone had offered to rescue her she would have refused the offer.

(3)

The ice-green, ice-cold waters of the Gulf of Finland, and the ship plunging and rolling, but driving on, cutting through the waves like scissors through green cloth. The dark forests and grey towers of Estonia tilting to the sky, then flattening out again as the ship's bows came up after each plunge. The ringing sound of the ship's engine, and the tremendous humming of the wind in the rigging, fusing like the instruments in a great orchestra. The gulls following in the wake of the ship, screeching and squabbling without impinging upon the essential harmony.

The hypnotic flow of water, slipping past, slipping past . . . ice-green, ice-cold in the Gulf of Finland, darkening on the evening tide in the Pool of London. Green water like a mirror. Mirroring a pale face and dark loosened hair. Marian, Maria, sleeping on her divan in the room above the river. Marian, Maria, like a dream at the bottom of the mind. The mind drowned in reverie under the green flow of water. Marian, Maria, asleep on her divan at the bottom of the sea. Marian, Maria, on the side of the angels against the forces of evil . . . The magic casements open on to perilous seas, Marian, Maria. Better ye become as a little child . . . smiling up confidently through the green flow of waters. Only a child can accept magic simply. In the heart of a child the world's wonder lives, beyond good or evil. Only a child can hear the temple bells of lost Atlantis ringing under the sea. Ringing in the vibrations of a ship's engine and in the wind in the rigging.

I will be there when you need me, Jenny Flower.

"Seek and ye shall find."

"Except ye become as little children ye shall not enter into the kingdom of heaven . . . "

May not the devil quote scripture?

The bells of lost Atlantis ringing under the sea. The waters of the Gulf of Finland, ice-green, ice-cold, slipping past, slipping past . . .

Chapter IX

Candlemas

O nce the succession of Sundays that was Christmas was over Jenny began counting the days to Candlemas. There seemed an almost unimaginable number of them. There were thirty-one days in January alone, apart from the pointless odds and ends of days between Christmas and New Year's Eve. As soon as Christmas was over, Jenny thought, you ought to get on with the New Year, the same as when the boredom that was Sunday was over you got on with Monday. Monday was a good day; it came all clean and fresh after the stuffiness of Sunday. It was like the smooth shining first page of a new exercise book, that always made you want to do your best writing, neat and careful and free of blots and crossings-out. On Monday you went back to school, you ran the streets again; on Monday the shops opened, everything came alive, people wore their ordinary clothes, and there was cold meat and pickles for dinner, because Monday was washing-day; on Monday, too, there was generally cold fruit pie and custard left over from Sunday. On Monday everything started fresh, and New Year's day was a super Monday. But that straggle of days after Christmas, when everything was over and nothing new begun—what was the *use* of them? On New Year's Eve you were allowed to stay up till midnight to see the New Year in—not that there was anything to see, and you were hustled off to bed the moment the church clocks had finished striking twelve, but before midnight you had the fun of declaring that you weren't going to bed until next year, and after you had gone to bed you lay listening to the bells ringing, and you fell asleep on the satisfactory thought that when you wakened it would be not merely a fresh clean new day but a fresh clean new year, a brand new exercise book with nothing written in it.

On New Year's Day that year Jenny opened the little pock-et-diary she had had in her Christmas stocking and looked at all the numbered days of January; she let them run through her fingers, day after day after day, until she came to February, and then in the little space in which, below the date, "Candlemas" was written in very small letters, she wrote in pencil in her best writing, "I wonder what will happen on this day." All through January, at every bedtime she drew a line through the diary space allotted each day, and crossed the number out in the table at the beginning. The crossing off of the days afforded her immense satisfaction; only there were so many of them. Even when you had crossed out twenty there still remained more than a whole week to work through.

When there were only a few more days to cross out she asked Mrs. Beadle, repeatedly, "Will he come at Candlemas?" and the old woman always answered, "For sure!"

Jenny would sit in class and look at Miss Drew, at her teacher's desk, and she would think, triumphantly, "He will come at Candlemas but she doesn't know!"

Once she asked Mrs. Beadle, "Where is he all this time?"

The old woman answered, impatiently, "How the devil should I know? Ask him yourself when you see him."

They talked of him in this way, but they never gave him a name.

January was always a bad month; it was all rain and sleet and slush; it was too cold for paddling in the river; it was dark after tea, and you had to stay indoors, and indoors there was nothing to do, at least that you wanted to do, and jobs were found for you to keep you out of mischief till bedtime. There seemed no sense in giving a month like January thirty-one days . . .

But somehow it came to an end; thirty one was crossed out in the January table, and February the first was easy to live through because it was a nice fresh new day, number one of a fresh new month, and the following day was Candlemas.

That it was Candlemas was Jenny's secret, shared only by Mrs. Beadle. Everyone knew when it was Christmas, but no one, it seemed, knew when it was Candlemas—no one except the people who made the diaries, and such people had no reality; they were abstractions, like kings and governments.

When Jenny came out into the sunny courtyard of the flats on the morning of February the second she had no knowledge of the religious and traditional significance of the day; it had not occurred to her to inquire into its meaning. Mrs. Beadle had said that it was a witches' sabbath, and a witches' sabbath meant a day when he would come; you did not know when or where, but you knew. He would emerge out of the day, somewhere, somehow, as surely as he had emerged out of the flames and the shadows of Hallowe'en. You couldn't, therefore, afford to risk missing him by going to school.

Jenny had not played truant from school since she had gone up into Miss Drew's class, but on the morning of February the second she sat at the top of a flight of steps above the river, listening to the school-bell clanging, and watching the barges, with a sense of rediscovered freedom. The vital thing, of course, when playing truant, was not to run into a copper or the school-board man. A copper was liable to ask you why you weren't at school; the school-board man was sure to. This meant you had to keep off the streets. You were safest at Mrs. Beadle's, but though you knew a way of slipping along the wharves to Ropewalk Alley you dared not do that this morning for fear of missing *him* . . . You had to hang about somewhere round the river, and you had to wish very hard, because by wishing very hard you could make things come true. You could stare into the eyes of a toad and wish it dead, and if you stared long enough and wished hard enough it would die. You stared into the river and watched the water slipping past, slipping past, darkly green, darkly cold, and you began to feel sleepy and far away, far away. The river was like a mirror; if you stared long enough you could see deep down into it, as in a crystal; you could see the person you wanted to see, if you stared long enough, wished hard enough. Green water like a mirror. Mirroring the stranger beside the forest pool, horns upon his head. The stranger smiling at her, approaching her, speaking to her, coming up out of the greenness of the water as he had come out of the greenness of the forest; coming up the steps to her, smiling, speaking . . .

"Hullo, witch!"

She got up and stood waiting for him. A few steps below her he halted, so that they were level. She laughed, happily.

"I knew you'd come!"

"Did you sit there summoning me up from the vasty deep?"

"I wished hard!" She tilted forward, flinging her arms round his neck; he caught her and held her to him.

"Where've you been all this time?" she demanded, burrowing into his shoulder.

"In hell."

"Was it very hot?"

"Hellish hot!"

"Flames and things?"

"Night and day, unceasing. I stoked the fires myself!"

She sighed, contentedly, then slithered down out of his arms, "Let's sit here and you tell me stories!"

She sat down and he seated himself beside her on the steps.

"What sort of stories, witch?"

"About foreign places."

"Travellers' tales—icebergs and volcanoes and forests full of wild beasts and bright flowers—is that it?"

She turned an eager face to him, and nodded.

He put an arm round her and she nestled close to him. The water slapped along the wharves gently, and when a tug approached with its barges laden with timber, cement, wastepaper, the water swelled up over the lower steps; you could watch it forever, and for ever listen to his voice, turning the river into the road to the sea, the road to the brightly coloured map of the world. You went aboard a ship called *The Seven Seas Spray*, you went slipping down the river on the morning tide, and soon you were in the open sea, "with Holland to starboard"; you came to the Kiel Canal; you saw it, very narrow, with the flat fields each side, dotted with small, neat red-roofed houses, like the illustrations to a fairy-tale. And it is all that, a fairy-tale, with mermaids under the ice-cold, ice-green waters of the Gulf of Finland and enchanted castles rising above the dark forests of Estonia, and princesses with long golden hair waving from grey towers, waving grey scarves above the trees, weaving in a dream, for lovers who never come, and the scarves fade into trails of mist, and the mists fade into the sky, and the water goes slipping past, slipping past . . .

A traveller's tale and a dreaming child, and in the wind upon the river the first breath of spring. The traveller told of ships, and the child saw them as golden galleons; he spoke of men and women who spoke in foreign tongues, and the child saw them winged and garlanded; he spoke of meadows, and she saw great spaces of flowers; he spoke of cities and she saw them decked with crimson banners.

All the morning they kept close to the river, loitering along the wharves, leaning on little iron bridges and watching the ships leaving their basins to "cross the road", watching the traffic of the Pool from wooden landing-stages and stone steps above muddy stretches of beach; he told her the names of ships, their cargoes, their destinations, or from whence they had come; they found the first primroses in the churchyard of a Scandinavian church with an onion-shaped dome and a clock with a blue face. It was a blue and gold day, of wind and sun, promise of a cold and bitter spring, but of this the stranger did not speak, and of such prophecies the child had no knowledge, and in everything there was the magic sense of wonder, of seeing everything for the first time in a world made new.

She talked a good deal of Mrs. Beadle, of her ancient books and magic charts, of the Evil Spirits and the Furies who could be called up if you knew how, and Mrs. Beadle did know how, "And one day I shall be able to, too, because people born on a witches' sabbath have special powers. One day," she added, proudly, "I shall have a Familiar and practise Ceremonial Magic! I shall understand the Tables and the Charts of the Planets, and I shall be able to call up Apollyon and Belial and all of them!"

"Including proud Lucifer himself?"

She looked at him, shyly, through her hair. "I call you Lucifer in my mind."

"Is that what you think—that I am Lucifer—Satan—the Devil?"

"I don't know what I think," she answered simply. She removed her hair from her eyes by brushing her head against his sleeve. "I love you," she added.

He smiled, and pressed the hand that clutched his. "It's as conclusive an argument as any."

At midday they leaned together on a wooden pier above a landing-stage used by police-boats. There was a busyness of tugs and barges, of swooping gulls, of lorries loading and unloading along the wharves, of quaysides busy with the commerce of ships. There was the hoot of tugs, the rattle of chains, the chugging of the engine of a crane, the throb of engines of the river traffic, and the air clean and cold and blue and brilliant, with a smell of mud-flats, of breweries, of ships, and the sea. The river was alive with the excitement of running out to the sea; the wind with the excitement of having swept in from it; it was the excitement of the ports of the world, with ships loading and unloading, the excitement of harbours crowded with shipping from the Baltic ports, the Mediterranean, the East. Small white clouds raced over the pale clear-blue of the sky, and small gold-flecked waves raced over the blue-gold river. It was a day in which to laugh and shout into the wind for the animal joy of being alive.

The tall, dark stranger who looked like a seaman, and the small thin child who looked like a gipsy, leaned on the wooden pier and ate fish and chips from a greasy newspaper, and dates from an ornamental box depicting palms and camels and men in Eastern robes, and they spat the stones into the river and had the satisfaction of landing one on the deck of a police-boat, and presently they went beachcombing along the muddy beach below a flour mill, and found a piece of comb, a blunt pencil, a broken pen-knife and various other useful articles.

They found a dead eel, and Jenny was reminded of the adder in the forest, then, following the association of ideas, she recounted how on Mrs. Beadle's charts she had found everything they had seen in the forest—the horns, the creeping thing that could have been the lizard, the flying thing that could have been the owl, the water that could have been the pool.

"But there were other things we didn't see—a flame, and a sword, and a crown, and a scourge. What's a scourge?"

"What did it look like on the chart?"

"Like a whip."

"A symbol of pain. But talking of crowns, let's go and look at the Crown Jewels in the Tower . . . "

The afternoon flowed away in endless bliss.

(2)

At the door of her room Marian stooped and stared. The figure at the window turned, smiling.

"You! How did you get here?" She hardly knew what she said. The beating of her heart seemed to fill the world.

"Forgive me. The front door was open and I came up the stairs. I knocked on your door and turned the handle. People who leave their doors unlocked encourage uninvited guests!"

She advanced into the room and placed her handbag and an armful of books on the table.

"When did you get back?"

"Early this morning. The first person I met along the wharves was Jenny—waiting for me!"

"How could she be waiting? She didn't know when you'd be back, did she?"

"She knew. She knew what day it is. Do you?" He smiled his crooked smile, but his eyes were gentle.

"It's the second of February. What about it?"

"It's Candlemas, and Candlemas is the first of the year's four great witches' sabbaths."

She frowned. "All that nonsense!"

He turned back to the window and looked out at the river, glinting in the pale late afternoon sunlight.

"Are you so sure it's nonsense, Marian, Maria? Do you really know where reality ends and fantasy begins? Are you quite sure the images of the mind have no reality? There is always the materialist explanation for everything, even for God—and God includes the Devil. You can say if you like that I came off a ship this morning and found Jenny Flower by chance, but you can't explain away the fact that she was waiting for me, quite convinced that I'd come, because it was Candlemas."

"That old Mrs. Beadle puts ideas into her head. She probably told her that February the second was Candlemas, that it was a witches' sabbath, and that you'd probably come back that day, and the child believed her." She spoke angrily, the old hostility roused in her.

"You'd say it was sheer coincidence, then, that I did come back the very day the child was expecting me? And that it was coincidence that each of the three occasions on which we've met has been a witches' sabbath—Lammas, Hallowe'en, Candlemas?"

"Of course! You'll probably now stage another romantic return on the next witches' sabbath—Midsummer's Eve, or whenever it is!"

He smiled, "No, Lady, earlier than that—May Eve."

"And you'll carefully arrange your reappearance on that date?" Her voice was contemptuous.

"By all means think of it like that if you prefer! But whether shall return or not will depend on whether I'm summoned—or, if you prefer it, whether I'm wanted."

"I suppose you'll say Jenny summoned you up on Hallowe'en at the Fair?"

"She was intensely excited by the fire scene; it was therefore natural she should see me. Certainly to her in that state it seemed the most natural thing in the world that I should step straight out of the flames to her, as this morning I rose up for her out of the water."

"I was not excited by the fireworks on Hallowe'en, but you materialised for me, too!"

"For you 'materialised' is the wrong word. For you I merely happened to be there. I don't stand in the same relation to you as to Jenny. You don't believe in the magnetism of desire; she does—though she doesn't think of it in those terms, but very much more simply. The first essential is faith. With faith all things are possible. Joan of Arc heard voices because she believed in voices and visions; to her, therefore, was vouchsafed the revelation denied to those who tried her. You're angry because you believe I'm deceiving Jenny, yet you yourself want nothing so much as to be deceived! You want me to give you a name to call me by—any name will do so long as I solemnly assure you it's true. You want me to fill in a background for you—any kind of background so long as it's comprehensible to you, something you can accept within strictly materialist bounds—in fact any lie will serve so long as I insist on its truth!"

He sighed. "Marian, Maria, you wanted me to come back, but now I'm here you can find nothing better to do than rebuke me for refusing to give you the conventional lies!"

She trembled with anger. "You who are the Father of Lies!"

He looked at her, curiously. "You realise the implication of those words?"

She buried her face in her hands. "Oh, I don't know what I'm saying! Why don't you go?"

"Because you don't want me to!"

"You're tormenting me."

"You'd be far more tormented if I took you at your word and went!"

He came over to her, drawing her hands away from her face, drawing her to him, but her mind's angry resistance made her body go rigid at his touch. She forced herself to look at him, and she said, with a passionate intensity, "I want you to go. I've never wanted anything so much in my life! As God is my witness—"

His hands fell away from her. He said, shortly, "There's no need to 'exorcise' me—I'll go."

At the door he looked back. She was still standing in the middle of the room, white and trembling.

Now it was he who was contemptuous. "It's been a very pretty little exhibition of Christian virtue triumphing over the powers of evil! Charming!"

She said, with that same intensity, "I never knew anyone could be so wicked!"

"Wickedness is all a matter of definition!"

"I never want to see you again."

"I'm sorry, because I'm afraid you must!"

"There's no must about it! There's such a thing as free will."

"There's also such a thing as the pattern in the carpet."

She looked at him. He smiled, ironically, blew her a kiss, and was gone.

She listened to him running down the stairs, heard his step in the short, narrow hall, and then suddenly she looked wildly round the room, as though she had been trapped in it—trapped in a terrible emptiness and silence in which the ticking of the clock and the stir of the pages of a magazine by the open window had no relation to the reality of that terrifying emptiness and stillness.

Her hands flew to her face again. She moved blindly over to the divan—where she had lain so many nights gripped with such fierce longing—and wept, and wept.

(3)

The grey endlessness of Wapping Highway; Shadwell Dock Steps swarming with children; the strip of muddy beach under the black hulk of a cement barge; the pale-blue sky impaled on the slender spire of a church; stretches of threadbare grass, a little terrace under clipped budding trees; the wind whipping along the river with a strong pungent smell of mud, and breweries, and brine—always that suggestion of the sea; the rattle of chains, the burr of men's voices, the clatter of moored barges in collision as the wake of mid-stream traffic washes in towards the wharves; tall chimneys belching black smoke, a conglomeration of crates, barrels, cranes, derricks; ships calling, men shouting, children shrieking and laughing, dogs barking . . . The grey grace of Tower Bridge with the great dome of St. Paul's behind, delicately beautiful as a Shotter Boys' drawing on stone, rising above the jumbled formlessness of commercial buildings.

Then Piccadilly, redeemed from triviality by a great spread of sunset making of Hyde Park Corner almost an Arc de Triomphe, and of the budding glades of the parks almost a Champs Elysées. The Elysian fields . . . the bells of lost Atlantis ringing under the sea. Pale face and loosened hair, the dream at the bottom of the mind, drowned in reverie, drowned in tears, the magic casements opening on to perilous seas in fairylands forlorn, and a chill in the first breath of spring upon the Elysian fields . . .

Hyde Park Corner in the sunset glow, and listless groups of people giving less than half their attention to the impassioned speakers preaching their various roads to salvation—the Catholics, the anti-Catholics, the Communists, the anti-Communists, a wild-looking old man with the ancient mariner's eye and a religion all his own, an emaciated female with shrill voice and ecstatic expression beseeching all to join her in the bosom of Jesus, an angry Irish nationalist with green, white and orange flag, a coloured man with flashing teeth and gleaming eye-balls. Men and women in spiritual and economic chains preaching freedom, preaching God, preaching anti-God. "Man was born free but everywhere he is in chains." Enough to make the angels weep (do you weep, Marian-Maria?) enough to make the devil spit blood . . .

Oxford Street full of pink lingerie and corsets and dawdling, shop-gazing, clothes-obsessed women, eagerly exclaiming young women, wistful-eyed older women with figures no longer suited to the whorish flimsy fineries, they for whom it is written on the clock-face, "It is later than you think."

The grey wilderness of the streets off Tottenham Court Road; the swing door of a familiar pub and inside the remembered inferno. However long you stay away it is always the same when you get back. As though the place never closed down; as though its patrons never went home, or, indeed, have any homes to which to go. Their home is there, in the heat and smoke and clatter, with the automatic piano grinding out the "old-time favourites"—*Daisy, Daisy, give me your answer, do!*—with a boisterousness that all but obliterates the tunes.

The usual clutter of Bloomsbury young men with beards and sandals and corduroy trousers, swearing by T. S. Eliot and the damp souls of housemaids; the usual young women with bright scarves and barbaric jewellery—mass-produced in the Midlands and retailed from the little Jew "antique" shops—and "artistic" hair-styles and make-up, flour-white face and scarlet mouth, trying to look like Epstein models, to show their intellectual superiority over the office and shop and factory girls who merely try to look like Hollywood film stars, or common or garden "tarts", the usual Eton-cropped Lesbians, tailor-made, with collars and ties, pockets in their skirts, husky voices, and "chappish" manners; the usual "pansies", scented, and swaying at the hips and discussing the Ballet with the usual over-emphasis—"My deah! The *most* lovely décor!"—the usual faded "queens" who had once been glamour boys themselves; and stirred in with it all a sprinkling of Bloomsbury personalities, a woman painter of some repute, a well-known journalist, an art critic, a young man who had written a "terribly amusing" novel, and the weary reviewer who had dismissed it in print in a couple of lines, and in person in one monosyllabic word. And leavening all this art and craft and intellectualism, the nondescript people who make up every pub scene—the stout middle-aged women drinking stout, the red-faced bowler-hatted men drinking beer and telling dirty stories in an illusion of maleness, flabby-minded, flabby-muscled—"hubbies", pornographic, hearty, devitalised; and rubbing shoulders with them the people whose lives are centred in "the tote", whose background is the race-course, the dirt track, "the dogs"; and the inoffensive people from stuffy domestic interiors, and the loud-voiced, showing-off people both of Bloomsbury and Suburbia.

And the snatches of what passes for conversation in human intercourse—

"I arst him—I arst him very nice—"

"The horrors of country life—"

"No nice girl goes on living with her mother—not once she's reached the age of consent, anyhow!"

"They've been tucking up together for some time now—"

"In this week's *New Statesman*—"

"You got to 'and it to ole Chamberlain—"

"Put a packet on the two-thirty—"

"Some sex-reform society or other. As though sex isn't perfectly all right as it is!"

"Karl Marx—that eminent Victorian—"

Oh wearisome condition of humanity! All huddled up together in the heat and smoke and noise and showing off—showing off like mad to hide the inner emptiness, the loneliness, the emotional and physical impotence; Lesbians with their sex-fear of men; male homosexuals with their sex-fear of women; heterosexual men and women mutually degrading each other with their drab promiscuity, their tawdry lusts, and all the lonely perverts looking for someone to share their cravings—cravings both monstrous and infantile, and the lonely masturbators, no longer seeking . . . Man, alleged to be made in God's image—and they say that God is not mocked!

"Why, this is hell, nor am I out of it—" and are these they "for ever damned with Lucifer"? What is hell if not the home of the damned? But Lucifer at least has looked upon the face of God, known Infinite Beauty, whereas these, grunting and guzzling in their human sty, what do they know of heaven or of hell?

Hell—electric trains to all parts every few minutes; good 'bus service . . .

Were you tempted of the devil, Marian, Maria, and did you cast him out into hell? And thereby bring ten thousand hells upon yourself?

Out there in the starry darkness, beyond this inferno, beyond this sprawling whoreshop of a city, the foxes call to each other in the hazel woods—clear as a reed the mating cry of the dog-foxes and full of a fearful compulsion the answering cry of the vixens, and the air clean and cool, and fugitive scents of primroses . . . but you refused to believe in magic, Marian, Maria, insisting on your labels, demanding an impossible recantation, and so we remain apart, each in our separate hells . . .

"O, thou art fairer than the evening air—" but if you insist on remaining rigidly enclosed in your angel-guarded morality, what can a poor devil do?

Chapter X

"Magic . . . Hath Ravished Me"

When Jenny got in at tea-time after her day's truancy Ivy was, in her own words, "ready for her", the school-attendance officer having called during the day. She seized the child the moment she entered the living-room, thumping her in the back.

"I'll teach you to play truant, you little devil!" she shouted at her, red in the face with anger.

Les looked up from his Meccano set. "You don't need to teach her that, Ma!" he said, and grinned. He had become very cheeky of late.

"You shut your mouth!" Ivy commanded, furiously, and then, to Jenny, "Take that! And that!"

The blows left red marks on Jenny's face, and the series of thumps in the back which followed the slaps on the face, made her feel sick, but she grinned at Les and Stan to show that she didn't care, just as she grinned at the other girls at school when a teacher slapped her.

"And now you can go to bed!" Ivy said, when her rage had spent itself. "No tea for you! Off you go!"

Jenny tossed her head. "I don't want any tea. I'm not hungry!"

As she turned to leave the room Ivy seized her again. "Don't you answer me back, my girl!" She struck her in the back again, so violently that she sent her flying across the room. Jenny stumbled and caught her head against the lintel of the door and fell. She lay for a moment stunned.

Les suddenly leapt up, his face white. "Cruel beast!" he shouted. Stan, seated beside him at the table, began to cry, frightened.

Ivy crossed the room and dragged Jenny to her feet. "Go on!" she shouted at her. "Go on, I say, get out!" She pushed the dazed child out of the room, then rounded on the boy.

"You're as bad as she is!" she cried. "You wait till your father comes in! He'll leather you!"

She was trembling with rage. The younger boy was sobbing hysterically, terrified by the storm which had broken over the home, reaching from Jenny to Les and likely, it seemed to him, to engulf him next.

Les gave him a shove. "Shut up!" he said. He felt sick. The scenes were common enough; one or other of them was always in trouble, and up to a point there was a certain excitement when one of them was going to "cop" it; a thump in the back or a box on the ears was nothing, but Ma had no right to knock Jenny down; for a moment he thought his mother had killed her, that her oft-repeated prophecy that she was sure that one day she would strike her "an unlucky blow" had come true.

Ivy made tea, but nobody wanted it, and as a result of the scene she had what she called a "splitting" headache. The boys were sullen, forcing down the thick slices of bread-and-dripping they were commanded to eat, and for which they were normally ravenous.

When Joe came in Ivy "let him have it".

"That Jenny's been playing truant again! I had the school-board man here! A nice thing! I gave her a hiding and packed her off to bed without her tea! She needs a good belting. She won't mind me!"

Les looked up sullenly from his plate. "Ma knocked her down," he said.

His father regarded him with that long, dark, slow look that alternately fascinated and maddened Ivy.

"You shut up," he said.

"I've had enough of young Les's lip, too," Ivy complained. "My head's splitting," she added.

Joe turned his dark morose gaze on to her. "Take a couple of Aspros," he suggested, laconically.

He went out of the living room and into the small box-room where Jenny slept.

She was lying on the bed humming. There was a swelling across her forehead where her head had struck the door.

Joe looked at her from the doorway.

"What you mean by playin' truant?" he demanded.

Jenny was silent. She slid her fingers down inside her dress to finger the hidden coral.

"You try it on once more and I'll tan the skin off your hide. Get me?"

She still didn't answer. The eyes she turned on him were dark stones. He felt her indifference and it angered him. It was something he understood; he had it in himself; it was in the Flower blood. Nell had it too. Nothing you or anyone else could say could make any difference. If you were a Flower you did what you wanted; people could shout and scream at you and it was so much water off a duck's back; you let them get on with it. He knew all about that. But he wasn't going to stand for it from a bit of a kid like young Jenny.

"You mind what I say, see!"

He advanced towards her, raising an arm, threateningly, but she did not flinch, and he suddenly turned and went out.

In the living room, sitting down to his tea, he said, heavily, "I've made her mind. You won't have no more trouble with her."

Ivy asked, anxiously, "You 'it her?"

He repeated, stubbornly, "I made her mind."

"I'd better go into her." She half-rose.

He snapped at her, "She's all right—I tole you, di'n' I?"

Stan sniffed, and Joe rounded on him. "What *you* snivellin' about?"

"Nuthin'," the boy whispered and lowered his eyes to his plate again. Under the table Les kicked his brother's foot warningly.

Ivy poured out her husband's tea. He ate in silence. The atmosphere was heavy with oppressed spirits. The alarm clock on the mantelpiece seemed to tick very loudly, and it was a relief when with a loud belch Joe finished eating and Ivy could clear away. Whilst she was busy in the scullery, washing up, Joe sat beside the kitchen range and picked his teeth; he frowned, but his mind was empty of thought. The boys got out their school books and tried to concentrate on their homework. There was the raucous voice of a distant radio giving the evening news, and the hoot of ships on the river.

In the scullery Ivy had a little cry. She felt upset. She could not forget that Les had called her, his mother, a cruel beast. No one could say she was a cruel mother, or even a strict one. She merely tried to bring the children up proper, to make them mind. Everyone said how well-behaved her children were—barring Jenny, but then Jenny wasn't her child. Les and Stan weren't little guttersnipes like most of the children in the flats; they were very obedient on the whole. Ivy asked no more than that of *any* child—that it should be obedient. Only it was no use "going on" at children unless you let them see you meant it. If she was crool, like Les tried to make out, why did all the children in the place come running to her? They were always in and out of her place; when they fell down and grazed their knees and elbows they'd come running to her before they went to their own mothers, and she was always drying their tears, putting ointment on their grazes, and giving them sweets, and playing with them. No one could say she wasn't fond of children. I love children, she told herself, passionately, dabbing at the crockery, the tears streaming down her face, her breath catching in quick hiccupy sobs, I love children, and it's not crool to make them mind . . .

When she had finished washing-up she blew her nose, vigorously, wiped her eyes, and prepared some bread-and-milk for Jenny.

Joe glanced up as she came into the living-room carrying the basin of bread-and-milk.

"I thought Jenny had better have something," she murmured.

Joe grunted. Les said, eagerly, "Let me take it in to her!"

"You get on with your home-work," she snapped.

In the box-room she could just see Jenny lying on the bed in the dusk. She had fallen asleep. Ivy set down the bowl of bread-and-milk, lit the candle on the chair beside the bed, and gave the child a shake.

"Here's your supper," she said. "Not that you deserve any!"

Jenny sat up, her hair falling over her face. She took the bowl from Ivy and began to eat, silently.

"When you've finished it get undressed and get into bed," Ivy commanded.

She looked at the bump on the child's forehead. It had turned blue. It ought to have some butter on it. Oh, well! It was probably too late to put it on now, anyhow, and it would only start the child feeling sorry for herself.

"Blow out the candle when you're in bed, mind," she said, in the same severe tone, "and don't forget your prayers."

Jenny nodded. When Ivy had gone out she obeyed all the instructions except the prayers. One of these days she would say them backwards; but not now; now she was too tired—full of the wind that had whipped along the river and the sun sparkling on the water, and the stranger telling stories of far-off and foreign places, and the water slipping past, slipping past . . . until you slipped at last into sleep as into a deep, dark forest.

(2)

She didn't go to see Mrs. Beadle for a few days. Calling in on the way home from school made her late home, and she wanted to avoid any more trouble for a bit. Saturday, when she was sent out to play gave her an opportunity.

It was a warm sunny afternoon and Mrs. Beadle was sitting on a kitchen chair at her front door, as were other inhabitants of Ropewalk Alley. Various of her cats sprawled about on the pavement round her, sunning themselves. Jenny came skipping along the dirty pavement and when she came up with the old woman climbed up into her lap.

"Here," the old woman protested, "Hop it! Come on, we'll go inside and make some tea."

They went into the dark evil-smelling house. In the narrow hall Jenny nearly tripped over the toad.

"He's taken to coming indoors," the old woman said, "I tell him it's spring and he ought to be outdoors looking for a mate, but he says he prefers the old woman!" She cackled, gently stirred the creature with her foot. "It's a wonder the cats don't go for him; but they seem to know he's no ordinary toad."

They came into the kitchen and the old woman pulled the kettle to the front of the range and poked the fire through the bars to encourage it to draw up.

"Did you see your friend at Candlemas?" she inquired.

Jenny nodded. "I stayed away from school specially, and I got a hiding for it when I got home, but I don't care. When will he come again?"

"When do you expect? The next witches' sabbath of course."

"When's that?"

"May Eve."

Jenny counted on her fingers. February, March, April—three months. "It's an awful long time—"

"It'll pass."

"What happens on May Eve?"

"Nothing specially—unless the coven meets."

"What's that?"

"It's a group that meets to raise the devil."

Jenny's imagination was stirred. "And does he come?"

"He comes all right, when those who believe in him are gathered together. He comes with horns on his head, every witches' sabbath—when the sabbath is kept."

"When do they come—the witches' sabbaths?"

"Well, you know them all now—you've just had Candlemas, and the next is May Eve; then comes Lammas on the first day of August—that was the day you met your friend in the forest with horns on his head."

"Yes," Jenny whispered, breathlessly. "Yes."

"The last of the year is Hallowe'en—your birthday. Don't you ever forget you were born on Hallowe'en, Jenny Flower! To be born on a witches' sabbath is to have special powers."

Jenny was silent for a moment, then she said, slowly, "Does it mean one day I'll be able to make spells?" Her voice was eager.

"If you believe. Faith is everything. You believed he would come back at Candlemas, didn't you, and he came back? Perhaps the coven will meet on May Eve; perhaps they will accept you as one of their band. If they do you'll receive the witches' mark and be given a familiar . . . "

The old woman rambled on, talking more to herself than to the child, spinning out the grey web of fantasy as a spider spins its web out of itself, but the web closed round the child, drawing her deeper and deeper towards the mysterious core of the Goetic life.

(3)

Ivy never inquired into the reason for Jenny's Candlemas truancy from school. She assumed a natural "naughtiness" in children in general and in Jenny in particular, and she fought an unending war against this naughtiness, attempting to quell it by the only method she knew, which was punishment and the perpetual threat of it. She assumed that Jenny stayed away from school periodically for no other reason than that she didn't like school, or anyhow liked it less than running the streets in freedom, which appeared to be a common childish failing. From time to time she heard rumours of Jenny having been seen in Ropewalk Alley, to which charges Jenny always stubbornly declared, "I never!" To this Ivy always made the stock answer, "You let me catch you, that's all!" This, of course, merely strengthened in Jenny the resolve not to be caught if she could help it.

Les and Stan began going to the Children's Club several evenings a week that spring, though Les was more interested in a church youth organisation commonly referred to as "the cadets". The "cadets" wore a "uniform" consisting of a pill-box cap and belt and bandolier. They marched to a band consisting of a drum and two bugles. They made quite a stir when they came down the street, and people ran to their doors and windows and exclaimed, "There go the cadets!" They made almost as much commotion as the Salvation Army, but they had a *panache* the Salvationists lacked. They marched for no particular reason, but purely for the love of the thing. There was some vague talk of inculcating Christian principles through organisation and discipline, allied with physical training, thus combining the welfare both of body and soul, but so far as the boys themselves were concerned it all began and ended with the wearing of the scrap of uniform and with the general military flourish of marching to brass and drum. Twice a week they marched merely for "exercise". On Sunday afternoons they marched to the Drill Hall, which was a gymnasium belonging to the church, and which was also used for Sunday-school treats at Christmas and for confirmation classes. At the hall the cadets learned

"First Aid" and "Signalling"; they also did "physical jerks", and took turns on the parallel bars and the ropes. Before they left, Mr. Wilson, their group-captain, a pale young man who was the Sunday-school superintendent, gave them a little talk on manliness and uprightness, clean thoughts and tongues, and the avoidance of something vaguely referred to as "bad habits", and then they marched home again. The hall was draped with Union Jacks, and there was a picture of King George V over the platform; round the walls were pictures of Lord Roberts, Lord Kitchener, Baden Powell, and General Gordon. Near the door there was a garishly coloured poster depicting a tall white man in a tropical suit and topee, and holding a Bible conspicuously in one hand, talking to a group of black children under a palm tree, with Jesus looking down, dimly, from the clouds, with a benign, approving expression. At the bottom of the poster were the words, "Suffer the little children to come unto me", and below that, in much smaller letters, "Church of England Sunday Schools Mission".

Every Sunday the group-captain urged the boys to think of themselves as the young soldiers of Christ, with the Cross of Jesus going on before, as it said in the hymn. They listened docilely to all this; it was all part of the proceedings; they had the feeling that it meant, really, as little to Mr. Wilson as to them—it was like the God-save-the-King they played at the end of the pictures—that for him, too, the real business was the marching and drilling, the First Aid and the Morse Code, the gymn and jerks and band practice. Mr. Wilson was "all right"; he was a "sport", and a "decent chap", and they all admired him marching ahead of them, tall and straight, head up and shoulders back, a leader to be proud of . . .

Kenneth Wilson's real strength with the children was his enthusiasm and his capacity for identifying himself with their make-believes. Away from the Sunday School and the boys' brigade he was a lonely and ineffective young man who spent his life adding up figures in the City and eating bad meals in dingy "digs" in Bermondsey. He was shy with "girls"—too much afraid of them to be capable of being attracted by them, though he had an attraction for them, because of a quality of helplessness that brought out the maternal in them; he had, also, a singularly sweet smile. In most situations he felt hopelessly inadequate, but the boys' brigade afforded him a sense of leadership nowhere else obtainable; through it he achieved a sense of spiritual and physical robustness, of virility. The "cadets", therefore, meant a very great deal to him. He was twenty-six, and already his hair was receding. It worried him, but then outside of his church activities everything worried him. He worried about his work if his landlady seemed a bit off-hand, or if a tea-shop waitress was curt with him; it worried him if the laundry lost one of his handkerchiefs; he worried if attendance fell off at the Sunday School, and if the vicar seemed less cordial than usual. His eyes held always this anxious, troubled look. He blushed, readily, and that worried him, too.

It worried him that the one woman with whom he did feel at ease disapproved of the one thing upon which he prided himself—his leadership qualities with boys. Marian Drew disapproved of the boys' brigade; she disapproved of it and she ridiculed it. "Playing at soldiers", she called it, and "encouraging militarism". As to "leadership" she would have none of it; young people too easily followed a leader, she declared; look at the youth-rally to a leader called Mussolini, and what had it led to—what *was* it leading to? Offer youth leadership and a uniform and they'll follow anywhere; what we needed, she insisted, was a movement to encourage youth to find itself, individually, not play follow-my-leader . . .

"Your boys' brigade keeps the children out of the club, where we try to encourage them to express themselves as *individuals* through something creative—concocting plays and producing them and acting them themselves. We have a drawing-class and a modelling class, and a weaving loom, and a potter's wheel, and a workshop—but you seduce them away from the creative—you offer them a pretence at a uniform and a pretence at a brass band, and martial music—and leadership! You appeal," she smiled at him, "to the worst in them—to the instinct for show and bravado; it's only a few steps further on in this direction before they're wearing jackboots—actually and spiritually!"

They had many such discussions, at the club, and in her room, where she gave him tea on Saturday afternoons—Sundays were taken up with Sunday School and the cadets.

He always fell back on the leadership of Jesus.

She reminded him, "Jesus didn't put his followers into uniforms and march them round the town! There was no swagger and bravado, no drums and trumpets, no outward show to attract—"

"People left all to follow him—to become his disciples—"

"To work with him—to spread the gospel of the way, the truth and the life. There was no brave music or even a distant drum in it! Only persecution and the shadow of Golgotha!"

He was troubled. He had to hold on to his beliefs; they were all he had; his *amour-propre* depended on them.

He was a nice, serious, sincere young man, Marian thought, but weak. She was sorry he had roped in Lesley Flower; he was a bright spirited boy, energetic and imaginative; it was chiefly through his efforts that the club had so good a stage, with skilfully arranged lighting—he had shown quite a flair on the electrical side. She had hoped for a lot from him; he helped to create the desired atmosphere amongst the young people, but his interest and enthusiasm for club affairs flagged when he joined the boys' brigade. Even when he was not marching and drilling with the "cadets" he was busy practising the bugle—he had to go down to the river to do this, as the people in the flats complained bitterly, which Ivy thought very unreasonable of them. "Anyone would think," she declared, "they'd never been children themselves!"

It seemed to Marian that both the Flower children were defeating her, but she was determined not to lose Jenny entirely if she could possibly help it. The loss of the boy to a militaristic youth organisation was much less serious than the loss of the girl to these strange, dark preoccupations with the Goetic life. The boy might well grow out of the ideas at present being inculcated in him; the girl looked like becoming more absorbed in her preoccupations—so perniciously fostered by old Mrs. Beadle and the enigmatic stranger—as she grew older. The muddled, well-meaning Kenneth Wilson was not the menace to the boy that the half-mad old woman and the preposterous stranger were to the girl. Didn't they realise what, between them, they were doing to the psyche of the child by the deliberate building-up of this Goetic fantasy? The old woman was illiterate and probably crazy, but *he*, whoever he was, was an educated person, a man of intelligence, and sane enough—he should know better! It was all very well to insist, as he did, that a child needs no persuasion to believe in magic, that it accepts it naturally, and that no one offers any objection to a child believing in fairy-tales and myths; he was encouraging a child to believe in a supernatural that was sinister and evil, that was associated with horrible rites which had actually taken place, which, amongst depraved people, might still take place as part of a perverted cult of "black magic". Even if no such rites were indulged in, if everything took shape and place in the mind, the neurosis remained—of being apart, outside of nature, predestined. An abstract perversion can poison and corrupt no less than a material one. It was all very well for Faustus to cry—

'Tis magic, magic that hath ravished me,

Faustus was doomed and damned as the price of his ravishment, and, poetry apart, such ravishment in practice means neurosis, the sick psyche, and possibly ultimate insanity. Perhaps in spite of his charm, his intelligence, his plausibility in argument, he was in fact mad? And thinking that, she could see him smile, and hear him murmur, "It depends. Lady, what you mean by madness . . . "

Oh, an impossible person! But she had been foolish to quarrel with him, to send him away; she should have kept him with her, tried to find out about him, tried to reason with him, for Jenny's sake. She must try to see him again when he came back on April 30th—as, with his flair for dramatic reappearances, he certainly would. She would lower her pride and try to find out from Jenny where he was to be found. Perhaps, even, he would call on her again. He had, after all, said that she had not seen him for the last time. It ought to be possible, somehow, to call his bluff, and somehow to break the spell he appeared to have put on Jenny—with the collaboration of old Mrs. Beadle. The important thing, clearly, was to keep in touch with Jenny out of school hours. She tried to persuade her to spend at least part of the Easter holidays with her at the vicarage; it would be of great value, she felt, to get the child into a new and healthy atmosphere. But Jenny was not interested; she looked forward to the Easter holidays as an opportunity of spending precious hours with Mrs. Beadle, learning the only thing she was interested in learning—the exercise of those special powers peculiar to certain people, of whom she was undoubtedly one, having had the good fortune to have been born on a witches' sabbath. Her curiosity over Mrs. Beadle's ancient books of magic, and her astrological charts, was growing; every scrap of information Mrs. Beadle deliberately imparted or carelessly let drop intensified this interest. She was increasingly convinced that the old woman had magic powers and that one day she would demonstrate them, and increasingly fascinated by the mysteries of witches' sabbaths, which always brought *him*—out of the forest, out of the fire, out of the water. Where would he come from next? That he would come on May Eve she did not for a moment doubt. She could hardly wait for the time to come, for the magic to happen. Keeping close to Mrs. Beadle she had the feeling of keeping close to him, because Mrs. Beadle understood about him; it was as though she knew him, and in some way she could not have defined she felt that they all belonged to the same world, she and the stranger and Mrs. Beadle, as surely as Miss Drew belonged to quite another. It was an idea to which, ravished by magic, she was continually returning.

Chapter XI

Pretty Lady

Nell's visits to her sister-in-law were very infrequent. She went to tea on the Sunday after Hallowe'en, and then not again until the Sunday after Candlemas, the following February, that is to say not for another three months. She never went at Christmas; she couldn't bear family gatherings, she declared. The November visit was primarily to take Jenny the new dress and the chocolates for her birthday. At Christmas she sent her a winter coat and a doll, with books for the boys, silk stockings for Ivy, and cigarettes for Joe. She was always generous with presents. She arrived unexpectedly on the Sunday in February, bringing a bunch of daffodils, newly in and expensive, a bottle of port, and sweets for the children. Ivy was washing her hair, not expecting "visitors", and was rather put out. Les was out with the "cadets". Stan and Jenny were somewhere outside; Joe had gone off to his ex-servicemen's club to play billiards and wait for the pubs to open. There had been a time when, with the children out of the way, Joe liked to have "a nice lay-down" on a Sunday afternoon, with Ivy along with him, but in recent years this friendly domestic custom had fallen into disuse. Ivy had grieved and fretted about it at first, then she had felt a little bitter and hard, and now she was indifferent; if Joe went off on his own it gave her a chance to get on with such odd jobs as washing her hair or turning out a cupboard.

"You've caught me, proper," she protested, as she answered the door to Nell. She had discarded her jumper, had a towel round her shoulders, and another one twisted turban-wise round her dripping hair. Nell was very smart as always, a chinchilla cape over a black velvet suit, a blouse of thick lace with a cascade of frills down the front, good gloves, stockings, shoes, handbag, a very modish hat, and the inevitable aura of perfume. Her clothes were all expensive and, each taken separately, in good taste; but the chinchilla was too much with the velvet, and the elaborate blouse too much with both. Even Ivy who always admired Nell's smartness was not deluded that she looked a "lady"; she had to admit that she looked like nothing so much as "a high-class tart". She had fine eyes, but they were too heavily made up; she had a pretty mouth, but it was too red—and too hard. Some of the red from her mouth came off on Ivy's cheek when she kissed her.

"How are you, dear? Don't mind me. I'll put the flowers in water whilst you finish your hair. If you like I'll get the tea—I'm a dab hand at thin bren-butter! I brought a nice bottle of port for you and Joe. A coupla glasses and the ole man'll quite fall for you again. I brought the kids a few sweets . . .

She flung her furs down into the nearest chair, carefully removed her hat and gave her hair a few pats, then opened her bag and took out a blue and silver enamel cigarette case and extracted a cigarette. Ivy fluttered about, confusedly, producing a vase for the flowers, whisking the *News of the World* out of the one easy chair—Joe's chair—holding her turban load of wet hair up with one hand, talking distractedly, "Nice of you to bring the daffs, but you shouldn't have. They must have cost the earth. Make yourself comfortable. I won't be a few minutes."

She hoped to have the scullery to herself whilst she finished her hair, but first Nell must come in to fill the vase with water for the daffodils, then, when she had arranged them and placed the vase in the middle of the table, she came and leaned in the doorway. The smoke from her cigarette clung unpleasantly to the steam and Ivy felt it at the back of her throat and it added to her irritation.

But Nell was quite unconscious either of the effect of cigarette smoke on steam or of Ivy's annoyance. She leaned against the door completely at ease and glowing with that sense of well-being which the prospect of a pleasant evening always gave her. Her satisfaction with life made her feel benign, and a little sorry for all those people—and they seemed to be the majority—whose lives were not such fun as hers. Most people just didn't seem to know how to live. They seemed afraid of life. And they were always thinking and worrying about the future instead of taking each day as it came. There was no sense to it that Nell could see. She had a "dinner date" in the West End that evening with a gentleman who was in the fur trade in the City—hence the chinchilla. He was a yid, of course, but say what you like about the Jews they were generous. This one, Max his name was, was young, not more than about thirty, and he had been good enough to tell her that he thought her wasted behind the bar; he could get her into a dress shop in the West End if she liked; working on commission she ought to do well. But though Nell appreciated the compliment she was not sure about it as a proposition. Odd as it seemed to some people she actually liked being behind the bar. She liked the rougher sides of life and the men who came in off the ships. These rich Jews were so sleek and elegant; they gave you furs and jewellery, and a good time, in bed and out, but though she could wallow in luxury like a cat in warmth there was another side to Nell Flower, that wanted something quite different—that did not want the smooth and sleek and perfumed at all; that could say to hell with it all, give me a sailor straight off a ship, a man out of the fo'c'sle, with his rough hands and his strong body that has known sweat and sun, and no fancy tricks in his handling of women, but a hunger that devours him and you with it. No

124

central heating and soft carpets in the places you went with him, but you hardly saw your surroundings—he saw to that! And afterwards you went out to some matey Limehouse sailors' café called Curly Charlie's, or some such name, and you ate a hearty meal of steak and chips, followed by drinks galore in a public bar, and you could see he was proud of you, for a fine classy bit of stuff, a sight above the foreign tarts in those houses at Marseilles, Port Said, Buenos Aires. And you'd look at him with pride, too, because, cloth cap and choker and studded belt and all, he was a man—a real man, not a tailor's dummy with soft white hands that have never done a day's hard work in their lives . . .

Still, you didn't always want the same thing, and once in a way it was pleasant to wrap yourself in chinchilla and black velvet and contemplate dinner in the West End with a sleek, suave "God-forbid" with a diamond signet ring.

She would have liked to have told Ivy about Max, but Ivy with her head covered with soapsuds and the shoulder-straps of her underclothes falling down over her arms looked so cross. And she would probably have disapproved anyway. Poor old Ive! She asked about Jenny.

Giving her hair its final rinse. Ivy said, "She's been a little devil lately—playing truant again."

She squeezed the water from her hair and tied it up once more in the towel turban.

"Let's go in the living-room," she said, "Then I can dry it by the fire."

Kneeling in front of the kitchen-range she added, "I gave her a good hiding, but she doesn't seem to take any notice of me, and Joe's too soft with her."

"Did you find out how she spent the day?" Nell inquired. "I mean if you know why a kid takes a day off from school it's kind of useful—a clue. I thought she liked school with this new teacher—that reminds me, I meant to have told you last time I was here, I saw her in a pub on Fair Day with some feller off a ship I knew years ago—I can't quite place him, but his face was familiar. When I told him that he laughed and said "Well it ought to be!" Cheek! A good-looking feller, tall and dark—I like them like that. But fancy picking up with a school ma'am! Said he'd met her at the Fair—she'd come up when he was talking to Jenny. What do you think of that?"

Ivy looked up, her face red from the fire; the wet towel in her lap, her damp hair hanging dankly about her shoulders.

"But how did he come to be talking to Jenny? I left her with her brothers when me and Mrs. Grigg went off to have a drink—she knows I don't allow her to talk to strangers!"

Nell laughed. "Well, ducky, whatever you allow, there she was talking to one, it seems! And it wasn't the first time she'd met him, neither. I asked him how he come to know the kid, and he said he'd met her in Epping Forest at a Sunday-school treat in the summer. Come to think of it she told me something about it—she got lost and he brought her home. But you needn't worry—the school-teacher came steaming up, it seems, and they musta got off with each other, for he took her off to the Seven Bells!"

Ivy rubbed her head vigorously with the towel. "I don't know, I'm sure. What can anyone do with a child like that?"

Nell threw her cigarette-end into the grate. "I can't see what you got to worry about. It was decent of him to bring the kid home when she got lost—you ought to be thankful. It was natural enough he should speak to her seeing her at the Fair—I can't see there's any harm in that. And, hell, she's only seven!"

"All the same—you read things in the papers. Little girls found interfered with in woods, and that."

Nell looked in the mirror and rearranged a wisp of hair. "Well," she said, "She wasn't interfered with, was she? Shall I make the tea—the kettle's boiling . . ."

They had a cup of tea together before the children came in. By that time Ivy had dried her hair and fixed it all up under a net—there was no doing anything with it when it was newly washed, she explained.

"It would pay you to have it done at a hairdresser's and have it set—save you a lot of trouble," Nell suggested.

"Fat lot of time I've got for the hairdressers," Ivy protested, quite indignant at the idea.

Nell didn't bother to argue the point. Ivy's was a stupid sort of life, anyhow, always working and worrying and scraping and saving and never enjoying herself, getting everything at second-hand at the pictures, making herself a slave to the kids—who would be better and happier if she didn't—never going anywhere, and letting herself get so dowdy. No kind of freedom. You might as well be in prison if you were going to live like that. But some people—most people—seemed to do that, get themselves imprisoned in their lives.

The children, when they came in, were delighted to see their Aunt Nell. She cheered the place up. All other relations were dreary and boring. They asked you how you were getting on at school, and if you liked school, and said you were growing, and when they were there you escaped out into the yard as soon as you could. But it was fun when Auntie Nell came. She made you laugh. She treated you as if you were a grown-up. And she was such a pretty lady, and she always brought you something. No other children in the flats, or for that matter in the whole neighbourhood, had an aunt who was so "posh".

Jenny ran to her with a cry of joy and jumped into her lap, flinging her arms round her neck, half strangling her.

"Oh," she cried, "you smell nice! You smell like flowers! Your dress smells nice and your skin smells nice and you are nice!"

She nuzzled her face against Nell's cheek.

"For goodness sake!" Ivy exclaimed impatiently. "Stop showing-off! Go out into the scullery this minute and wash!

What've you been up to? Your hair's a sight, and no one would think that dress was clean on this morning! You needn't tell me you came straight home from Sunday School!"

"I did, then!" Jenny protested, and appealed to Stan, "Didn't I? We come straight home together!" When you did so many wrong things it was unbearable to be accused of things you didn't do.

"She's all right," Nell said, quickly, before Ivy could weigh-in with her don't-answer-back. "She only wants her hair-slide fixing. Come here, ducks, I'll do it—"

She took a comb from her handbag and combed Jenny's untidy hair and refixed the slide, smiling at her. "Now, when you've given your face a wipe you'll look a treat!" Ivy went on at the kids too much; she was always on at them. You couldn't expect kids of that age to be clean and tidy all the time; it wasn't natural.

"She's a dirty little tike," Ivy insisted. "Go on—off with you! You too, Stan."

Jenny climbed down from Nell's velvety knees reluctantly, stroking the cloth as she slid down. Everything about Auntie Nell was so soft and scented. She followed Stan out to the scullery. Sharing the enamel washing-up bowl in the sink they agreed that it was "lucky" Auntie Nell had come. What was "unlucky" was that the dreariness of Sunday should pass unrelieved, or be aggravated by "relations" to tea. It was extra lucky for Jenny that Nell had arrived, or she would have been smacked for coming in so untidy and for answering back.

Nell livened up the Sunday afternoon tea considerably. She talked and laughed freely and easily, told about films she had seen, and about queer characters who came into the bar, and treated Les as though he were a young man, listening respectfully to his opinions of films and film-actors, and not making fun of the "cadets", like some grown-ups did, or being "down on it" like his mother—on the grounds that it was "all a lot of nonsense, parading about"—but taking a proper interest.

He kept his bandolier and belt on during tea for her benefit; he would like to have worn his cap, too. His mother kept spoiling things, of course, by interrupting to assert that he was "only showing-off", but Nell was always on his side. "I'm *interested*," she would say, firmly, and turn to him again as though she really were. And Ivy would think bitterly, "Can't resist playing up to anything in trousers, even if it's only a school-boy and her own nephew!" To make up for all the snubs from his mother Nell pretended to be surprised to learn that Les was not yet fourteen, and strongly supported his contention that he should have long trousers at least for Sundays—he had been agitating for "longs" for months, and his father didn't see why not, as he was tall for his age, but Ivy stubbornly insisted that he couldn't have them till he was fourteen. Les wished Aunt Nell was his mother. Only somehow he couldn't think of her as a mother—a mother was someone who nagged you and thwarted you in everything you wanted to do; his mother had said no when he wanted to join the cadets, but Dad had come to his rescue there; he had put his foot down; Dad believed in boys' brigades; they were manly, he said. But if only by some miracle you could have a mother like Aunt Nell! Someone who was interested in what you did, someone you could talk to, and who was on your side! Someone young and pretty and gay . . . It was funny to think she was Dad's sister. He was such a dry old stick! But in a way you could tell they were related; they had the same sort of eyes; queer eyes, really, that seemed to see right into you, and they had the same way of ignoring anything they didn't want to take notice of; you felt that they'd both do what they wanted to do, whatever anyone said, Dad in a quiet secret sort of way, Aunt Nell in an open be-damned-to-you way.

Even the morose and sulky little Stan responded to Auntie Nell. She won him over by the simple process of hugging him, presenting him with an assortment of cigarette cards, and behaving as though he were really a most lovable little boy.

There was competition to walk with her to the 'bus when she left in the early evening. Les wanted to escort her alone; he would be proud to be seen with such a "swell dame"; if only he had "longs" people might even take her for his "girl". Stan said that if Les went he wanted to go, too, and Jenny also clamoured to be allowed to go, but "just me, not the others!"

Nell also wanted Jenny to herself. "I can't have you all trooping along," she said, "so let it be Jenny this time, then I can give her a telling-off for playing truant from school last week!"

She gave Ivy a wink and gained her support. "She doesn't want the whole pack of you hanging on to her," Ivy said, briskly. "Go and tidy yourself, Jenny. Put your best coat on. Hurry up!"

There was no hurry, but Ivy could never resist urging the children to hurry, any more than she could resist telling them to "stop it" when they were most enjoying themselves.

On the way to the 'bus Nell asked, "Why did you play truant the other day? I thought you liked school now you were in Miss Drew's class?"

"School's all right, but I wanted to see someone."

"The someone you were talking to at the Fair when your school-teacher came up?"

"How did you know?"

"He told me himself!"

Jenny stared at her in wonder. "Do you know him too?"

"I knew him before you were born."

"What's his name?"

"I don't remember."

"Miss Drew doesn't know it either. Nobody knows!" There was triumph in her tone. "Mrs. Beadle calls him Lucifer. Do you think he really is Lucifer?"

Nell laughed. "I shouldn't be surprised! He's proud enough! But what's Mrs. Beadle got to do with it?"

"She tells me about him. She told me he would come back at Candlemas, and he did. The time before was Hallowe'en, and the next time will be May Eve. Did you know I was born on Hallowe'en?"

"I knew you were born on the thirty-first of October."

"That's Hallowe'en. It's a very important day. It's a witches' sabbath."

"Does that make you a witch?"

"If you believe in it. It's no good if you don't believe."

"I see. And you believe you'll meet—Lucifer—again on May Eve, do you? Where will you meet him this time? Does it mean you'll play truant again? I shouldn't if I were you."

"I'm not going to. I shall go to Mrs. Beadle's. He'll find me. He didn't know where I'd be last time, but he came."

"Where did he come?"

"Up out of the water."

Nell looked down at her. "You're a funny kid."

"I was born on Hallowe'en," Jenny reminded her, simply.

They walked on in silence for a little, then Nell asked, "Do you see Old Mother Beadle very often?"

"Saturdays, mostly. But you won't tell? Ma wouldn't like it. She says she ought to be locked up. Miss Drew doesn't like me seeing her, either. She says she's a bad influence."

"She would!" Nell was instinctively on the side of the lawless and godless against the law-abiding and God-fearing. The deep antagonism of class-difference rose up in her, and of an opposing moral code. The school-ma'am, the "lady", the vicar's daughter—he had told her that—the professing Christian, the social-worker—but for her fine clothes she would have obeyed the impulse to spit.

"Ma Beadle's all right," she said. "A bit cranky, but she's got her wits about her, all the same, and her heart's in the right place. You can give her my love next time you see her. But don't let on to your ma I said it was all right to see her. No point in causing trouble."

Jenny was elated. Now they each had a secret to keep; Auntie Nell would not give her away, and she would not give Auntie

131

Nell away. They were on the same side, not the side of the angels, with Miss Drew and everyone who wanted you to be what they called "good", but the side of the fallen angels, along with Lucifer.

She tugged at Nell's hand with a sudden urgent pressure. "You come to Mrs. Beadle's, too, on May Eve, then it'll be a party!"

Nell smiled. "Perhaps, I don't promise. It's a long way off yet. Three whole months!"

"I shall keep on reminding you," Jenny said.

When they parted at the 'bus stop she flung her arms round Nell's neck, kissing her wildly on her scented cheeks, her painted mouth. She was her pretty, pretty lady, her darling Auntie Nell . . .

"I love you," she cried, "I love you, I love you, I love you!"

Nell said, when she could get her breath and had disengaged herself, "I'll need a new lot of make-up after that lot!" but she was laughing, and her eyes were softer than any man ever saw them.

Jenny skipped all the way back home, along the tramlines of the grey Jamaica Road, along the narrow sunless lane between the warehouses. Not since her day's truancy from school had she felt so happy. Auntie Nell was on her side, on the same side as Mrs. Beadle and he whom she called Lucifer. They belonged to the same secret world—the strange dark exciting world of secret things, of spells and sorceries and charms, of that darkness in which magic was worked, and of which Lucifer was the proud Prince.

Chapter XII

May Eve

Somehow there was an end of February, and of the wild March days, and the softer days of April, and at long last it was the last day of April. Jenny crossed out all the numbered days in her diary and finally approached the longed-for ringed-round date, Saturday, April 30th.

That it fell on a Saturday had at first seemed to her an advantage, since Saturday was the day she could most easily slip away to Mrs. Beadle's, whilst Ivy was doing the Saturday afternoon shopping for the week-end, and the boys had gone off to play by the river. But half-way through April it was decided that as May Day fell on a Sunday it would be a good plan to hold the school's May Day celebrations on the Saturday afternoon. These celebrations consisted of dancing round a Maypole in the school playground, and doing a selection of Morris dances, before an audience of parents. If the day turned out wet it was done in the school-hall. Jenny liked the Maypole dancing; it was fun weaving in and out amongst the red and yellow and blue and green ribbons, till they were all tightly plaited round the pole. You wore a holland smock for the occasion—the smocking of which had been your needlework lesson for weeks beforehand. If you were to be a "boy" dancer you wore a white linen hat with your smock; if you were a girl you wore a milk-maid bonnet. As Jenny was small she was chosen for a girl. Every class had a maypole dance, the higher-up classes doing the more complicated dances, producing the more intricate patterns amongst the ribbons. But though she normally enjoyed the Maypole dancing the decision to keep May Day on the Saturday worried her. If her mother came to watch the dancing she would be expected to walk home with her, and she would be unable to escape. It was unthinkable that her mother shouldn't come; she enjoyed any kind of an "outing"; there were so few in her life. She would do her week-end shopping in the morning, or on Friday, even, so as to be free to come. Jenny knew that she had written to Auntie Nell telling her she was going and suggesting she might be interested to go along. But she and Auntie Nell had to meet someone at Mrs. Beadle's . . . ah, if only it were possible to send a letter!

Then suddenly it came to her—Mrs. Beadle could call up Evil Spirits, and wasn't Lucifer an Evil Spirit, a Fallen Angel, the greatest of them all? Why shouldn't she call him up on Friday? What was the use of being a witch and knowing magic if you didn't get what you wanted by your magic? Her heart beat very fast with the thought. What was it like to call up an Evil Spirit? Was it very terrible? Would there be thunder and lightning and the curtains blowing out in a wild wind, as in a Boris Karloff film? She shivered, but not with fear. She was not afraid of lightning; a thunderstorm thrilled and excited her; she always wanted to run out into it . . .

She was resolved to go to Mrs. Beadle on Friday, on the way home from school. She looked at Miss Drew a good deal during the lessons that day, and she thought, "*He* is coming back to-day, but she doesn't know!"

Marian looked a good deal at Jenny that day, too, deeply troubled. She was convinced that the stranger would come back the following day, that he would make a point of doing so, and she wondered how and when Jenny would meet her "evil genie"—for thus it was she had come to think of him. And indeed, she asked herself, how else was it possible to think of him? She wondered whether Jenny would stay away from the Maypole dances; but would she dare? Her mother would almost certainly be coming—which would give her a chance to meet her and have a word with her about Mrs. Beadle. She decided to walk part of the way home with Jenny that evening and try to find out what was in the child's mind, and whether Mrs. Flower would be coming to-morrow.

At four o'clock when she had the children stand as usual for the evening hymn—

Lord keep us safe this night—

she was suddenly aware that Jenny was standing with tightly closed lips and a curious expression on her face. She was white, and her skin seemed tight-drawn, and her dark eyes were like burning coals in her head. It was, it suddenly came to Marian, a positively demoniac expression!

May angels guard us while we sleep—

That was absurd, of course. Jenny Flower was always a wild-looking little thing, and in her wilful way she probably never did sing the evening hymn; it was just that she had never noticed before . . . Why should she refuse to sing it this night rather than any other? This, after all, was not May Eve. To-morrow was May Eve. But to-morrow she would not be able to keep her witches' sabbath—that preposterous make-believe. Supposing she was up to something to-day? Perhaps Mrs. Beadle was in touch with him and had warned him to stage his reappearance to-day instead?

Jenny was quite unperturbed when Miss Drew attached herself to her in the playground when she was leaving.

"I'm going your way this evening," Marian said. "I thought we might go along together."

"All right," Jenny said, laconically.

"Is your mother coming to-morrow afternoon?" Marian asked.

"I 'spect so."

"It's May Eve, isn't it? What about your friend? Isn't he due back then? Will he come, too?"

"I don't know."

This isn't getting us far, Marian thought.

She tried again. "You won't let us down by playing truant to-morrow, will you?"

"No."

"Is that a faithful promise?"

Jenny resented being made to promise something she had every intention of doing, and made no answer. As her mother would be going along with her what chance would she have of not going?

"I asked you a question, Jenny."

Still Jenny did not answer, and her resentment increased. Miss Drew had no right to try and force answers out of her out of school; she had no authority over her out of school-hours.

I suppose, Marian reflected, one shouldn't try to make a child promise anything. They walked on in silence and came to Ropewalk Alley. Then, abruptly, Jenny said, "I'm going to see Mrs. Beadle before I go home." There was no defiance in her voice; it was merely a statement.

Whilst Marian was hesitating over what answer to make, Jenny added, "I'm meeting my Auntie Nell there." She had had a sudden fear that Miss Drew might insist on coming with her, and she didn't want her to; she didn't belong; she belonged to that quite other world.

Marian felt balked. She had been right, it seemed; the child was up to something. She was going to meet him there this evening instead of to-morrow. It seemed almost criminal to be allowing the child to go unhindered to that evil old woman, to meet that hard-faced aunt, and him—an unholy trinity if

136

ever there was one! But what could she do? The child probably wouldn't stay long; the aunt would probably have to be back at the Seven Bells by opening time, and he would probably leave with her. She might wait about on the off-chance of catching them when they came out. In that case there'd be only about half an hour to wait. It would be hateful seeing him again, of course, especially with that woman, but she ought not to miss the opportunity—nor even the possibility of it—of making another appeal to him to leave Jenny alone, to abandon this pernicious game of make-believe he was playing with her . . .

She said good-bye to Jenny and walked on. She would walk to the end of the High Street and buy an evening paper, then stroll back. She might even, it occurred to her, meet him on the way to Mrs. Beadle's. It would be much easier speaking to him without Nell Flower.

Jenny left Miss Drew with a sense of escape. She ran down the steps into the alleyway and skipped along the dirty pavement. The sky was full of golden light. People sat at their doorways taking the last of the sun. They smiled and nodded to each other and remarked what a warm evening it was, real spring. Ah, yes, it was spring, soft and warm and beautiful and exciting. There were daffodils even in Ropewalk Alley, in window-boxes, and in bowls on the sills inside the dingy rooms.

Mrs. Beadle was not at her door, but the door was open and Jenny ran in. To her surprise and delight she found Nell there, seated by the window in the back room, her perfume overriding the familiar stale smell, her bright clothes decorating the room like flowers. To-day she was not wearing her grand West End clothes, but a scarlet beret perched jauntily on her dark hair, and a tight-fitting scarlet jacket over a short black skirt. Round her neck there was some kind of bright gold ornament, like two snakes twisted, and a similar ornament at her wrist. She looked lovely, Jenny thought, and ran to her, ignoring Mrs. Beadle.

"What made you come to-day? Did you guess it would be to-day because of the Maypole to-morrow?" Without waiting for the answers she began covering Nell's face with impetuous kisses.

"Your Auntie has a right to call on me without telling you, I suppose," Mrs. Beadle observed, drily.

"You wouldn't think so, would you?" Nell laughed, pushing Jenny away from her. "Lay off, you brat! I've got to go to work in these clothes presently!"

But it didn't matter what she said, because she smiled and her eyes were soft.

"What have you come for, if it comes to that?" Nell inquired. "I thought Saturday was your day for playing witches."

"But I can't come to-morrow," Jenny reminded her, "and so I wanted Mrs. Beadle to call him up to-day." She turned to the old woman, her eyes burning. "You will, won't you? You can do it! You know you can do it!"

The old woman looked at Nell and winked. "Hark at her!" she said.

Jenny went over to her and began tugging at her.

"You must!" she insisted. "You must make him come quickly, to-day, now, instead of to-morrow. There won't be another chance till Lammas, and that's not till August. You must do it!"

She was filled with a terrible urgency. Mrs. Beadle couldn't fail her now. Somewhere at the back of her mind was the unformed thought that if she failed her now everything would be gone for ever.

"You've only got to call him," she repeated. "I'll draw the circle for you—"

"Don't be silly," Nell said, sharply, and to Mrs. Beadle, "Don't encourage her in the nonsense, Ma!"

But Mrs. Beadle was looking at the child, a long strange look, and sweat had broken out on her yellow wrinkled forehead.

"We'll try," she said, in a curious tone, a loud hoarse whisper. "But we must have darkness. Darkness. Draw the curtains—"

Nell realised that the last remark had been addressed to her and started. "It's going too far," she protested, but she turned and drew the dirty green serge curtains, as though under some compulsion.

Mrs. Beadle took a box of matches from the mantelpiece and struck a light, then moved over to the dresser and held the match to a candle in an enamel holder. Then she pulled open a drawer and took out a black cloth, which she spread on the table. From a cupboard beside the range she took a crystal and placed it in the centre of the table; then fumbled in a pocket in her ragged old skirt and brought out a piece of chalk which she handed to Jenny.

"Draw the circle right round the table," she instructed. "Nothing can happen outside the circle."

She stood holding the lighted candle whilst Jenny went down on her knees on the dirty linoleum and began to draw the circle.

"I don't know what you two think you're up to," Nell said, uneasily, "but you won't get me inside your old circle! No funny business for me!"

Neither the old woman nor the child answered her. They were both completely absorbed. When the circle was completed Mrs. Beadle stood the candle beside the crystal and drew Jenny close to her. She made a pass with her hands over the crystal and then took Jenny's hands and laid them on the table.

"Lean forward right over the crystal and look deep down into it. Don't take your eyes from it. Think about him. First we'll repeat the Abracadabra together, then I'll say the incantation, and then he will appear in the crystal. He will be here in this room. You mustn't move out of the circle or take your eyes from the crystal or your thoughts from him. Are you ready?"

"Yes," Jenny whispered. Her body was ice cold.

She bent over the crystal that glowed like a lamp in the dim room. Gazing into it was like gazing into a pool of golden light. A deep sea of fire. Somehow through that sea of light, that glowing fire, he would come, Lucifer, Prince of Darkness, Lucifer the Light-Bringer . . .

"Abracadabra," the old woman began to chant, and Jenny intoned with her, "Bracadabra, Racadabra, Acadabra, Cadabra—"

Outside the circle of light Nell watched, trying to tell herself that it was all a lot of nonsense, like those fake séances, all a lot of old woman's hocus-pocus, and a shame to take the kid in with it, but fascinated by the intensity of concentration in the two faces peering into the crystal, fascinated by the incantation, the invocation of the unknown. There might be something in it, she thought, uncomfortably, you never knew. The old woman was queer, supposed to have second-sight, and she knew people who swore by the fortunes she told from the crystal . . .

The Abracadabra came to an end, and the two gazing into the crystal did not move. The old woman began her invocation. "Most unholy Lucifer, Prince of Darkness, Lord of Light, appear now before us, thy most humble servants and adorers, we beseech thee. Forgive us our virtues. Lead us into temptation. Deliver us into evil. Kingdom the is thine for. For ever and ever, and never and ever . . . "

The old woman's voice faded into a mumble and Jenny ceased to hear any distinct words. The golden sea of the crystal had become all fire; it seemed to be drawing her into it, deeper and deeper. There was a rushing in her head as though she were drowning and the waves washing over her. Down, down, into the golden sea, the golden fire, deep down, deep down, until there, at the bottom of the sea, at the heart of the fire, he stood, smiling; coming towards her out of the flames of Hell, holding out his hands to her, growing bigger and bigger, until he filled the world . . .

"Hullo, witch!"

She tried to reach the hands he held out to her, and knew a pain like a sword driven into her heart. She gave a cry, tilted forward, and there was a blaze of light . . . She was in his

140

arms and sunlight poured through a window on to her face, blinding her.

Nell stood by the window, the drawn-back curtains still in her hand. She was trembling.

"What the devil—?"

No one took any notice of her. The old woman was bending over the child.

"There, there, it's all right now. The pain had to come—the witch's mark. But it's all over now, and he's here, and you're his . . . for ever. Nothing can ever take you from him now!"

Nell dropped the curtains and rushed over to the old woman and grabbed her arm.

"You damned old fool! Shut your damned cackling! Can't you see you've frightened the kid nearly to death? It's her heart—her lips are blue—"

She pushed the old woman aside and bent over the child herself, brushing back her hair and asking her if she were better, if the pain had gone, if she wanted a drink of water . . .

Mrs. Beadle laughed. "There's nothing wrong with her that you can cure, Nell Flower, or any doctor either!" She hobbled back to the range and began stirring the brew in the big pot.

Jenny smiled up into Nell's anxious face. "I'm all right," she said, "Reely I am! I had a big pain, but it's gone now." She was as white as paper, but her smile was like a light, and the same light was reflected in her eyes.

"He did come, you see!" she said, triumphantly. "He always said he would come when I wanted him!"

Nell said, scornfully, "He timed it very nicely, I admit!" To him, she said furiously, "These games have got to stop! A bit of make-believe's all right with a kid, but this is going too far!"

He smiled. "It seems you have an alliance with our school ma'am after all, Nell Flower! Who would have thought it?"

"The kid thinks the old woman's a witch and called you up out of the crystal. Tell her it's not true, dam' you! Tell her

141

you came in at the front door in the ordinary human way, by chance, just at the right moment!"

He smiled down at the child in his arms, her head against his shoulder.

"You heard what your Auntie Nell said, little one? I came in at the front door in the ordinary human way!"

Jenny smiled as at a joke shared. "I saw you in the crystal."

He looked at Nell. "It's not a bit of use your telling her she didn't see me, you know, when she knows that she did. She's not going to believe you against the evidence of her own eyes."

Nell said passionately, "You've hypnotised her, between the two of you! I'll take her home. What's more I shall tell Joe and Ivy that she's been here and they'll take good care she never comes again!"

He said quietly, "You'll do nothing of the kind, Nell Flower. You will not say a word about anything that has happened here to-day, or even about her being here."

She tossed her head. "What's to stop me?"

"Your fear of me."

"I like that! Why the hell should I be afraid of you—*sailor?*"

"Because you don't quite know who I am, and you're afraid I might tell you, and it's something you couldn't bear to know, and because the secret you kept from Jenny is known to Mrs. Beadle and to me, as well as to Joe and Ivy, and you don't want it told, do you?"

"Blackmail, eh? Think yourself smart, I suppose?"

He got up, still holding Jenny in his arms.

"*I* will take Jenny home!"

At the door of the kitchen Mrs. Beadle came forward and produced something from the folds of her apron and pressed it into Jenny's arms. It was furry and alive. It was a black kitten.

Jenny laughed, happily. "Is it my familiar?"

"What do you think?"

"What's its name?"

"Anything you like. It's a male."

"I shall call him Satan!"

"Ivy won't let her keep it," Nell said, curtly.

Jenny smiled at her. "Don't be cross, Auntie Nell. I did see him in the crystal, honest I did! Without a word of a lie!"

Nell went over to her.

"You mustn't come here any more. Promise me, Jenny! You said you loved me. If you love me truly you'll promise me!"

It was his turn to be contemptuous. "Now who's trying blackmail?"

The old woman said, "She might promise, but it won't stop her coming. She belongs to him now, and she'll do what he says. And so will you, my girl!"

"I don't want to promise," Jenny said, simply and caressed the kitten.

Nell turned away.

"Good-bye, Auntie Nell," Jenny called, from the hall, but Nell made no answer.

When they were alone Nell rounded on the old woman.

"You old bitch! Between you you'll kill her! It was her heart when she pitched forward like that, I tell you! The strain was too much for her heart . . . "

"You can call it what you like. No doctor can do anything about it. It's the witch's mark. You get it in all the old witch-craft confessions—"

"Jenny's only a kid—"

"The youngest witch ever burnt at the stake was a child of eleven. St. Gregory himself tells of a child of five who saw evil spirits and confessed to it."

"Oh, in those olden days "Nell said, vaguely, feeling that she was being unfairly taken out of her depth.

"Human nature doesn't change," the old woman replied. "In the seventeenth century in this country two sisters of the name of Flower confessed to being in communication with the devil and were burnt at the stake—did you know that?"

"I didn't know it, but what's it got to do with it? There musta been plenty of people called Flower. It doesn't follow our lot were descended from that olden-days lot!"

"It doesn't necessarily follow, but on the other hand it might, and how else do you account for your Jenny being so interested in these things?"

Nell retorted, bitterly, "Because she had the bad luck to fall in with you!"

"Don't forget that before I ever set eyes on her she'd already met someone in the forest with horns on his head—on a witches' sabbath!"

"Children imagine things!"

"Why should she imagine horns? Why didn't she imagine him wearing a golden crown or a bowler hat or a wreath of flowers?"

Nell felt that the argument had got out of hand. She tried to bring it back to a level on which she could cope with it.

"A child like that ought not to have her imagination encouraged, and that's what all this crystal business is doing, and keeping up this pretence that that feller is someone special. It's bad for her heart—you seen it for yourself!"

"You can have a doctor examine her heart, and you'll find that he will discover nothing wrong with it. There'll be a red mark above it that he won't be able to account for. He'll probably say that it's a birth-mark that's been there all the time and that you've never noticed. You'll know how true that is. So will Ivy."

"I'll believe about the mark when I see it!"

The old woman cackled. "You'll have to! Seeing is believing, isn't it? That's why Jenny believes she saw him in the crystal and that he came up out of it You'll say he just walked into the house in the ordinary way whilst Jenny and I were crystal-gazing, but you weren't crystal-gazing and you didn't see him come in."

That, anyhow, Nell thought, was an easy one. She said quickly, "I was watching you two, and the room was dark. I didn't hear him open the kitchen door."

"Because he didn't open it! And I'll tell you another thing—you saw him walk out of here with Jenny in his arms, but if you go outside into the broad daylight and ask anyone sitting at their doors if they saw a man pass with a child in his arms they'll say no. Because they haven't seen him!"

"Expect me to believe that?" Nell's tone was derisive.

"I don't expect you to believe anything. You can go outside and ask them. There's one more thing—that school-teacher has been waiting in the High Street this last half-hour to catch him, and at this moment he's passing so close to her that she can feel the rush of air; it's made her shiver in the warm sunshine; she has said to herself that someone must have walked over her grave—because that's what people say when they suddenly shiver for no reason they can understand. Lucifer's brushed past her with the witch-child in his arms and she hasn't seen him, and she has felt his passing without knowing it. If you go now you'll find her still standing there, waiting . . . "

Nell stared at her a moment longer, then shivered herself.

"Oh, Lor'," she said, "I'll be going. You give me the creeps . . . "

People looked at her with interest as she came out into the sunlit alley. She was a smart piece of goods. They knew her well enough by sight and some even saluted her by name.

"Afternoon, Nellie."

"Evenin', Nell."

I've a good mind to ask them, she thought. Just to prove it. But of course they'd seen him, and then she would look silly. They'd say to themselves, "Does she blinkin' well think we're blind?"

All the same—nothing like proving a thing. Just for your own satisfaction, like . . .

At the end of an alleyway she suddenly stopped and inquired of a woman who nodded to her.

"You saw that feller who come out of Mrs. Beadle's a few minutes ago with a kid in his arms?"

"A feller with a kid in his arms? I can't say that I did."

The woman turned to the group in the next doorway, "Any o' you see him?"

A man answered, "Can't say as I noticed. A few minutes ago? We bin here ever since you arrived. Was you wantin' him or sutthing?"

She said confusedly, "Oh, it's nothing much. He left something behind, that's all. Funny you didn't see him go—"

She hurried on, not wishing to have them agree with her that it was funny.

As she came out into the High Street at the top of the steps she saw the school-teacher look at her wrist-watch and then walk away.

(2)

Jenny slept that night with the black kitten lying on her chest. Ivy had raised only a half-hearted objection to it. She was fond of cats, and it was a pretty little thing. Jenny said she had found it on the way home. She played with it all the evening, and Ivy laughed at its antics; she had to admit that it was "sweet"; but it would have to go outside at bedtime, she said. But when bedtime came and Jenny took the kitten through with her Ivy made no comment. She had the feeling that there would be a "scene" if she tried to turn the creature out, and she told herself that it was not weakness on her part to want to avoid this, but simply that it wasn't important enough to stand out about. Giving in she compensated herself by the thought that it just showed that whatever some people might think—that they should call her a "cruel beast", which was something she would never get over—she was really a very indulgent mother.

It also weighed with her that ever since the trouble in February Jenny had been a fairly good child, no more playing truant, no more coming home late and dirty from school, or setting out late, through "dawdling"—a common crime in the young—never pulling a face when sent on errands or given the cutlery to clean to keep her out of mischief. There was no doubt, Ivy thought, that she had learned her lesson after the February upset. And she didn't want an upset now, with the "do" at the school the next day; she wanted the child to be at her best, a credit to her, with all the other mothers there, and she wanted to be at her best herself, and a scene upset her so, gave her a headache for days after. And if the kitten kept the child in a good humour, well, let her have it. "Though, mind you," she felt constrained to say, as she tucked Jenny up for the night, "one mess in the house and out it goes!"

Jenny slept the deep sleep of pure contentment—the sleep she had slept at Candlemas, and before that at Lammas and Hallowe'en, but now everything then tentatively suggested was proudly stated. Everything was true. Nothing had failed. Faith was confirmed. There had been no betrayal, nor now ever could be. She laughed happily because "Satan's" nose was cold against her cheek. Of course it was cold—what else would anyone expect it to be?

She moved in a dream in the morning sunlight, her heart singing. Ivy, rushing about trying to "get everything done" before going out in the afternoon, nagged at her incessantly, but it didn't matter. Nothing mattered now, in this new and splendid certainty of belief.

Then, suddenly, in the middle of the morning, it occurred to Jenny that if Ivy went to the Maypole dancing she would meet Miss Drew. Even if she refused to point out her mother to the teacher, the other girls would if they were asked. Most of them knew "Jenny's mother" by sight. Then Miss Drew would tell about her going to Mrs. Beadle's yesterday, and there would be a scene like there was after Candlemas, and ever afterwards it would be made difficult for her to go. Between them they might even manage to get Mrs. Beadle sent away—locked up. Her mother must be prevented from going to the school that afternoon. With a little shiver Jenny realised that she could only stop her now by putting a spell on her. Had she the strength? Had she the power?

She had read in Mrs. Beadle's ancient books, and Mrs. Beadle had herself told her, a great many ways of putting a spell on someone; many of them were too elaborate for practical purposes—they involved possession of the dried blood of a bat, the eyes of a toad, ground snakeskin, mandrake root, hairs from the tail of a pregnant mare. But there was another and simpler magic, by which you took something from the person upon whom you wished to put the spell and transferred the evil through it to the owner. It might work now; it must work!

She slipped into the scullery when Ivy was in another room and snatched from the clothes-horse behind the door the red cotton handkerchief which Joe used to wear to work and which lately Ivy had taken to tying round her head to keep the dust off her hair when she shook the mats. Jenny took it with her and the kitten into the W.C.—the only place where she could lock the door and be sure of privacy. She was ice-cold all over her body and her face had assumed a set look, her eyes burning with a terrible intensity. Without smiling and without pleasure she played with the kitten, roughly, until it put out its claws and drove its small sharp teeth into her hand. Deliberately she let it draw blood, and she felt no pain. She wiped the blood on the handkerchief, then pressed it to her forehead and whispered over and over again, her eyes closed, "You have a headache; you have a terrible headache; you will have to lie down this afternoon; it is coming on you now, a terrible headache; you will have to lie down . . . "

When she let herself out of the W.C. she was as white as after the crystal-gazing, but quite certain. She went calmly back to the scullery and replaced the handkerchief on the clothes-horse, then resumed her task of peeling the potatoes for the midday meal.

Presently Ivy came into the scullery and took the handkerchief from the clothes-horse and tied it over her head. She sighed. She felt a headache coming on; it was the bad time of the month, of course. It would have to come to-day of all days!

She picked up the scullery mats and went out on to the balcony to shake them. The shaking made her headache worse; it felt as though it was going to be one of her sick headaches, the blinding kind. If it didn't get better she wouldn't be able to go this afternoon; she would have to lay-down . . . It was all this rushing about that had done it, of course, at the very time when she ought to be taking things easy . . .

By dinner-time Ivy knew that she wouldn't be able to go to the Maypole dancing. Her head throbbed so that she could hardly see. She served the children's dinner, put Joe's on a saucepan of hot water on the range to keep hot, and went into her bedroom. Jenny would have to get herself ready. She could do no more. She drew the blinds against the bright afternoon sunlight and gave herself up to her misery, feeling too ill even to be disappointed at being done out of an "outing".

Jenny looked at Ivy's white face whilst she served the dinner and she felt nothing except triumph. When it was time to leave for the school she went into the bedroom where Ivy lay and asked her to button her smock for her and see if her hair was all right.

Ivy heaved herself up from the bed with a groan, fastened the smock at the back, and sank back again. "You'll do," she said.

"You'll do," Jenny repeated to herself, as she skipped in freedom across the courtyard and out into the sunless lane.

You'll do. You'll do. But you mustn't do it too often or you might lose your power. You might use it all up. You must save it for when you badly need it. Lucifer could appear any time, but he only comes at the proper times, on witches' sabbaths, or when someone with the power of witchcraft calls him up for a special reason. Mrs. Beadle could call him up whenever she liked, or any of the Spirits, but she would only do so when it was important. Magic, she had once told Jenny, was not to be used like a conjuror's box of tricks. That was abusing the powers granted us by the Prince of Darkness; it degraded the great dark secrets. You could be cast out of his Satanic Majesty's kingdom as he himself had been cast out of God's celestial kingdom, and if that happened you were utterly damned, since then you belonged to neither God nor the Devil, and had no home in Mankind; then you had visibly upon you the mark of the cloven hoof which you could never hide, and you might as well be dead. Ah, that was terrible to think about, and you didn't want to think about it on May Eve when you had successfully worked your first spell and bells rang in you, chiming. You'll do, you'll do . . .

When she reached the school she saw a number of people already sitting on the rows of chairs arranged in the playground, and a platform covered with red bunting and set with small gilt chairs and vases and pots of flowers, and at each side tall palms. The gilt chairs were for the May Queen and her attendants and for various local personages—councillors and educational authorities and such—who were to give tone and weight to the occasion. The May Queen was elected each year by the vote of the whole school. The vote was for the prettiest girl, but there was a rule that she must also be a "good" girl; a girl who had not a good-conduct record could be disqualified if the head-mistress thought fit, but as the school knew the rules this never happened. The two girls who got the next highest number of votes were appointed her attendants. The school subscribed to provide the May Queen with a long white silk dress, white shoes and stockings, and long white gloves; the same train served each year; it was of green satin and painted with apple-blossom. The Queen was crowned with a wreath of apple-blossom, and she was presented by some distinguished local person with a bouquet. Her attendants were expected to provide their own white dresses and shoes and stockings, but if her family could not afford to equip her she was helped. There was no rule about it, but it was always one of the older girls who was chosen to be Queen.

The Maypole waited, crowned with blossom, and its ribbons tied in to the pole. Girls raced about in various kinds of fancy dress—the Maypole and Morris dancers in their smocks, "Irish jig" dancers, in emerald skirts and white blouses with red scarves draped round their shoulders and knotted on their young bosoms, "Highland fling" dancers in Tartan kilts, Welsh dancers in tall black hats—of cardboard—with red cloaks and striped aprons. Teachers, arrayed in smart dresses such as they never normally wore to school, rushed about almost as madly as the children—though with less enjoyment—rounding up their classes.

At one side of the platform there was a piano at which different teachers were to undertake to thump out the requisite jigs, reels, marches, and old-English folk-tunes. It was all very exciting, Jenny thought, and she was free to enjoy it to the full, without the shadow of any possible meeting between her mother and Miss Drew. If Miss Drew said anything to Auntie Nell she was quite sure she would "get her answer", for though it was true Auntie Nell didn't like her going to Mrs. Beadle's, she'd never stand for being lectured by any school-teacher about it. She was completely confident that, when it came to the point, her darling Auntie Nell would be on her side. She would be late, of course; she wouldn't be able to get away till the bar closed, and that wasn't till half-past two, and then she wouldn't be able to leave immediately. She would miss the march-past, headed by the May Queen with her attendants holding up her train, with all the dancers following. She would also miss the "infants' " dances, but she should be there by the time Jenny's class was round the Maypole.

Jenny was seized by various girls who said, "Miss Drew's looking for us," and when the teacher had her dancers lined up she stopped by Jenny to inquire, "Is your mother here?" Jenny told her, "Ma couldn't come. She's got a sick headache." It was difficult to keep the triumph out of her voice. Marian thought, "I seem fated not to meet Mrs. Flower! Anyhow, whatever the child got up to yesterday she looks healthy and happy enough to-day!" For the time being she had other things to think about, in any case. "May Day" from the teachers' point of view was a nerve-wracking and exhausting business . . .

At last it all got started, a good twenty minutes after the scheduled time, but getting all the groups of children together was like rounding up flocks of sheep, despite the fact that they had all been instructed to report to their respective teachers as soon as they arrived and to stay by them . . . but as the teachers themselves raced about, rounding up stragglers, there was inevitable confusion. However, at last the notable personages filed on to the platform, and a teacher took her place at the piano and banged out a march, and then the march-past began, led by the May Queen—ordinarily Gladys Thompkins—looking very red and self-conscious, but, everyone was agreed, also "very sweet". Gladys's mother watched with tears in her eyes. Gladys looked lovely; like a bride; she wished Dad could have been there; but you could never get Dad along to anything. Well, for one thing he hadn't got a decent suit to go anywhere in. What can you do on three pounds fourteen and eightpence a week with six children and the rent alone seventeen-and-six a week? Still, there were to be some photos taken, and Gladys would be given three copies, she understood, and then Dad would be able to see. But he should've come; he could've looked through the railings if he didn't like to come inside . . . Mrs.

Thompkins humped the baby higher up in her arms so that he could see Gladys, so that he could wave to her, our Gladys looking like a bride . . . Oh, but for the sick dread that there was yet another baby on the way Mrs. Thompkins could have been supremely happy that sunny Saturday afternoon . . . She didn't know what Gladys would say when she knew; she was a good girl, but she was only thirteen, and the young were so hard, they didn't understand—how could they?

No one thought Jenny Flower looked "sweet", not even Nell who arrived in time to see Miss Drew's class weaving its way in and out amongst the coloured ribbons. Nell wanted to laugh when she saw Jenny; she looked such a little ragamuffin. All the other little girls looked so neat and clean and cared-for; but though Jenny's dress was as new and as clean on as theirs it looked very much the worse for wear by the time Jenny was round the Maypole, For one thing she had fallen down twice, sprawling full length, before she had ever got to the Maypole. She and a few others had got bored watching dances they had seen rehearsed so often during the past few weeks, and between the march-past and their own contribution to the programme had started racing about at the back of the playground. Also she had done her hair herself and her parting was zigzag, and she had lost her slide, so that her hair was all over her face. Finally, owing to Ivy's attack of migraine Jenny's white gymn shoes had not been cleaned and were a dirty grey amongst the other children's clean white shoes. She was the black sheep in the flock all right, Nell thought, but she looked very happy one-two-three hopping in and out amongst the coloured ribbons. It was a pretty sight, she thought, and the kids enjoyed it—though it got a bit boring for the grown-ups after a bit . . . unless, of course, you were one of those who "loved" seeing children perform, which she wasn't. When she caught Jenny's eye she waved to her, and Jenny grinned. The sight of Auntie Nell there in the crowd filled her cup of happiness to overflowing.

When Jenny's class had finished its dance Nell slipped away. There was nothing else to stay for, so far as she was concerned. On her half-day she would meet the kid from school and tell her how nice she looked, just to please her.

Jenny had already pointed out her smart and beautiful "auntie" to various of her friends, so that Nell's early departure was not as great a loss to Jenny as it might have been, though she had hoped to see her afterwards.

As it was, instead of Auntie Nell she had Miss Drew attached to her once more, at the end of the afternoon—Miss Drew asking her if she had seen her friend yesterday.

Jenny tossed her head. "That would be telling!" she said.

"Of course it would," Marian replied, "that's why I asked you."

"P'r'aps I did and p'r'aps I didn't!"

"You're so cheeky to-day, I think you must have done!" Marian said, resolutely smiling.

"Well then, I did, if you must know," Jenny said, unable to resist the sense of power it afforded her to be able to say it.

"Shall you see him again?"

"I don't know. I might."

"If you do, will you tell him I particularly want to see him and ask him to call on me?"

"I might—if I remember."

"It's important, Jenny." She tried to keep the note of pleading out of her voice, but it crept in.

Jenny was aware of it and it added to her triumphant sense of power.

I won't tell him, she thought, I shouldn't dream of telling him!

She had no idea whether she would see him again or not. He had made no promise, and she hadn't asked him, so full had been the cup of yesterday's happiness. Unless he suddenly appeared when she was on her way home she didn't see how she could see him again before Lammas, another three months away—too remote to contemplate.

When she got in Ivy was still lying down. She had sent Les out to do the shopping, to his great disgust, as she felt unequal to it.

"How did everything go off?" Ivy inquired, when Jenny came cautiously into the bedroom.

"Fine," Jenny answered. "Auntie Nell was there, but she didn't stay."

"Done up to the nines, I suppose, as usual?"

"She wore her red things."

"Makes her look common," Ivy said, and raised herself on the bed.

"Pull up the blinds," she ordered, "I'll get up and make tea."

Jenny asked as she went over to the windows, "Is your head better?"

"Not quite. But better than it was. Not thumping, anyhow." Then, looking at Jenny in the sunlight let into the room, "You look a sight. I hope you looked a bit better than that round the Maypole. Go and wash yourself, for goodness sake, and tell Les to put the kettle on the gas. Look sharp."

Ah, but it didn't matter, it didn't matter; she had been defeated for the afternoon . . . hadn't she, Satan, my darling, my darling? She picked the kitten up and pressed it to her face. We worked it between us, didn't we, my darling, my precious lovely familiar?

She went to bed happily again, taking the kitten with her as before, but this time she did not immediately fall asleep. It was May Eve, a magic night, in which anything might happen.

She lay very still, staring at the darkness, stroking the kitten lying on her chest, listening to its contented purring. Lucifer, she whispered, Lucifer, if you could come and say good night to me . . . It's so long till Lammastide . . .

She lay staring at the pane of window, listening to the noises all round; the low burr of her parents' voices from the living-room, smothered laughter from the boys' room, the sounds of radio from the surrounding flats, sudden noises in the streets—bursts of laughter, the distant clangour of trams in the Jamaica Road. Presently there was the hum of Ivy's sewing machine, and the clatter of her scissors on the table. She fell into a light doze.

When she opened her eyes all the sounds had ceased, even the trams. The kitten had left her chest. She could dimly see it silhouetted against the lightness of the window-pane.

She meant to whisper "Satan" to call it back to her, but in her drowsy state she whispered, "Lucifer!" . . .

Then she was aware of him standing at the foot of her bed, very tall and dark and filling the room, filling the world. She could not see his face. He had horns on his head as that time in the forest.

"You must go to sleep, Jenny," he said, gently.

"Kiss me good night."

She felt his darkness closing over her like great wings, and his kiss cold on her forehead. She sighed contentedly and felt the deep, dark waves of sleeping going over her like the dark river slipping past, slipping past . . .

Chapter XIII

The Dark Forest

During the next few days Nell was very much exercised in her mind, she who prided herself on not being a "worrier". Serving drinks behind the bar of the Seven Bells, resting on her iron-bedstead at the top of the house, riding in trams and 'buses, even when dressing herself for an evening in the West End, she could not get the events of that Friday evening out of her mind. That people sitting in their door-ways in Ropewalk Alley that fine evening had not seen a man leave Mrs. Beadle's with a child in his arms, though they saw her, Nell Flower, plainly enough a few minutes later, had shaken her. And then seeing the teacher waiting, just as Mrs. Beadle had said she was—how had the old woman known that? Well, but plenty of people believed she had second-sight; there was nothing in that; that was something you might easily believe in, like fortune-telling. You could get over that, but not this other business. She felt that she must know now whether Jenny really had some strange mark above her heart—some mark that had not been there before and which could not be accounted for in any ordinary way. But how could she find out? She couldn't ask Ivy outright; it would start too many questions. Ivy bathed the children on Saturday night—the one night Nell couldn't get time off, or she could have timed a visit for bath-time and insisted on bathing Jenny herself. She could ask Jenny if she had the mark, but the child would be sure to say "Yes".

She met her from school several times that first week in May, watching for any effects on her health of the crystal-gazing experience, but there was no sign of anything wrong with the child. She was as full of life as she had been at the Maypole dancing. She would see her from afar tearing down the street, chasing other children in the road, swinging round lamp-posts, shrieking and yelling as lustily as any other healthy gutter kid. When she saw Nell she would come rushing towards her with eager cries. She did not hold it against her that she had disapproved of the happenings at Mrs. Beadle's and of her going there. When Nell asked her did she still go she answered fearlessly, "Sometimes on Saturdays—when I can." It was something, Nell thought, that she didn't lie to her.

"I don't know what you find to do there," Nell would say. "What *do* you do?"

To which Jenny would reply, child-wise, "Mess about."

"What do you mean—mess about? Crystal-gazing?"

"Oh no!" Her tone was quite shocked, and very emphatic, and Nell felt rebuked.

"What then?"

"Lots of things. Sometimes Mrs. Beadle lets me look at her books and explains me things. Sometimes we just play with the cats. She lets me taste her herb teas and gives me pieces of cake. I tell her about school—"

She broke off and looked at Nell with the air of one who really cannot enumerate everything, particularly when it should be obvious anyway.

"Lots of things," she repeated.

It sounded innocent enough. The things Mrs. Beadle would "explain" would be all "nonsense", of course, about sorceries and charms and magic and all that, but no more harm, really, when you came to think of it, than all the fairy-tales they stuffed kids' heads with. After all, witches and spells came into the fairy-tales. As long as there was nothing to frighten or upset a kid, and probably if Ma Beadle had known how the crystal-gazing would have shaken the kid up she wouldn't have done it. There was no real harm in the old girl She was fond of Jenny, anyone could see that . . . and the fact that Ivy and the school-teacher disapproved of Jenny going there was a very good reason why she, Nell Flower, should stick up for her! You were on one side or the other in this life, as she saw it; on the side of the angels, that is to say on the side of the good, starchy respectable people, or on the side of the people who didn't give a dam'—the people who were no angels and didn't pretend to be or want to be, and these were the really decent people, the people you could go to when you were in trouble, whether it was money or the police or being in the family way. It was not to be wondered at that Nell Flower's daughter should prefer old Ma Beadle to the prim Miss Drew, or the strict Ivy.

As to *him*, dam' him, she was probably worrying herself unnecessarily. He had brought the kid home from the Sunday-school treat when she'd got lost, and she'd spent a perfectly harmless day with him that day in February, and apparently he'd taken her safely home on the last occasion. The meeting at the Fair was obviously pure chance, and obviously he couldn't have known he'd find Jenny there when he'd come along to Mrs. Beadle's the other evening, and slipped into the kitchen unobserved when they were all so engrossed in crystal-gazing. Then, of course, when Jenny had expected to see him appear in the crystal, when he showed up in person it was a bit of a shock for her . . . a silly trick to play on a child, really, but the old girl had meant no harm in timing it just when he would be arriving. As to the people not seeing him when he carried Jenny away down Ropewalk Alley, people often didn't see things right before their noses . . . One way and another you could explain it all. Even the horns. Just some game they played in the forest, no doubt. If she ever met him again, and she supposed he'd be in the Seven Bells again next time his ship was in, she'd remember to ask him . . .

As the weeks wore on and the whole incident dimmed she found it increasingly easy to explain everything away in perfectly natural terms, but still she had to satisfy herself about the mark on Jenny's body. Just to know it wasn't there. For of course it wasn't, and it was silly even to think about it. But there was nothing like settling a thing once and for all in your own mind.

"You don't know who I am," he had said. Well, how should she? She met dozens of different seamen in a week, and this one she hadn't seen for years. He was just a feller off a ship she had once known—how intimately she really couldn't be expected to remember. Apparently he knew that Jenny was her kid and that she didn't want Jenny to know. Well, as he knew Ma Beadle it wasn't anything very remarkable that he knew, for she had gone to her to try and procure one of her herb concoctions for an abortion. It was unusual for the old girl to talk; still, you never knew; he might have got it from some other girl who knew Ma Beadle and knew that she, Nell, had been there—these things had a way of getting round. He needn't have been so dam' knowing and sinister about it. But then he was the kind that liked to be a bit dramatic, you could tell that, with his sudden appearance on special occasions. Men were great kids, really. Nell always found it difficult to be angry, for long, with an attractive man . . . and he was attractive, no denying it! It wasn't only his looks, either, but something about him that was more than that—the way he had of walking, as if he owned the earth, and something in his manner—what was the word? Well, masterful, really. And a man ought to be like that, Nell thought, or you couldn't respect him; and what was the good of a man you couldn't respect?

In spite of all this there was that persistent curiosity about the "witch's mark", which refused to be dismissed as "nonsense". Then, suddenly, with the hot weather in June, she had an idea. She sometimes spent a little time with Jenny in the new gardens above the river. In common with the other children

Jenny paddled at the bottom of the steps and along the strip of beach under the hulls of the barges. Some of the children wore bathing costumes . . . Nell bought one for Jenny, and as soon as she had bought it, of course, the hot weather promptly ceased. She felt a little ashamed of her eagerness to help the child into it; she had the guilty feeling of having plotted against her, and it was almost a relief that the heat-wave had ended.

However, it came back, in a thunderous uncertain fashion, heat without much sun, and as soon as it came she met Jenny from school and showed her the costume and suggested that she might like to go to the gardens and splash about on the beach in it.

Jenny was delighted with the idea. She had often wished she might have a bathing costume, instead of having to content herself with tucking her dress into her knickers.

In the gardens Nell helped Jenny undress discreetly behind a bush. She pulled her frock up over her head and then the child was standing in her little cotton vest and knickers. Off with the knickers first and slip quickly into the lower half of the costume, said Nell, directing operations, and then pull up the upper half of the costume and slip the vest over her head . . . These instructions Jenny clumsily obeyed. Nell pulled the vest up over her head, and then she saw what she now knew, somewhere at the back of her mind, she had expected to see—a dull red mark above the child's heart.

"What's this?" she said, touching the mark. "Knocked yourself?"

Jenny looked down at her body. "It came that day I had the pain at Mrs. Beadle's," she said. "Mrs. Beadle calls it the witch's mark."

Nell said quickly, "That's all nonsense. It'll go. I expect you were playing some rough game and gave yourself a bang."

"If you press it I can't feel anything there. You could pinch me there and I wouldn't feel it, and if you stuck a pin in I wouldn't feel it, and it wouldn't bleed!" Her tone was boastful.

Nell frowned. "I don't believe it! How d'you know?"

"Mrs. Beadle told me. 'Sides I've tried it. After she told me I went home and stuck a needle in out of Mum's sewing box, and I didn't feel it at all, and it didn't bleed."

Nell said, "I suppose the flesh has gone numb or something—dead tissue, I expect—"

She pulled the rest of the bathing-costume up and fastened it on the shoulders, and Jenny raced away through the sunshine and down to the water.

Nell picked up the little heap of clothes and discovered that she felt sick.

But by the next day she had satisfied herself that it was simply that the child had knocked herself in some rough game and destroyed the tissue. She was not quite sure what that meant, but it was an expression she had heard used. When you applied that medicinal vinegar to a wart you "destroyed the tissue". She had heard that it was what deep-ray treatment did to malignant internal growths. Well, then . . . With that "Well, then", she pushed the whole matter to the back of her mind. The kid was as lively as a cricket; nothing the matter with her. Kids were always knocking themselves about in some way or other. Alternatively, discolorations did sometimes come in the skin for no reason you knew anything about. Maybe old Ma Beadle with her second-sight knew about this mark that had appeared on Jenny's body, and of course being a bit cranky she had made a magic mystery of it. You could really find an explanation for everything if you exercised your brain-box a bit . . .

Ivy had also noticed the mark on Jenny's body and decided that it was a "knock". When she asked Jenny if she knew how she got it the child merely shrugged, and upon her assurance that it didn't hurt Ivy thought no more about it. You'd go grey before your time if you worried and fussed about every bruise and scratch a child managed to collect one way or another, in one place or another.

(2)

In July Joe had a week's holiday with pay, and, the schools having broken up, the Flower family took its annual holiday at Southend. Neither of them had any ambition to go further afield, even if they could have afforded it. Southend suited them very nicely. It was a short journey and easy to get to. It had all the amenities of the life they were used to—plenty of pubs and cinemas, fun fairs for wet days, and in addition there were the beaches, the whelk-stalls, the pier—what more could you want than a pier over a mile long and with an electric train running along it?—and the pleasure-steamers. Southend, Ivy was fond of declaring, was a "god-send" to "people in our position". She had no hankering after the country. She was a Londoner born and bred, and the quietness of the country got on her nerves; it made you feel you wanted to talk in a whisper all the time, like going into a church; and it was so tiring on the feet. You had to walk so far to get anywhere, and when you got there it was nothing much—just more fields, more lanes, or some little tin-pot village, with a one-eyed little shop that sold everything and nothing, and was no more than somebody's front room. Besides, Ivy was afraid of cows, and the fields were full of the brutes, and when it wasn't cows it was horses. The children had their taste of the country once a year with the Sunday-school treat, and they must be content. On the whole they were; they didn't really know much about "the country" except for that one day a year out at Epping Forest or Box Hill, or some such near-London place. They were London kids, and of their generation, and Woolworths, and the cinema, and crowded streets, were their natural element. For them milk had very little relation to any animal in a field; it came out of a bottle, or very often, out of a tin. If they thought about it they knew there must be the wheatfields before there could be bread, but it was the baker shop in the High Street, not the field of corn that was a reality to them. Meat was the joint at the butcher's, not the sheep or bullock in a field. They had never seen peaches on a wall; peaches were flat, yellow things with hollow centres that came out of tins, just as pineapple was syrupy cubes out of a tin. They knew that there were two kinds of beans—green beans that grew on allotments and that were also sold in greengrocers' shops, and beans that were one of Heinz 57 varieties and came in tins. If you had asked them where they were before they were in the tins they would probably have said "in the factory". Everything came from shops and factories, and had no relation to the land. "The country" was a far-away green place related only to Sunday-school treats. It was Epping Forest and Box Hill—all right for a day, but no use if it rained, and nothing like the fun that Southend was. You wouldn't choose to go to the country for a holiday if you had the chance of a place like Southend.

Except Jenny, and Jenny was a queer one. Jenny thought there was no place in the world like the country. She would like to live in a forest with a river running past, she said. She would have a little house with the forest behind and the river in front. She would watch the barges going down the river to the sea, and when she was tired of looking at the river and the barges she would go into the forest and sit by a pool and look at the water-lilies, and the frogs hopping in and out, and watch for dragon-flies, and she would listen to the birds until she knew every single one by its songs and calls. In the spring there would be primroses in the forest, thick clumps of them . . . she had never seen them but there was a coloured picture in a "nature" book at school showing just how they were amongst the dead leaves and twigs. Later on there would be bluebells—the whole floor of the forest would be covered with them; there was a picture of that, too; it must be wonderful to see bluebells growing like that. In the summer there would be honeysuckle in the woods, and in the hedges of the open spaces that were as much a part of the forest as the trees; there would be pink wild roses, and cows-parsley in the ditches, and wild mint with a purple flower and a strong smell in the swampy, places; there would be sunny open places with buttercups that came up to your knees and left a yellow powder on them—she knew how it was in the country in the summer. It was warm and still and golden, and towards evening full of shadows and strangeness. In the autumn there would be berries, the wonderful purple and vivid green and yellow of the deadly nightshade, and the honeysuckle turned to scarlet berries, and the leaves all red and brown and yellow; it must be wonderful in the forest in the autumn. And then in the winter it would be all bare and you would see the shapes of the trees and the wind would come through them as it came through the spars and the rigging of ships, and the pool would be covered with ice, all the creatures that lived in it locked in. Sometimes the ground would be covered with snow, and snow would be lying along the branches of the trees, and it would all look like an illustration to a fairy-tale; the trees would cast long purple shadows on the snow, and at the end of winter, when the ice had melted, and the pool and the river and the forest streams were full from the winter rains, and you could begin to notice the buds swelling on the trees, then he would come, Lucifer, Prince of Darkness and of Light, and he would smile and take your hand, and it would be as though someone had lighted candles in your head, and in all the forest glades. Everything would be splendid and shining—and different . . .

It was an endless fantasy with Jenny that summer. She wished with all her heart that they were going to the forest for the week's holiday, but to go away at all was an adventure. She liked paddling in the sea, and now that she had a bathing-costume she would be able to bathe; Les had said he would teach her to swim; she would like that, too. She liked the electric car along the pier, she liked going in the steamers, she liked all the penny-in-the-slot machines—the house on fire, with the firemen and their ladders and hoses, the execution scene, in which, after the penny had dropped the victim jerked out of his dungeon and the executioner awaited him with bloodstained block and axe. She liked being lifted up by Les to look through a thing called a stereoscope, at what were supposed to be "rude" pictures, for adults only—the pictures showed saucy ladies in big old-fashioned, tightly-laced corsets and black stockings, with high-heeled shoes. This form of amusement seemed to be popular with boys of Les's age, and a little older, and with men with drooping moustaches and bowler hats. Jenny couldn't see what was particularly rude about the pictures, unless it was rude to see a lady in her stays; but on the beach you saw them in bathing-costumes that showed ever so much more of their bodies—that showed their belly-buttons—and no one seemed to think this was anything but "smart".

Southend was not beautiful, like the forest, but it was fun. You had a wooden spade and a painted tin bucket and you dug in the wet muddy sand and made castles with moats round, or turned out "puddings" from your bucket; you found shells and pieces of sea-weed, and crabs and picked mussels off the rocks; you sat on the beach and let the pebbles run through your fingers whilst you sucked Southend "rock" that said Southend right the way through, and your mouth got all hot and pepperminty, and then you coaxed for an ice-cream cornet when you saw the man coming round, trudging over the shingle . . . Dad lay on his back with a newspaper over his face, dozing a good deal of the time, until "they" opened. Mum sat writing post cards, and you spent a lot of time looking at other people. At a quarter to one and a quarter to five promptly you all trooped back to the boarding-house—the whole beach cleared—and Mum was always saying what a treat it was to eat a meal you hadn't had to cook yourself. You hung your wet towels and bathing-costumes from the bedroom windows, and there was sand all over the bedroom lino.

But when all this was said in Southend's favour, you still wished you could have spent the week at the forest, exploring the deep avenues, listening to the birds, listening to the silence, looking for witches' bane, hemlock, dragon-wort, crimson and orange toadstools, watching for the dragon-flies with their brilliant bodies and their shimmering wings.

If Joe had had his way every year he would have spent the holiday at home. He didn't see the point of traipsing off to Southend or anywhere else. If you stayed home you could loaf about, take it easy, get up when you liked, go to the dogs or the dirt-track if you felt like it, or take a trip out to Hampton Court or Kew or one of those places. Southend was all right, but what was wrong with London—good ole London?

This sort of talk would make Ivy very angry. It was just like a man, she would say, thinking only of himself; holidays at home might be all right for *him*—but what rest would it be for *her*?

"All right, all right," Joe would say, "We're not *'avin'*'em at 'ome, are we?"

But that he could even give it a thought, Ivy would think, resentfully . . . She was hurt as much by the things he might have done as by the things he actually did.

When they got back from Southend it was only two days to go to Lammas, but this was something in which only Jenny was interested. All the time she was away she worried about "Satan". She had wanted to take him with her, but Ivy wouldn't hear of it. You couldn't take a cat to a seaside boarding-house; who would mind it all day when they were "down at the beach"? Or did she think they were going to cart it down there? The people in the next flat would feed the cat, and if it found its way back to wherever it had come from whilst they were away, well, so much the better; you were best off without animals in the home; they were only a nuisance, and a great "tie".

Jenny would have liked to have taken Satan back to Mrs. Beadle whilst she was away, but could see no way of arranging it. To her relief, when she got back the cat was still there—as Les, who did not like cats said, "As large as life and twice as ugly." Satan was not, as cats go, particularly attractive; in three months he had lost his first kittenish prettiness; he was going to be an ugly thing when he was fully grown, Ivy declared, and that reminded her, he ought presently to be "seen-to". Tom-cats that were not seen-to became scrawny brutes, and attracted all the she-cats of the neighbourhood. Jenny didn't know what having a cat seen-to meant, till Les, source of all the facts of life, explained to her in private, and then she was horrified.

"It doesn't hurt them," Les assured her.

"But it's wrong," Jenny said, passionately. "It *must* be wrong!" She clutched the kitten to her, protectively. No one should ever, ever do anything to him.

Les said, jauntily, flaunting his sophistication, "I dunno. What you've never 'ad you don't miss, they say!"

That meant nothing to Jenny; she could only feel, instinctively, that the thing was wrong, a mutilation, something that was not "meant". . . And it should not be allowed to happen to Satan, who was part of herself, her familiar.

(3)

Jenny decided that her tryst with the stranger on August the first would be the steps where she had waited for him at Candlemas, and she was determined to go there as soon after breakfast as she could escape from the flat. During the school holidays Ivy gave the children slices of bread-and-dripping to take with them when they went out to play on fine days, so that they need not come back in the middle of the day, an arrangement which gave her, she said, a chance to "get on". They could have a proper meal in the evening, a bit of cold ham with their tea, or some tinned salmon. But before they were allowed out to play they were liable to be sent on errands, or given odd jobs, such as cleaning shoes, shelling peas, top-and-tailing gooseberries, polishing cutlery and door-handles, turning out the toy-cupboard. On that Bank Holiday Monday, however, Ivy found no chores for Jenny to do, and she was able to get out immediately after breakfast, with her slices of bread-and-dripping wrapped in a piece of yesterday's *News of the World*, and an apple bulging the pocket of her pullover. Les went off to meet one of the "gang", as the "cadets" were known to each other off-duty. Stan wanted Jenny to go paddling with him under the barges and looked as though he were going to cry when she said she wanted to go off on her own. He pulled a long face and threatened to "tell Ma". Jenny called him a "soppy kid" and taunted him with being a cry-baby and a "tell-tale", and ran off and left him—she had long ago decided that it was the only tactic to employ with Stan and people like him, who "tacked on", or tried to, when they were not wanted.

She was not first at the tryst. She found the stranger leaning on the rail at the top of the steps. He was looking at the water with a far-away expression and did not hear her come running up to him. She tugged at his arm and he turned and smiled at her.

"Hullo, witch."

She clung to him. "I didn't think you'd be here first. Have you come off a ship?"

"Not this time."

"Where've you been all this time?"

"The Back of Beyond. Let's go and find Miss Drew."

"Miss Drew?"

"Yes. We're going to take her to the forest. She doesn't know it yet, but we are!"

Jenny was filled with dismay.

"She won't come. I 'spect she's gone home for the holidays, anyhow." She hoped, wildly, that she had. But he dashed that hope immediately.

"I saw her this morning. I was going down to the Pool in a barge and she was throwing bread to the gulls from her window. It was what gave me the idea."

"I'd sooner we took Auntie Nell."

"Auntie Nell isn't built for forests, and she has to be in the bar at eleven in any case. Come."

He took her hand and they turned their backs on the river.

The day was overcast for Jenny, though there was always the hope that Miss Drew wouldn't want, or wouldn't be able, to come. But she had the feeling that whatever Miss Drew wanted wouldn't count.

Marian had not gone home for the first weeks of the holidays because Miss Hawkins and Miss Pritchett had gone away for a holiday together, and if Marian also went there would be no one—except Kenneth Wilson—to look after the club, and it was generally felt that though dear Kenny was so good with boys, he was not likely to be so good with the girl members of the club, particularly the older ones. And it was very important during the school holidays, particularly the summer holidays when the children ran the streets, to keep the club open all the time.

So Marian was there on that summer morning when the two unexpected visitors mounted the dark stairs to her room. When she opened the door to them she was startled.

"Oh," she said, "you!" It was at him she looked.

"I'm sorry," he said, "but I warned you I was afraid you'd have to see me again. You know what to-day is, of course?"

She did know; she had been wondering. But she said, deliberately, "It's August Bank Holiday—if that's what you mean!"

"It's Lammas," Jenny supplemented.

"I know," Marian said, "a witches' sabbath. But I'm a non-believer, so why call on me?"

"Because, Lady, sometimes those cast out of heaven remember the bliss they once knew, and then, very badly they hope an angel will take pity on them, to bring them back if only for a few hours. To-*day* a fallen angel asks a good angel, very humbly, if she will come out to the forest, chaperoned by this very little witch."

"I'm sorry," Marian said, "but I can't leave the club."

"You can leave it by the simple process of shutting it up, and then the children will run wild by the river and in the streets and do the things they really enjoy doing instead of the rather boring, priggish things that grown-ups like them to do. No natural child wants to play with a potter's wheel when it can muck about in a nice bit of mud and water under a barge. Ask Jenny."

"Is Jenny a good example of what you call a natural child, do you think? Or, rather, aren't you and Mrs. Beadle between you doing your best to make her into an unnatural one?"

He sighed. "Don't you know, yet, lady, that you can't put anything into a child, you can only bring out what is there? Oh you teachers, you teachers, you don't know the first thing about children or about teaching! Come out to the forest, Marian, Maria, and give the children a day off for once, free of all that moral influence that so demoralises them!"

"You don't think you're demoralising Jenny, by any chance?"

"If I said no you still wouldn't agree, so why ask me? Out in the forest there are birds and rabbits and lizards and dragon-flies and foxes, all of whom have no morals whatsoever, good or bad, and are not concerned with anything but being alive. Out there we might also be similarly concerned. You'll find us quite good company, Jenny and me. We've brought our bread-and-dripping and we'll willingly share it with you! Also half our apple."

Marian laughed—and was lost.

When they were all in the train together Marian was suddenly very happy. Wasn't this what she had hoped for, wanted, that they should all three be friends, so that there should be an end of jealousy on Jenny's part, and so that gradually she might break down the "unhealthy" element between the man and the child—the unhealthy fantasy, as she thought of it. She had been right to come, she told herself. Nothing but good could come out of the day.

Jenny sat by the window alternately frowning out at the houses flying past and at Miss Drew. The light in her with which she had gone to keep the tryst was quenched. She was filled with black thoughts. One of these days she would put a spell on Miss Drew. Ah, but *could* she? If *he* had Miss Drew under his protection then surely anything that she—a very little witch, as he had said—might do would be useless? But she would not always be a very little witch. One of these days she would be as old and wise as Mrs. Beadle. But long before then she would know a great deal.

She leaned back against his shoulder, kicking the edge of the seat opposite, where Miss Drew sat, with the big toe that poked out of her broken gymn shoes, and raising a small dust. Miss Drew smiled at her, but Jenny continued to scowl. If there had to be anyone else to-day, why couldn't it have been her darling Auntie Nell, her pretty, pretty lady? Then three would have been company as much as two . . . Instead of which there was a lot of grown-up conversation in which she had no part, which shut her out.

"Isn't it," said Marian, "time you told me your name and dropped all the mystery?"

"Without what has been called 'the willing suspension of disbelief' it would be pointless to tell you. Until then any name will serve. With that suspension of disbelief you will *know*."

She mocked him, "Art thou indeed Lucifer, Prince of Darkness?"

"To the blasphemous parody, Lady, I give the blasphemous answer, 'Thou sayest.' "

Had she been guilty of blasphemy? She hardly knew. Her education had been such that Biblical quotation, and therefore

Biblical parody, came easily to her, as Shakespearean quotation and parody came to others.

She was silent a moment, then she said, "In Freudian psychology it would be called 'an obsessive neurosis', or, more simply, a delusion. Every lunatic asylum is full of people who believe that they are the Shah of Persia or the Messiah or something of the kind. Some, no doubt, claim to be Lucifer."

He smiled. "No doubt. In the kingdom of the human imagination there are many mansions. Are you prepared to say where fantasy ends and lunacy begins? You are prepared to accept enchantment at the poetic and romantic level, the bewitchment of love and beauty, the magic of night and the stars, *la clair de lune*, and all that—but at what point does magic, which we regard as sublime, degenerate into witchcraft which we regard as perverted? Are Virgil's 'hoary simples', culled 'with brazen sickles at noon of night', magic or witchcraft? Black magic or white?"

She could meet him there. " 'Rites obscene' is surely the verdict?"

"She was very beautiful, that Queen of Carthage, and there's a certain tenderness in that picture of her at the high altar . . . " He broke off, then asked, abruptly, "As a good Christian you believe in the Virgin Birth, and that Christ worked miracles— and still does to-day?"

"Yes, of course—about to-day, you mean at Lourdes? I don't know. I've never been or met anyone who had, but the power of faith is very great . . . "

"The power of imagination is very great! If you can believe in the divine mysteries, and the divine power to work miracles, logically you must accept the other side of the picture—the infernal mysteries and infernal power. Once you leave the materialist conception of it you accept its mystery, once you get outside of what the scientists call natural laws anything may happen—even magic! If you are going to acknowledge angels you must acknowledge devils, too! You can't have the realms of light without the abyss. Once you accept God you accept the Devil, and the 'fatal lightning' that smote the earth when God cast Lucifer out. If there's 'that of God', as the Quakers say, in every man, there must be that of the Devil, that spark of the Satanic lightning, along with it."

He turned to Jenny fidgeting restlessly, fretfully, at his side.

"All this is very boring for such a very little witch!" He lifted her up on to his knees. "I'll tell you a story, shall I?"

"Yes." Jenny leaned her head back against his shoulder, contentedly. Now he was in possession once more; now it was Miss Drew who was shut out, which was as it should be.

"Once upon a time there was a little girl. She was very lonely, because she had no brothers or sisters, and she lived in the country, where nothing ever happened. There were no cinemas and no buses and it was very dull, because she had not yet learned to be interested in dragon-flies and things. One day when she was leaning on the garden gate, very lonely, and very bored, a stranger came down the road, and seeing the little girl leaning so dolefully on the gate he stopped to talk to her. He—"

"What was he like?" Jenny interrupted.

"Oh, he was quite ordinary, really. He wasn't young and he wasn't old; he wasn't tall and he wasn't short. He wasn't well-dressed, but he wasn't in rags. If you were to judge by his clothes you would say he was a farm-labourer in his best suit, or a sailor just off a ship, and as a matter of fact that's what he really was—just a very ordinary seaman. He stopped to talk to the little girl, and he asked her why she wasn't at school, and she said because there wasn't any school to go to; and she asked him where he was going, and he said nowhere much, because there was nowhere much to go to, and that seemed to make them 'quits', and from that moment they were great friends. They had a lot of things in common, they found. They were both lonely and bored; they both hated rice pudding; they both liked swinging on gates, and they had neither of them

ever seen a unicorn or a white elephant. Also they were both
inclined to believe that there were no such things. Then they
got to talking of strange things, such as dragons, which, said the
man, the Chinese used to pickle and considered a rare delicacy;
and basilisks, which were serpents hatched out of a cock's egg,
which of course made them very rare, as you didn't often get a
cock laying an egg . . . Well, the stranger told the child a lot of
interesting things like this, and about the foreign places he'd
been to. Some of the places had beautiful names, like Cathay,
and Kashmir, and Isfahan; he told her about Arabia, and the
tents of the Bedouins; he told her about the wild horses of the
Caucasus racing over the wide steppes with their long tails and
manes flying; he told her about the Don Cossacks who rode like
the wind, and about the gipsies on the great plain of Hungary,
with their flashing eyes and bright clothes and wild music; he
told her about Sicily where the oranges hang on trees and the
goats graze in the olive groves with a tinkle of bells; he told
her about meadows of asphodel, and the wine-dark Ionian
sea . . . The child didn't know what half the things he talked
about were, but it was all a kind of poetry, and it painted pictures
in her mind, and she didn't feel lonely or bored any more, and
when the stranger had gone she thought over all he'd told her,
and waited for him to come again. He didn't come very often;
he had to go sailing the seven seas, but he always came back
sooner or later, and he always told the child about where he'd
been and the things he'd seen, and the child came to love him
very much, and to look forward to seeing him again. And so
the years went by, and from being a little girl she became a big
girl and she loved the stranger more than ever, so that at last
she thought she couldn't go on living with her parents, but that
next time the stranger came she would have to go away with
him and marry him and be with him always—that is to say all
the time he wasn't sailing the world. So when he came again she
told the stranger this, and he put his arms round her and kissed

her, and the girl thought she would die of happiness, but the stranger was very sad. He said 'I love you, but I cannot marry you, for though I am the prince of this world I am not of this world.' The girl didn't understand what he meant, but then, as she often didn't understand what he meant it didn't worry her. Then to make her understand he looked down at his feet and commanded her to look. She looked and saw what she had never seen before—that he had cloven hooves—like a goat. The girl knew what that meant. Only the Devil had cloven hooves. But she loved him and it was too late now to alter that, and she said, 'I don't care who you are, I love you and I don't want to marry anyone but you!' He said, sadly, 'If you marry me you will become a witch and you will be damned for ever.' And the girl said, 'Very well, I will be a witch and be damned!' He said, 'It means you will never be happy with human beings again,' and she replied, 'I wasn't, anyhow.' He said, it means when you die you will go to Hell,' and she answered, 'I shall be with you, and nothing else matters.' So then the Devil won her for a bride, and her soul for Hell, and they lived happily ever after."

Jenny looked up at him. "And when she died did she go to Hell and burn in hell-fire?"

"When she died she went to Hell. She went right down into the flames and the Devil came to her there and took her hands and asked her, 'Does it seem very terrible to you here, my heart's Love?' And she laughed, and said, 'If this is Hell, why then it's only another name for Heaven after all!' "

"I suppose she didn't feel the flames because she was a witch?" Jenny suggested.

"She didn't feel the flames because she was all flame herself, loving him."

He looked at Marian, smiling faintly. "A very moral story, you see, Marian, Maria."

She returned his smile. "As you would say, it all depends what you mean by moral."

"Naturally. Everything is a matter of definition, God and the Devil, Heaven and Hell, miracle or magic, enchantment or witchcraft . . . As they say at the pictures, that is where we came in—and this is where we arrive . . . "

(4)

It was one of those perfect days which sometimes occur in England in August, warm and still, with a sense of high summer, of harvest fullness. It is only in towns that August is arid and sultry. Out in the country the cornfields are beautiful with their golden sheaves leaning together to form little tents ranged in long rows. There is still honeysuckle in the hedges, and in cottage gardens there are still a few roses, and the warm glow of marigolds, and a golden shine of sunflowers. The year is mellowing into orange and gold; a rich, full harvest sweetness lies over everything, and there is still warmth in the sun.

As soon as they stepped out of the little station Jenny drew in a deep breath of the clean air as though it were the scent of flowers. "It all smells different!" she exclaimed.

They got away from the Bank Holiday crowds straggling on the outskirts of the forest as though wishing not to lose contact with pubs and 'buses and everydayness, and came into the great avenues full of green twilight, and the open spaces that trapped the sun. They came to the pool and unpacked the food they had brought with them. Marian had supplemented Jenny's bread-and-dripping and the solitary apple with coffee in a thermos flask, hard-boiled eggs, tomatoes, brown bread-and-butter, home-made cakes, peppermint creams. There were still wild yellow irises at the edge of the pool, and a froth of small white water-lilies on its surface. A huge blue dragon-fly flashed over and then hovered with glistening opalescent wings poised above the brown rod of a bulrush head.

"Oh, the pretty thing!" Jenny exclaimed, enraptured, "the pretty, pretty thing!" and did not flinch when it darted forward, making, it seemed, straight for her face.

"I wish it would settle on me!" she cried, and was glad Les and Stan weren't there, because they would want to catch it and stick a pin through it and put it in a box, as they did with butterflies, whereas Jenny wanted it to live for ever, flashing in the sunshine. It wasn't like a thing of this earth, but like a faery thing . . .

When they had eaten their food they wandered about for a time on the common land picking and eating blackberries, and then plunged into the deep glades of the forest where the trunks of the beeches were like great grey cathedral pillars, and bird-song emphasised the stillness. Whilst they were sitting on a fallen tree-trunk in a grassy clearing a grass snake slid past their feet, causing Marian to shrink back with a shudder.

"It won't hurt you," Jenny said. "Even if you picked it up it wouldn't hurt you. You could twist it round your wrist like a bracelet. Even an adder doesn't hurt you unless you touch it." She appealed to the man. "That's true, isn't it? We found one last time and it didn't hurt us."

"All the same," Marian insisted, "there's something obscene about any snaky thing! It seems natural for human beings to recoil from them."

"It's not really, you know," he told her. "A child has no instinctive revulsion to a snake, or fear of it. I knew an English child in Africa once who used to be given his breakfast on the bungalow verandah every morning. The nurse could never understand why when she came to collect his dishes he always asked for more, and even when she increased the quantity the first time he was just as hungry when she came to clear away. One morning she went on strike and said he couldn't have more; he had had enough. The child said he hadn't had any at all, and when she asked him why, what did he mean, he said,

'Because a pretty thing comes and eats it.' The pretty thing was a black mamba! When it was killed the child cried."

"I would have cried too," Jenny declared.

"It's a completely horrifying story," Marian said.

They had tea at a farm-house, where Jenny saw cows milked for the first time in her life. She stood watching, fascinated, and then there came into her mind something she had read in one of Mrs. Beadle's books, about a spell that dried the milk up in cows, or caused them to produce soured milk, and as she thought this a bat fluttered out of a dark cobwebby corner of the rafters and flapped across into another corner of the byre, and it seemed to Jenny like her own dark thought escaped from her head and become a black, ugly, living thing, and suddenly she didn't want to watch the cows any more, but to be out in the bright warm sunlight where birds sang and delicate white and yellow butterflies fluttered like petals drifting on the summer wind. It was Marian's hand she took as they turned to leave the cow-shed.

The farmer's wife served them tea in a tiny parlour that smelt of musty books and dried rose-leaves—the musky smell of a room seldom aired, and in which old scents, of yellowing books and pot-pourri and lavender, are preserved. On the bulging blue-washed walls were framed texts, and a sampler, and old-fashioned photographs. There were round tables covered with knickknacks, and a yellow plush sofa, and stiff chairs with white crocheted antimacassars. There was deep crocheted lace round the immaculately clean white table-cloth, and forget-me-nots and moss-roses sprigged over the thin china cups. Marian was terrified that Jenny would break one of the cups—they were obviously part of the best tea-service, and were probably a wedding present of thirty years ago.

But Jenny handled the cup reverently. It was pretty. She would not wish to break such a pretty thing. She had not known that cups could be like that, so thin, and with little flowers all over them. She was used to thick, white crockery and enamel mugs. She would like to have spent a long time in that room examining all the things in it. There was a stuffed owl in a glass case, his perch surrounded by dried grasses and leaves. There was a ship in a bottle. There was a cupboard with glass doors and inside the cupboard all manner of interesting things—fancy cups and tea-pots and shells, a box made of mother-of-pearl, a silver shoe with a velvet pad in it so that it could be used as a pin cushion. On the wide window-sill of the room there were flowering fuchsias, and geraniums with scented leaves, adding to that lovely, musty, fusty shut-up smell that somehow made the room special and apart from everyday life. If you opened the windows and aired the room, Jenny thought, you would let something out, something that was as much a part of the room as the stiff old-fashioned tables and chairs and the muslin curtains tied up with yellow satin ribbons, the low sagging ceiling, and the old black beams that supported it. Jenny was resolved that when she had the little house of her own, with the forest behind and the river in front, she would have a "best" room like this one.

When they were leaving, the farmer's wife smiled at Jenny playing with a kitten in the rickyard visible from the window, then asked Marian, "You've only got the one?"

Before Marian could explain the man said, quickly, "Only the one."

"An only child is lonely, I always think," the woman said. "Three's a nice number. But there, of course, you have to think of the expense . . . "

When they were outside, walking towards the rickyard, Marian said, "Why did you say that?"

"Several reasons. It pleased her. She liked to think we were a nice young married couple with our little girl. Also it saved explanations. Finally it was a nice idea—one of those lost lovely impossible ideas, that you should belong to me and that Jenny should be our child."

She said, a little shaken, but making an effort at banter to disguise the fact, "And make-believe is your speciality, anyhow, isn't it?"

Jenny came running up to them and he made no answer.

But later, when they were walking in the forest and Jenny was ahead of them, wordlessly his fingers closed on hers as she walked by his side, and she did not withdraw them. The Hallowe'en episode came back to her, her heart quickening, painfully, with the memory, and her mind said No, no, not all that again; he is mad or wicked, or both. At best an impossible poseur. I don't want him. I only came to-day for Jenny's sake. But her blood was stirred as before, and something in her insisted, even if he hadn't had Jenny with him you'd have come. you're only glad the child is with you because you're afraid of your response to him.

When the sunshine began to grow mellow with evening, and the warmth to go out of the day, Jenny ceased to run on ahead and the chill that seemed to rise up out of the ground and creep down out of the sky seemed to envelop her, dulling her body and greying her spirit. Coming back to the others she saw their linked hands and wanted to smite them apart with a clenched fist.

Their hands automatically fell apart as she came up to them, but it was too late; she had seen and she knew that they had not wished her to see, and it intensified the black hate she felt for Miss Drew. Her hate and anger did not touch the man, despite the fact that he was responsible for Miss Drew being there; it was she who was the enemy. She could have refused to come. She had no right there. She didn't belong.

She slipped her hand into his and he looked down at her.

"Tired, Jenny?"

She said in a small dispirited voice, "It's getting cold. Let's go home."

This time there was no owl, no feeling of mystery and strangeness, and instead of being borne along in his arms, with that excited sense of being safe from lurking dangers, she trudged wearily at his side.

He reminded her, "Last time you didn't want to go home."

"Last time was different."

"Every time is different. Nothing can ever be the same."

"That's beyond a child's understanding," Marian protested.

He was silent, and a pervasive sadness crept down amongst the trees with the withdrawal of the sunlight and the slow deepening of the shadows.

Jenny lagged increasingly, and suddenly he stopped and dropped down beside her, drawing her to him.

"Jenny," he said, "Jenny," and there was a curious yearning in his voice.

She clung to him, her small light body suddenly taut, her thin arms in their strangling grip round his neck.

He picked her up and carried her the rest of the way.

"She's too big a girl," Marian urged.

"She's a little feather of a thing."

From the shelter of his arms Jenny peered out at Miss Drew, her dark eyes bright with malice and triumph.

In the train, drugged with the day in the fresh air, she dozed, leaning against his shoulder. Nobody spoke.

When they were nearing the station the man said in a low voice; whilst Jenny still dozed, "You'll stay with me after we've seen Jenny home, Marian, Maria?"

"I'm not drinking any more sailors' drinks with you, if that's what you mean!"

"We'll do anything you like—except open that children's club!"

It was still light when they reached Fenchurch Street station.

"You won't be late in this time, Jenny."

"No." But she found no comfort in the fact.

Outside the flats he bent and kissed her forehead.

"Everything's all right, Jenny. You know what Mrs. Beadle told you."

"It's a long time till Hallowe'en."

"Three months. Remember the girl in the story. In the end they were together always."

She nodded, and then without a word to Marian ran off. In the end they were together always. She repeated it in a sobbing whisper under her breath. That was what she had to remember in all the lonely wastes of the times in between.

When Jenny had gone he looked at Marian.

"Well?"

"Whatever we decide to do I'd like to go home first and leave the thermos and tidy up."

"I have a suggestion. I'll leave you at your door and then go and buy food and we'll picnic in your room. I'll buy a cold chicken and a bottle of wine and some fruit and whatever I can find that is delicious—"

"No wine—I don't want to sing you 'Adeste Fideles' with the wrong words!"

"I'd sooner the wrong words than the right ones, you know that! Of course I shall buy wine! Champagne if I can get it! And if you tell me you don't see the difference between it and your father's home-brewed cider I shall never forgive you!"

"But it probably will taste the same to me! It'll just be wasted on me!"

"Nevertheless, it's gay and we shall drink it, and before the evening's out you'll acknowledge that it's different—and that there are worse ways of going to the devil!"

She made a last effort. "But I've no intention of going to the devil!"

He laughed. "You know what the road to hell is said to be paved with, don't you?"

She looked so dismayed that he took her hand. "It's all right, Marian, Maria, it's not you who is the girl in the story! Don't worry! Only believe in magic a little—just for to-night!"

They parted outside the children's club and she went slowly up the stairs to her room. She was troubled. It was all quite wrong. She should have sent him away. Instead of that, within an hour he would be back . . . and she would believe in magic against all intellectual judgments.

He was mad. He was a poseur. And he had the conceit of the devil! She started—why "of the devil?" These expressions one found oneself using . . .

Nevertheless at the sound of his step on the stair her heart quickened.

And when he came into the room and set his packages down on the table and took her into his arms she knew that man or devil, right or wrong, this was bliss.

Part II

Prince of Darkness

*"We have made a covenant with death,
and with hell are we at agreement."*

– Isaiah xxviii, 15

Chapter I

The Book of Magicke

For a year after that first encounter in the summer of 1931 the Stranger always reappeared in Jenny Flower's life on each witches' sabbath—Hallowe'en, Candlemas, May Eve, and Lammas—as we have seen, but after Hallowe'en 1932 he did not come again for a year. He did not come at Candlemas or on May Eve, and by Lammas Jenny was desperate, thinking he had abandoned her, and she went to Mrs. Beadle and begged her to conjure him up into the crystal that she might at least see him and perhaps speak with him.

The old woman refused, and remained unmoved equally by Jenny's anger and by her tears.

"He'll come when he's ready," she insisted, stubbornly. She tried to explain that a conjuration is not to be undertaken as lightly as a telephone call; there had to be a good reason for anything so serious as invoking the powers of darkness. Jenny stormed and wept, but the old woman remained adamant.

"I'll call him myself!" Jenny said.

The old woman shrugged. "He won't come."

Jenny got out the crystal, lit the candle, drew the circle, repeated the Abracadabra and the appropriate conjuration for the day, passionately beseeched, passionately concentrated and willed, but nothing happened; the golden fire glowed in the heart of the crystal, but it did not draw her down into it; it remained merely light reflected in a crystal.

Then Jenny turned on the old woman, sprang across the room at her like a cat, clawing her, shaking her.

"You've put a spell on it! You've put the Evil Eye on it!" She was sobbing wildly as she made the accusation.

The old woman shook her off. "You'll learn wisdom one day," was all she said.

On Hallowe'en, her ninth birthday, she met him again at the Fair. She was standing in the crowd waiting for the roundabouts to stop so that she could go on it with Les and Stan, when she felt a hand on her shoulder. She turned round and looked up into his face.

"Why didn't you come before?" she demanded, clinging to him.

"There was no need. And I gave someone a promise that I wouldn't."

"Miss Drew!"

He made no answer, but drew her away from the crowd and picked a way through to the dark edge of the fair where the wagons were parked. He lifted her up and sat her on the dusty floor of a trap, then brushed back the hair from her forehead.

"Jenny, at Sunday School don't they teach you about guardian angels who look after you all the time, though you can't see them?"

"I don't believe in all that!"

"But you believe in fallen angels. A fallen angel can be a guardian angel to those he loves. If ever there's a bad time, Jenny, I shall find you." He folded her to him, suddenly. "Oh, my little one, don't you know that if you cried I should hear you a thousand miles away?"

"I did cry—when you didn't come at Lammas. I tried to call you up, but nothing happened."

"I know you cried. I know you called me. D'you think I didn't know? D'you think I didn't hear? But I couldn't come because I'd given a promise."

"If I'd made a promise I didn't want to keep, I'd break it!"

"If you made me a promise would you break it?"

"Not if I made it to you—that's different."

"Of course it's different. When you make a promise to someone you love it's always different. It's what they call in witchcraft a binding. My promise was that kind of promise."

Jenny was silent. The fair music throbbed on the cold air and the sky was full of lights and stars, but the world was black all round her and inside her. He had made a promise to Her—to Miss Drew. She had kept him away from her. Her heart beat fast with anger and hate.

He bent and kissed the top of her head, holding his face a moment in the dark tangle of hair with its childish smell of the school-room, sweetish, like the smell of a cat. She clung to him, her face turned in to his chest.

"I love you," she said. "I hate her, but I love you."

He pressed her close.

"Believe in me, Jenny. Don't try to summon me. Don't grieve when I don't come. One day you'll need me and I shall be there. And one day we shall be together always. But first you have to grow up, like the girl in the story. Here's your birthday present—you can say a gipsy gave it you."

He took her left hand and slipped a ring on to her little finger, then cupped his hand round hers so that she could see how the stone gleamed in the dark.

"The Hungarian gipsy I got it from called it a cat's eye," he told her.

She gazed at it, fascinated. "Is it a charm?"

"If you believe it is. Now, I must take you back or your family will start a hue and cry for you."

He lifted her down. She stood, clinging to his belt, looking up at him.

"When will you come again?"

"I don't know. But I shall come."

He took her back to the roundabouts, and when they reached the crowd gathered round them propelled her towards the front. When the swirl of horses, ostriches, swans, gilded cars, slowed down he lifted her up on to the wooden steps, put coppers into her hand, waited whilst she scrambled up on to the back of an ostrich. She clung to the brass rod rising up from the ostrich's back, looked back and smiled at him, then the merry-go-round began to move again and she was whirled away from him . . . When after what seemed a long time she climbed down to earth again he was gone.

Whilst she was still standing dazed and giddy a hand grabbed her, shook her, and an angry voice exclaimed, "You little devil! I've been looking for you everywhere! Where've you been? Why can't you keep with the others?"

She was given a thump in the back and pushed through the crowd to where Stan and Les waited, full of virtue, having kept together as instructed and come straight back to the appointed spot where Ivy waited.

The boys were given sixpence each and allowed to go off on their own to see the fireworks. Jenny was taken home, as a punishment. She didn't care. The high spot of the evening was over. He had come and gone. Surreptitiously she cupped her right hand round her left and looked at the ring. It was a cat's eye shining in the dark. It was magic if you believed in it, and she did believe.

(2)

In the room above the river Marian said, "Thank you at least for your promise to stay away from her for a year. Though you probably undid all the good work by going in search of her to-night."

"I didn't promise not to come back on Hallowe'en. I had to find her to-night."

190

"Why 'had to'?"

"It's her birthday. The anniversary of the date of birth of someone you love is as important to you as to them, surely?"

She said, as though she grudged him the acknowledgment, "You do love that child, don't you? I wonder why."

"They say the devil loves his own, don't they?"

She frowned. "You know I don't like you to talk like that!"

He smiled his ironic smile. "Say, then, that I love her because she's lost and damned like myself!"

"That doesn't make it any better! *Why* is she lost and damned—in your opinion?"

"Because her name is Jenny Flower. Because she has the poisoned blood of the Flowers in her veins. Because her ancestors were burnt at the stake as witches—the Christian Church having laid it down that 'thou shalt not suffer a witch to live'."

He spoke violently, his eyes hard.

She looked at him, distressed. "That her ancestors were burnt as witches doesn't prove they were! They were probably quite harmless creatures."

"They're unfortunately not harmless to Jenny."

"They should be—they've been dead long enough!"

"You don't really believe that the dead can do no harm?"

"I don't believe in evil spirits, if that's what you mean!"

"It's not what I mean. But it makes no difference whether you believe in spirits or not, good or evil; you can't escape the fact that the spirit of a dead person survives death—the spirit of the past, people call it, because they shrink from calling it what it really is, which is the spirit of the dead that still has power over the destinies of the living. One day Jenny will know about her ancestors, and then their spirit will reach out to her, across the centuries, and there'll be no escape from it. She'll be filled with perverted pride, and a terrible fascination. Why do you suppose the dark mysteries of the occult fascinate her so much already, whilst she's still

191

a child? She was lost and damned from the moment of her unhallowed birth, I tell you!"

"But why should she know these evil things of the past?"

"Because the moving finger writes, and having writ—"

"You mean it's all predestined? I don't accept all that. I refuse to accept that the whole pattern of a human life is pre-arranged—that living is merely working-out of a pre-arranged pattern. I believe we make the pattern as we go along—of our free will."

"Free will! There's no such thing! We have only the illusion of self-determination. We work out the pattern according to the temperaments with which we were born, and according to the influence of environment working on that temperament—plus the pressure of external things—circumstances—beyond our control. Character determines destiny, and blood determines character, and Jenny happens to have the Flower blood in her veins. Even if the women burnt at Lincoln were good, harmless creatures, even if they were in any case nothing to do with these twentieth century London Flowers, the psychological factor still remains— they would still reach out across the centuries, ultimately. The influence of those dead, tortured women can be nothing but evil, and because of her blood she is readily responsive to evil. In another age we should say that Jenny Flower was possessed of the devil, beyond salvation. But it's nothing to the possession that will seize her presently, when she knows the truth!"

"It's horrible! She must be protected from knowing!"

"That's impossible! There's no protecting people from their destinies!"

"That's fatalism!"

"Say then that there's no protecting people from their fellow-creatures—man's inhumanity to man!"

"There's something besides that—human goodness. That of God in every man."

"D'you really believe that—in your heart?"

"I try to. It's difficult sometimes, particularly in the face of things like brutality, stupidity, meanness—all the ugly things, violence, anger, hate—"

"Including just anger, and hatred of injustice?"

"Yes. Hate is purely destructive—a spiritual violence."

They had so many of these ethical discussions, leading nowhere except into the cul-de-sac of their opposing viewpoints. Always in the end they held out their hands to each other across the gulf of their dissimilarity. It was something that they could reach each other across the gulf. Something? It was everything. And there were points at which all the clear-cut lines and fine edges of right and wrong faded and fused, and all that held firm was personal integrity, and in this the devil himself might hold his own, and an angel falter in self-distrust.

But always when he was gone from her she was deeply troubled. For her he was not, as for the child, a romantic stranger with a gift for story-telling, to be accepted simply in the present, without reference to the past or the future, nameless and without background; for her it was more difficult, her adult mind not apt for that "willing suspension of disbelief" necessary for unquestioning acceptance of him as a dark presence, a smile, ironic or strangely gentle, a nameless lover bearing gifts, a man in the flesh but inhumanly isolated in the present. Either he was a man wilfully—and exasperatingly—enigmatic, or he was something more, and that he should be something more was unthinkable. That, at least, was the word she used— "unthinkable", but her mind, nevertheless, continually groped at the edges of thought beyond material conceptions. She was troubled, not only on her own account, but on Jenny's. She wanted, passionately, to take her away from the life of the dockland streets, away from the old beldame of Ropewalk Alley and the barmaid of the Seven Bells; to give her a new world, a new orientation. It came to her with a sense of despair that children's clubs were not the solution; they were merely oases in the wilderness, and the children must live in the wilderness and only come occasionally to the oasis. The need for Jenny Flower, as for so many of the children, was a quite new environment. If Jenny could grow up with Gwen's children at the vicarage! Environment was admittedly not everything, but it counted. It counted enormously. At present Jenny knew no world but the squalid teeming one in which she lived. If she could only take Jenny home with her for a part of the school holidays. Let her run wild in the cherry orchards instead of the grey streets, live in an atmosphere of love . . . She wouldn't come, Marian knew, if she asked her, but if *he* would—Jenny would do anything for him. She resolved to discuss the matter with him after that Hallowe'en conversation, but it was another year before either she or Jenny saw him again, and it was not until the following year—the summer of 1935—that she was finally able to realise her dream and bring Jenny to the vicarage, and by then, though she did not know it, it was too late.

(3)

It was too late because by then Jenny knew a great deal more about the Goetic life than she had known eighteen months ago when the conversation between Marian and the stranger had taken place.

Ever since Mrs. Beadle's refusal to make another conjuration in the crystal Jenny had been determined to acquire all the secrets of the mysteries for herself, and every available spare moment she was at the cat-ridden house in Ropewalk Alley poring over the ancient books and charts of magic, and extracting information from the old woman. A book which called itself *The Magus* offered "A Complete System of Occult Philosophy". It was over a hundred years old, and the s's were all printed like f's, which made it very difficult to read, but

Jenny would lie for hours on the floor in Mrs. Beadle's upper room struggling to distil the essence of wisdom from the big yellow pages. The great book dealt exhaustively with every kind of Secret Myftery; it explained the Cabala, the Operations of Good and Evil Spirits, All Kinds of Cabaliftic Figures, Tables, Seals, and Names, with their Ufe, likewise the Times, Bonds, Offices and Conjuration of Spirits. It dealt with Celeftial Influences, and the Magic Properties of Metals, Herbs, and Precious Stones, and every aspect of Alchymy and Natural Magic—Amulets, Charms, Enchantments, Binding, Sorceries, Magical Confections, Magical Lights, Candles, Lamps, etc. It gave the formulas for the making of Suffumigations for raising Evil Spirits, Familiars, or the Souls of the Dead, with full instructions as to the Appropriate Places for the purpose. It gave the forms of the Exorcisms, Benedictions and Conjurations, for every day and hour of the week, with the Manner of Working Fully Defcribed.

From this Book of Magicke Jenny learned that "he that works magic must be of a constant belief, be credulous, and not at all doubt of the obtaining of the effect", also that magic is stirred up "by a strong imagination, by a daily and heightened speculation, and, in witches, by the devil". The words were long and difficult, but she got the sense of them, and there was in her that daily and heightened speculation. "Every magical faculty," she read, laboriously, from the ponderous book, "lies dormant, and has need of excitement, or stirring up; which is always true, if the object whereon it is to act is not nearly disposed, if its internal phantasy doth not wholly conform to the impression of the agent, or also if the patient be equal in strength, or superior to the agent therein". She learned, also, that often the spirits called up do come, though they are not always visible, which comforted her, curiously. She learned the uses of the blood of basilisks and the venom of toads, the tongue of a water-frog, the tooth of a mole.

She looked long and long at the faded parchment prints depicting the fearsome faces of the Evil Spirits—Daemons, Veffels of Wrath, Fallen Angels, and the careful drawings of the Symbols or Characters of the Evil Spirits. She would take paper and pencil and draw them herself, until she could draw them from memory. She could repeat the conjurations for every day of the week, and knew the Familiar Shapes of all the Spirits.

She ran wild in the streets like any other dockland child, paddled and bathed in the river, at the foot of the wharf stairs, under the hulk of the moored barges, along the strips of muddy beach; she went to the cinema, played hop-scotch on the pavements and in the courtyard of the flats, set booby traps for policemen, knocked at doors and ran away, collected cigarette cards, swapped marbles, sucked sherbet out of paper bags with a stick of liquorice, gathered under railway arches and in alleyways with other giggling, whispering children for obscene exchanges of the facts of life, chalked up words on walls . . . in all such external ways she was no different, neither better nor worse, than any other East End kid. At school her writing and spelling were bad, and her examination papers carried low marks, but it was not, Marian knew, lack of intelligence but lack of interest. She exasperated her teachers one after another because for all her brightness she was always at the bottom of the class. She talked in class, she played up the teachers, cheated when she could, was very often late, and occasionally played truant. She was not popular with the other children. She stole their sweets and marbles, she cheated in the games they played together, and she had a vicious temper. She was not afraid of anyone, adult or child. Surrounded by an angry gang of children whom one way or another she had wronged she would fight like a cornered rat, her small wizened face distorted to a quite extraordinary savagery. Whatever happened to her in these scraps she never cried, or gave any indication of pain, and however much punishment she took she always had an air of emerging as the victor . . . There was a certain gutter *panache* about her.

She loved only two people—the stranger and Nell Flower. Mrs. Beadle was important to her, but she did not love her; she never wanted to hug and kiss her again after her refusal that Lammas; there was a hardening, then, in her attitude to the old woman, and it increased as time went on. She began to see her, even, as a dirty old thing, as she became increasingly aware of Nell's scented elegance and showy beauty. But she was dependent on Mrs. Beadle for more than Goetic knowledge; spiritually she stood to her in the relation of a mother—and a mother from whom she was not yet weaned. Nell she loved, because she was different—as different from the every-day world as the forest was. She smelt like flowers, in a world that smelt of breweries, tanneries, fish-and-chips, bug-ridden interiors, unwashed bodies. She was colour amongst all the grey. Gaiety amongst all the drab. And though she never said it in so many words you knew that she was on your side, and, when you thought that, you wanted to skip and sing and nothing else mattered—not arm-slappings at school, the boxes-on-the-ears and thumps in the back at home. That she had ever felt Miss Drew to be on her side, ever felt drawn to her, she had long ago forgotten. Miss Drew was kind; she never punished, or "lectured", and it wasn't worth while playing her up because she never seemed to notice it; but all the same she was the enemy; she had been that for a long time, but now she was not merely the enemy but a highly dangerous one. She kept *him* away. She made him promise not to see her, Jenny, and he promised because he loved her. This he had said, and it was a pain in Jenny like the pain of the witch's mark on her body, and when she thought of it, and felt this pain, she seemed to feel it there. Then she would press her hand to that strange red mark above her heart and her face that had been soft thinking of him would become hard and wizened again.

On her tenth birthday she met him for the last time at the Fair. He brought her a little bracelet designed like a snake, and he told her that he would not see her again for a long time —not next year, not the year after, nor the year after that, and each year as he enumerated it was the lash of a whip throbbing in the witch's mark above her heart, that mark insensitive to physical hurt. It was the scourge of the magic chart. Not next year, nor the year after, nor the year after that. You couldn't think so far. You couldn't live so long. The unimaginable closed round her and her body was ice-cold. She turned her face into his chest and whispered, "Where will you be all that time?"

"In hell most of the time, I expect."

"I don't want you to go!"

He stroked her hair. "I shall come back. I shall come back when you need me. But you're still such a little witch! You've got to grow up. You'll do it better without me!"

She was silent in her helplessness. He held her close to him and the music of the roundabouts, rising and falling, rode on the night wind. It was a dark night. It was going to rain. There was already the spit of it on the air. The naphtha flares on the stalls blew out wildly in the scurries of wind. The noise of the fair sounded very far away.

"During the holidays next summer," he went on, "I want you to go away with Miss Drew. It is lovely country where she lives—much nicer than the forest. It will be good for you and you'll like it."

"Why must I go? I don't like Miss Drew any more."

"Miss Drew is the best person you know."

"If I've got to go away why can't I go with my Auntie Nell?"

"Because she's not what I want for you. You will go with Miss Drew, and I shan't come to you, but I shall be very close to you all the time, especially at Lammas."

She did not speak. Her small thin body shook with the storm of sobs that rose up in her.

His arms tightened round her. "Jenny," he said, "Oh, Jenny, my little one!"

Suddenly he caught her up m his arms and carried her back to the noise and lights and crowd.

This time he carried her up the wooden steps of the roundabouts when they slowed down and seated her on a horse with flying mane and fierce scarlet-painted nostrils, and climbed up behind her.

That was the last she knew of him for over three years, the wild ride through the night with his arms round her, the whirl of light and music in the black night, that brief ecstasy at the heart of pain. At what point he dropped off she never knew, but when the roundabouts finally came to a standstill she sat alone clinging to the brass rod that still gently rose and fell in the wooden horse's back, and when she climbed down into the dim confusion of the crowd he was nowhere to be seen.

She pushed her way through the crowd, sobbing, and several people turned and looked after compassionately, murmuring to each other, "Poor little thing, she's lost!"

Not far away, in a room above the river, there was his conversation:—

"I did what you wanted. I told her she must come to you during the summer holidays, and that she would not see me again for three years."

"How did she take it?"

"I think it broke her heart. It's a terrible thing to break a child's heart, let me tell you."

"Children soon get over things."

"That's what adults always say, I know. They've forgotten their own childhood. Forgotten 'the lonely dreams of a child'. It would have been no more difficult to hit that child over the head than do what I did to her to-night!"

"I'm sorry you feel so badly about it, but I'm grateful to you for doing it. I'm convinced that it's the right thing to have done. Now we shall see how she will develop."

"Yes, we shall see!" His voice was bitter.

"You think it will make no difference if you don't see her?"

"Why should I prophesy? We're going to see, aren't we? In the battle for the soul of Jenny Flower the forces of good look, at the moment, like winning! But you know what the militarists say—you can win the battles and still lose the war!"

"Or lose the battles and win the war?"

"If you lose the battles in the next few years you won't win the war!"

"You think that what you call the forces of good are bound to lose, don't you?"

"I tell you I refuse to prophesy! You must see for yourself—after all, the whole monstrous business is your idea! I only know that if the child were in this room now and I said to her very solemnly all the things you'd like me to say—if I said to her, I am nothing remarkable; I am an ordinary man like anyone else, a seaman off a ship, and Mrs. Beadle didn't conjure me up that time, I merely happened to arrive at that moment, and the horns I wore in the forest were merely some I'd picked up, and I didn't come up out of the river that Candlemas, I was on the beach and merely walked up the steps, and you merely dreamed I came to you in your room that night, and I come back on witches' sabbaths only as part of a great game of make-believe—I tell you if I told her all that, very solemnly, she wouldn't believe! *That* for her would be the make-believe! She has been touched by the fatal lightning. She *knows*! She has *seen* the stranger in the forest with horns on his head, she has *seen* him come up out of the river, she has *seen* him at the foot of her bed when she willed him to come, she has *seen* him materialise out of the crystal and felt the pang of a terrible initiation in her own body *seen* she carries the mark of it above her heart, and she will carry it till she dies, and you can account for that pain and that mark in any natural way you choose, and you cannot alter the nature of the experience for her!"

"According to you any hallucination is to be accepted as reality?"

"Hallucination *is* reality for the person experiencing it—the only reality. Everything exists only in relation to oneself. What I, personally, feel, see, hear, experience in my mind and body—this for me is the only reality, the only truth."

"There must be some ultimate truth. Reality must have substance!"

"Who is going to determine ultimate truth? Are you going to say a vision has no reality because it has no substance—that St. Joan didn't hear voices because they came from no human throats? Words! Words! The only reality is what I personally apprehend, in my body, in my imagination. Well, you have nearly four years in which to work on the soul of Jenny Flower—free of the dark satanic influences!"

He smiled his ironic smile. "If you believe, as you say, that you can't put into a child, but only bring out—very well, we shall see what you will bring out! If at some time you hear a sound of harsh satanic laughter across your cherry orchards you will remember this . . . "

There was no meeting, then, of hands or spirits across the gulf. He left her abruptly, and she did not see him again until the winter of 1937.

Chapter II

Visit to the Vicarage

When Ivy heard that Miss Drew wanted Jenny to spend a few weeks of the summer holidays with her at her home she was delighted. The summer holidays were always a problem because they were so long, and because it was light until ten o'clock at night, and the children just ran wild. Now that the boys went to the club several evenings a week, and Stan had his boys' brigade to attend, they did not present such a problem during the holidays, but nothing, it seemed, could induce Jenny to go the children's club, and rumours reached Ivy that she was seen "hanging about" Ropewalk Alley a good deal, though she always denied this—and Ropewalk Alley meant that dirty old woman who ought by rights to be locked up.

Miss Drew wrote to Mrs. Flower asking should she call in one afternoon after school to discuss this idea of taking Jenny home with her, or would Mrs. Flower prefer to call in at the school one day for a chat? Ivy preferred to call at the school. She didn't want Miss Drew, or any school-teacher, poking about in her place. Not, mind you, as she said to Mrs. Grigg, that she had anything to be ashamed of. "We may be poor, but we *are* clean," Ivy declared. Mrs. Grigg confirmed, loyally, "You keep your place lovely! I don't know how you do it with three children paddling in and out all day! You've nothing to be ashamed of, I'm sure! Still, I know how you feel. I'm the same

202

meself. People in our station," she added, vaguely, to which Ivy replied, "That's right."

So Marian met Mrs. Flower at last and thought her a very nice little woman, and Ivy found Miss Drew "very pleasant" and not at all "la-di-da", like so many school-teachers; she was very pleased that Miss Drew mentioned about Mrs. Beadle.

"From the little I know of her," said Marian, "I can't feel she's a good influence."

"She certainly is not!" Ivy said, emphatically: "I've strictly forbid my Jenny to go there. But of course you never know what they get up to once they're out of your sight. It's why I'm very pleased, I'm, sure, for her to spend some time with you. I'm very grateful to you, Miss, and Mr. Flower asked me to send you his best respects and say the same." Joe had said nothing of the kind, but Ivy said for him what she felt he ought to have said—what, being anyone but taciturn Joe Flower, he would have said. Joe, when told that Jenny's teacher offered to give her a few weeks' holiday at her home had merely observed that it would be one mouth less to feed for a time.

"To keep her away from Mrs. Beadle is one of the reasons why I want to take her with me," Marian said. Then she showed Ivy some photographs of the vicarage, one taken looking across the cherry orchard in blossom, and one from the rose-garden, and some pictures of Gwen and her babies, and Ivy exclaimed what a lovely place the vicarage looked, and what a pretty girl Gwen was, and how sweet the babies were, bless them, and what a lucky little girl Jenny was to be going to such a lovely place.

"You see," Marian said, "it's no use just forbidding Jenny to go to Mrs. Beadle's, or to any place like that; what we've got to do is to get her so that she doesn't want to."

"Improve her tastes, as you might say?" Ivy suggested, brightly. She was being very careful not to drop any aitches or say "didn't arf" or "not arf" or anything "common" like that. She prided herself that she could "talk nice" when she liked. She had bought herself a new pair of gloves for the interview with the teacher—nice, neat brown kid. Her hands were a "sight". It was the black-leading, and the vegetables; vegetables stained the hands terrible, and what with that and the black-lead and the soda . . . though she had no patience with those who didn't use it. She sat with her hands in the tight new gloves, clutching her shabby old black handbag, remembering to speak nice and making an effort to answer up brightly to everything the teacher said. She has a nice face, she thought, a *good* face. She'd be about thirty. About the same as me, but I look a lot older. But then she's had an easy life; no worries, no children . . . It must be funny to be thirty and never have had a man . . . She pulled her mind back to the present.

"Would I have to get her any special clothes—for the country, like?" she asked.

"She ought to have some strong shoes, that's all," Marian said. "But I don't want you put to any expense, so perhaps you'd allow me to see to anything like that?"

"It's very kind of you, I'm sure," Ivy said quickly. "But there's no need. If you would just let me know the things—"

Marian replied as quickly, "What she wears to school will do very nicely." She realised that she had blundered in her offer to supply the shoes.

Ivy left the interview both pleased and worried. She was pleased that she had got on so well with Miss Drew and that Jenny was going to such a nice place, and worried because although Miss Drew had said the clothes Jenny wore to school would do nicely Ivy knew that they wouldn't. Jenny's underclothes were a disgrace, and her nightgowns were rags. She'd need a regular trousseau if she was to be sent away at all decent. Well, Nell would have to fork out. It would be no use asking Joe for a bit of extra.

She wrote to Nell asking her to tea and telling her about Jenny's vicarage holiday. Nell came round and "forked out" five pounds.

"Are you sure you can spare it, dear?" Ivy asked, genuinely anxious. Five pounds was a terrible lot of money. It was more than Joe earned in a week. It was a sum that took months to save.

"Plenty more where that came from," Nell assured her. Her gentleman friend in the fur trade in the city was still about . . .

Nell was amused by the idea of Jenny at the vicarage.

"I don't want to go one bit!" Jenny told her, vehemently.

Nell said, "Never mind, ducks, you'll like it when you get there! Everyone'll make ever such a fuss of you!"

"You'll have to say prayers night and morning and grace before and after meals!" Les told her, grinning.

"That won't hurt her," Ivy said, shortly, and, as Jenny wiped the jam from her mouth with the back of her hand, "Perhaps she'll learn some decent manners whilst she's there!"

When the children were out of the room, Ivy said, lowering her voice to the confidential note, "I couldn't help thinking while I was talking to Miss Drew what you told me about seeing her in the bar with that feller. I never woulda believed it! She doesn't look the sort, you must admit! A common seafaring feller, you said?"

"I didn't say, he was common. A petty-officer, probably. A cut above the usual crowd."

"Funny if she should be hanging-on one of your cast-offs!"

"I don't see what's funny about it," Nell said, bored. "Everyone is someone's cast-off, come to that!"

Ivy was a little nettled. "It doesn't follow. If a woman's— pure—" she coloured slightly, "she's not anyone's cast-off. The same with a man."

Nell brought out a flap-jack and began powdering her nose.

"They say that when a unicorn meets a virgin it falls down dead."

Ivy fell for it. "There's no such thing as unicorns."

Nell laughed. "Aren't there, dear?" She got up, brushing the flecks of powder from her skirt. "I must be going. Where's that kid of mine?"

"Sh!" Though there was nobody in the flat Ivy didn't like such things said out loud.

When they walked to the 'bus together Nell said to Jenny, "You don't want to make up your mind you won't enjoy it at the vicarage. It's a lovely place, by all accounts, and Miss Drew's all right, isn't she? Kind, and all that."

"I hate her!" Jenny said, violently. "She made him promise not to see me, and now he isn't coming back for years. He said I was to go with Miss Drew. I'll be thirteen when he comes back. He said not this year, nor the year after, nor the year after that."

Nell stared at her. "When did you last see him?"

"On my birthday, at the Fair. He took me on the roundabouts."

"And he said he was going away all that time?"

Jenny nodded, her eyes filling with tears. Nell saw the tears and put an arm round her shoulder, hugging her to her.

"He'll be back before then, you'll see. Fellers that go off to sea never know when they'll be back."

"It's not to do with going to sea," Jenny whispered, struggling with the lump in her throat, "It's to do with *her*! He stayed away a whole year before because he promised her. I wish she'd die! I wish she'd die!"

"Shut-up!" Nell said, "That's not a thing to say. She's probably right. Stop sniffing and blow your nose! Have you got a hanky?"

"Yes," Jenny said, meekly, and tugged a grimy handkerchief down from a leg of her knickers.

"Blow hard!" Nell commanded.

Jenny blew hard, stuffed the handkerchief back in the knicker leg, and they walked on in a silence punctuated by an occasional sniff from Jenny.

Nell was on the side of the angels once more. She was glad Jenny was going to the vicarage. She was glad Miss Drew had been able to exert her influence and send him away. He was no good to the kid. He mightn't do her any actual harm, but she was better off without him. He hadn't been in to the Bells since that upset at Mrs. Beadle's. She had wondered where he had got to. Keeping the school-teacher company, most likely. Oh, well, live and let live. All the same, she was glad he was fading out on the kid for a bit . . .

Jenny was aware that Nell had gone over to the other side. Now it seemed to her she had no one, and she was filled with desolation. She had no one but Satan. Well, if she was to go to the hateful vicarage he should go too. Wasn't he her familiar? Her servant? Her servant. An idea stirred in her mind.

There was no impetuous embrace at the 'bus-stop as on previous occasions. When the 'bus came and Nell bent and kissed her she barely noticed it; there was no response in her. The dark idea was shaping in her mind, excitingly. It might be a good thing to go to the vicarage after all. In the end they might all be sorry they had been so keen for her to go. Even *he* might be sorry . . .

(2)

It was a fresh, cool summer morning when Marian called for Jenny in a taxi—an unnaturally clean and tidy Jenny, her feet stuck into large brown shoes, very new and stiff, her newly washed hair severely brushed back from her face and securely fastened with a large new clasp. Everything she had on was new and clean, and she was acutely uncomfortable. The cotton dress was a little too long—to allow for growth, Ivy said—and flapped round her knees; the knickers that matched it were also a little too large and felt baggy and bulky; the new vest irritated her skin; and her hair was so tightly drawn back that it hurt. It was going to be a lovely day, and if she hadn't got to go away with Miss Drew she could have gone bathing in the river; Les was teaching her to swim. She held Satan in a piece of sacking. The sacking was tied round his neck and he also was acutely uncomfortable and rebellious. Ivy was hot and cross with the struggle to be ready in time for Miss Drew.

When she saw the taxi draw up at the gates of the courtyard she grabbed Jenny and her cheap bulging suitcase, determined to get out into the yard before the teacher should start coming up the stairs and into the flat, which at that time of the morning was not fit for visitors. Marian was in fact just crossing the yard towards the block of flats when Ivy emerged, pulling Jenny along behind her, the boys following. Ivy was in a thoroughly bad temper but she arranged her face into a smile as she greeted Miss Drew.

"You've got a lovely day for your journey," she said, and then to Jenny, glaring at her, "Isn't that a thrill for you, going off in a taxi?"

"I wisht I was going!" Les said eagerly, and pushed his way into the cab.

Ivy screamed at him. "Now then, young Les, just you come out of that!"

Marian said quickly, "Let him come, let them both come—I'll drop them at London Bridge."

"They're too untidy," Ivy protested, torn between maternal pride which did not like the children to be seen any distance from home in an unkempt condition, and a longing to be rid of them and have the place to herself if for only for half an hour.

"They're all right." She smiled at the hesitating Stan. "Jump in!"

They were arranged at last, the boys on the tip-up seats, Marian and Jenny opposite, Satan still struggling and miaowing in his sack on Jenny's lap. Ivy kissed Jenny on the forehead and told her to "be a good girl". Various neighbours waved from the balcony, Mrs. Oliver slatternly as usual in a bedraggled kimono, little Mrs. Grigg trim in a clean overall, a fat woman wearing a workman's cap and a sacking apron, a number of children. When they passed the flour warehouse the boys waved excitedly with cries of "There's Dad!" Joe Flower stood at the bottom of a chute down which the sacks of flour slid from the warehouse into the lorry. He had a sack over his head and trailing down his back, and was white from head to foot. He smiled slightly and waved as the taxi rolled past, the boys waving wildly from the window. He was a little embarrassed by the family demonstration in front of his workmates.

Jenny sat silent, withdrawn into herself.

"Coo, you ain't arf lucky," Les kept saying, over and over again. "I wisht I was going!"

But it was the taxi drive and the train journey that appealed to him, Marian thought. He wouldn't like it at the vicarage. He was essentially a London kid; the country would bore him. Marian looked at his alight, eager face, and thought how different he was from Jenny; he was the complete extravert; there was nothing withdrawn or secret about him. The younger boy was secret and withdrawn, but not in the way that Jenny was; you didn't feel any mystery in him; what his silent exterior enclosed, you felt, was very little; the room of his being was dark and locked, but if you could open it and turn on the light you would find nothing there; whereas with Jenny the inner room was crowded with every kind of strangeness.

They dropped the boys at London Bridge, though they begged to be allowed to come further. Jenny sat looking out of the window at everything that was new and strange, and she heard the teacher explaining and pointing out, "Those are the Law Courts", and "This is the Strand", but it was all like a film she didn't understand, a lesson in which she was not interested.

Marian had, carefully, secured the tickets in advance, so that at Paddington they went straight to the train. She had booked seats. and Jenny had a window-seat. The compartment filled up and people smiled encouragingly at the cross-looking little girl and said kind things about "poor pussy" in the sack. Jenny stroked the cat's black head and glowered at her fellow-passengers.

"It's all strange to her," Marian felt constrained to say at one point, in explanation of Jenny's persistent refusal to answer the remarks made to her.

Jenny had had a fight to be allowed to bring Satan. At first Ivy wouldn't hear of it. "What next?" she had demanded. Right up till the morning of departure Ivy had held out about the cat, and at last Jenny had torn off her new dress and thrown herself down on the floor and declared that she wouldn't go if Satan wasn't allowed to come. Ivy had beaten her—Joe, fortunately, had already left for work. Jenny had kicked and screamed—whilst the minutes ticked on bringing Miss Drew and the taxi nearer and nearer. Not until Ivy had given in, and Les had been sent to find a sack and sew the cat up in it for the journey, had Jenny consented to put on the dress, wash her face, and allow herself to be made ready for the journey.

Ivy had a raging headache and Jenny was full of a black hatred by the time the taxi arrived.

When the train came out into the country round Oxford Jenny could still feel the slap of Ivy's fingers on her face, and her breath was still coming up in small catches of hiccupy sobs at intervals, so that Marian looked at her and wondered.

"The child has been crying," she thought. "Does she hate it so much coming away with me? Is it really such a cruel thing to cut her off from *him*, root her up from her own world?"

She comforted herself with the thought that when they got there Jenny would like it. What child could fail to?

She opened a packet of sandwiches, and offered them to Jenny, but Jenny refused them. Presently she fell asleep, her breath still coming in the little sobbing catches.

The Reverend Charles Drew took the vicarage pony and trap and Charlie Two to meet his daughter and her small protégée, whom the twins had already, in advance, christened, "the dead-end kid". He took his grandson because he felt that the presence of another child might made the "dead-end kid" feel more at home.

But Jenny stared as blankly at little five-year old Charlie Two as at the vicar himself. Charlie Two was not like any child she had ever seen. It was not simply that his hair was flaxen silk and his small face like a wild rose, but that he seemed to Jenny to be in fancy dress, with his sky-blue trunks held up by scarlet braces, a scarlet handkerchief knotted round his throat, and blue and scarlet sandals on his feet. Jenny glowered at him, but he smiled engagingly and reached out to stroke the cat.

Charlie One had been instructed by his family not to roar at the dead-end kid and frighten her. At which he had snorted and said she would probably frighten the wits out of him. Which she did.

She was an unprepossessing-looking child, he thought, and wondered why of all the available East End children who could do with a country holiday Marian had had to bring this one. He smiled at her nervously as he told her to jump in. Marian kissed his forehead, drew a deep breath of the country air, and said it was wonderful to see the country again.

They drove off and Marian asked after the family, and the cherry crop, and the neighbours. Old Miss Ellswood got no better, he told her; she had scared them all the other night by getting up out of her bed whilst her sister was asleep and walking stark naked down to the blacksmith's. She knocked the blacksmith and his wife up and there she was standing naked in the garden with a candle in her hand, like something raised from the dead, Mrs. Blacksmith said. Her sister thought she would have to be put away. No more news except that they'd had fifty to the children's tea-party and it had gone off well . . .

On either side the narrow leafy lanes the cherry trees stood darkly green, no longer heavy with their crimson fruit, but full of summer still, the long grass beneath them starred with flowers—marguerite daisies and wild canterbury-bells and lupins and red sorrel. In the near distance thickly wooded hills flowed gently along the edge of the sky; the clearings were full of bracken, and the thatched cottages with their bright gardens had an air of dozing in the sun. A soft golden light lay over everything. The grey wilderness of Wapping Highway, Shadwell, Rotherhithe, Limehouse, Stepney, seemed a thousand miles away.

Jenny looked at the woods and thought of the forest, and that she would not see him this year, or the next, or the year after, and her heart felt hard and cold in her, like a stone. She did not want to be with these people. She did not belong. Then she remembered her secret plan, and her mouth tightened, giving her face the malicious wizened look.

As they turned in at the shady vicarage drive with its tall old elms and straggling wild rhododendrons, Mrs. Drew came out of the porch to meet them, followed by Gwen with her youngest child in her arms. Mrs. Drew wore a large old Chinese sun-hat, and looked, Marian thought, like the illustration of a witch in a fairy-tale. She kissed Jenny and exclaimed admiringly about her cat, then bore child and cat off into the house.

Satan, released from his sack, stretched his limbs and eagerly gave his attention to the saucer of milk set before him. Jenny allowed herself to be taken to a bathroom, used the W.C., and washed her face and hands. Mrs. Drew stood by smiling, making small friendly conversation, and thinking, "Poor little thing, it's all so strange to her."

They all assumed that Jenny's silence meant that she was shy, and they all endeavoured to set her at her ease. But Jenny was not shy. The strangeness of everything did not worry because it did not interest her. She ate the food set before her. She answered questions. Yes, she had been to the country before. Yes, she liked it. Yes, she had seen cows milked. And then, to everyone's dismay. No, she didn't like babies. It had been assumed that the little sister of Charlie One, and the small new baby only a few months old, would interest Jenny, make her feel at home. The plan to take her up to the nursery after lunch, therefore, fell through, and Marian conducted her round the gardens and grounds instead. There was a little delay in finding Satan and Jenny refused to go without him. Gwen came with them on the tour of the grounds, pushing the baby in a pram, the two other children running ahead.

Presently they sat in the rose-garden and the two sisters talked, whilst Charlie One and his little sister ran about, and Jenny sat bored, playing in a desultory fashion with Satan, now fully recovered from his uncomfortable journey.

Presently she picked him up and strolled away.

"You won't get lost, will you?" Marian called after her, a little anxiously. Jenny shook her head. She was, if they had but known it, utterly lost already in that strange world.

When she was out of earshot Gwen observed, rocking the pram gently, "She's a strange little thing, isn't she? D'you think she'll settle down here? What are the bad influences you wrote about?"

Marian began to tell her about Jenny's association with Mrs. Beadle and her curious preoccupation with witchcraft.

"She looks rather like a child-witch," Gwen said.

Marian told her, too, about the stranger—though not of her own encounters with him.

"Of course it's all the most colossal make-believe, but it's not good for her. It's why I wanted to get her away, and made him promise to stay away from her. By the time he comes back, if he keeps his promise, and I feel he will, she'll be adolescent and grown out of it all."

Whilst this conversation was taking place in the sunny rose-garden Jenny, clutching Satan tightly to her, turned into the dark drive and came out into the lane. She was looking for something. She was looking for a field in which there was a haystack; they had passed it in the trap, coming along. She did not pass that particular field, because she was on the wrong road but she found another field with a haystack. She climbed over the gate into the field, throwing Satan over in advance. She went across the field to the stack, and where a chunk had been cut from it forming a ledge, climbed up to pull down some of the straw thatching. Then she sat down on the ledge and began twisting the hay and straw together, her face passionately intent. She sat so long plaiting the straw together that the sun had begun to go down before she left the stack, carrying a small straw doll, on the feet of which were a pair of baby's knitted shoes which she had taken out of the pram when for a moment she had found herself alone beside it after lunch, before they had set out for the rose-garden.

When she climbed over the gate into the lane she saw Marian coming towards her. She hid the doll between the cat's body and her own.

"Jenny—where did you get to? You gave me a fright! I thought you were lost! It's gone tea-time. You shouldn't go off like that, you know, till you know the place a bit."

Jenny was silent. Back at the house she made the excuse that she wanted to "go somewhere". She went to her room and hid the straw doll under the mattress of her bed.

(3)

Jenny was a fortnight at the vicarage before she did anything with the straw doll. Gwen remarked several times that she couldn't think what had happened to baby's little knitted shoes she had left in the bottom of the pram. At the end of a week it was a little woolly jacket she was looking for. Both Charlie Two and the little girl denied having gone off with these things, and Gwen made no more inquiries. Things did sometimes just disappear, and turned up again later.

Jenny gave no trouble at the vicarage. No child could have been more docile or unobtrusive. "A perfect little angel," Mrs. Drew said. But Marian was uneasy. This was not Jenny Flower as she knew her, this quiet child who never smiled, ignored the other children, never played, but just sat or walked about with her cat in her arms, answering questions, but never addressing a remark to anyone. Marian had the feeling that she was merely waiting for the days to pass so that she could go home again. If that was so then the "angels" were being defeated. She remembered, then, what the stranger had said about winning the battles but losing the war, and was troubled. She took Jenny for walks; she showed her all the sights of the countryside, took her to call at cottages, took her shopping at the tiny stores that were merely the front room of a cottage, took her for drives in the trap, took her deep into the forests and showed her where the charcoal burners lived like forest hermits in improvised huts and looked askance at strangers, took her to church on Sunday—the youngest Morgan baby in the pram now, under the lectern—a highly polished brass eagle with spreading wings. David tried to show her how to play the harmonica in Larry Adler fashion, and Joan tried to interest her in the piano-accordion. Mrs. Drew piled her plate at tea-times with home-made strawberry jam in which the strawberries were whole, convinced that hitherto the child had known only bread-and-scrape. She squandered pounds of butter and sugar making toffee and "fudge" for her. Jenny watched the sweet-making with interest, and she ate the results with pleasure, but she did not warm to Mrs. Drew. She did not warm to any of them; she thought Gwen pretty—though not as pretty as Auntie Nell. At best she did not mind them; but she was not interested in any of them. They were none of them anything to do with her. In the evenings when they sat on the weed-grown terrace outside the house singing songs whilst Joan played the accordion—Mrs. Drew and Gwen always with mending or knitting in their hands whilst they sang or listened—strange feelings would stir in her with the music. Then she would remember the roundabouts at the Fair, the wild whirl and plunge, the feeling of being cut off from the earth, and the music throbbing in your blood, like a heart beating, or a pulse. Then she would remember the dark forest and the owl crying, crying, and the sense of excitement and danger. Then she would remember the crystal, drawing her deeper and deeper into its fiery heart, till *he* came up out of it, and the sword drove into her heart and she was in his arms. Then she would remember May Eve and the coldness of her body, and the strange, frightening, exciting power. Her body would grow cold again, remembering these things, and when she went up to bed, after Marian had been in and kissed her good-night and blown out the candle, she would pull the straw doll out from under the mattress and take it into bed with her, pressing it to her cold body. But always something in her seemed to say that the time was not yet. It was as though she were waiting for something.

If she knew what she was waiting for she did not acknowledge it. But she did nothing with the doll until Lammas.

That night after Marian had gone she took out the doll; the night was not yet quite dark and she could see well enough to make up a bed on the floor, with the pillow from her own bed for a mattress, and the counterpane several times folded for bedding. Into this bed she slipped the doll, wrapped in the baby's knitted jacket and with the little bootees on its feet. Then she took the cat and put it on top of the doll and held it there, whispering over and over again into its black fur, "The baby is smothering; the baby is smothering." The cat began purring and "kneading", as cats do, salivating at the mouth. The saliva dropped on to the doll, and the cat lifted its forefeet, its claws extended, its body vibrating with a smooth slow rhythm, and all the time Jenny repeated, her face white and set, her eyes closed, her body ice-cold, "The baby is smothering, the baby is smothering."

When the cat ceased its kneading she lifted it up and put it outside the door, then got back into bed, leaving the doll in bed on the floor.

She lay still for a little while staring at the patch of light that was the window. She could make out the cedar tree in the garden, black against the pale sky. Now she admitted to herself the knowledge that this was Lammas. I shall think of you all the time, he had said, and especially at Lammas . . . If he should appear at the window, smile at her just for a moment! But she could not will it; she had no strength left; power had gone out of her.

Suddenly somewhere in the house a baby cried; there was a scurry of steps, a slamming of doors. In a flash Jenny was out of bed, had whipped up the doll's bed and the doll and taken them back with her into bed.

She was barely settled before her door burst open and Marian flung the cat into the room.

"You must keep your door shut, Jenny," she said, sharply. "Your cat got out and into the nursery and was sitting on the baby's face. It might have smothered her!"

She went over to the window and closed it at the bottom.

"We can't have the brute getting out again through the window," she said.

"Has Satan hurt the baby?" Jenny asked, faintly, peering out over the bedclothes.

"He's scratched her face, and if the poor little thing hadn't wakened up and cried she could easily have been suffocated!"

When Marian had gone Jenny took the cat into bed with her and lay fondling it. Satan, her darling Satan, her faithful servant; her familiar . . .

"It worked!" she whispered to herself, ecstatically. "It worked!"

It had worked on May Eve, and it had worked at Lammas. These were only small things. She hadn't wanted to kill the baby;

she had only wanted to test her power, to know, to have this triumphant certainty. May Eve could have been a fluke, but this was no fluke. Now she knew for certain that she had this power. Now she need not hate Miss Drew any more, because she was confirmed now in her power. Miss Drew was no longer the enemy, because she could be got rid of, sent away. "Sent away." . . . Beyond that Jenny's mind refused to go. She gave a deep contented sigh and fell into an exhausted sleep,

In the morning the chief subject at the breakfast table was how in the night the baby had nearly been smothered by Jenny's cat. David said that it was well-named Satan. Mrs. Drew said poor thing it knew no better, but all the same she had read in the papers of how babies had been killed by cats getting into their cradles or cots and squatting on their faces. They ought to lock the cat up in the coal-shed at night to make sure it was in a place where it couldn't get out.

Jenny said suddenly, violently, "Satan isn't to be locked up at nights!"

Mrs. Drew answered patiently, "You see, dear. I'm so afraid that even if you close the door of your room he might get out of the window, and we can't keep the nursery window shut—the baby must have air, and so must you. We can't keep all the windows closed because of the cat."

Jenny was silent, but after breakfast when she was alone with Marian, walking with her to the post, she announced, "I want to go home!"

Marian looked at her with dismay. "You've only been here a fortnight. I thought you would stay the whole time and we'd go back together."

"I want to go now," Jenny insisted.

"Is it because of Satan? Perhaps we could shut him in the kitchen; he'd be warm and comfy there, and he couldn't get out from there."

"All the same I want to go."

Marian reminded her:

"*He* wanted you to stay here, didn't he?"

"He didn't say I was to stop all the holidays. He would let me go home now, if I wanted to."

Would he? Marian wondered. Would he? The feeling of defeat came back to her. It was obvious that Jenny wasn't happy here. The only time she had smiled was when they had called at the Misses Ellswood's, and the mad Miss Ellswood's sister, as dirty and crazy looking as the other one, had peered into her face, pinched her cheek, and asked her had she come to see the two old witches, and wasn't she frightened. Then Jenny had smiled, and said she wasn't frightened, she liked witches . . . It had seemed an outrage to Marian that Jenny should smile at that dirty, crazy, old crone and stare stonily at golden Gwen, their sweet mother, and Gwen's wild-rose children. It was obvious that old Miss Ellswood spoke to something in her condition, and all this beauty and peace and gentleness didn't and that was all there was to it. It looked as though "the forces of good" were defeated. She sighed.

"I'll put you on the train to-morrow and wire your mother to meet you," she said. "We'll send the wire now."

Jenny's face lit up, and as clearly as though he stood before her Marian saw the stranger's ironic smile, heard the harsh satanic laughter across the cherry orchards.

Chapter III

The Wharves of Sorrow

Marian made no attempts to win Jenny Flower over to the "side of the angels". Her faith in the influence of environment was shaken. The two weeks at the vicarage, it seemed, had not made the slightest impression. It was true that two weeks was a very short time, but she felt that two months, two years, would have made no difference. Jenny had that capacity for going inside herself and closing the door and staying shut away inside herself indefinitely—all her life, if need be, Marian felt. Now, it seemed to her, there was nothing she could do; Jenny refused to go out with her at weekends, though she invited her to the Zoo, to Kew Gardens, to Richmond, to the Forest, and she stubbornly refused to come to the club. "I've failed with her, dismally," Marian thought. "And it's my own fault. I've always known that you can't do anything with a child unless you're on its side, and I haven't been. I wasn't on her side over Mrs. Beadle—or over him. And she knew it. I disapproved, and a child needs approval. All the time. I'm no better than all the mothers who say they love children and show their love by nagging them and boxing their ears and messing up their psyches without knowing it! But it wasn't only that she felt my disapproval; she was jealous. There was nothing I could do about that!"

She tried to find comfort in that thought, and some sort of defence of herself; but it was no good. Something deeper than this surface defence insisted, "You need not have intruded. You could have left her to him. Let her go to the devil, some people would call it, but then, as he would say, you must define what you mean by Devil. And that's something about which you've never made up your mind. Some people would say that *you* had gone to the devil—you, the professing Christian, with your illicit love . . .

With that thought the blood would come up into her face, the old sense of guilt sweep her. There were times when she felt a passionate need for confession. For confession and absolution. Times when the routine collective confession of the Church of England service seemed not enough. "We have erred and strayed from Thy ways like lost sheep . . . We have done those things we ought not to have done, and left undone those things which we ought to have done. And there is no health in us." You could repeat it with an impassioned sincerity, and still it was not enough. What then? There was the need for atonement. At-one-ment. Wholeness. Integration. "What must I do to be saved?" Cast out the memory of those unhallowed Hallowe'ens, that lovely Lammastide. "Go and sin no more." Well, he had gone away now for years, and it was two years since that lovely Lammas when she had surrendered her mind to the "willing suspension of disbelief", and after their last meeting, now almost a year ago, they had parted in anger, unable to reach out across the gulf between them. By the time he came back, if indeed he ever did come back, perhaps she would have found "salvation" in one form or another; in the meantime there was this sense of defeat, of failure, of disintegration and emptiness. Life seemed drained of satisfaction, spiritual and physical. She envied Miss Pritchett and Miss Hawkins, and even Kenneth Wilson, because they had created some core of satisfaction in their lives; they had no doubts as to the value of the things they were doing. Nor had she, until she had failed with one small child, and then everything she had believed in seemed to collapse, everything seemed futile, and oneself the most futile thing of all. One went to the devil in spite of oneself!

And the world, it seemed, was going to the devil as fast as it could go. All over Europe men were marching. It was no longer any question as to whether there would be another world-war or not, but merely when it would come. The sinister year 1936, with the dress-rehearsal for the coming world-war taking place in Spain. And one went on sitting behind a school-teacher's desk filling children up with useless information, running a children's club and increasingly obsessed with the thought, "In a few years' time all these adolescents will be part of the marching, the uniforms, the regimentation, the hell-let-loose . . . " She took small groups of children to see *The Insect Play*, and they were amused, and all the audience was amused, when red ants and black ants in turn declared that war had been forced upon them and disputed over a blade of grass. They were all agreed that the whole idea of war was crazy; but they all knew at the back of their minds that it was coming; they knew it fearfully and impotently . . . and they sat there applauding the satire and letting the reality come. As though they were hypnotised into inaction. Fascism and the New Order in Europe; Democracy and Freedom; the clash of ideologies, and idealists all. The whole fabric of civilisation crumbling . . . and one fretted about the disintegration in one's futile self. Ah, better to go on blindly marking the children's exercise books; it was not more futile than anything else. What could it matter that a child called Jenny Flower was doomed and damned when a whole generation was everywhere? What matter the lack of peace within oneself when the peace of the whole world was running out fast, through open sluices?

Lucifer and the Child

(2)

But for Jenny Flower, living out her life amongst the docks and wharves, the three and a half years from the time of her return from the vicarage to the Hallowe'en that was her thirteenth birthday and the end of her noviciate, were full of an exciting potentiality. She read more and more deeply of the Book of Magicke, with increasing understanding and an increasing sense of power. She no longer respected Mrs. Beadle as the source of all knowledge. She discovered that there was a great deal that Mrs. Beadle did not know. At times she even seemed to her little better than an old fortune-teller and crystal-gazer. Of the deeper implications of the Goetic life she knew little or nothing, and by the time she was thirteen Jenny knew a great deal, including the fascinating fact that two who might have been her ancestors were burnt at the stake as self-confessed witches.

At thirteen she was still thin and undersized, and from Ivy's point of view more unmanageable than ever. She was quite extraordinarily conceited. She was not vain about her appearance as young girls often are; indeed she was not interested in her appearance; she had none of the usual young girl's vanity, but she had a colossal vanity regarding her knowledge of the supernatural, and an almost paranoiac sense of potential power, intensified by her knowledge of the seventeenth-century Flowers. At school she had the utmost contempt for the other girls, particularly for the ones generally regarded as the "clever" girls, and a similar contempt for the teachers; they thought they knew everything, and they knew nothing. She had more power in her little finger than they had in the whole of their bodies—all of them put together. They knew only the surface things, it seemed to her; nothing of the dark mysteries underneath. From time to time she put small comparatively harmless spells on them, to reaffirm her faith in herself. She would steal a girl's glove and take it home, and next day the girl would come to school with a painful whitlow on her finger, or would have pinched her finger in a door, or cut or burnt it.

She loved no one except Nell, but her she loved unchangingly, uncritically. Nell merely laughed when she told her she "couldn't stick" the vicarage after a fortnight.

"I didn't think you would," she said, "but I thought we ought to see whether it would do you good or not. I ought to have known it wouldn't! Your name isn't Flower for nothing!"

And still as the years went on and Jenny grew from an undersized child into a thin, awkward adolescent, Nell searched in her face for the sign she sought; and still it seemed to her that Jenny wasn't like anyone but herself—Jenny Flower, strange and dark and secret, as though she were not an ordinary child at all but a changeling—except, of course, that you didn't believe in that sort of thing.

Ivy watched Jenny with increasing misgiving. It was quite common for girls of her age to get out of hand; usually they were boy-mad, like Mrs. Oliver's Doris, only a year or two older than Jenny; they were mad on clothes and lipstick and going to dances, and tried to make out they were older than they were. And that they were given to irritability and short-answers in the home you took for granted. But Jenny was neither boy-mad nor clothes-mad; she seemed equally indifferent to her personal appearance and to the opposite sex. She was not irritable, but her manner at home was intolerable all the same, in its contemptuousness.

Ivy complained bitterly to Joe, "That girl doesn't care that much—" snapping her fingers together—"for any of us! She treats us all as though we're dirt! One of these days she'll rile me so I shall take and tell her she's nothing but a bastard!"

"Fat lot of good that'll do her," Joe muttered.

"Take her down a peg or two!" Ivy was bitter.

"She'll get some of the conceit knocked out of her when she starts earning her living," Joe said.

Jenny was his sister's kid; she was a Flower; something in him felt compelled to stand up for her in spite of everything. And Ivy's nagging got on his nerves a great deal more than Jenny's contemptuousness. Jenny didn't talk much; that was something. She just moved about looking and behaving as though she despised the lot of them and at times he didn't blame her. For her, as for him, Ivy's nagging was water off a duck's back, so that there was a kind of unspoken alliance between them.

Jenny felt this alliance, vaguely, at times, but she was indifferent to Joe on the whole. He was quiet, lived shut up in himself; that was something. If you couldn't be gay and lovely like Auntie Nell you had best keep your mouth shut and make yourself as unobtrusive as possible.

When Nell came to the house Jenny would have the feeling of doors opening in herself, of buds opening out, drawbridges let down; then the cold closed look would leave her face and she would smile, and the colour would come up into her pale face; then she would be happy, excited, gay. And when Nell had gone, and she was silent and cold and closed again, Ivy would nag, "You can be nice enough when your Auntie Nell's here! Nice as pie you can be when you like! She ought to see you as we see you!"

Jenny would give her a cold, insolent look and as often as not say nothing. Why waste words on fools, she, the descendant of Margaret and Philippa Flower!

She spent an increasing amount of time at Mrs. Beadle's. There was nothing to do at home, whereas at Mrs. Beadle's there was always plenty to do, for if you lived for a hundred years you would never master all the mysteries of necromancy and the other secret arts. You could talk to old Ma Beadle; you could say whatever came into your mind without her thinking you mad or wicked or both—though of course according to general ideas you were both, as she was—and as *he* was . . . You could talk about him—that was another reason for going there.

And you weren't treated as a child. To be treated as a child when your head was stored with the wisdom that was as old as the world was intolerable. And Mrs. Beadle's was the only place where you could rest. No one else knew how much you needed to rest, how tired you got, going round all the time with your head laden with all that dark knowledge, and your body charged with all that unused power, and all the time the terrible longing in you that was like a fire burning you up . . . and then people wondered why you were so pale and thin! Ah, if only he would come back! Surely he must come soon. This was the fourth year he had been away. Soon she would be thirteen; soon it would be Hallowe'en again. She would sit beside the fire in Mrs. Beadle's kitchen sometimes, leaning back in a chair, her arms hanging down limply over the sides, not thinking anything, sitting still and silent as in a trance, with a sense of the tiredness flowing out of her finger-tips, streaming from her in a relaxation she could know nowhere else. The old woman would bring her cups of herb-tea and croon over her with a strange maternal tenderness. "So tired," she would murmur. "Poor little one. So tired . . . " But Jenny would be far away and not hear her; cold green waters went flowing over her, flowing over . . .

She went to Mrs. Beadle's the day before her birthday. She was keyed up and excited. Would he come to-morrow? Would the time be up to-morrow? Where ought she to wait for him—there or down by the river? In the morning or in the evening? Mrs. Beadle had no answers for her restless, feverish questions, and Jenny knew the futility of asking them, but to be with the old woman was to be in a sympathetic atmosphere nowhere else available, and it brought her that much nearer him.

She stayed late into the night; for the last few months she had taken to staying later and later. She would get home at the same time as though she had been to the last house of the cinema; sometimes she would pretend that that was where she had been, but Ivy never believed her.

"You've been with that dirty old troll!" she would storm, and Jenny would toss her head and say, "All right, then, that's where I've been! What do I care what you believe? In future I shan't tell you." Whether she lied, told the truth, or said nothing, there was the same scene when she got in late. But she didn't care. And the night before her birthday she was later than she had ever been, and she was more tired than she had ever been, and it was pouring with rain outside, and she finally announced her intention of not turning out. She might as well be hung for a sheep as a lamb, she declared.

She spent the night on the sofa in the front room of the dirty little house, got up late, since it was Sunday, drank herb tea with Mrs, Beadle in the kitchen, and arrived home just as the boys were leaving the house for the church-lads' "parade", Les with his "uniform" proudly buckled on, Stan the admiring and faithful camp-follower. Joe had gone for a stroll until opening time.

Jenny went in prepared for a storm, and it broke over her immediately. Ivy's face was quite savage as she confronted the girl. She had been working herself up all night.

"You dirty little stop-out!" she screamed at her. "I wonder you've got the face to show up again! You think I'll stand for this, do you? You think because your mother's a whore you can start your games at thirteen! You dirty little slut!"

Jenny stared at the livid face. "A whore?" she said.

"You know what I mean well enough! There's no filthy thing you haven't known since you were about seven years old. Whore, I said—street-walker, slut, common prostitute! That's what your mother is! You can stare! I'm not your mother—thank God!"

"Not my mother?"

"You heard what I said! Am I a whore? I'm a respectable married woman, I am, and you know it. But your mother was a whore before you were born and she's one to this day! As to who your father is it's more than she knows! So now you know, my fine lady! A bastard's what you are, and one that doesn't know its father. Put that in your pipe and smoke it, my girl!"

Ivy was white and trembling, exhausted with her fury. And a little frightened. All these years she had kept the secret, and now it was out. She clattered the breakfast things together on an old japanned tray.

Jenny stood silent a little longer, then she said, faintly, "Why doesn't my mother know who my father is?"

"Why do you think? Because whoever he was he wasn't the only man in the night's work! He was probably some drunken ship's greaser—what would you expect of a sailor's tart?"

Jenny was suddenly aware of the pain like a knife above her heart, and of feeling violently sick. And in the midst of it, of the cat brushing against her legs.

She bent and picked the cat up, then without a word turned and walked out.

Chapter IV

A Witch Has No Tears

Jenny went straight back to Ropewalk Alley. She ran most of the way, clasping the cat to her, splashing through puddles, running like a wild thing pursued.

Mrs. Beadle's front door was open, as usual; Jenny went straight in and through to the kitchen. She found the old woman where she had left her an hour ago, sitting beside the range, a cup of tea in her hand, cats rubbing themselves against her knees. Jenny stood at the door, her face white, her eyes wild, her hair wet from the rain falling in lank wisps and streaks about her face. Her shabby shoes were sodden with the rain, her light stockings splashed with mud; the belt of her coat hung loose; she looked what she was, unwashed, uncombed, distraught, a "dead end kid", but one at whom demons tore.

The old woman looked up in mild surprise.

"Brought me the Sunday papers?" she inquired.

Jenny ignored the remark. She came over to where Mrs. Beadle sat and stood over her, glaring down at her,

"I want to know who my mother is. You got to tell me! If it's true she's not the old cow that brought me up, who is she?"

The old woman stared at her.

"Who told you Joe and Ivy Flower aren't your parents?"

"She did herself. She said I was a bastard. She said my mother was a sailor's tart."

She began to sob, great breath-taking sobs coming up from the pit of her stomach, without tears, her face screwing up, her whole body tormented.

"You don't want to upset yerself," the old woman said. "There's plenty better than you been born bastards."

"She said no one knew who my father was. He could be any dirty greaser off a ship. Saying things like that to me! It's not true! I got to know who my mother is and then I'll find out. If it's true I'll kill her! Oh yes, I will—you think I'm just saying it. I'll kill her, I tell you! You needn't think I couldn't do it, because I know I can! You don't think I got that witch's mark for nothing!"

She rushed over to the cupboard, still sobbing the deep dry sobs, and got out the crystal.

"We'll soon find out. Come on! Don't sit there staring! Where's the candle? Give me the chalk! Get the curtains drawn, you old fool! We'll soon find out!"

The old woman rose, lit the candle for her, drew the curtains, produced the chalk from her pocket. Jenny crouched on the floor drawing the circle, and the darkened room seemed filled with her sobbing breaths.

When she bent over the crystal there was complete monomania in the intentness in her face. She was no longer sobbing, but her breath came in a long deep-drawn hissing. Her body was ice-cold. She was in the grip of a terrible hysteria.

The old woman stayed outside the circle, watching her, and in her own eyes there was the same maniac intentness.

Jenny leaned over the glowing crystal and babbled the conjuration for the day of the week, then commanded the evil spirits in the name of Lucifer, the Most High, Prince of Darkness and of the World, to reveal to her the face of her mother.

The crystal was a ball of fire drawing her deep down into its flaming heart. This, then, was the meaning of burning in hell-fire.

"My mother," she whispered, "My mother! Show me, unholy Lucifer, Lord of all the World, and the dark kingdoms of the infernal. Show me her face, she who bore me, she of whose flesh I am . . . "

Words and phrases of which her conscious mind knew nothing swam up to the surface. She had become an automaton of the unconscious.

Slowly the golden fire in the crystal folded back, assumed form, and she looked down into the smiling face of Nell Flower. The painted scarlet lips parted.

"I am your mother," they said. "I don't know who your father was. Why do you suppose I am always searching your face, except to read the secret there?"

It was not Mrs. Beadle who lifted her up from the table as she collapsed across it, wracked by the sword in her heart, but for a few moments as the wild frenzy swept her she did not know who it was.

"Poor little thing," Mrs. Beadle murmured, drawing back the curtains, letting in the grey day, "Better for her if she could cry, but tears are not for her."

He held her to him whilst the terrible tearless sobbing ravaged her thin body.

He said, "She'll never weep again. It's the end of her noviciate," and his voice was sad as the grey rain weeping along the grey river.

At the sound of his voice she opened her eyes.

"You!" she cried, and clung to him as though she were drowning. "You shouldn't have gone away for so long! All that time! It wasn't any good my going to the vicarage—I hated it. I had black thoughts there."

His arms tightened round her. "I know. I know. But it's past now. I won't leave you for so long again."

"Never?"

His smile was sad. "Never is a big word. But not for long."

"You said one day we'd be together always!"

"One day we will." He got up, lifting her to her feet. "We'll go from here."

"Where will we go?"

"Across the river, to Paradise Court."

Jenny stooped and picked up Satan in readiness to depart.

The old woman looked at him. "She's thirteen to-day, not sixteen. You better be careful——"

He gave her a look of the utmost contempt, and without a word took Jenny's hand and they went out, followed by the old woman's cackling laugh.

Chapter V

Paradise Court

R opewalk Alley was not more squalid than Paradise Court, approached by Love Lane. There was something dehumanised about the dirt and drabness of Paradise Court, yet human beings bred there, lived out their lives there, and when the time came were sorry to die. Children grew up there—lane and court rang with their laughter and shrill cries; men and women knew passion and desire there; they loved there—perhaps it was not love as the poets understand it, with little beauty or tenderness to it, but still it served them very well, and what are the cinemas for but to supply those elements in which life is deficient? Bugs and rats abounded in Paradise Court; the bugs you could get used to, but not the rats; you couldn't leave a thing out over-night; it was sickening. You could move—if you could find a place to go; but could you? And rents were cheap in Paradise Court; so was human life—but that is cheap everywhere.

Number Ten, to which the stranger took Jenny, was a dilapidated house rented by a coloured seaman with a delicate-looking white wife and a swarm of mulberry-coloured children. This family lived on the ground floor and the remaining rooms were furnished with an iron bedstead and a chair and rented to seamen, white or black, who slept in the rooms but fed with the family. They were at sea most of the year, and when they came ashore what more did they need than a bed to sleep in and a meal on the table? In this way they lived very cheaply and surprisingly comfortably, all things considered. Their plates were piled high with salted beef and carrots and potatoes; there was plenty of good strong black tea, and margarine never found its way to the table, always butter; Pete prided himself on having always the best of everything. Plenty of good West Indian cooking; plenty of salted beef, plenty of rice; yes, *sir!* And take things where you found them. Pete found a gas-cooker in an upstairs room; the whole floor had been used as a flat at one time. He charged a slightly higher rent for this room with the gas-cooker, because, as he explained to prospective tenants, here you had heating; you had only to light the oven and leave the door open and you had as good a gas-fire as you could wish for! And if you were tired of life you could always turn on the gas without lighting it. Every convenience! And Pete's magnificent teeth would flash out in his black face. He liked a joke. Yes, *sir!*

There was no convenient gas-cooker in the stranger's room, but he had imported an oil-stove, and there was a chest-of-drawers minus the drawers which Pete had picked up cheap one day from a junk dealer and brought home on a wheel-barrow. It was, as Pete pointed out, just as useful without the drawers, because you could shove all your things into the spaces where the drawers had been, and you hadn't got the fag of pulling the drawers out; also you could see at a glance what you'd got.

The stranger's room was the grandest in the house. Pete often took people up there, when the owner of the room was away, to show them this splendour which had come to dwell in his humble midst. There was an embroidered Indian silk cover on the bed, sewn with gold thread and gay as a peacock's tail. There was a small Chinese table in the middle of the room inlaid with mother-of-pearl ("Worth a fortune!" Pete would say, proudly.) On the mantelpiece, and cluttering the top of the chest-of-drawers were jade and ivory carvings, pieces of amber, tortoiseshell, crystal. A crimson Spanish shawl, richly embroidered, hung down over the front of the chest-of-drawers, concealing the fact that it had no drawers, (The chest's lack of drawers always occasioned a ribald joke from Pete, and that would lead him on to assert that there were three outstanding things about the Arabs—that the men had no religion, their horses no bridles, and their women no drawers . . . That the first two statements, at least, were manifestly incorrect did not trouble him. He was a walking encyclopaedia of mis-information on all things, historical and topical.) But the most impressive feature of the room, so far as Pete was concerned, was the number of books in foreign languages, and not foreign languages such as a lot of people might know, such as German, French, Spanish, Italian, but the more unlikely foreign languages, such as Persian, Japanese, Amharic, Hindee. As there was no accommodation for these books they were stacked up from floor to ceiling and lay in heaps along the skirting. Crowning touches of refinement to the room were a portiere curtain across the door of heavy green silk with a tarnished golden dragon sprawling over it, and at the windows shabby red curtains that when drawn at night, and with the gas lit, looked very "rich", said Pete.

It was an odd assortment of things viewed by the grey daylight, that showed the brown stains in the dirty striped wallpaper and the dust and dirt and rain-tears of ages on the sash window. It looked what it was—the room of someone who inhabited it very little, merely using it for occasional shelter and for the storing of possessions. A battered suitcase full of clothes lay open on the floor in one corner, and a bulging seaman's sack was propped up in another corner. There was also a tin trunk, on the top of which was a collection of tins and crockery. There was a washhand-stand with jug and basin and a grey towel hung over the back. The window was closed and the room smelled stalely of rank Virginian cigarettes.

For Jenny it was all beauty and delight. Nothing at the vicarage, with its shelves of books, its flowers, its coloured pottery, its hand-woven rugs, its good old-fashioned furniture, had interested her in the least; but here everything was exciting, every smallest thing touched with wonder. The view from the window was over a maze of junk-filled backyards.

Jenny walked about fingering everything reverently, whilst her host lit the oil-stove and put a tin saucepan of water on top. Presently the room filled with the good smell of coffee. Jenny took off her muddy shoes and curled up on the bed with its exotic cover and he brought her dates and biscuits on an enamel plate, coffee in an enamel mug. She sat with her back against the head of the bed, and he seated himself on the bed facing her, and it was as much a picnic as the meals beside the forest pool.

When it was over she stretched out luxuriously like a cat, relaxed and happy. Satan purred contentedly at the foot of the bed. The stranger lit a cigarette and regarded her with great tenderness.

He said, after a moment, "Does it matter so much that your Aunt Nell turns out to be your mother? I thought you were fond of her. And she's very pretty."

Jenny's lips tightened. "A sailor's tart," she said, bitterly, all her gutter knowledge of sex working in her. "I daresay she still is! She makes up like one. I hate her! I never want to see her again. Dirty slut!"

He was silent a moment, then he said, "Miss Drew is pure and good, but you hate her too."

"Her!" Her voice was all contempt. She lay still a moment, frowning at her thoughts, then she reached out and took his hand and pressed it against her cheek.

"I love only you in all the world," she said. "I shall love you always!"

He smoked in silence whilst she held his hand against her face. Suddenly she said, "There's something else I know, that I haven't told anyone yet. I know about Margaret and Philippa Flower, and their mother."

"How did you find that out?"

"In one of Mrs. Beadle's books. It's why my mother's bad. All the Flower women are bad."

"Your mother isn't a witch."

"She entices men. It's a kind of witchcraft." She was silent again, and then, "All witches come to bad ends, don't they?"

"They can't be burnt at the stake any more."

"There are other things as bad. People get murdered in woods. They get burnt alive in fires. They're found drowned in rivers. A witch never dies in bed."

She sat up, suddenly, "Where am I going to live now?"

"Where you were living before."

"She won't want me."

"Yes, she will. If you go anywhere else she'll bring you back."

"I could run away."

"Not yet. It would be no good. You're still at school."

"When I've left can I live with you?"

"Not till you're sixteen. And not then if the people who legally adopted you object. But much may happen in three years."

He got up abruptly. "The sun has come out. We'll go out. We haven't walked yet along this side of the river."

Before they went out he put a small coral bracelet on her wrist.

"You see," he said, "I didn't forget your birthday."

She said, bitterly, "My mother never does, either. But I don't want anything more from her."

They loitered along the wharves, leaned on wooden piers, watching the wind whipping up along the river, watching the shipping, and a music of foreign names was woven into the day as he talked—Port of Spain, Costa Rica, Rio de Janeiro, Nikolaistadt, Haparanda. They stood watching the timber ships coming up with the tide—steamers from the Baltic and White Sea ports, with towering deck-cargoes of planks, and he talked again of the deep forests and the lonely lakes, and she was a child again thrilling to a traveller's tale.

They took a 'bus to Hyde Park and walked down through the park to Kensington Gardens. They scuffled through the dead leaves under the trees and walked beside the water, and there was a splendid moment in which a swan came gliding down the air with a loud honking and white wings spread. It came at such a speed that it seemed it must crash upon the water, the great wings buckle up, but its timing was perfect, its precision a poem; its breast was laid upon the water as gently as soft music upon, the air.

Jenny laughed aloud with pleasure. Now there was no hate in her, no bitterness, no darkness of horror and disgust, no malice; she was a happy child, laughing in the pale sunlight of an October day. The day begun in ugliness was now all beauty. The weeping willows were golden beside the lake; there was the sudden crimson flame of a sumac tree; there were birds wheeling about the sky like blown leaves; and accompanying it all the cries of children at play and an excited barking of dogs, with the bass note of traffic, muffled and remote. Kensington Gardens was not the forest, but it was full of forest joys—great trees whose grey trunks were like cathedral pillars, dry twigs and leaves crunching underfoot, polished horse-chestnuts burst from their hard green cases, the twitter of birds, a pervading sense of peace. Jenny clung to her companion's hand and time flowed over her unmeasured. This, then, was happiness, just to be with someone you loved in peace, safe from the bruising fingers of the world. It was as simple as that.

After a while they left the gardens and lunched in a teashop full of steam and clatter. People looked at them, the tall man in his rough seaman's clothes, and the little pale untidy girl.

The man was attractive, the women thought; "unusual" was the word that came into their minds, for their conception of male good looks was derived from the films. The child could be his daughter, and yet somehow they felt that she wasn't, because the happiness that radiated from her, and the tenderness in the looks the man turned on her, were not as between father and daughter . . . With the speculation strangeness was released into the room full of steam, and the clatter of tea-cups and twittering chatter of what so-and-so said at the office, and the price of jumpers and the bargains at the sales, and boyfriends and films, and they thought it was because the man was "unusual" that they had to keep looking at those two, because there is never any name for the impact of strangeness on the commonplace, that *je ne sais quoi* that ripples the surface of everydayness and sets up unaccountable disturbances in the imagination and the blood.

Jenny and her companion returned to the Gardens after they had lunched, and the afternoon melted timelessly away. There was a golden and crimson sunset that gave a glory to the city streets and for a brief moment lifted the hearts of the scurrying crowds before they dived down underground into tubes or trooped into the hot airless dark of cinemas or scrambled for 'buses. It lifted them for a moment from their preoccupations— money, sex, food, clothes, emotional complications, domestic worries—gave them a moment of wonder and delight, lifted them, then, fading, dropped them back to earth again.

As the light faded the swans became luminously white, like drifts of snow on the steel-grey water.

"Ah, the pretty things," Jenny murmured, "the pretty, pretty things," and was reluctant to turn her back on them. It was easy to believe that when night came they would turn into princesses with streaming hair.

Dusk crept in a lavender mist in the glades of the tall trees, and the lights came out along the edges of the Gardens.

"I must take you back," the stranger said.

She made no protest, only clung silently to his hand. She was at peace now; nothing could invade the secret world she inhabited.

They returned to Paradise Court and fetched the cat, then went back under the tunnel to the other side of the river.

Back in her own world Jenny said, "Shall I be seeing you again soon?"

"I shall be here for a little while," he told her. "Come when you can."

"I could come to you instead of going to Mrs, Beadle's."

After all, what did she want with the old woman now? Now that she was sure of her power—that dark power which she had forgotten all the golden afternoon—and he was there, across the river?

"All right. If I'm not in the door will be undone."

They left it at that. He came almost to the flats with her, then bent and kissed her forehead, and almost before she had realised it was gone.

Chapter VI

Poison Ivy

After Jenny had gone Ivy sat down and had "a good cry", then she made herself a fresh pot of tea. She was so upset she felt as she told Joe afterwards, "downright ill". "I didn't ought to have said what I did to her," she brooded. "On her birthday, too! But she riles me so! Stopping out like that! At her age, a mere bit of a kid. Even if it was with old Ma Beadle it's not right, and I won't have it! She knows I won't have her going there, but she goes on defying me. I suppose she's gone straight back there now. Defying me."

All the same, as the day wore on she was resolved that if Jenny had gone back to Mrs. Beadle she would overlook it this once. After all it was her birthday. You don't want upsets on birthdays. Her birthday, and she hadn't given her the nice little suede handbag she'd got for her, with a little silk handkerchief from the boys tucked inside. She could take her prayer and hymn books in it to Sunday School; it would be handy, too, when she went to the pictures, for her hanky and her money. She was getting too big to tuck her hanky up her knickers. Soon, she supposed, she would refuse to go on wearing those kind of knickers anyhow; want something prettier, more grown- up; still, time enough for that when she left school and was earning her own money. Till then she would be a school-girl, a child, and dressed accordingly. Though of course she wasn't, strictly speaking, a child any more. Not for more than a year now. You'd never think such a little thin bloodless thing would mature early like that, as she said to Mrs. Grigg. But of course, as Mrs. Grigg pointed out, it was all to do with how you were made, and for all she was so thin and small Jenny always seemed older than her years.

She had been silly, really, she thought, after several cups of strong tea and a couple of aspirins, to fly off the handle at the kid like that. After all, thirteen was an awkward age, neither child nor grown-up. Jenny had been very rude and tiresome lately, but weren't they all, at that age? And she might be a lot worse; at least she didn't give her cause to worry about boys and that. She wasn't interested in them. In fact from the remarks she let drop when anyone had a baby she seemed to think the whole business disgusting. Well, it was in a way. Still, if everyone thought like that the world wouldn't go on. But better for a young girl to think like that at first, perhaps. Better than being like Mrs. Oliver's Doris, not yet sixteen and in the family way, and married to that bit of a boy of seventeen, a nasty little bit of work with plum-bloom suits and getting tight at the pub on Saturday nights as if he was a grown man. A fine husband for a young girl! "But what can you do, mate?" Mrs. Oliver had said. "He got her in the fam'ly way; it's up to him to keep her. *I* can't. If he comes in the worse for drink on a Saturday night and knocks her about it's her own look out. She should have thought of that before! Her father created something shocking when he knew how she was. 'You get her married in double-quick time,' he says to me. So what could I do?"

They'd had to go to court to get permission for two such very young people to get married, but the bench raised no difficulties when they knew the girl's condition, and for once Ivy had been on the side of the social workers and Miss Drew who had urged Mrs. Oliver against marrying her daughter up to such a worthless youth. Two wrongs would never make a right, they urged; because the girl had made one false step there was no good purpose served in pushing her into a marriage of which no good could come; they could arrange for the child to be adopted; then young Doris could make a fresh start; she would still be only sixteen when the baby was born.

But Doris's parents wouldn't hear of it. They had enough troubles without adding bastards to it. It made them look ridiculous as it was Mrs. Oliver and her daughter being in the fam'ly way at the same time.

So little Doris Oliver was married to young Freddie Reece, as worthless a lout as ever wore a plum-bloom suit and lounged on a street-corner on a Sunday afternoon chi-iking anything that went past in a skirt, a gutter-rat with a sewer mind, and Ivy Flower was upset more than on Doris's behalf. The whole business had an upsetting effect on her. At nights she could hear the young couple laughing in their room, so thin were the walls between; and sometimes she heard her crying and the young husband saying things that even too much drink couldn't excuse. Whether they were happy or quarrelling their proximity disturbed her. Ever since they had been married and the boy had come there to live she had been unable to get them out of her mind. Pushing a couple of mere children into bed together, that's what it was; Mrs. Oliver ought to be ashamed of herself. When she heard the girl laughing she would fill with an excited kind of anger; the brazen little hussy—even being in that condition couldn't cure her, it seemed. When she heard her being bullied by the boy she would fill with an excited kind of disgust and pity.

She tried to discuss it with Joe, but the subject bored him; he couldn't see why Ivy should get so excited over the business.

"It's their affair, ain't it?"

"He could have been let to marry her for the sake of the kid's name, but not pushed into bed with her like that—by her own mother of all people!"

"Natural they should want to be together, ain't it?"

"Not in children of their age!"

"Children or no, it seems they can make a baby!"

"Don't talk dirty!"

He laughed, dourly, "Jealous is what you are, it strikes me!"

Nice thing to say to me, his wife, Ivy thought resentfully, recalling the conversation. It had made her cry at the time. She seemed to have had a lot of fits of crying lately; her nerves were bad, what with young Jenny being so tiresome, and being so fidgeted by the newly-married young couple, and Joe seeming hardly to notice she was there, except to put the meals in front of him, and see he had a clean shirt to his back Sundays . . .

When Jenny came in from her rapturous afternoon she looked quite different from the girl who had walked out white-faced and tight-lipped that morning. It was not merely that, at the stranger's suggestion, before leaving Paradise Court that evening she had washed her face and combed her hair, pulled up her stockings and brushed some of the mud stains from them, but her whole expression was different; her eyes were soft, there was a little colour in her cheeks, her lips were parted; she looked—it came to Ivy in a flash of bewildered realisation—almost pretty.

It was tea-time and Ivy allowed Jenny to take her place at the table without comment. She brought the birthday present from the next room and laid it, wrapped in tissue paper, on Jenny's plate.

"Many happy returns," she said, belatedly.

Jenny unwrapped the present, fingered the little bag, opened it; caught the whiff of cheap scent on the gaudy little handkerchief. Ivy watched her, eagerly.

"The bag's from Dad and me," she explained, "The boys bought the hanky between them."

Jenny looked at Les, smiling faintly. "Thanks," she said.

"No expense spared," Les murmured in his cheeky way.

"It was my money too," Stan reminded her, a little sulkily, feeling that he was being left out.

"Thank you too," Jenny said. To Ivy she said nothing. She pushed the handbag and tissue paper aside and went on with her tea.

Ivy was hurt, but resolved not to show it. There'd been enough upset for one day. Then she noticed the coral bracelet. She reached out a hand and touched it.

"Who give you that?"

"A friend," Jenny answered, laconically, and Les said, "A boyfriend—what you think?"

"Shut-up," Jenny said, but without anger.

"You seem always to be getting bits of jewellery given you on your birthday—last year it was a gipsy give you a ring at the fair; the year before that a serpent bracelet. Where you bin all day?"

"Out!" Jenny answered.

"You don't say!" Les mocked.

"She thinks it's smart to be rude," Ivy said. She decided to let the matter drop. If she'd been a girl to run after boys there'd be some point in pursuing the matter; as it was she supposed she'd spent the day with old Ma Beadle and that it was she who had given her the bracelet and Jenny didn't like to own up to it . . . Let it go. Let everything go for the sake of peace and quiet. There'd been enough upset for one day.

Presently she said, "Your Auntie Nell's having a velveteen dress made for you, but it won't be ready till next weekend. She'll come in for tea to-day week, likely, and bring it with her."

The soft look left Jenny's face, like a light suddenly turned off in a room.

"I shan't be in."

Ivy stared at her, her temper rising.

"Oh! You won't indeed! And where d'you think you're gallivantin' off to with your auntie coming to tea? Who's give you permission to go out every Sunday I'd like to know."

Jenny stirred her tea in silence.

"Answer me!" Ivy commanded.

Jenny said in a low voice, "After what you told me this morning you can't stop me doing anything any more."

The boys gazed with inquisitive curiosity at Jenny.

"What's all this?" Les demanded.

"You mind your own business!" Ivy snapped.

Joe came in; Ivy went into the scullery to refill the kettle; the conversation lapsed. Ivy knew herself defeated.

After tea Ivy said, "I thought perhaps we might all go to the pictures, being as it's Jenny's birthday."

"That's an idea!" Les said, eagerly.

Jenny said, "I don't feel like the pictures. I want to go to bed early. I'm tired,"

"Don't you feel well?" Ivy demanded, suspiciously.

Jenny told her, brutally, "I could have sicked me heart up this morning, but I'm all right now. I just want to go to bed."

Ivy flushed slightly. Jenny seemed somehow to have got the upper hand now that she knew she wasn't her daughter.

It ended with Ivy taking the boys to the pictures, and Jenny sitting with the cat on her knees opposite Joe, belching and picking his teeth over the last unread scraps of the Sunday papers until "they", blessedly, opened once more. They never had much to say to each other, those two. For one thing Joe had not the slightest idea what you said to a girl of that age. He could talk to his boys, help them with their model aeroplanes and meccano sets, discuss the boys' brigade with Les, foreign stamps and marbles with Stan. He could talk to the other men at work, at the ex-service men's club, and in the pubs, about the political situation. He could even make sufficient conversation, of a purely domestic nature, with Ivy. He never made any attempt to talk to Jenny; he couldn't when she was a child, and he felt even more remote from it now that she was neither child nor adult. For one thing he didn't feel that any conversation was called for short of such things as "Chuck that box of matches over", or "What about making a cup of tea?"

For some time after the others had gone out that evening Jenny sat in silence, stroking the cat, looking into the fire. Then when Joe folded his paper, having exhausted its contents, and reached for his pipe on the mantelpiece, she said, slowly, "You're really my uncle, aren't you?"

He was startled. "What's all this? Who's been putting ideas into your head?"

"My Aunt Ivy told me this morning. Your sister's my mother!"

Joe was deeply embarrassed. What had Ivy wanted to go and tell the kid for? Everything was all right as it was.

He mumbled something about it being difficult for her not being married, "So we brought you up as ours." He looked at her bleakly. "I can't see what's the odds," he added.

Jenny half buried her face in the cat's neck.

"I liked her better than anyone. Now I never want to see her again."

Joe pressed the tobacco down in his pipe. "I can't see as it makes any odds," he repeated, helplessly.

Jenny looked up, her eyes hard, the look of hate on her face, thinning her mouth, tightening the skin across her cheek-bone.

"She disowned me," she said, passionately. "Would you like to be disowned by your own mother? And know that your father might be anyone of any number of men? It's horrible! People say that people like old Ma Beadle ought to be locked up, but it's people like my mother who ought to be locked up!"

"Go easy," Joe murmured, a glint in his eye, "Go easy."

Jenny got up, the cat on her shoulder. "It's horrible to know such a woman is your mother. It makes you wish you could die and be born again, of someone else. It makes you feel—" she hesitated a moment, then brought out the word, resolutely, "dirty".

Joe sprang up. "Here," he said, "get out. Get out of this before I put you out!"

Jenny stood motionless, her head high. "Go on, then, hit me! It won't be the first time! Your name is Flower, too. It's all the same bad blood."

Joe turned away. "Get out," he repeated, but this time sullenly, defeated.

In her room Jenny lay for a long time in the darkness without undressing, the cat clasped in her arms. She felt terribly tired. Presently she would sleep, and because it was Hallowe'en her spirit would leave her body and go to its final resting-place. In the morning she must try to remember where her spirit, free of the shameful, humiliating flesh, had gone; perhaps it would find *him* . . . There must be a way of letting your spirit free of the body at other times than Hallowe'en. If you were free of your body you could float above the world, go anywhere, you could move amongst the stars, or glide with the swans over the silver water; all the peace and the beauty of the world would be yours. You could find the green waters of the Gulf of Finland, and the deep Baltic forests . . . Your body would be left lying in the bed, but you would be far away, roaming the world. It wouldn't matter, then, that you were born of a whore, and that your father was the-devil-knows-who. Yours would be the world, and the kingdoms thereof. You would be one with your beloved, the Prince of Darkness . . .

(2)

In the room above the river Marian said, "It isn't any good, you see. I'm not apt for that willing suspension of disbelief you demand. Either you drop this mystery once and for all and tell me who you are, or it's Good-bye."

"But if I told you, you wouldn't believe me. You would simply say I was mad. It's much easier to make you believe a

248

lie. I could have told you a convincing lie long ago. I could tell you one now. You would be satisfied. But to use your phrase, I am not apt for the willing suspension of my pride."

She made a helpless gesture with her hands.

He sighed. "It couldn't be, of course. I always knew it couldn't be. The desire of the moth for the star. But it's more than that. The longing of Lucifer for that heaven he once knew, and to which he can never return."

There was a stricken silence between them, and then she said, "What about Jenny?"

"She knows everything now. Including the fact that her mother is Nell Flower, and her father unknown. She is filled with hate and horror and disgust of the flesh. But this afternoon we saw the courts of Heaven open in the sunset, and swans settling like drifts of snow on silver water. These things she carries in her too."

She stared at him, utterly dismayed.

"What's to become of her?"

"The end that was destined for her. Witches don't die in bed."

"Witches!" She was impatient.

He reminded her, "It's you who like the definitions and the labels!"

She said, resolutely, "In another year she'll be leaving school—getting a job. It will take her mind off all this business of her parentage, her ancestors. In the meantime, if you really care about her, you won't play on her adolescent susceptibilities—her imaginativeness—"

He sighed. "Lady, Lady, all these discussions, all these words going to and fro between us, and still we go round in circles! Must I remind you yet again that it's not a question—ever—of playing on the imagination, but of what the imagination responds to! If its response is to what is commonly called the supernatural it won't respond to what is called the natural. All these cut and dried phrases! Natural and supernatural—two sides of the same medal, two different kinds of imagination! Jenny Flower will follow her daemon—we can none of us do any more, or any less!"

"I shall go on trying to help her."

"It's no use. You can evoke nothing in her—except hostility."

She was silent, and then said at last, with difficulty, "It's good-bye, then—we've nothing more to say to each other."

"Yes. We shan't meet again. I'll remember your goodness—in hell."

She said, bitterly, "You keep it up, don't you? I suppose it's as good an act as any!"

"An act! How much simpler if it were!"

At the door he looked back and his smile was ironic.

"Good-bye, Marian, Maria. There's no need for regrets. We did storm the gates of heaven in our rare moments! Give the devil his dues!"

He blew her a kiss and was gone. She stood motionless listening to his step upon the stairs that he would never mount again. She wanted to tell herself "I am glad", but there was nothing in her heart or mind but the greyness and emptiness of a loss that was like death—*le petit mort*; but this time no resurrection . . .

Chapter VII

Night-Riding

Joe naturally assumed that it was Ivy who had told Jenny that Nell was her mother—he had in fact understood this from what Jenny had said. Ivy, tackled on the subject that night, after the boys had gone to bed, admitted that she had told the child that she was not her mother and that her mother was "no good", but swore to God she had not brought Nell's name into it. A moment's thought as to who might have told her and she decided that it could only be Mrs. Beadle. Nell had gone to the old woman when she was wanting to get out of the trouble in which she found herself; she might have told Mrs. Beadle that Jenny was her child, or the old woman might have guessed . . . Joe mumbled that he couldn't see that it mattered who had told the kid; the damage was done now. The kid was turned against Nell. Nell had better be told to keep away from the kid—anyhow for a bit. Ivy thought so too. She didn't want any "scenes". She wrote and asked Nell to come and see her one afternoon before the child came out of school; it was urgent, she wrote, "as Jenny now knows you're her mother and is turned against you".

Nell didn't answer the letter and she didn't come. She was "fed-up". She didn't doubt that Ivy had let the cat out of the bag in one of her fits of temper. As if life wasn't difficult enough, Nell thought. Ivy was a fool. She didn't feel like going round to listen to Ivy's explanations and excuses; nor did she feel like

251

facing Jenny's angry reproaches and accusations. If the kid was turned against her there was no point in seeing her any more. She'd send some clothes from time to time. She'd given up hope of reading the secret in the child's face, at least for the present. Perhaps in years to come, when Jenny was grown-up, she might run across her and read in the adult face what she had failed to read in the child's. You never knew. They were bound to meet again sometime. It was a deep conviction of hers that you met everyone again sooner or later, that you'd never seen the last of anyone, or of any place.

She had a brief discussion of the matter with Joe when he came into the Seven Bells during the week. They were agreed that Ivy was a fool, but that no good purpose was served either by discussing the matter with her or running into the child—not for a bit, anyhow. Nell and Joe reached this decision in a very few words. They felt that they understood each other. There was something in being brother and sister. The same blood flowed in them both.

Although Ivy mentioned that Nell wasn't coming to tea next Sunday after all, but was sending the dress, Jenny went out; she didn't trust Ivy; it was probably a trick to get her to stay in and meet her mother, she thought, and she was determined not to. As passionately as she had loved her she now hated her; as beautiful as she had seemed to her she now seemed horrible. She went instead to Paradise Court.

She became a familiar figure running up the bare, dirty stairs of No. 10 to the room at the top. Very often there was no one there; then she would wait a little while, looking at things, or merely lying on the bed, her shoes carefully removed so as not to soil the peacock-coloured cover, content merely to be there. If he didn't come she didn't fret; he would be there another time; he hadn't gone away—that was the important thing. Sometimes when she was running up the stairs Pete's black face would bob out from a ground-floor room.

"Yo' fren ain't there, Missy," he would tell her. "Just yo' come right in along this here tribe and take a bite to eat."

Pete's wife had no objection to the addition of the white child to her own brood. She was good-natured, easy-going, indifferent. Peter treated her as merely the eldest of a difficult crowd all of whom had to be bullied for their own good. The children "minded" him; but Lily took no more notice of his commands than they did of hers.

Jenny ate with them a good deal; as much as she liked anyone she liked them; they didn't worry her; they never questioned her comings and goings; she could be silent with them. Pete required nothing of her except that she should "eat up", and this she was always glad to do. Lily accepted her as she accepted any stray cat that came around; there was always milk and scraps for a stray cat, because she was "fond of animals"; there was always a smile and a meal for Jenny because she was fond of children. She was fond of them; she had no emotions stronger than that. She was twenty-seven and had been pregnant every year since she was seventeen—that there were seven instead of ten children was accounted for by two miscarriages and the fact that one child had died in early infancy—and bearing her brood seemed to have drained her of vitality. She was lily-pale and lily-languid, and as content in Paradise Court as a cow in a field. She often declared that Pete had enough energy for them all.

Pete knew his top-floor tenant as Mr. Smith. He didn't for a moment believe that that was his name, but he was not interested. So long as a man paid his rent regular one name was as good as another—yes, *sir*!

Gradually Paradise Court completely replaced Ropewalk Alley in Jenny's life. There was no longer any reason for going to see Mrs. Beadle. She felt that she had nothing more to learn from her, that she had now as much power as she would ever have, and that it would increase as she grew older. The lamp was now turned completely inwards; for a little while she had "gone out" to Marian Drew; and for a longer time to Nell Flower; now apart from the stranger there was no one, and she did not so much go out to him as draw him into herself, allow herself to be absorbed in him. Increasingly reality and fantasy fused, so that as time went on he was not more real to her in his room at Paradise Court or walking by the river with her, than he was when out of the intensity of her longing she recreated his presence in her room at home. In his physical presence she lived in a dream; in dreams she knew his physical presence. She no longer needed circles and invocations and crystals to summon him; he materialised now out of her passionate desire. Willing it she could see him quite clearly at the foot of her bed, smiling at her, holding out his arms to her, lifting her from her bed, carrying her away through the window, floating with her high up over the roof tops, holding her close as he had held her when he carried her through the darkening forest. It was immaterial how or where they met, whether on the materialist or the visionary plane; what was important was that they should meet, and she did meet him, and increasingly as adolescent yearning intensified, rode with him great storms that raged in space, knew with him the shadowless mountains of the moon.

When in a book of poems at school she came across "Kubla Khan" she experienced the authentic thrill of enchantment, and an exultant recognition. Who understood better than she the cry of "woman wailing for her demon lover"? Who better equipped to comprehend the building of a vision in a dream? Did she not in day-dreams and night-dreams build those domes in air—

That sunny dome! those caves of ice!
And all who heard should see them there.
And all should cry, 'Beware, beware!
His flashing eyes, his floating hair!

Weave a circle round him thrice,
And close your eyes with holy dread,
For he on honey-dew hath fed,
And drunk the milk of Paradise.

It was the only poem which had ever meant anything to her, and it fascinated her, endlessly. Mystic Xanadu became as real for her as Wapping Highway—in a sense it had greater reality for her, for she could walk Wapping Highway without being aware of it, without seeing it, but the moment her mind turned to Xanadu she saw that sunny dome, those caves of ice, and walked in those gardens "bright with sinuous rills, where blossomed many an incense-bearing tree". Knew the enchanted whole, (twice five miles of fertile ground, with walls and towers girdled round). The stranger had given her many strange faery kingdoms, but to this one she came alone, and in it she came and went alone, spending long hours in the caverns measureless to man, and wandering by the sunless sea. She had only to lie in the darkness at night, close her eyes, and summon the vision, and her spirit left the shameful and hated flesh and floated out through the window and up to the stars . . .

She did a good deal of sleep-walking at this time, but this she did not know. Ivy was afraid to lock her into her room for fear she should get out of the window on to the balcony and "catch her death of cold". She tried giving Jenny sedatives in her cocoa at bed-time, but it made no difference. Jenny still walked in her sleep, night after night, and in the morning was pale and shadowy-eyed. People walking in their sleep gave Ivy "the creeps". There began to grow up in her mind the idea that Jenny would be better away from home—which was self-deception, for what she meant was that she would be relieved to have Jenny away from home.

She need not have worried, as it happened, for soon after she left school Jenny ran away.

Chapter VIII

The Didiki

Jenny finished the Christmas term at school, and then, to everyone's astonishment, agreed without a murmur to Miss Drew's suggestion that she should go "anyhow for a little while", to help Mrs. Drew at the vicarage—an arrangement which seemed to Ivy "ideal"; the only alternative—since she wanted her away from home—was for Jenny to "go into service" with strangers, and it was a responsibility, sending so young a girl away from home to strangers. But at the vicarage she would not be amongst strangers; Miss Drew would be there during the holidays; she would be surrounded by "good influences".

Jenny had her own reasons for agreeing to the plan. In January Lucifer—for she now thought of him by no other name—was going away again, and he would be gone till the end of the year, or anyhow till next Hallowe'en. She had to fill in the time whilst he was away. But she had no intention of staying long at the vicarage; the vicarage was merely the gateway of escape. Actually she stayed longer than she had intended. She stayed until Easter. In those few months her conduct was exemplary. She washed dishes, peeled potatoes, wheeled the baby in the garden, did mending, ran errands down to the stores, and even helped the vicar weed the garden. She remained as on her first visit, unknowable, untouchable. She never smiled, except sometimes when she was playing with Satan—she had refused to leave home without him; she was allowed to have him in her room at the vicarage provided she kept the door closed and only the top of the window open. She spoke only when spoken to—except to crazy old Miss Ellswood, but of this the Drews were unaware. Old Miss Ellswood was a substitute for Mrs. Beadle. Her sister had now been "put away", and she was lonely; Jenny visited her when she could and managed to spend some part of almost every day in her dirty kitchen, munching seed cake, stroking Satan, and letting the old woman babble on. She had nothing to say of any interest to Jenny, but the girl felt at home in that dirty kitchen with the mad old woman. Miss Ellswood did not seem to her in her madness more crazy than anyone else, and she was a great deal more companionable. In the girl the old woman found an unwearying and uncomplaining audience for her wrongs, which were mostly imaginary; she had a persecution mania; everyone was suspect, everyone in league against her; everyone was in league with the Devil . . . everyone except the pale wizened little witch who worshipped him. But Jenny did not speak about herself; the old woman's monologues did not encourage conversation, and Jenny was quite content to sit enclosed in silence. It was not a withdrawn silence such as enclosed her at the vicarage; it was as though she let down the drawbridge from the secret tower in which she dwelt, but was not concerned to cross it; the old woman crossed it and Jenny sat within, listening and not-listening, but content. Here was somebody who demanded nothing of her; someone outcast from other people, cut off from them by her strangeness, and therefore like herself under the protection of the dark angels of the abyss.

Everyone at the vicarage made resolute efforts to break through the shell with which Jenny surrounded herself. They were all resolutely friendly, resolutely patient. Mrs. Drew treated her as a child and gave her sugar and butter with which to make toffee, and presented her with a hand-painted cardboard egg containing marzipan eggs at Easter; Gwen treated her as an adult and took her walks with her, and on occasional shopping excursions into the town; the twins when they came home determinedly took her dark silent presence for granted and greeted her with cheerful affection; the vicar tried all tactics from ignoring her to booming at her, demanding hadn't she a tongue in her head, and they all might have been addressing themselves to a stone image.

"She's a strange little thing," Mrs. Drew would say. "One never seems to break through to her, try as one may."

"You try too hard, Katie," the vicar roared at her. "Mistake to with children. Ignore them. Let them come to you. They will in the end. They're like wild animals—no confidence in humans. You've got to gain their confidence. Can't do it by coaxing—makes them suspicious."

These principles, so sound in general, did not, however, work with Jenny. She was well aware that they were all trying hard to win her round, and she had no intention of being won. She despised them all. Miss Ellswood had the immense virtue of accepting her as she was, wrapped in her silence.

At Easter, when Marian came home for the holidays, Jenny wrote to Mrs. Beadle and instructed her to send a telegram calling her home. She composed the wording herself— "Return immediately, good job awaiting you here, Ma." Mrs. Beadle carried out the instructions and Jenny showed the telegram to the Drews.

"I'll have to go," she said. "I expect it's that clerical job in the office of Dad's warehouse. He always said there might be a chance of getting me in later on."

Marian was inclined to keep Jenny at the vicarage until there had been some correspondence with Mrs. Flower, but both the vicar and Mrs. Drew were opposed to this.

"If they've taken the trouble to send a wire they want her at once," the vicar roared. "Probably want to start her immediately after the Bank Holiday."

"It's a pity," Marian said. "Just as she was settling in here."

"She wasn't settled in," the vicar shouted, a little impatiently. "She was merely putting up with it."

"Of course that sleep-walking is a worry," Mrs. Drew said. "Perhaps it's best she should be in her own home. If anything should happen to her here—"

Ivy had said nothing about the sleep-walking when she had accepted Miss Drew's offer. It seemed a pity to risk losing a good chance of settling Jenny away from home, and perhaps, she salved her conscience, she wouldn't do it away from home . . .

The day after the telegram arrived Jenny was taken to the station with her small suitcase of clothes and put on the London train; she had to change a few stations down the line. She changed at this station, but not to get into another train. She walked away into the deep woods resolutely, with the air of one in familiar country.

A week or so later Mrs. Beadle posted in London a letter to Mrs. Drew purporting to come from Mrs. Flower. The letter was to thank Mrs. Drew for all she had done for Jenny and to say that she had arrived back quite safe and settled down in the warehouse office. The Drews who had never seen Ivy's hand-writing accepted the letter in good faith. From time to time Jenny wrote to Ivy to say she was quite well and all right.

All that spring, summer, autumn, Jenny lived with a family of Didiki in the woods. These people, despised by the true Romanies, are neither tramps nor gipsies. When they can get derelict cottages cheaply enough they live with roofs over their heads, and any house they inhabit immediately becomes a slum. When there are no such places to be had they put up rough shacks in the woods, and shelters—they are hardly tents—of sacking and old rags; they usually have a pony and cart or two, and people say, "Look—gipsies!" but though they have gipsy blood they are not gipsies, any more than the caravan nomads are gipsies, and these people are a grade lower even than the caravan dwellers. They live as best they may; the women make clothes-pegs and send the children into the villages and towns with them; they hawk bunches of primroses, "pussy-willow", cowslips, bluebells, in season; they tell fortunes at fairs and race-meetings, and because they are addicted to the wearing of beads, brass ear-rings, and gaudy scarves, people take them for gipsies and give to them where they would not give to the ordinary tramp or beggar. They are a wild, rough people; the men poach rabbits—and anything else they can get; the women work an effective line with sprigs of white heather and babies that may or may not be their own at their breasts. They spend their lives dodging the police and game-keepers, and they are always on the move; even those who live in houses never stay long, and "shooting the moon" is a common practice with them.

Jenny had no difficulty in getting herself accepted as one of themselves; she was dirty and unkempt enough, and there was a hardness about her which commended her to them. She gave the family to which she attached herself her few clothes and the few shillings wages she had brought with her from the vicarage. She told them she had been working as a servant and had run away; that her home was in London, but that she wasn't going back because her parents beat her. When they found she could tell fortunes with cards, read hands, and knew all the formulae of magic, they were delighted. She needed very little coaching from them to become a great success at fairs and race-meetings; she gave racing "tips", read, palms, sold bunches of wild flowers, and sometimes simply begged, whining and wheedling with the true professional touch, "Spare something for the poor gipsy girl, kind lady! Kind gentleman! Cross the gipsy's palm with silver and you'll have good luck . . . " And with her bracelets and the cat's eye ring, and a gaudy silk scarf round her neck, she looked the part.

Through Herefordshire, Worcestershire, Warwickshire, Gloucestershire, Shropshire, she went with this family who called themselves Robbins. The family consisted of an elderly couple, their son Jim and his wife Sue, and their four young children, and a younger son, of about seventeen, Davy. The boy was dark and slim, with an insolent kind of good looks; there was something sly about him. He looked curiously at Jenny when she first joined them, but after the first few days seemed not to notice her. He was a "handy" poacher; he was also quick-fingered at fairs and in the matter of street-stalls. Jim was thick-set, brutal-looking, and a bully. He hawked logs from his pony-cart when he could get them, or went round collecting "old clo' ". He accepted Jenny because he saw in her an asset. Everything she earned he took off her with the same matter-of-factness that he took the money from the clothes' pegs, the begging, the fortune-telling, that constituted his wife's trade. The old couple did very little; the old woman cooked the food and cleaned the plates and occasionally washed a few rags in a stream or pond; the old man collected firewood and made clothes' pegs; the boy was the most energetic; it was chiefly his efforts that provided things for the pot. Sue was lazy and lecherous and good-natured. She was also extremely dirty, and her rags of clothes were safety-pinned together. Her brown face had a weather-beaten look, the skin tight-drawn across high cheekbones. She had blue eyes and brown hair that when clean was probably golden and which now showed golden streaks. She had a small tight mouth and her eyes were crafty. When she laughed, which she did readily, she revealed magnificent small white even teeth. She wore a number of gold rings on her dirty fingers and there was a jingle of silver bracelets at both wrists when she moved her hands. She was good-looking, in her unkempt, animalish, fashion. She was friendly towards Jenny, even affectionate, but Jenny hated her and shrank from her; for her she exuded everything that was horrible; she was of the flesh, and the fact was emphasised by her blatant pregnancy. The sound of her voice and the man's together in their ramshackle tent would fill Jenny with loathing.

Jenny stayed with the Robbins not so much because she liked the life as because she preferred it to life at the vicarage or at home, and she had somehow to get through the months of waiting. She was often cold and wet and hungry, and in her moments of awareness of Sue and Jim in relation to each other, full of bitterness and hate, but she was able to get away a good deal, into the forests, on her own, her cat in her arms, and then—and then only—she would feel at peace. Then there would be the feeling of the Dark Forest all round her again; the Dark Forest in which Lucifer had first come to her, with horns on his head; in which she had first heard the screech-owl and first known the fear and excitement of great mysteries.

In all that time she made no attempt to summon Lucifer. He had said he would return, and implicitly she believed him. She had only to live through the days till then, and she was living through them in a way which suited her well enough. She had the forests; she was able to be alone—she was free; no one ever required her to wash, or to comb her hair; no one tried to win her over or induce her to play with the children; and there was a certain malicious satisfaction in all the cheating and begging from all the respectable people who lived in neat houses, wore shoes to their feet, and were so clean and tidy. You were the rubbish, the riff-raff, the outcast, but it was you who won. they who were fooled . . . Everything that was anti-social in her responded to the life of the Didiki; the life offered outlet for all her contempt of the good decent people, the people of Miss Drew's world, the people who were on the side of the angels; she had her revenge on them every time one of them, out of kindness, crossed the "poor gipsy's" palm with silver in return for the lies she told them.

In the autumn the Robbins headed for London; you were better off in towns for the winter, they said. War and the black-out overtook them. It was a cold and wet and miserable trek, ending in a Mitcham slum, in a house already overcrowded with people of their own kind. There was only one room available and they "dossed" down on mattresses on the floor. It had no significance for Jenny that Davy laid his mattress next to hers. She never thought about him; he was merely one of the family. Even when in the middle of the night she felt his hands on her she thought for a moment he had merely thrown his arm over her in his sleep. Then suddenly she realised his intention and sprang up. He tried to pull her down to him and she drove her teeth into his hand. He released her with a yell. There was a general waking, a cursing and swearing; someone struck a match. She was sobbing her dry sobs, full of hate and fear and revulsion. The old woman called her to her side and she crept under the cover beside her. The old woman soothed her. Sue laughed. Davy went out to rinse his bleeding hand under the tap in the scullery adjoining . . . The family settled down again.

In the morning Jenny put on her shoes; washed her face and hands; forced a bit of broken comb through her matted hair, took half a crown out of Jim's pocket hanging on a nail from the door, grabbed the cat, and when they were all occupied one way or another slipped out.

She found a tram that would take her almost to the door of Paradise Court.

Chapter IX

Return to Paradise

Pete stuck his head out of the scullery as Jenny entered
the dark narrow hall of No. 10.

"He ain't back yet, Missy. Any day now. But you
come right in along this here tribe—I'se just frying the Sunday
sausages this minute."

So it was Sunday. Until then the days of the week had had
no names.

She went into the stone-floored scullery and watched Pete, a
large faded blue apron tied round him, frying the sausages. By
the copper Lily, with a dreamy air, was bathing the youngest
child in a tin bath.

Jenny said, "I want to ask you if I can stay here. I'll work,
I'll scrub out all the lodgers' rooms and do their washing and
anything you like, only I don't want to go home. I've been away
the last six months—in the country."

Pete jabbed a sausage and turned it over. "They sure is
done to a turn," he exclaimed with satisfaction, then looked
at Jenny.

"Sure, you can stay! But there's been a party here inquiring
about you—it seems like you was missed, sister!"

Jenny asked quickly, "Who was it?"

Pete looked inquiringly at Lily.

"Old Ma Beadle," Lily replied. "Everyone knows her. The
old girl who hangs out in Ropewalk Alley. It seems your ma

was round there asking for you, and old Ma Beadle come round here thinking you might be here—on account of him." She jerked her head to the ceiling. "It was a while back now," she added. "During the summer."

"I'll go round after breakfast," Jenny murmured.

Mrs. Beadle's front door was open as usual and the old woman was sitting beside the range, a cup of tea in her hand, the cats brushing themselves against her legs, exactly as Jenny had last seen her.

"Where've you sprung from?" the old woman demanded as Jenny came into the room.

"I got back last night," Jenny told her. "The people I was with have come back for the winter. I didn't want to stop with them any longer. I went to Pete's and he said you'd been round there in the summer, asking for me. What happened?"

"Your ma wrote to the vicarage several times and got no reply, so she went round to see Miss Drew at the school. Then the cat was out of the bag."

"Are you talking about my mother, or my Aunt Ivy?"

"Your Aunt Ivy! She's more your ma than the other one. Your Aunt Ivy, then! A fat lot the other one cares where you get to."

"What happened?"

"Your ma—I mean your Aunt Ivy come round here asking if I knew your whereabouts. It seems Miss Drew put it into her head to come and ask me. Miss Drew said the police should be informed—but Joe wouldn't hear o' that. Good riddance to bad rubbish is what he said!"

Jenny's lips tightened. "What about her?"

"She was upset. Cried. Said she'd always tried to be a mother to you and this was how you rewarded her. Bad blood would out, she said."

"I'll go and see her, when he's out at the pub to-night." Jenny said. "I don't want her nosing round again. She can know where I am and make up her mind to it. I left a few clothes there and

I could do with them. I've only got what I stand up in. He ought to be back soon. It must be getting near Hallowe'en—"

"We're a week off it. Have some tea?"

Jenny shook her head, but she seated herself opposite the old woman and held out her hands to the fire. Satan settled in her lap purring.

"Have you seen my precious mother lately?"

"She's been here a few times—bringing friends for fortune telling, and other things. She'd heard you was missing, but seemed to take it light. Said you'd turn up again. The proverbial bad penny, she said. Old soldiers, and all that. You know how she is."

Jenny lips formed into a thin narrow line. She said nothing, but sat caressing the cat with long smooth strokes.

"He looks none the worse for his wanderings," Mrs. Beadle observed. "He's a fine-looking creature."

Jenny lifted her head. "What would you expect?" she demanded. "You don't suppose my familiar would be a miserable mangy thing, do you?"

She looked round the grimy kitchen and was suddenly filled with a longing for the room of the peacock bedspread, and the tarnished dragon.

"I must go," she said. "I'll look in sometime. So long."

Back at No. 10 Paradise Court she went straight up to the beloved room. She looked with love at the bedspread, the curtains, the dragon embroidery across the door, and then stopped short. In the middle of the chest-of-drawers, amongst the jade and amber and ivories was a little photograph of Marian Drew in a leather frame.

Jenny stood staring, her lips tight, her eyes seeming to sink into her head, the skin of her face to be stretched more tightly over the cheekbones. Then she took the picture into her hands and peered down into the gentle eyes and spat on the faintly smiling mouth.

She dropped down on to her knees, crushing the photograph in her hands, her breath coming in quick sobbing gasps. She pressed the cat against her body, and the photograph against the cat's body. She was ice-cold but she did not shiver.

She repeated the conjuration for the day and invoked the Evil Spirits.

"She must go away," she whispered, over and over again, "She must go away and never come back."

Then for the first time she repeated the Lord's Prayer backwards and everything grew black. She had a momentary awareness of the rush of blood to the back of her neck and of a feeling of intense sickness before she fainted.

When she came to she was lying where she had collapsed on the floor. She sat up feeling weak and ill; then she saw the photograph in its leather frame on the floor, and remembered. She got to her feet, picked up the photograph and replaced the picture on the chest-of-drawers. Then took the cat in her arms and went downstairs to sit beside the fire. She sat so close to the fire that the damp of all her nights in the woods and under hedges steamed out of her clothes, yet still she felt cold.

She did not go out till the evening. The blackout did not trouble her; she had a cat's eyes in the dark. On the way to her old home she pushed open Miss Drew's front door and put the cat on the stairs, pulling the door to after her.

At the flats Ivy opened the door a crack, anxiously; it would be a warden about the blackout, she thought.

Jenny said, impatiently, "You can open the door—it's me," and pushed her way in to the lighted room that was momentarily blinding after the darkness outside.

Ivy stared at her in amazement.

"Yes, it's me all right," Jenny said, in her short, bitter way. "Are you alone?"

"Yes. Dad's at the Bells. The boys are in next door." She looked Jenny up and down, shocked by her unkempt appearance.

"What've you been up to all this time? You look dirty enough for a gipsy!" The old familiar nagging tone was back in her voice. "I've been worried to death," she added. "I wonder you got the face to turn up again! You're filthy dirty—"

Jenny said, curtly, "You needn't worry; I'm not stopping. I came to get those few clothes I left behind. I got nothing but these. And to tell you I'm living with a family over at Rotherhithe—working for my keep. Later on I might go and work in a café. Anyhow I'm not coming back here. I just want my things."

Ivy went white with anger. "A bit of a kid like you—not fifteen yet—dictating what you'll do—"

"You don't want me here, and I don't intend to be here, so we'll cut all that out. My things still in my room, or have you traded them for a pot of ferns?"

"They're still in your room. There's that velvet dress and your winter coat—"

"I don't want the dress. You can send it back where it came from."

"It's never been worn," Ivy protested.

"And never will be, unless you give it away or wear it yourself. Have I got any underclothes?"

"You took them all with you. I could let you have some old ones of mine to make do with."

She followed Jenny into the little room. She said, "The water's hot if you'd like a bath. You could change and leave your dirty things here—"

Jenny had the bath and washed her hair. When she was dressed in the clean clothes she went back to the living room and knelt in front of the fire to dry her hair. Ivy picked up a towel.

"I'll dry it for you."

Jenny submitted, and suddenly the tears welled up in Ivy.

She said, in a choked voice, "I don't know why it should all turn out like this—I did my best. I always wanted a little girl—"

She broke off, laid aside the towel, and fumbled for a handkerchief in her belt.

Jenny picked up the towel and went on with the drying.

She said, briefly, "You adopted the wrong kid, that was all."

Ivy blew her nose.

"I'll get you a comb," she said, and went out.

She came back with the comb and began to comb out the knots in Jenny's hair, as gently as possible.

"This is still your home," she said, at last. "There's no need to live away. I'd be prepared to try again, if you would. P'raps now you're older—"

"No," said Jenny. "You mean well, but it's no good."

Ivy went on combing, sniffing occasionally, and presently Jenny said, "It'll do now," and got up.

Ivy looked at her. She looked much older than six months ago, she thought, and she had such a hard look; not like a young girl. But they were all a bit like that nowadays, the young girls, all a bit hard. Look at the one next door—a mere kid, but a married woman, and hard as nails.

"What made you go off?" Ivy asked.

"I got fed up."

"Where did you go?"

"I lived with the Didiki in the Wyre Forest at first."

"Didiki? That's kind of gypsies, isn't it? Very rough . . . "

"That's it," She looked at Ivy derisively. "Anything else you'd like to know?"

"Not if you don't want to tell it," Ivy answered, bitterly.

"That's all right, then. I'll go."

"You could have a bit of supper," Ivy suggested. "The boys will be in soon. You might like to see them. You used to be fond of them, especially Les—"

"I thought they were my brothers."

"They're the same kids, whoever they are!"

"It's not the same for me. They're nothing to do with me."

"You're hard, Jenny. I don't know why you should be so hard—"

"Don't you?" Her smile was as derisive as her voice. She picked up the bundle of clothes.

"Perhaps you'll look in sometimes," Ivy hazarded.

"I shouldn't think so."

When she had gone Ivy sat down in the chair beside the fire and had a good cry. Jenny's quick light step went pattering away along the corridor, down the steps, and across the yard.

Out in the black darkness Jenny had a feeling of "purification". She felt more than physically clean; she felt clean inside.

She stopped at Miss Drew's front door and put her head into the darkness and called her cat. It came running to her down the stairs and she took it up into her arms, rubbing her chin against his silky head. Darling Satan; darling, darling Satan . . .

(2)

When Marian got in from the children's club that evening she found a black cat in her room. It reminded her of Jenny's cat. When she sat down it sprang up into her lap. She fondled it, absently. She had a raging headache and a sore throat and ached all over. It felt like 'flu. There was a lot about, and she couldn't afford to have it; there was so much to do. She gave the cat a saucer of milk, heated herself some soup, took some aspirins, and went to bed with a hot-water bottle. She left the door open so that if the cat should suddenly remember its way home it could go. She felt she could do no more about it, or herself. She felt ill. She felt quite extraordinarily ill.

She passed a feverish night and felt even more ill in the morning, but was determined to go to school. It looked bad, she thought, just to ring up and say you couldn't come. In any case she would have to get up and dress to go out and telephone; might as well go on to the school once you were up and out. She got to the school, but came home at mid-day.

On the way she posted a note to her club colleagues to say that she was afraid she'd got 'flu and wouldn't be able to go to the club for a few days. She was alone all that afternoon and night with a high temperature.

She thought, "One could die like this and no one would know." She felt a little sorry for herself. After all, people did die of 'flu; any number of them. Well, as well die in bed of 'flu as be caught by a bomb and die under a heap of rubble in the coming air-raids. Because of course they were coming; it was only a matter of time, and everyone knew what to expect, because they had all seen what had happened in Spain. There had been Guernica. There would be Guernicas all over England. They would be safe at the vicarage; that was something to know your loved ones were safe; the tide of war would never flow as far as that. Though spiritually it had already reached there, filling her father with a sense of the futility of trying to let in that little light he counted so precious; and as the war progressed, intensifying in savagery, destroying all values, it would be harder than ever for him to believe, as he had to believe, that man was capable of salvation . . . Once you ceased to believe that a light went out in you, the light by which you lived. But the lights were going out, one by one, in people, and all over the world . . . It was getting darker everywhere; in this room, everywhere in the world . . .

Miss Hawkins and Miss Pritchett came to see her in the morning, with a doctor. She was taken to hospital by ambulance in the afternoon; she could not stay there with no one to look after her, they pointed out when, feebly, she protested at the "fuss".

Later in the day Jenny called round; she wanted to know; she had to know. The front door was closed, and whilst she was banging on it a woman came out from the fried fish shop next door and said that if she wanted Miss Drew she'd bin took off to hospital that afternoon, by ambulance. Her friends had come round with a doctor that morning. They said it was 'flu, but more likely it was pneumonia . . .

Jenny buried her face in the cat's neck. "She mustn't come back," she whispered, passionately, "She mustn't come back!"

(3)

Somewhere near at hand someone was singing "Adeste Fideles", a young clear voice, pure as a bell—

O come all ye faithful.
Joyful and triumphant,
O come ye, O come ye to Bethlehem;
Come and behold Him
Born the King of Angels,
O come let us adore Him,
O come let us adore Him—

Then there was the great triumphant swell of the organ, mounting to the beams of the little old church where the birds nested, high up to the old beams, to the great cathedral arches of the trees . . . in the forest, full of summer and the twitter of birds.

"We did have our moments. We did storm the gates of Heaven. Give the Devil his dues . . . "

Ah yes, give the Devil his dues; there are the infernal as well as the divine miracles. The two sides of the same medal; two different kinds of imagination . . . two versions of the same hymn.

The Queen was in her counting-house,
Counting out her money—

It was David singing, of course; David with that catch of laughter in his voice . . . and that was Charlie One coming in with a roar.

Blasphemy? Ah no. What was sacred was inviolable. There were things at which even Richard with his gay sophistication did not laugh; his heart was amongst the cherry orchards however many continental bars he propped up, however many cafés he sat at, being cynically amusing about his vicarage background. He had to come home when the cherry orchards were in flower, though spring was beautiful in Paris and Vienna, and the apple-blossom at Heidelberg was world-famous. Is it really you, Dick? Have you really torn yourself away from Montparnasse? But Paris is emptying, of course. The war is coming. There are waiting-lists for passages to America; everyone going home, hurrying before the gathering storm, hurry home. You too, Marian. Marian, Maria. No, no, that was all last year, the fatal Munich year that merely postponed everything now the war was already here; the lights had already gone out and the world was plunged in darkness.

Are you really Lucifer, Prince of Darkness? Prince of this world and Son of the Morning—the opposite sides of the same medal. But one learns wisdom too late. One means so well and does so badly; always this sense of personal failure. Jenny—what is to become of her? If she follows her daemon it will lead her to the Devil. But they say the Devil loves his own, and she needs love; she needs it so terribly . . . and the Devil is all a matter of definition.

Someone crying. Why should anyone cry when it is so peaceful here under the trees; under the cherry-trees—

Trees where you sit
Shall crowd into a shade . . .

No need to cry; no need to worry; you have only to suspend disbelief, and believe in magic, just for to-night, and love wraps you round like a benediction, in the fading light, the gathering shade . . . into which one sinks, so tired . . . so gratefully . . . and there is only the river, flowing past, flowing past . . .

(4)

The woman from the fried fish-shop said, "The 'ole neighbourhood susscribed for a wreath. Lovely it was! She was very popular with the mothers as well as the children. They 'ad the prefect from each of the senior classes at the school to march in procession, and that nice Mr. Wilson from the Sunday School brought 'is church-lads along, all in uniform. In the church they played a Christmas hymn—her fav'rite I s'pose it was. Her family requested it. Her father's a clergyman. He seemed very cut up, poor gentleman. But they didn't none of them wear black. Seems funny, don't it? Her two sisters was there in all the colours of the rainbow. A red scarf round 'er neck one of them wore, if you please! And the two children of the other one running about amongst the tombstones whilst the coffin was bein' lowered! You'd think coming of a family to do with the church they'd a bin brought up to know better, wouldn't you? It's one of these new modern ideas, I s'pose, like not bindin' the mothers up after a confinement, and all this imminising they go in for in the schools nowadays. Meself I like a funeral to *be* a funeral, with proper funeral horses and plumes and deep mourning and no colour in the wreaths. Still, it was a nice touch to 'ave the church-lads there and to play the Christmas hymn, though it's a way off Christmas yet . . . Yes, Mister, the Church of St. John down by the river. You won't 'ave no trouble in findin' the grave—it's piled that 'igh with wreaths . . .

But nothing from me, Marian, Maria. Piled high on your grave beside the river are all the flowers I never gave you. Did you find, at the end, that willing suspension of disbelief—that ultimate belief in the power of the fatal lightning, accept that hell no less than heaven has its miracles? Did you find that atonement, that at-one-ment you sought? At the end did you hear the bells of lost Atlantis ringing under the sea, Marian, Maria? Do you know that they buried you on a witches' sabbath, the unhallowed festival of Hallowe'en, the day on which we met and on which we parted? Was it all nothing but coincidence after all?

(5)

She waited in his room. She lit the oil-stove and drew the curtains that were now lined with black material. She knew that he would come. To-night he would come, and he could not bring *her* with him, nor could he go to her. Not even in death could he reach her, because hers was the Kingdom of Heaven; body and spirit she was gone from him, forever. She lay beside the river but she would never again see the first primroses pushing up in the long grass on the unkept graves. You had seen the wreaths piled high on her grave and they were the wreaths of your triumph. You were fifteen and in full command of Satanic power. And now you had used your power to the utmost; now you were damned beyond all redemption. But you were triumphant, and you were free. You had known the scourge, and this, now, was your crown.

Her hands went up and down the cat's smooth black back in long caressing movements, almost voluptuously. She had brushed her hair and put on the red dress. It was faded and stained but it was her best. She had tied a red ribbon round her head and wore all her jewellery. In a glass on the mantelpiece was a red tulip and a white carnation she had stolen from the grave.

The moment he came into the room she saw by his face that he knew. He looked grey and haggard. He stood a moment at the door looking at her, and she was suddenly afraid. His face without tenderness or light looked lean and wolfish. But he said, as usual, "Hullo, witch."

Then he saw the flowers on the mantelpiece. He asked sharply, "Where did you get those?"

"From her grave. I went this afternoon, after the funeral."

"You knew she was ill?"

"Yes."

"Did you pray for her?"

"Yes—backwards!" The words were out before she was aware of what she had said.

He gave her a long look.

"So you are a witch, after all?"

She tossed her head, arrogant. "Did you ever doubt it?"

He sat down beside the oil-stove and did not answer. She came over and sat on the floor, her head against his knees and sighed, contentedly. He laid a hand on her head. After a moment he asked, "What have you been doing all this year?"

She told him, and concluded, "And now I'm living here, helping in the house."

She looked up at him. "Now the war's come you'll stay here, won't you?"

"Is it likely that when hell's let loose I'll be out of it?"

"Pete says the loss of merchant ships is terrible."

He made no comment and they sat in silence for a while, then suddenly he put a hand in a pocket and brought out a silver girdle and dropped it down over her shoulder into her lap.

"I remembered your birthday," he said.

The belt was of chased silver, with an elaborate jewelled buckle.

"It's Caucasian," he told her. "The buckle was designed to carry a dagger."

She raised herself and fastened the belt round her thin waist.

"It's beautiful," she said rapturously, then still kneeling, seized his hands and pressed them to her face.

"I love you," she said, then looked up at him, her eyes shining, her face soft with happiness. "Now we have only each other, haven't we?"

He gave her a long, curious look, then repeated, "Yes—now we have only each other," and his tone was expressionless.

She sighed contentedly and sunk down against his knees.

He sat stroking her hair, absently, staring hollow-eyed into space.

Chapter X

Inferno

He went away again in a few weeks, but now Jenny did not fret about his absences; she was like a contented wife who knows that her man will return in due season. She lived under the same roof; she could go into his room and finger his possessions, assuring herself of his living reality in the flesh. And at nights she could ride the sky with him, to the utmost ends of the earth.

Sometimes when she heard Pete talking of the losses to merchant-shipping caused by U-boats and mines she would have momentary fears, since he was flesh for her as well as spirit and she loved him in the flesh, longing, like any woman for a lover or a loved husband, for the sound of his step upon the stair, the feel of his hands touching her hair, for his hands to press against her cheeks, against her lips, for the sound of his voice, and his tall dark presence that seemed to fill the whole world. In the flesh she worshipped him, in an asexual passion of loving. But in the spirit he was the Prince of the World, Son of the Morning, the Day-Spring from on high. In him in the spirit all mystery was vested, all the splendours of infernal power. That, when he chose, he should assume the shape of man and dwell amongst men was the counterpart of the accepted miracle of Jesus taking unto himself flesh to dwell amongst us. Strange to accept the miracles of heaven and deny the miracles of hell. Now she lived with him in two worlds, the material, and that strange phantom world beyond the bounds of the material, that invisible world for which there is no name, since to call it fantasy, or dream, or imagination, does not suffice, emotion being involved in experience of it, and its phenomena charged with such meaning that the whole texture of the real world is changed, such commonplace things as a curtain blowing out in the wind, or a second glance from a stranger in a crowd, becoming endowed with diabolic significance, exciting, terrifying, sinister, or possessed of a fatal and terrible beauty.

That he should come and go seemed most natural to her. That he should have any time for her at all when the whole world was his kingdom was the miracle of miracles, source of inexpressible pride and the utmost humility. That in his physical self he should go away in ships also seemed most natural, since he was the eternal traveller. Of his material activities she thought scarcely at all; the books in his room were merely the symbols of his learning, as the jades and ivories and ambers and Oriental embroideries were of his wanderings. She was herself very little concerned with the material world. With the Didiki she had known cold, hunger, discomfort, but it had all mattered very little to her; she could go without food without much hardship, was indifferent to what she ate, and had no feeling for comfort. Living with Pete and his family she knew hard work, squalor, discomfort, but as experience it was much less real to her than the nights when with her cat clasped against her thin body she experienced an ecstasy of the spirit known only to saints and demons. Scrubbing floors, washing clothes, waiting her turn in stinking fried fish shops, eating coarse food, lying on a hard bed, immersed in the grunt and sweat of Paradise Court—all this was so much trivialia; as experience it did not count; what counted was that release of spirit into invisible worlds, in which experience was so intense that it was absolute. Then you knew the meaning of Absolute Power; then, your being fused with that of the Prince of Darkness, you were the equal of God.

At fifteen she was completely enclosed in her invisible world; all the years had led up to this; the lamp of the spirit instead of shining out more and more as she passed from childhood to adolescence was turned more and more inward. In another they would have said of her that she was "possessed". From this invisible world she emerged only when her lord—for so she thought of him—returned; and then she emerged only as far as his shadow reached.

Once she saw her mother walking in the street, tippeting along on her high heels, slender legs flashing in their sheer stockings, her skirt about her knees, her shoulders rich with furs, her lips bright as poppies. She was absorbed in her thoughts and, on the other side of the road, did not see Jenny. Jenny looked hard at her, and if Nell had returned the look Jenny would have spat; but Nell did not break out of her reverie and went on her way unaware of her daughter's hatred and contempt. It was a pale cold Sunday morning in the early spring of 1940. Nell was no longer at the Seven Bells. She had been "directed" into a factory and worked on aeroplane parts. She didn't mind; the money was good, and it wouldn't last for ever. Going into the Bells on the other side of the bar gave you another angle, so to speak. And you got Sundays off. Poor old Joe was sweating on the top line waiting to be called-up. Good thing, too. Get him away from Ivy's nagging tongue for a bit . . . Thus Nell on her way to catch a 'bus for the West End, unaware of the hate being directed at her from across the road. That was the last time Jenny saw her mother.

At Candlemas and May Eve Jenny was amused to call on Mrs. Beadle. She felt, she said, on both occasions, in the mood for evil spirits. She brought a number of candles and stuck them everywhere, all over the dresser and the mantelpiece, and amused herself with the crystal and the spirits until the room was full of evil, and she was filled with exultation. She laughed excitedly, her eyes crazed, a mania of power working in her.

The old woman sat outside the circle watching her, muttering, aware that she no longer commanded respect, and that her powers were held to be negligible now that the young witch had finished her noviciate, and learned all she could from her. Now into the crystal Jenny could summon the great goat, witness the obscene ritual of adoration, and in her hatred of the flesh she exulted in these obscenities and perversions, because they mocked the flesh, were a travesty of that relationship which bound men and women and was dear to them. Now the great witches' sabbaths filled her with a wild restlessness and excitement. She lighted candles, but her desire was for flames leaping to the sky. She invoked the evil spirits, but in those wild moods her desire was to be one with them, riding great storms of thunder and lightning. And all the time she was burnt up with her longing for him who was prince of them all.

By day she was silent, composed, biddable. She bathed the children, washed and ironed their clothes, did the shopping—Lily having no energy—allowed herself to be ordered around by Pete in his great evening orgies of cooking, swept out the lodgers' rooms. She had no trouble with the men who came to the house; she did not attract them; she was to them "only a bit of a kid" and anyhow too tight-lipped, flat-chested, and bloodless. Except on the great days when she was expecting *him* she took no trouble with herself, often not even troubling to wash. When he was due she went down to the public baths, put on clean clothes, brushed her hair, tied the red ribbon round her head, put on the stained and faded red dress; then and only then a little colour would come up into her cheeks, a light into her eyes and her lips soften and relax. Then she had all the outward signs of a woman in love. But of all that business of being in love as commonly understood she wanted nothing; it had no part in her life. Passion for her meant a fever of longing, an ecstasy of power. The only kisses she had ever known brought no glow to her body. They were ice-cold—*cold as the lips of Lucifer*—and their coldness went deep down into her and possessed her in a terrible chastity.

He came back in the first week of September—Saturday, September 7th, 1940—and when she heard his step on the stair she threw open the door and ran down the stairs and into his arms and settled there like a bird in its nest.

In the room he put her at arm's length from him, holding her by the shoulders, looking at her intently.

"You're getting a big girl," he said.

She said, eagerly, "Soon I'll be sixteen!"

He smiled, his face full of tenderness. She was arrayed in all his gifts—the coral necklace and bracelet, the snake bracelet, the cat's eye ring, the Caucasian belt.

" 'Too sad for a child; too young for a lover'."

He murmured the words sadly.

She followed him up, quickly. "I don't want a lover—I hate all that!"

"I know." He pulled her close to him, folding his arms round her, and she rested her head contentedly against his shoulder. "There shan't be any lovers, Jenny."

"I only want to love you—for always."

"You shall."

"And you'll love me? For ever?"

He stroked her hair. "For ever and a day. Listen!"

They moved a little apart.

"A siren," Jenny said, carelessly.

"D'you go to a shelter?"

"No. Lily takes the kids over. They spend the night there. Pete stays out in the street. He's a warden. I stay wherever I happen to be."

"You don't want to go downstairs?"

"Not unless you do."

"Then we'll stay here."

The guns opened up.

"It's only like a heavy thunderstorm," Jenny said.

"A little more dangerous."

"You can only die once."

"Some people like life and want to live a long time," he pointed out.

"Some people like being alive in their bodies. I don't, except when I'm with you. When you're asleep your soul leaves your body and goes where it pleases. When you die it's left it for good. It can never go back. It's free."

"Once you're dead you can't sit holding hands like this."

She sat on the floor, leaning against his knees, the cat in her lap.

"You don't need. Because then you can be with the person you love always."

"That's what you believe?"

She lifted her head. "I *know!*"

The bombers zoomed overhead; the guns cracked and thundered in a terrific bombardment. It went on all the afternoon. The house shook with the force of the gunfire and the crash of bombs.

Jenny's eyes were alight with excitement, as during a thunderstorm.

He murmured, " 'We have made a covenant with death and with hell are we at agreement.' "

He went over to a corner of the room and pulled out a battered portable gramophone. There were a few records in the tray on top; he lifted them off and selected one and put it on the machine. The words were in Latin, but Jenny recognised the tune immediately.

"A hymn!" she said, in disgust. He motioned to her to be silent, and the great sweep of "Adeste Fideles" filled the room; the golden choirs of angels sang in exultation against the crack and thunder of the guns.

He went over and stood by the window. He was back in an Autumn night with a spit of rain on the wind. He could

hear her saying, "And then we all join in the chorus, led by
the vicar himself—

And down came a ruddy great blackbird,
And down came a ruddy great blackbird,
And down came a ruddy great blackbird
And pecked—off—her nose!

And he could see the vicar wandering about the great old
house set amidst its cherry orchards humming it to himself,
or breaking out into a great roar . . .

When the disc had spun round for the last time Jenny
pleaded, "No more hymns! Tell me a story about the Gulf of
Finland and the great forests."

"I'll play it for you. Listen!"

They spent the rest of that shattering afternoon listening to
records of Sibelius symphonic poems.

She saw again the swan alighting on the water, the dragon-fly
quivering opalescent above the summer pool. She saw grey
towers rising from dark forests and princesses waving from
the battlements; she saw Xanadu and the gardens bright with
sinuous rills and sweet with incense-bearing trees. She heard
the bells of lost Atlantis ringing under the sea . . . and all the
time the house shook and rattled with the guns.

It ended only to begin again with more savage intensity
in the evening. The afternoon raid had left the sky crimson
from the fires—a superb target for the night. Balls of fire went
drifting over the sky; chandeliers of living flame, like some
tremendous fireworks display. Screaming-bombs fell with a
din like sheets of tin being wildly shaken. There was the rattle
of machine-guns, and the ferocity of the anti-aircraft guns.
There was explosion after explosion and a sense of the earth
being ripped open. The bombers zoomed over, endlessly;
the upper air was nothing but this monstrous trundling,

and all the time the guns leaping up as though they would tear down the sky.

A bomb fell very close and the house seemed to heel over like a ship in a gale. There was the scurry and clangour of fire-engines and ambulances charging down the street. It went on like that all night.

At Jenny's suggestion those two in the top room at No. 10 Paradise Court put out the light and watched the inferno from the window. Eastward the sky was like some savage sunset. Every now and then volumes of crimson smoke wreathed with flame shot up and unfurled against the flaming backcloth of the sky. Shrapnel pinged on the roof like a monstrous hail.

"London's burning!" Jenny whispered, ecstatically. It was as though she had waited all her life for this tremendous conflagration. Here was hell let loose at last, the raging inferno beyond all imagination. She looked at him and saw his face lit by the crimson glare; it seemed to her that he had horns on his head, as that first time.

He pulled her away from the window as the engine of a bomber faltered and, it seemed in the same moment, the 'plane dived.

In the crash that followed, so far as they were concerned the earth split wide open. The windows had gone, and naked flames fled across the place where they had been. There was a hole through the roof and the far wall had collapsed. Smoke was coming from somewhere. In the street there was a commotion of bells, a grinding of brakes, a confusion of shouting voices.

"We've been hit," he said. "Or the house next door has. We must get out."

The door had been torn off its hinges and was jammed awkwardly across the sagging floor. He tugged at it, forcing it outward. The landing and staircase were in darkness and thick with smoke. "I'll strike a match," he said, but there was no need, for flame shot up suddenly out of the smoke.

"We might make it," he said, "Quickly. I'll carry you. Keep your face in under my coat, away from the smoke."

He put an arm under her knees and lifted her as he had lifted her in the forest that summer evening nine years ago, and she knew again the same fusion of excited fear and confidence.

The staircase held as far as the next floor; beyond that it burned like matchwood. He darted into a room and made his way through swirling smoke to where the window had been. Flames licked across it. He put her down beside the wall and leaned from the window regardless of the darting flames. He was seen. There were immediate shouts, and a busyness with ladders.

He turned back to her where she stood by the wall with her face buried in the cat's fur.

"They've seen us." He pressed her close to him, trying to protect her from the smoke. "You're not frightened?"

She looked up at him.

"No." She smiled.

He smiled back at her and she felt his kiss cold on her forehead and the smoke blowing across their faces.

There was a clatter of ladders going up against the wall of the house. A ladder reached the sill of the room where the two waited just as the floor collapsed taking them with it.

Chapter XI

Revelation

Only Mrs. Beadle knew where Jenny was living. On the Sunday morning the inhabitants of Ropewalk Alley, finding themselves still alive after the horrors of the night, began asking each other where the bombs had fallen and going out into the ravaged city to see for themselves. In this way, during the course of the day, Mrs. Beadle learned that Paradise Court had "gone". Immediately she wrapped herself in her old shawl and went round to where she knew Nell Flower was living since she had left the Seven Bells. It was a long tram ride, as Nell had moved some distance further down the river to be near her factory, and it was one o'clock before the old woman arrived and found the shabby street in which Nell lived.

Nell was just going out. She had got up late and wanted to get out before "they" shut. She was putting the finishing touches to her toilet when the frousy landlady showed Mrs. Beadle up to her room.

She exclaimed at the sight of the old woman, "Good Lord, Ma, what brings you here? Bombed out? Lord, what a night! I don't know why we're still alive!"

"A lot of people aren't," the old woman answered her, "I came to tell you Paradise Court's wiped out. There was a lot killed. I thought we might go along to the hospital together. Jenny was living at No. 10."

Nell ceased the vigorous darkening of her eyelashes and stared.

"What was she doing there, for goodness sake?"

"*He* lived there. There was a nigger let rooms and he and his wife let her stay with them, working for her keep."

"So that's where she got to! Why didn't you tell me, you old devil?"

"She asked me not to. She didn't want you coming around, she said. You know how she turned against you when she found out."

Nell tossed her head, and the old woman was reminded of Jenny. It was easy, to see where the kid got the trick from.

"I heard. She needn't have worried her head. I'm not all that maternal." Her tone was hard, and again Mrs, Beadle was reminded of Jenny. There was the same tightening of the lips too.

"All the same you ought to know whether she's dead or alive. Joe and Ivy ought to know. They legally adopted her. If we found out you could let them know."

"Why didn't you go to them instead of coming to me?"

"You're her mother, when all's said. And there's him."

"Him! I can't even remember his name!"

"All the same he was something to you once."

"Not more than any of the others."

"Somewhere there's one was more to you than the others. The one that got you with child. Supposing it was him?" The old woman edged closer to her, lowered her voice. "Supposing that accounted for his interest in her and the great feeling she had for him?"

The colour came up in Nell's face, crimson under the pink of the rouge. "Supposing this and supposing that!" she cried, irritated. "For God's sake let's get out before the pubs close. I need a double brandy after last night!"

The old woman said tartly, as Nell bundled her from the room, "It was no worse for you than for anyone else!"

"I daresay! But my nerves are bad . . . " What she meant was that she was thoroughly disturbed by the old woman's suggestion as to the possible paternity of her child.

They went down the stairs and out into the street, empty with Sunday, scraps of paper blowing forlornly in the gutters. There was still a glow in the sky over the Surrey docks, and the wind blew a smell of burning along the river.

"God, what a night!" Nell repeated.

They went into the saloon bar of a pub on the corner. It was packed and everyone was talking about the night's "blitz" and exchanging bomb stories.

"I tell you straight, I thought my last minute had come!"

"They say you never hear the one that's going to get you . . ."

"Sitting on the double-you and shot straight out into the street. True as I'm standing here!"

"All the ceilings down and not a scrap of glass left in the 'ole bloomin' 'ouse . . . "

"The Gov'ment'll 'ave to do something, 'undreds still wanderin' about after it was light with no place to go—"

"Seemed to circle round and round right over our house."

"I can't stick it. I tell you straight, I can't stick another night like that. Everyone's got to 'ave sleep. You can't work without sleep—"

"Thank God I'm not behind the bar," Nell muttered, sipping her drink. "I bet those girls are sick to death of everyone telling them how much worse it was for them than anyone else." The drink warmed her and she began to recover her good nature.

"Knock it back, Ma, and have another," she urged. "They'll be calling time in a few minutes. And it's the second one that does you good."

They had their second drink and came out into the pale sunlight at closing-time.

"We must have a taxi," Nell declared.

They walked a little way and picked one up on the main road.

Nell said, as they neared the hospital, "Of course there could be something in what you said—about Jenny's father. You'd need to see them together to tell. The only time I ever did was at your place, and then I was too wild—but funny you never thought of it before." She looked at the old woman in sudden suspicion.

"I did."

"You never said anything."

"I had my reasons."

Nell said, ironically, "Like a bit of mystery, don't you?"

Mrs. Beadle made no answer, and they finished the journey in a speculative silence.

There had been a procession of people since early morning at the hospital, haggardly studying the casualty lists of dead and living nailed up outside, and they were still coming when Nell and Mrs. Beadle arrived. Some went in and were taken up to the wards; others went along a corridor in a different direction. Many of those who came back along that corridor were in tears; a few of the women sobbed and moaned hysterically.

Nell and Mrs. Beadle stared at the lists, Mrs. Beadle screwing up her eyes in the effort to see. Nell settled her chinchilla afresh on her shoulders to distinguish herself from that drab crowd. She told herself that it was all a lot of nonsense their having come. Of course the kid would be all right; she would have gone to the shelter with the rest of the people in the house.

When she saw the name, JENNY FLOWER, amongst the list of those who had died since being admitted to hospital she stared blankly.

"See it?" the old woman muttered at her elbow, peering forward.

"Yes. Half way down the left-hand column. Died since admission to hospital."

The old woman pressed forward then. She had to see for herself. Other people, also anxiously studying the lists, were annoyed at the dirty old thing pushing her way in front of them.

289

"Steady on, mother," they said, and asked her who she was shovin' . . .

When she had satisfied herself that the name really was there she turned back to Nell.

"Better go in."

They went up the steps and into the stone-floored entrance-hall.

"Smell of disinfectant," Mrs. Beadle murmured, and made a face of disgust.

Nell approached one of the hall-porters.

"We've come about a young girl who died here after admission—"

She gave the name and particulars, replied that yes she was the child's mother, then she and the old woman were following the porter down the corridor, away from the wards. Nell went a little pale. Gruesome was the word that came to her. That's what it was—gruesome. Mrs. Beadle looked at her.

"Like me to go in for you? I've done layin' out. It don't mean nothin' to me."

"It's all right. I'm her mother, aren't I?"

"A fat lot that means to you," the old woman thought, but she said nothing. Nell was full of a kind of superstitious dread, but she was determined no one should guess. She gave a final shrug to the chinchilla before following the porter into the mortuary.

There was nothing after all so very frightening about it. Nothing gruesome. Everything was neat and decent as a hospital ward, if only the place hadn't been so cold. Like a tomb.

The attendant was quietly business-like.

"Could you identify the gentleman that was found with the little girl, ma'am? The two bodies were found together."

Nell answered resolutely, with the coldness of the tomb in her own body, "Perhaps—I don't know—I'll see—"

The attendant turned back the tops of the cloths on two slabs, side by side.

Nell steeled herself to look. But again it was not so very dreadful. Nothing so very terrible about death, after all—they could both have been asleep. The terrible change had not yet set in. There seemed, even, a little ironic smile about the lips of both . . . The same smile.

Nell Flower searched the face of her child for the last time, looking from it to the face of the man, and back again. Why had she never noticed it before—the same slant of the brows, the same nose, the same curve of the thin lips, the same high cheekbones? Now that they both lay so still, side by side like that, it was like the page of a book laid open for anyone to read, she thought. Or was it only because the old woman had put the idea into her mind that she saw the likeness? The doubt came into her mind, flickered there a moment, and was gone. Deep down in her she knew. Beyond any doubt. And now she remembered him. She had never known his name, but one thing other than that he had got her with child had distinguished him from the others—the strange, unnatural coldness of his lips.

> *Begun in "Southern England" in June 1944,*
> *and finished at the Tudor House Hotel,*
> *Tewkesbury, October 1944.*

Acknowledgements

The publisher would like to thank those who helped see
this book into publication: Nathalie Boisard Beudin,
Rob Brown, Lorena Carrington, Anne-Sylvie Homassel,
Meggan Kehrli, Ken Mackenzie, Rosanne Rabinowitz,
Jim Rockhill, and Cathy Faulks-Hart, without whose
support this book would not have been possible.

Lucifer and the Child was first published by
Jarrolds Publishers Limited, London (1946).

About the Author

Ethel Mannin (1900-1984) was a best-selling author born and bred in South London. Her first novel, Martha, was published in 1923, having first been entered in a writing competition. She continued to write at an astonishing pace, producing over fifty novels during her long career, plus multiple volumes of short stories, autobiographies, travel and political writing. Mannin was also a lifelong socialist, feminist, and anti-fascist. She died in Devon at the age of 84.

SWAN RIVER PRESS

Founded in 2003, Swan River Press is an independent
publishing company, based in Dublin, Ireland, dedicated
to gothic, supernatural, and fantastic literature. We special-
ise in limited edition hardbacks, publishing fiction from
around the world with an emphasis on Ireland's contribu-
tions to the genre.

www.swanriverpress.ie

*"Handsome, beautifully made volumes . . .
altogether irresistible."*

– Michael Dirda, *Washington Post*

*"It [is] often down to small, independent, specialist presses
to keep the candle of horror fiction flickering . . . "*

– Darryl Jones, *Irish Times*

"Swan River Press—cutting edge of New Gothic."

– Joyce Carol Oates

*"The redoubtable Brian J. Showers [keeps] the
myriad voices of Irish fantasy alive there in Dublin."*

– Alan Moore

EARTH-BOUND
and Other Supernatural Tales

Dorothy Macardle

Originally published in 1924, the nine tales that comprise
Earth-Bound were written by Dorothy Macardle while she
was held a political prisoner in Dublin's Kilmainham Gaol
and Mountjoy Prison. The stories incorporate themes that
intrigued her throughout her life; themes out of the myths
and legends of Ireland; ghostly interventions, dreams and
premonitions, clairvoyance, and the Otherworld in parallel
with this one. It is so easy to dismiss them, as some have,
merely as part of the narrative of "Irish nationalism" of the
time, but it is the supernatural elements that make them
much more. She would revisit these themes in later works
such as her classic haunted house novel *The Uninvited*
(1941). To this new edition of Macardle's debut collection,
reprinted for the first time in ninety years, we have added
four more tales of the supernatural.

> *"Beautifully written, with a fine air for the music of
> language and vivid descriptions of the landscape."*

– Black Static

> *"A beautifully presented and valuable resource for anyone
> interested in Irish history, culture or literature."*

– Dublin Inquirer

THE LURE OF THE UNKNOWN
Essays on the Strange

Algernon Blackwood

The Lure of the Unknown is a collection of Algernon Blackwood's essays, talks, reviews and anecdotes exploring encounters with the strange and unusual or, in Blackwood's preferred word, the "odd". They include his first attempts to investigate alleged haunted houses, his association with such luminaries as W. B. Yeats, "A.E.", and Gurdjieff; his thoughts on telepathy, reincarnation, elemental spirits, other dimensions, and his beliefs in what lies beyond our normal perceptions. These writings reveal not only Blackwood's diverse experiences, but his depth of reading and analysis of the unexplained. Few of these essays have been reprinted beyond their first publication or their broadcast on radio and television. They provide another dimension to an understanding of one of the great writers of the supernatural.

"This is an essential book for any Blackwood fan."

– Washington Post

*"A beautifully designed edition . . .
a fascinating glimpse of Blackwood's ideas."*

– Fortean Times

*"An excellent collection of occasional writings by one of
the most gifted and charming authors of supernatural fiction"*

– Supernatural Tales

THE UNFORTUNATE FURSEY

Mervyn Wall

The forces of evil have launched a determined offensive on the sanctified precincts of Clonmacnoise, and gain a bridgehead in the cell of Brother Fursey. But the hapless monk is so tongue-tied with fright that he cannot utter the necessary words of exorcism. When the other monks discover this, poor Fursey is expelled, and sets forth on the first stage of his travels accompanied by a fantastic procession of cacodemons, hippogriffs, imps, furies, and other dreadful creatures, not to mention the elegant gentleman in black who is their commander-in-chief. Described by critic E. F. Bleiler as a "landmark book in the history of fantasy", Mervyn Wall's *The Unfortunate Fursey* remains a classic of modern Irish literature.

"Wildly fantastic, intensely satirical, and wickedly comic."

– Irish Times

"An extremely readable, entertaining and pertinent novel."

– Dublin Inquirer

"For anyone who doesn't know Fursey,
this opportunity to do so is not to be missed."

– Dublin Book Review

www.ingramcontent.com/pod-product-compliance
Lightning Source LLC
Chambersburg PA
CBHW051125190726
48290CB00006B/1696